KU-742-780

Lynda La Plante was born in Liverpool. She trained for the stage at RADA and worked with the National Theatre and RSC before becoming a television actress. She then turned to writing – and made her breakthrough with the phenomenally successful TV series *Widows*.

Her fourteen novels have all been international bestsellers. Her original script for the much-acclaimed *Prime Suspect* won awards from BAFTA, British Broadcasting and the Royal Television Society as well as the 1993 Edgar Allen Poe Writer's Award.

Above Suspicion and *The Red Dahlia* have been ratings winners for ITV in 2009 and 2010.

Lynda La Plante has been made an honorary fellow of the British Film Institute and she was awarded a CBE in the Queen's Birthday Honours list in 2008.

Visit Lynda at her website: www.LaPlantebooks.co.uk

COLD HEART

Lynda La Plante

**POCKET
BOOKS**

LONDON • SYDNEY • NEW YORK • TORONTO

First published in Great Britain by Macmillan, 1998
This edition published by Pocket Books, 2010
An imprint of Simon & Schuster UK Ltd
A CBS COMPANY

3 5 7 9 10 8 6 4 2

Simon & Schuster UK Ltd
1st floor
222 Gray's Inn Road
London WC1X 8HB

www.simonandschuster.co.uk

Simon & Schuster Australia
Sydney

A CIP catalogue record for this book is available
from the British Library

Paperback ISBN: 978-1-47111-050-4
Australian trade paperback ISBN: 978-0-85720-140-9

Printed and bound by
CPI Group (UK) Ltd, Croydon, CR0 4YY

For my beloved father

ACKNOWLEDGEMENTS

I sincerely thank Suzanne Baboneau, Arabella Stein and Philippa McEwan at Macmillan, and the real Lorraine Page whose name I borrowed. Thanks to Gill Coleridge, Esther Newberg, Peter Benedek, and especially to Hazel Orme. I'd also like to thank my team at La Plante Productions: Liz Thorburn, Vaughan Kinghan, script and book editor, Alice Asquith, researcher, Nikki Smith, Christine Harmar-Brown, and Ciara McIlvenny.

With thanks for their contribution to:

Geoffrey Smith
East Hampton Police Department
Sergeant Gilmore and Lieutenant Salcido of the Beverly
    Hills Police Department
Dr Ian Hill, Department of Forensic Medicine, Guy's Hospital
George W. Clarke, San Diego District Attorney's Office
Tom Rowland of Thomas Rowland Associates
Kathy Byrne of the Chicago Film Office
J. B. Smith of the New Mexico Film Commission
Kerstin Chmielewski from the Berlin Tourist Office
Sotheby's Press Office, New York

But above all my thanks go to a very admirable lady who brought me the story of her life.

THE BULLET blew off virtually his entire face. He was naked, but he appeared to be wearing swimming trunks because of the band of untanned skin which they usually covered. His arms and legs were spread open and his body floated face down. She watched with sick fascination as the blood continued to spread like the petals of a poppy, wider and wider; he was brain dead, but his heart still pumped, and continued for longer than she had calculated. Suddenly his outstretched arms jerked, his fingers clenched and unclenched, and he gave a strange guttural snorting sound, as if his throat were clogged with blood. A few seconds more, and she knew he was dead. Only then did she move away from the edge of the pool.

The bentwood sun chairs were replaced neatly, his towel folded. His sunglasses she put back in their case, and his half-smoked cigarette she left in the ashtray to smoulder and die – slowly, as he had. She wrapped her hand carefully in the edge of her floating silk chiffon wrap to remove the glass she had used, slipped it into the deep pocket of her jacket, then walked soundlessly across the velvety lawn, past the sheets of lead and lumps of rock that Harry Nathan had considered to be sculpture,

1

to enter the house through the garden doors. She took the glass from her pocket, rinsed it and replaced it in the kitchen cabinet. She was fast, meticulous, knowing every inch of the kitchen, even wiping the taps in case she had touched them inadvertently. She surveyed the immaculate kitchen, making sure nothing was left out of place, and then, still barefoot, she returned to the garden the way she had come. By now, Nathan's cigarette had burned itself out, the ash extending for a curved inch and a half in front of the butt. She made her way round the edge of the pool, not even looking at the body, which still floated face down but was now drifting almost in the centre of the deep end. She looked round furtively before picking up the weapon, a heavy Desert Eagle, still wrapped in a silk headscarf. Then she hurried towards a small shrubbery, full of topiary trees clipped into strange geometric shapes that were clearly meant to echo the sculpture. She was careful not to step on the soil but to remain on the grass verge. She fired the gun into the shrubs then quickly tossed it free of the scarf, to land just in front of the first row of plants.

A bird screeched as the sound echoed of the weapon firing, and she thought she heard someone scream in the house, but she didn't go to investigate, didn't even glance back, intent on getting out of Nathan's estate and knowing it would take her at least five minutes to reach her car, parked further down the avenue. She did not put on her shoes until she was standing beside the Mitsubishi jeep. She bleeped it open with the alarm key and gave only a brief, guarded look around to make sure she had not been seen by anyone before she got inside and inserted the key, her hands rock steady as she turned it. The engine sparked into life and she drove off. Harry

Nathan was dead and she was now a wealthy woman, about to regain everything he had taken from her and more. She would savour for ever the look in his eyes when he had seen her take out the heavy gun, seen him step back, half lifting his hands in submission, and then, as she pulled the trigger, there had been a second when she saw fear. She would relish the fear, because she believed that, without doubt, she had just committed the perfect murder.

CHAPTER 1

12 August 1997

LORRAINE PAGE of Page Investigations had not, as yet, moved into a new office, though she had already used part of her cut of the million-dollar bonus from her last case to move from the tiny apartment in Los Angeles she had shared with her former partner Rosie, who had now married Bill Rooney, the ex-police captain who also worked with them. The couple had recently departed for an extended honeymoon in Europe.

The lost feeling hadn't happened for a few days. She had been so caught up in making plans for the wedding, choosing what they would both wear, and the laughter when they forced Rooney to splash out on an expensive suit that had made the rotund man look quite handsome. Everything had been 'fun', particularly now that they had money to spend.

It was not until Rosie and Rooney had departed for their honeymoon that it really hit home: Lorraine missed them. Waving goodbye at the airport had almost brought the tears that didn't come until a few days later. She had been sitting in Rosie's old apartment, now hers, looking at the wedding photographs, and she had no one to share them with, no one to laugh and point out how funny it had been when Rooney spilt champagne on his precious new suit. There was no one who would understand the three of them standing with solemn faces and their glasses raised. Rosie's and Lorraine's had, of course, contained non-alcoholic champagne, but they had raised their glasses for a private toast to their absent friend, Nick Bartello, who had died on their last case.

The photographs, like the small apartment, held such memories, some sweet, some so very sad, but they had made Lorraine decide to buy another place. It had not been an easy decision but she couldn't stand the ghosts – it made the loneliness even worse.

Lorraine's new apartment was on the upper floor of a two-storey condominium built on an old beach-house lot right on the ocean front in Venice Beach, one of four or five blocks where the little houses were so closely packed together that there was no room for front or back yards. Walking round the kooky old bohemian neighbourhood, she found she had already fallen for its lively energy and charm, and she loved the close proximity of the beach. Lorraine didn't think of herself as 'kooky' or 'bohemian'; in fact, in her neat suit and blouse she looked slightly out of place, but the neighbourhood reminded her of when she had been married. It had been tough, trying to juggle her job as a rookie cop and bring up two young kids while her husband studied at home and worked nights in the local liquor store. Money had always been tight, but friends had not, and there had been so much love. Lorraine had money now and she wanted, needed, more friends like Rosie and Rooney. Deep down she ached for all the love she had lost.

While viewing the new apartment, she had caught a glimpse of herself in a full-length mirror. Staring at her image, from the well-cut blonde hair down to her slim ankles in low Cuban heels, the ache had suddenly surfaced, making her gasp. It didn't matter how long ago she and Mike had been divorced, how long it had been since she had seen her daughters, the pain was still raw. In the past she had obliterated it by getting drunk but she was stronger now. She could still feel the dreaded dryness in her mouth and feel herself shaking, but she forced herself to follow the real-estate agent round the rest of the apartment.

'I'll take it,' she announced. 'Just one thing, though. Do the other residents allow dogs?' She lit a cigarette. Tiger, the wolfhound/malamute crossbred canine who had belonged to poor dead Nick Bartello, was now Lorraine's responsibility, and she needed to be near an open space where she could exercise him – clearly, the beach would be perfect.

'I don't think that would be a problem. I presume—'

'Tiger,' Lorraine interjected, using her right hand to indicate with a patting motion that Tiger was about the size of a toy poodle.

'I presume he's house-trained. The landlords of the head lease do have a proviso with regard to animals.'

'Oh, yes, he's the perfect gentleman indoors, professionally trained, exceptionally obedient.' Crossing her fingers behind her back, she hoped that this would soon be true. She didn't want to risk losing the apartment: it felt right, it felt safe.

'I think I could be happy here,' she said softly, and flushed with embarrassment: it sounded stupid. But the agent smiled warmly, eager to do the deal but rather surprised that this elegant, if rather nervous, woman hadn't even asked to see the kitchen. Lorraine insisted they drive to the real-estate office to finalize the sale. She

7

required no mortgage, and arranged a banker's draft for the full amount.

'I'd like measurements of all the rooms so I can order furniture, curtains . . .' She wafted her hand and, as she did, the agent noticed there was no wedding ring – in fact, she wore no jewellery at all. As Lorraine stood up and bent forward to pick up her purse, her silky blonde hair slid forward, revealing a jagged scar that ran from the corner of her eye, a scar that make-up couldn't hide.

Driving back to Rosie's, she recalled her assurances about Tiger. It had proved impossible, to date, to house-train or instil any kind of normal dog behaviour into him. Rooney and Rosie had both tried, but he had become a liability during the pre-wedding arrangements. He would either attack anyone who came into the house, or disappear for days on end, and no matter how long they all cajoled him and fed him biscuits, he point-blank refused to wear a collar. Eventually, Lorraine had booked him into a kennel for extensive schooling with a former police-dog handler. If this failed it was unanimously decided that he would be joining his old master Nick Bartello – nobody had been able to train that son-of-a-bitch either.

When she got back to the apartment, Lorraine contacted the kennels. Tiger was progressing but they suggested an extra two weeks' training. They did not elaborate and Lorraine was quite pleased – she needed time to furnish the new apartment. She decided not to take anything from Rosie's place but to start from scratch and buy everything new. At the same time she had resolved to do something about her scar, the scar that reminded her of who she had been, of what she had been. She no longer needed to force herself to look at

8

the ugliness it represented. She wanted to put her past behind her, once and for all.

Lorraine felt as if she was high – she could hardly sleep. The shopping trips to the Beverly Center to buy furnishings and fittings were like stepping back in time. She selected everything she thought she would need, from a bed, dining table and large white sofa to wine-glasses, lamps, dishes and silverware, and arranged for it all to be delivered to the apartment. She wanted every-thing to be ready for her release from the clinic and she didn't want to lift anything, carrying anything or move so much as a book.

The surgery was extensive. She had decided to have a full face-lift, which was done at the same time as the operations on her scar, which was deep and required skin grafts. She decided to remain at the clinic, pampering herself with beauty treatments, until the wounds had healed. She was still paying for Tiger's 'rehabilitation' and the kennels were beginning to worry that he would become a permanent fixture, but Lorraine assured them that she fully intended to take him back.

When the surgeon, who had not allowed her to look at herself, finally held up a mirror to her face, she wanted to celebrate, to kiss and hug everyone close by.

'You're a very beautiful lady, Lorraine,' the surgeon said softly, as she cocked her head from side to side, drinking in her smooth, scarless cheek, her perfect eyes, the taut skin beneath her chin. He leaned in close. 'Mind you, I can't take all the credit. You have a wonderful bone structure. I just did a little suction beneath your cheekbones, ironed out the laugh lines,' he continued, pointing out what his magic knife had done, taking pride in his work. He asked the nurses their opinion, but

Lorraine didn't hear: she felt as if she was looking into her soul and it made her gasp.

'Happy?' the surgeon asked, lifting his funny bushy eyebrows.

'I used to look like this,' she whispered, wishing Rosie could be there to see the new Lorraine.

While in the clinic, Lorraine had worked out and eaten well and, on her release, she felt fitter than ever before. She gave her entire wardrobe to charity and hit the designer shops with a vengeance. She had never spent so much, so fast. She had always had good taste but now she went for quality, and for the first time in her life she never looked at the price tag. Next she bought a brand-new Cherokee truck and a second-hand Mercedes, the car she had always dreamed of owning. It was in perfect condition, with only twenty thousand on the clock, immaculate leather upholstery, CD player and telephone. As she flicked open the make-up mirror it lit up and she sat smiling at herself, her new beautiful self, as the salesman hovered.

'Yep, this'll do nicely.'

By mid-September, she had found a comfortable office in a small three-storey complex on West Pico Boulevard. Los Angeles had its rapidly changing fashions in office buildings, as it had in pizza toppings and nail extensions, and although the building had only been erected five years ago, the gleaming mirrored exterior was already considered behind the times. But as far as Lorraine was concerned this was an advantage, as it brought the rental more within the range she felt justified in paying. There was a smart lobby and a pleasant Filipino doorman, good security and – the biggest advantage – right across the street was Rancho Park with acres of grass for Tiger to run in. She thought about him, but kept putting off calling the kennels to say she would collect him.

The air-conditioned office, tastefully decorated and filled with plain ash furniture, also boasted an en suite bathroom and kitchen, plus a reception area furnished with sofas and coffee table. 'Page Investigations' was printed in letters of gold leaf on the main entrance door by the electronic, security-coded entryphone. The letter-headed paper, cards and office equipment were chosen with meticulous care. Only the old computer hardware from her last office was retained.

Ready to begin work, Lorraine deliberated over the wording for newspaper and magazine advertisements before committing to six-month runs. She then contacted three secretarial agencies, and asked that applicants should send their CVs before she interviewed them.

By October, appointments had been scheduled with the three applicants she felt were most suited to the job. Still running high on her own adrenalin, she didn't see them all: midway through the first interview she decided to offer the job to Rob Decker, even though she had really wanted a woman.

Decker was about twenty-eight, tanned, blond and good-looking, had worked mostly for television executives, had even tried acting himself, and his account of his unsuccessful thespian attempts made her laugh. He had a top shorthand speed, understood computers, and had a deep, laid-back voice that harked back to his theatrical endeavours. He was fit, with a tight, muscular body, and was wearing an expensive fawn linen suit, pale blue shirt and suede shoes with no socks. He had a Cartier wristwatch but, thankfully, no other jewellery. He carried his CV and other details of his varied career –

knowledge of weapons and shooting skills – in a soft leather briefcase, with his karate certificates and gun licence. With her history, Lorraine would have found it difficult to acquire a licence, but it wasn't the fact that she would have a gun-toting secretary that impressed her – she just liked him.

Decker was relaxed but not too relaxed, respectful but not obsequious, and when she asked why he had applied for the job he shrugged, admitting without any embarrassment that it sounded better than working tables at a bar and that money was short. His last employer had refused to give him references which had made it difficult to get a decent job since. Lorraine was confused: she had references from his last employer in front of her on her pristine desk. Rob nodded towards the paper, and said he had typed it himself. When she asked why he had no references from his last employer, he told her that he had refused to go down on him and, equally candidly, that he was homosexual. Then he had laughed and added that she probably knew that already, and probably he had not got this job either.

'Yes, you have.' Lorraine surprised even herself. She hadn't given it as much thought as she should have.

Decker's handshake was strong and he assured her that he would not let her down.

'I hope not, Rob. This is very important to me – I want the agency to succeed more than you will ever know. Maybe when you get to know me better you'll find out why, but in the meantime, when can you start?'

'Why not right now? We need some plants in here, and I have a contact in a nursery – I get the best, half-price.'

Lorraine arranged salary and office keys, discussed hours, and then, almost as an afterthought, asked if he liked dogs. He told her another anecdote, about when he had worked in a poodle parlour, and she said that Tiger was not exactly a poodle and needed firm handling. Just before Decker left he seemed suddenly vulnerable, and Lorraine liked him for that too. She knew Rob Decker would become a good friend.

The following morning, Lorraine looked over her office. As promised, Decker had bought two ficus trees in copper buckets, a mass of pink and white impatiens in a glazed terracotta planter, and a deep square plain glass vase, which he had filled with Casablanca lilies and placed on the little table in Reception. The whole place seemed to have come alive. He had left on her desk a note of the cost of each plant and a receipt, plus watering instructions. He had also bought coffee, tea, cookies and skimmed milk, and a new percolator, which he insisted was his own, so that not only was there a sweet fragrance from the blooms but a wonderful smell of fresh coffee.

There were no calls and no work on offer, so at lunchtime Decker and Lorraine went off to buy some exhibition posters and prints from the Metropolitan Museum of Art shop, as the office walls were bare. He also talked Lorraine into stopping off to pick up an elegant uplighter to put in Reception, a swing-arm graphite lamp, a violet glass ashtray for her desk, and – having divined her sweet tooth as though by magic – a jar of jelly beans. By three o'clock their new purchases were on display. The advertising had, as yet, failed to generate any work, but she was not disheartened, she knew things would take time, and during the afternoon they had been able to get to know each other better.

Lorraine never divulged everything about her background, but Decker knew she had been a cop, and knew

13

she had had a drink problem. In fact, he was such a good listener she felt that she had told him more than she really should have, but he was equally forthcoming about his life and his partner, with whom he had lived for eight years – Adam Elliot, late forties, a writer for films, TV or washing-powder commercials, still hoping to crack the big time before he turned fifty.

They left the office at six. Not one phone call had come in: it was Thursday, 26 October. Decker had asked Lorraine if she would like to have dinner over the weekend at his place, but despite the offer of masala chicken and chocolate pie, she had declined. She felt that perhaps she should keep a little distance between them.

Friday was just as silent, telephone-wise and job-wise, and they had talked even more, had lunch together again and discussed how they should rethink the adverts. Decker suggested they use Adam to reword them in a way that might grab a potential client. Again Lorraine refused his offer of lunch or dinner over the weekend. The initial buzz of her getting her new life together began to dry up. She didn't feel so confident any more and even her new face began to annoy her: she was so used to flicking her hair forward over her scar, but there was nothing to hide any more. She began to wonder if it had all been make-believe and that the old Lorraine still lurked ready to pull the new one down.

She wished she had accepted Decker's invitation, as she was alone the entire weekend, going over her accounts, totting up her bank balance. She was still in good shape financially as well as physically, but she had spent a lot of money on pampering herself and seeing it in black and white made her a little scared at her foolishness. Maybe she should have taken her time, but it was too late now – the money was gone. She had just over two hundred thousand dollars in her account, a lot, but at the same time she knew that, realistically, she could not keep the office and Decker running without some finances coming in: the outgoings would drain her savings. Still, any new venture needed time. But despite her forced optimism, something was eating away at her. She awoke one night with a faint voice in her head, telling her over and over she didn't deserve this new life. As if on cue, the phone rang. It was three o'clock in the morning.

'Hello,' Lorraine said suspiciously.

'Hi, blossom, how's things?'

'Rosie?'

'Yeah, guess where we are? No, I'll tell you, Vienna! My God, Lorraine, it's *unbelievable*!'

Lorraine lay back on the pillow as Rosie listed, at full volume, the restaurants and sightseeing tours. It was so nice to hear her voice, even if it was ear-splitting. She sounded so close, as if she was in the next room. 'Eh! How's life? You found a guy?'

'Nope, not yet, but I'm looking.'

'Well, you make sure you don't get one that snores!'

Lorraine smiled as Rosie continued to fill her in on the trials of sleeping with Rooney, never once pausing for breath. 'Hey, you there? Or I did I just bore you off the phone?'

'No, Rosie, I'm still here, making notes in case I meet my Mr Right.' She could feel Rosie's smile. She gave her the new address and phone numbers, and she could hear Rosie repeat them to big, bulbous-nosed Bill Rooney. Then she put Rooney on the phone and he complained

15

about the cost of the call and then said, so softly, in a voice she would never have expected from the old, hardened cop, 'You know, Lorraine, I've got a lot to thank you for. Not just for making us a load of money, but if it wasn't for you, I'd never have met the woman who's made me happier than I ever thought possible.'

There was a long pause and Lorraine could hear his heavy breathing at the other end of the line.

'I love her so much,' he mumbled, and then repeated it, sounding almost in tears.

Rosie grabbed the phone, laughing. 'He's drunk – but he tells me that every day. Nice, huh? Hey, I better go. We'll send you postcards, bring you presents and . . . Oh, yeah, can't wait to see your new place.'

Lorraine said goodbye. It didn't matter that Rosie had shown little or no interest in what was happening in her life because right now it didn't feel too wonderful and she couldn't see anyone in her future saying they loved her. Lorraine was lonely – deeply lonely.

The following morning she went to her local AA meeting, the only social life she had. She still couldn't rid herself of the feeling of isolation: it didn't make her want to drink, but it made her think, and face the fact that she had no friends. She started thinking about her ex-husband and his family. She had not seen her two daughters for a long, long time, and though they knew where she was, they had made no contact. She often thought about going to see them, but always talked herself out of it. She didn't want to disrupt their lives any more than she knew she had already.

She was glad when Tiger's trainer, Alan Pereira, called to say that the dog training was now complete, he would bring Tiger home. Lorraine perked up, even put on some make-up, then laughed at herself. Some weekend date, the return of Tiger.

Tiger was returned, subdued, wearing a collar in rainbow colours, his coat freshly washed, and his teeth cleaned. She had not realized how big he was, or how thick and beautiful his coat. She'd also forgotten his piercing large blue eyes.

'You got one stubborn son-of-a-bitch here,' Alan said, and Tiger's blue eyes were doleful as he first sat, then went through sit, stand, stay and heel. Lorraine was even more impressed when, on the command 'Bed,' Tiger slunk to a flower-printed foam basket and lay down.

He remained quiet, head on paws, as she cooked her supper, came like a lamb and sat when she slipped on his lead to take him for his evening walk. He performed his necessary functions, returned, ate his meal and even returned to his bed. It was about twelve o'clock when Lorraine was woken up by something tugging at her sheets. She sat bolt upright to be met with Tiger's face, and to see his two massive front paws on her bed. 'Bed. Go to bed *now*.' He slunk to the door, tail between his legs, nosed it wider open and disappeared.

In the morning she woke to find the dog's prone body stretched out beside her, with just six inches between them, comatose and snoring gently. Lorraine nudged him and, still with eyes firmly shut, he gave a low growl, his jaw opening a fraction to reveal his cleaned white fangs. She thought of Rooney snoring, and smiled, but then said with great authority, 'Bed, go to your bed. *Now*.' The tail thumped, just a fraction. 'I mean it, you're pushing your luck. Step out of line, pal, and it's the big kennel in the sky, you understand me? You're only on remand, Tiger.'

He was motionless, eyes closed, just a flicker of his tail. 'Okay, you can stay . . . just for a few minutes, you hear me?' She lay there, feeling the huge weight of him beside her, then squinted at the bedside clock. It was six o'clock. 'You know what time it is?' she said, turning on her side. She went back to sleep and at some point between the hours of six and seven thirty, that six inches closed. When she next opened her eyes, he was sleeping nose to nose with her, one paw gently resting across her chest.

'I don't believe this . . .' But she couldn't resist rubbing his ears. Cleverly, he never opened his eyes, just gave a long, satisfied sigh.

Before they went out for a morning jog, Lorraine discovered that Tiger had chewed two of her new shot-silk cushions and destroyed his floral bed. On returning, he was not interested in dog food, but devoured her cereal, nuts and fruit with natural yogurt. He followed her into the bedroom, nosed open the shower door, and padded after her while she dressed. He remained at her heels throughout the day, sat close to her on the sofa watching TV, and no amount of loud yells made him return to the living room when she got into bed. He wasn't a fool, and instead of climbing onto the other side of the king-size bed, he lay down beside it. But he was right next to her in the morning, his breath hot on her neck.

'Hey, this has got to stop, pal,' she said, but then blew it by hugging him close, and he knew he had got her. She just could not resist his love, because that was what she felt from the giant animal – love, pure, unadulterated

18

love – and by Monday morning they had, although she hated to admit it, already got into a routine. All his training, with the exception of allowing her to slip on his collar, had gone out of the window. Tiger had moved in on Lorraine as no man would have dared to, and he loved her with a passion. He sat in the passenger seat of the Cherokee, his nose out of the window and his ears blown back by the wind.

Decker was overwhelmed by Tiger, who growled at him, teeth bared, until Lorraine shouted at him, 'Shut up! This is friend, this is Decker.'

'Jesus Christ, Mrs Page! He's enormous. What on earth kind of breed is he?'

'Mixed, wolfhound and—'

'Donkey?'

Tiger was not too sure about Decker or the office. He made a slow tour of each room and cocked his leg on one of the ficus trees.

'You sure as hell aren't a poodle,' Decker said warily, but when the telephone rang his attention was distracted. He snatched it up – this was the first call that had come in.

'Page Investigations,' he said coolly, as a pair of ice blue eyes stared him out across the desk top. 'May I have your name? Mrs Page is on the other line right now.' Decker jotted down 'Cindy Nathan', glaring back at Tiger.

'Who is it?' Lorraine whispered, from her office doorway.

'A Cindy Nathan, just wait a second.' Lorraine watched as Decker flicked the phone onto speaker and

19

held it for one beat, two beats as he grinned and gave her the thumbs-up sign.

'Cindy Nathan, that is N-A-T . . .' said a low voice, spelling out the surname.

'I have that, Ms Nathan,' said Decker, 'and may I ask what your enquiry is about?'

'It's not an enquiry, I want Lorraine Page – is she there or not?'

Tiger gave a lethal growl, but as Lorraine pointed at him, he shut up.

'I'm sorry, Ms Nathan, but, as I said, Mrs Page is on the other line. If you could just tell me what your enquiry is. I am Rob Decker, Mrs Page's secretary.'

'Really? Well, Rob, as soon as she gets off the other line, get her to call me. It's urgent.' She dictated a number, and hung up.

Decker swore, scribbling down the numbers.

Lorraine threw up her hands. 'Jesus Christ, did you get the number? If that was our first case you just lost it.'

He leaned back in his chair. 'You don't know who Cindy Nathan is?'

Lorraine was furious. 'No, I don't. There's a lot of people I don't know, Decker. I had a long time when I didn't recall my own name. So who is she?'

'She's Harry Nathan's wife.'

'Really, and who the fuck is he?' she snapped.

'The head of Maximedia, the movie studio, though they do a lot of other stuff too. He used to be married to Sonja Sorenson.'

Lorraine leaned on his desk. 'I never heard of her either.'

Decker rolled his eyes to the ceiling. 'Lorraine! She's big in the art world – she owned a gallery on Beverly

Drive but moved back to New York after they divorced. Harry Nathan used to do spoofy, goofball comedies – *Killer Bimbos Ate My Neckties* kind of thing, though lately it's been more like *Ate My Shorts*, if you get what I mean.' He gave her a meaningful look. 'Not exactly family entertainment, shall we say? So, you want to call her? Or would you like me to connect you, ma'am?' He jotted the number on a yellow sticker holding it up on the tip of his forefinger. Lorraine snatched the note and banged her office door closed – only to have to open it again as Tiger threw himself at it barking.

'Get out,' she yelled. Then she sat down at her desk. 'She said she wanted me to call her?' she called to Decker.

The intercom light flashed. 'Yes, Mrs Page, and she seemed a trifle hyper. Shall I get Mrs Nathan on the line for you, Mrs Page?'

'Yes!'

Cindy Nathan was in her silk Hermès sarong, barefoot, clutching the mobile phone and staring into the deep end of the swimming pool. Henry 'Harry' Nathan was floating face down in it with a thin trickle of blood still colouring the bright blue water. She heard the police sirens, saw the Hispanic servants hovering by the industrial glass-brick doors with which Harry had replaced the former french windows and leaded diamond panes.

Her phone rang.

'Cindy Nathan,' she answered flatly.

'This is Lorraine Page. You called me and . . . hello? Mrs Nathan?'

Cindy's voice was barely audible. 'Yes.'

'This is Lorraine Page, of Page Investigations.'

'Are you a detective?'

'Yes, I run an investigation company.'

'I want to hire you, because I'm just about to be arrested for my husband's murder.'

'I'm sorry, could you repeat that?'

'I didn't kill him. I didn't kill him.' Cindy stared at the body. 'I need you, please come immediately.' She reeled off an address, then hung up.

Lorraine stared at the phone, then shouted to Decker, 'She's hung up, did you get that?'

'Yep, I got it. Maybe she read the advert – probably in *Variety*.'

Lorraine replaced the receiver and walked into Reception. 'What did you say?'

'I ran an advert for you in the *Hollywood Reporter*, plus one in *Screen International*, *Variety*—'

'What?'

Decker rummaged around his desk and laid out a fax. 'I told you Elliot was good. He suggested the wording.'

'Elliot?'

'My partner, Adam, but I always call him Elliot, he always calls me Decker. I said we needed him to beef up our adverts, and . . .'

Lorraine's face had tightened. 'What?'

'They only ran yesterday, I told you. I said he was good.'

'Lemme see,' she said tightly.

'Sure, you paid for them.' Decker passed over the fax.

Lorraine read it in disbelief. It was not really an advert, more a treatment for a TV show: 'The best, the one

22

agency that caters for the people that need discretion . . .' highlighted '. . . money no object . . .' highlighted again '. . . clients too famous to name, PRIVATE INVESTI-GATION means what we say – PRIVATE. If it's blackmail, stalkers, drug abuse, underage sex, call us – no case too small, too dangerous, too notorious. We issue a confiden-tiality contract as standard.'

Her jaw dropped as she read the list of high-profile cases with which Page Investigations was supposed to have been involved. 'My God, this is disgusting.'

'Good, though.'

'But it's a pack of lies. You can't say we worked for these people when we didn't. I've never read anything so ridiculous.'

'Maybe, but you'll never get anyone to query it – most, as you will see, are dead. We can say we acted for River Phoenix, but who's to know we didn't because he can't . . .'

Lorraine re-read the list of dead movie stars, studio producers, executives, bankers, politicians – even Jackie Onassis' name appeared. 'This is a gross distortion of facts,' she said.

'Yes, I know, but we got a result. Cindy Nathan.'

Lorraine leaned on his desk. 'You should have run this by me first. This is illegal, unethical, and we could be sued. These people may be dead, but they'll have rela-tives, and lawyers. Pull the adverts this morning, Decker.'

'Will do, Mrs Page.'

She turned at her door, serious. 'You never do this kind of thing again. You have to have my approval for any advert, in fact, for anything going out of this office. Is that clear? I'll call in when I know more – and give Tiger a walk if I'm not back this afternoon.'

'Yes, Mrs Page.'

She closed her office door as Tiger threw himself at it.

Lorraine got into the Cherokee and drove rapidly through Century City to take the short cut behind the Beverly Hilton and into Beverly Hills: she smiled, as she always did, as the signs of wealth and ostentation began to increase as steadily as the gradient of Whittier Drive. As the properties grew larger, hedges and trees grew thicker to keep out prying eyes, but behind them could be glimpsed a pick-and-mix assortment of architectural styles. The more traditional bungalows and hacienda-type dwellings rubbed shoulders with mock everything else – Dutch colonial and Cape Cod-style, art-deco, Tudor follies, steel and glass boxes that had been futuristic thirty years ago.

Lorraine knew she must be getting closer to the Nathan property. She was now on the borders of Beverly Hills and Bel Air, and after a quick glance at Decker's directions, she drew up at the enormous bare metal gates, with Gestapo-style searchlights mounted on the posts. A man was waiting for her. 'Are you Lorraine Page?' he asked.

'Yes, I am.'

He was thin, balding and nervous. 'I am Cindy Nathan's lawyer. She has insisted I speak with you, but I want you to know that I have already contacted my own investigation advisers and all this is now in the hands of the police. They have taken Mrs Nathan in for questioning but I'm sure she'll be released without charge as soon as the facts have been established. Right now, the position is . . . very confusing.'

Lorraine nodded. 'I'm afraid it is. You see, I don't know exactly what has happened.'

'She shot her husband. Harry Nathan is dead. The police are at the poolside now, there's forensic and paramedics and . . . I can't allow you to come inside. I have to go to Mrs Nathan.'

Lorraine smiled. 'Maybe I should come with you, as Mrs Nathan was adamant that I speak with her.'

'That is impossible. You will not be allowed to see her. As I said, this is police business now.'

'Really?'

'Yes, there's nothing you can do here. I will, of course, pay you whatever retainer was agreed, but as I said, the police are taking care of this now. So if you would let me have your fees to date.'

Lorraine hesitated. 'Do you have a card?'

'I'm sorry, yes, of course.' He passed it over. 'The police are not allowing anyone access to the premises.'

Lorraine looked at his card: Joel H. Feinstein, attorney at law. 'Fine, I'll send you my invoice – but just as a matter of interest, is Mrs Nathan being held at the Beverly Hills PD or elsewhere?'

Lorraine drove east on Santa Monica Boulevard, and turned left on Rexford into the bizarre new complex of heavy romanesque arches and colonnades that now housed the Beverly Hills police department. She knew it was unlikely that she would be allowed to see Cindy, even if she announced herself as a private investigator engaged by Mrs Nathan. She was thinking about what moves she could make when an officer she knew, who had done some private work for her on a previous case, walked up to the car parked directly in front of her: James Sharkey, still as fat as ever, still hauling his pants up over his pot belly.

'Hi, how ya doing?' She locked her car and headed towards him. For a moment he didn't recognize her, then gave her a brief nod while digging in his pockets for his car keys. When she asked about Cindy Nathan, he started to unlock his filthy, dented Pontiac. 'I need ten minutes with her,' Lorraine said quietly.

Sharkey laughed and shook his head. He was about to open the car door when Lorraine moved closer. 'You on the case?' she asked.

She knew he was, just by his attitude and the way he looked furtively around the parked cars. He jangled his keys.

'Meal break. Lady is pretty shook up – not talking straight and asking for raspberry milk-shakes . . . with chocolate topping.' Sharkey wasn't putting himself on the line, but she could take the lady her milk-shake, maybe palm the female officer, Joan, who was sitting her. Sharkey pocketed five hundred dollars and Lorraine went for the milk-shake. He had promised he'd have a word with Joan. He lied, he always had been a cheap, lying bastard, as Lorraine discovered when she had to pay another two hundred to persuade Verna to take a toilet break.

Cindy was not held in a cell but in an interview room in the basement of the station. Lorraine walked in and put down the hideous-looking drink.

Cindy was very young, so small that Lorraine towered above her, with a heart-shaped face as perfect as her superwaif figure. Even though she wore no make-up and her blonde hair was twisted into a knot and secured with what appeared to be a barbecue skewer, all of Lorraine's plastic surgery, health clinics and exercise paled beside this woman, who was so astonishingly beautiful. Added to her perfect features was a sweetness and vulnerability, whose impact was immediate. Perhaps the reason she had called in response to the advert run by Decker was that she was as innocent as she looked.

'I'm Lorraine Page,' Lorraine said calmly.

Cindy's brow puckered. 'I'm sorry, who?'

'I'm a private investigator. You called my office, we spoke earlier.'

'I didn't do it! I didn't kill him, and Mr Feinstein won't believe it.'

Lorraine sat down and took out a notebook. 'Do you want me to investigate the circumstances of your husband's death, Mrs Nathan?'

'I guess so. I mean, can they keep me here? I've told them everything I know. Is this for me?' She prodded at the froth on the milk-shake with her index finger, then licked it.

'I don't know what has been agreed, Mrs Nathan. Just tell me about what happened. Did you make a statement?'

'I can't remember. I called the police and I called Mr Feinstein and told him I found Harry in the pool. I was sleeping and . . . then I heard the gunshot. I guess that was what I heard. It wasn't all that loud, though, just a sort of dull bang.'

Lorraine was making notes but keeping half an eye on the open door. 'Then what did you do?'

'I got up and went onto the patio. I could see the pool, I saw Harry and I called out to him. He looked like he was swimming, floating but . . . well, he didn't answer, so then I went back into the house, and through the sun room, and . . .' She chewed her lip. 'When I got closer, I could see the blood, an' he wasn't swimming at all, and he had no trunks on, face down.'

'Did you touch him – I mean, go into the pool?'

'Oh, no. I ran back into the house, I was hysterical, an' then I called the cops.'

'Then you called my office?'

'What?'

'After the police you called my office.'

'No, no, I never called you. I thought maybe someone had called you for me, understand? I mean, why would I call you?'

It was odd, Lorraine thought. Cindy Nathan was behaving very strangely for someone whose husband had just been murdered, especially when she was a prime suspect and about to be charged. She seemed more distracted than upset, twice unfastening her hair and retwisting it round the wooden spike, asking why there wasn't a straw for the shake.

'So you did not ask me to meet with you?'

'No, I just said so. What's going on?'

Lorraine tapped her notebook. 'Well, I don't know either, but if you want me to look into your case, if you feel you need me—'

'Do you think I should have someone? I mean, are you a lawyer?'

'No, Mrs Nathan, I'm a private investigator, as I said.' Lorraine handed the girl her card, but she hardly looked at it.

'I don't know what I should do – maybe wait for Mr Feinstein. He'll tell me what I should do. Right now I'm all confused.'

'It must be terrible for you,' Lorraine said quietly.

Cindy lifted her delicate shoulders. 'Mr Feinstein'll sort it out, I guess.'

'I hope so, and please feel free to call me if you do want me to investigate the death of your husband.'

Joan returned, crooked her finger at Lorraine then jerked her thumb, indicating for her to leave, sharpish.

Cindy didn't even look at Joan. 'Right now I'm more worried about what's going to happen to me, because I didn't do it. I never shot Harry, but a lot of his friends won't believe it.'

'Why?'

Cindy Nathan gave that little shrug of her shoulders again. ''Cos I was always threatening him. I never got around to doing anything, though.'

'Well, somebody did. You're sure it was your husband in the swimming pool?'

Joan became slightly aggressive. 'Come on, don't get me in trouble. Out now.'

Cindy Nathan's wide, cornflower-blue eyes stared at the wall. 'Yes, yes, it was him, face down. It was Harry, all right.' And two big tears rolled down her cheeks.

Lorraine went out of the building, down the curving walkway that looked more like the approach to a smart office complex than a police department. As she bleeped open the Cherokee with her alarm key, she saw Cindy Nathan's lawyer standing by a black Rolls-Royce, parked on Rexford, arguing with two uniformed police officers. So heated was their exchange that they paid Lorraine no attention as she drove past.

*

The following morning, Decker was already brewing coffee and collecting the leaves the ficus trees seemed to shed every night when Tiger bounded in, almost knocking him off his feet.

'I've got all the newspapers. Mrs Nathan was released without charge last night. She's front page in most of the tabloids.'

Lorraine glanced over them. 'Well, until I hear back from her, there's not a lot I can do. She was very . . .' She frowned. She'd been thinking about her meeting with Cindy Nathan since the early hours. 'She wasn't exactly flaky, just, I don't know, not reacting the way she should have. I mean, she didn't seem to understand . . .'

'The trouble she's in?' Decker enquired, carrying Lorraine's coffee into her office.

'Yeah, I suppose so. Maybe she was in shock. They give any more details about her?'

'They certainly do. It was her automatic, by the way, slug taken from Nathan's head.'

'What?'

'She also inherits the house and about half of Maximedia, as his widow,' Decker said.

'Well, she won't if they can make a murder rap stick to her.'

'Mmm, well, according to the *LA Times*, it looks like that's a sort of foregone conclusion.' He rummaged through the paper to find the rest of the leading article from page one. 'Apparently Cindy Nathan threatened to shoot her husband last month at Morton's restaurant. They had a big slanging match in front of a packed dining room, and they had to drag her out.'

Lorraine sipped her coffee. She was now leafing through all the various papers, in which Decker had marked the relevant stories in green felt-tipped pen. 'She said she never called us,' she remarked, lighting a cigarette.

'Well, that's ridiculous. Of course she did. And we've got it taped.'

'*You taped the call?*'

'All calls. I protect you at all times, ma'am.' He slipped his headphones on.

'Play it for me, would you?' Lorraine continued reading, glancing at the pictures of Cindy Nathan being assisted into the lawyer's Rolls with her hands covering her face. The press had worked fast: they also had numerous glamour shots of her – she had been in a TV soap for a few weeks, but most of the photographs were sexy poses in swimsuits and lingerie. 'Shit, she's only twenty years old,' Lorraine said, not that Cindy had looked older – it just surprised her that she was so young. At the bleep-bleep of the answerphone she looked up.

Decker was searching for Cindy's call. He eased off his headphones. 'I fucked up, I can't find that call.'

'Jesus Christ, Decker, this is important. We need that recording. Cindy Nathan said she never made the call to the office. If Cindy didn't make that call, somebody did, someone who knew Harry Nathan was dead – maybe because they had shot him, understand, sweetheart? *That call is very important.*'

Decker was flushing bright red. 'You spoke to Cindy on the phone and met her. Did you think it was the same voice? I mean, do *you* think she made the call?'

Lorraine lifted her hands in the air. 'I dunno . . . and I'm not wasting time thinking about it. Like I just said, let's move on. I'm down seven hundred dollars on this fiasco.'

Decker was dispatched to get any back issues of articles on Cindy Nathan, and Lorraine read every newspaper. Harry Nathan had been married three times and there were photographs of Kendall Nathan, his second wife, a thin, dark woman who looked to be in her late thirties, and Sonja Sorenson, the sculptress, a tall, formidably elegant woman with prematurely white hair. Lorraine clipped out the pictures and the accompanying coverage, then tossed the rest into the trash can.

The phone rang and made her jump but she waited a moment before she picked it up. 'Page Investigations,' she said brightly.

It was Decker, speaking from the car phone. 'Hi, it's me. Turn the TV on. It just came over the radio. Cindy Nathan's been arrested for the murder of her husband.'

Lorraine hurried into Reception and switched on the TV. There was Cindy Nathan, almost hidden by a battery of cameras, being hurried into the police department. Feinstein, her lawyer, his arms wide, was trying to protect his client. She looked tiny and frightened, in a simple white linen button-through dress and carrying her jacket.

Lorraine sat on the edge of the sofa with Tiger at her feet. Then she shot up, tripping over Tiger as she snatched up a tape and rammed it into the video machine. At that moment Decker returned. 'Quick! Video this, will you?' She passed him the remote control. They recorded the coverage of Cindy Nathan's arrest every time it was screened – a lot was repetitive but they learned that she came from Milwaukee and had left at fifteen after winning a beauty competition. A few modelling jobs followed, and then her short stint in the soap drama *Paradise Motel* in which she played a chambermaid, not very well.

Harry Nathan was more handsome than Lorraine had expected, a tall, lean, muscular man with dark hair, worn quite long, and a dazzling, though somehow charmless smile. The still photographs of him were glamorous, mostly taken at society functions, premières, Oscar nights, with celebrities on his arm. His associates from the studio said in interviews that Nathan would be greatly missed by all who had ever had the pleasure of working with him, and his secretary, in floods of tears, was so distraught she could hardly speak.

Lorraine continued to watch the news coverage at home. It said nothing new. There was no mention of where she was being held pending arraignment.

Nathan was a self-made millionaire and renowned art collector, who had moved from making commercials to directing zany comedy movies, which had been a big hit back in the eighties. He had then turned his attention to producing rather than directing, and had moved gradually towards cheap, adult-oriented movies on the verge of porn.

Lorraine was about to call it a night when, channel-surfing, she caught an exclusive interview with Harry Nathan's second wife, Kendall. It struck her that there had been neither comment nor reaction from the woman who had been married longest to Harry Nathan, Ms Sorenson.

Kendall Nathan whispered that she was deeply shocked by events, and also felt compassion for Cindy. She had been married to Harry Nathan for four years and knew better than anyone that he had been difficult to live with, but their divorce had been amicable, and she had continued to enjoy a deep friendship with her ex-husband. They had also remained business partners.

33

Then she gave a tremulous smile, her voice breaking. 'Harry was always an honourable man whose many friends will be devastated, as I am, by his tragic and untimely death.'

Most people would have focused on Kendall's performance as a grieving woman, but Lorraine was trying to ascertain whether it could have been Kendall who had called her agency.

The morning newspapers were full of the update on the shooting, and as there were no other job prospects Lorraine and Decker cut out all the articles and pinned them together with the previous day's.

At twelve they had a call from a Mrs Walgraf asking for an appointment with regard to her divorce.

At two o'clock another appointment was booked and, to Lorraine's astonishment, a third call came in at four. The next two days were busy.

After being held at the Cybil Brand Institute for Women in the female facility of the Los Angeles County jail, Cindy Nathan was duly arraigned on charges of murder, pleaded not guilty, and was released on bail, security set at three million dollars. No one saw her leave the courthouse, as she was taken out through a small back entrance because of the number of press waiting outside. Her lawyer read a statement on her behalf: she was innocent and begged to be left alone to mourn the loss of the husband she adored. She would give no further press statements or interviews in the lead-up to the trial as she was pregnant. Feinstein assured the press that he was confident that all charges against his client would be dismissed, and that Mrs Nathan needed rest and care.

Her pregnancy was in the early stages and the stress of her arrest had made her ill. She was now fearful, Feinstein ended, that she might lose the child for which she and her husband had prayed.

Three weeks after Cindy Nathan's release, Lorraine had traced one missing daughter, and had discovered that Mrs Walgraf's husband had obviously been preparing for his divorce for many months before his wife had become aware of his intentions.

Mrs Walgraf did not have the money to pay Lorraine, who would not press her – she felt sorry for the woman.

'Well, let's hope we get something a bit more financially rewarding next,' Decker said.

Lorraine yawned. It was almost time to leave. Tiger was stretched out on his back on the pretty cherry-coloured sofa in Reception, his legs in the air. 'He's not supposed to get up on that,' she said, irritated.

'I know, my dear, but you try and shift him!'

The phone rang and Decker snatched it up. It was the main reception downstairs. He listened, then covered the receiver. 'It's Mrs Nathan. She's downstairs. She wants to see you.'

Lorraine smiled. 'You know, I thought I'd hear from her again. Ask her to come up.'

Lorraine put on some fresh lipstick and ran a comb quickly through her hair. She was just checking her reflection when Decker tapped and opened her door. Tiger was barking and tried to get into the office between Decker's legs. 'Mrs Nathan to see you, Mrs Page. Sit!'

Tiger slunk off to the sofa and lay flat on it with his head on his paws.

Decker closed the office door and returned to his desk, wishing he could be privy to the conversation. He was beginning to like the job. He'd been worried during the past week as there had been little to do, but now he couldn't wait to make a quiet call to Adam Elliot to tell him who had arrived.

Cindy Nathan wore dark glasses, a short powder blue princess-line dress, low, peep-toe shoes in white patent leather, and a silver chain and padlock, fastened tightly, like a dog collar, round her neck: a gift from her loving spouse, Lorraine had no doubt. She didn't have a purse, just a small white-leather billfold.

'Please sit down. Sorry about my dog. He's supposed to be trained, but he hasn't got it quite right yet. Can I offer you tea or coffee?'

'No, nothing, thank you.' She was perched on the edge of the chair.

'How are you?'

'Oh, I'm fine, get sick in the mornings, but they say the first few months are the worst,' Cindy said. 'Do you have children?'

Lorraine nodded. 'Two daughters. They live with their father.' She said it quickly, wanting to avoid a long conversation about births and pregnancies.

'Harry's other kid didn't live – this would have been his only child. It would be terrible if it was born in prison.'

Lorraine looked at her fingers. 'Do you think that's a possibility?'

'That's why I'm here. I need someone on my side.'

'What about your lawyer?'

'Oh, I have a whole team of lawyers, LA's best.'

'And what do they say?'

'Oh, they seem pretty sure I did it. They don't say it, it's just how they ask me all these questions, over and over.'

'Do you know what the evidence is against you, Mrs Nathan?'

Cindy looked down at her toenails, painted electric blue. 'Well, the gun was mine.'

'Are your fingerprints on it?'

'Yes.'

'And they have the gun?'

'The police found it in the shrubbery by the pool.'

'Did you fire it, Mrs Nathan?'

'Yes.'

'But you've said you did not kill your husband.'

'Yes, but you asked if I fired it and I did,' Cindy said, with a childish sort of exactness. 'A few times, just practising. Once I fired it at Harry, but I missed and there were blanks in it anyway.'

Lorraine picked up a pen and twisted it in her fingers. 'Did you fire your gun on the day your husband was found dead?'

'No.'

'Where did you leave it the last time you used it?'

'In our bedroom, on my side of the bed, in a silver box. Harry had guns all over the house – he was paranoid about security. He had a licence, and he even had a gun in his car.'

'Could I come out to the house, Mrs Nathan?'

Cindy nodded. 'Will you say that you're going to give

37

me a massage? I don't want them to know. I don't think they would like it, you know, me hiring you, without telling them.'

'Who are you referring to, Mrs Nathan?'

'Oh, the lawyers and the staff.'

Lorraine leaned back in her chair. 'Did you love your husband, Mrs Nathan?'

'Yes.'

'As his widow, are you his main beneficiary?'

'I get the house and the stock he had in the company, and his second wife, Kendall, gets his share in the gallery on Beverly Drive, though the will says that if there should be issue of our marriage, then the kid would be the main beneficiary and I get a lot less. The most valuable stuff is the art in the house – Harry was a collector. Feinstein says it's mine as part of the contents of the house, but Kendall's got some attorney to write claiming she and Harry agreed to split it so her half wasn't his to leave. There's something about Sonja too, but Feinstein says it won't add up to more than a few mementoes. It's all very complicated . . .' Her voice trailed off.

'I'll come and see you tomorrow, all right?'

Cindy nodded, then opened her wallet. 'You gave me your card, so I got the cheque all ready. All you got to do is fill in the amount. I don't know how much you charge, but I want you to look after me, exclusive, so that will be extra, and I'll pay extra because I don't want you to tell anybody that you're working for me. If it gets out, I'll deny it, and I'll get one of my fancy lawyers to sue you. Do you have client confidentiality?'

'Of course.'

*

Decker ushered Cindy Nathan out of the office and into the elevator, while Lorraine remained at her desk, staring at the looped, childish writing. She had suggested Cindy engage her on a weekly basis, and said it would be three hundred dollars a day plus expenses.

Cindy had counted on her fingers, then leaned over to use Lorraine's felt-tipped pen. 'I'm going to pay you five thousand dollars a week, and I want you for a month to start with. Then, if everything works out all right for me, I won't need you any more.'

When Decker returned, Lorraine held up the cheque between her fingers. He took it and looked stunned.

'Shit! Twenty grand! What in God's name do you have to do for that?'

Lorraine perched on the side of the desk. 'Long time ago, one of the boys arrested this old guy for passing dud cheques. When he was questioned he shrugged his shoulders and . . . he was crazy. He'd found the cheque book in a supermarket.'

'I don't follow. What's that got to do with Cindy Nathan?'

'I think she's crazy – the elevator's certainly not quite going to the top floor. I wouldn't be surprised if that cheque bounced. On the other hand, she's a wealthy widow.'

Decker chuckled. 'Well, hell, let's bank it first thing in the morning, and if she's out to lunch we're laughing.'

Lorraine clicked her fingers to Tiger. 'Yeah, you go ahead and do that. Oh, that phone call Cindy denies making.' Decker nodded. He still felt awful about the recording.

'Cindy has quite a high-pitched voice. If she got hysterical, like she'd just shot her husband, it's likely her voice would go up a notch. Whoever made that call, if my memory serves me well, had quite a deep, almost throaty smoker's voice.' She gave him that cock-eyed, smug smile. He said nothing.

Lorraine still hovered at the doorway. 'Did Mrs Nathan come with a chauffeur?'

'I have no idea,' Decker said. As the door closed behind her he shut his eyes, tried to remember the voice. Had it been deep, throaty as she had just said? He could not remember.

According to the doorman in the main lobby, Cindy Nathan had walked into the building. He had seen no driver, and she had not left keys for the valet-parking facility. She had asked him which floor Page Investigations was on, and then used the intercom phone to the office. 'I'm sorry if I did anything wrong,' the doorman said apologetically.

'You didn't,' Lorraine replied, as she left, with Tiger straining at the leash. But she knew intuitively that something was wrong. Nothing quite added up. She felt good, though, and she was twenty thousand dollars better off. Page Investigations was up and rolling.

CHAPTER 2

LORRAINE ARRIVED at the Nathans' mansion with her CD playing Maria Callas singing *Madame Butterfly* at full volume. The door was opened by a middle-aged Mexican maid who ushered her into the cool hallway and motioned her through an archway framed by a broad-leafed twining vine growing around two carved pine pillars. Looking up the floating stairs, Lorraine saw several modern art works. Whether they were valuable or not, she couldn't tell.

Through the archway was a shallow flight of pink polished granite steps leading down to the main living area of the house. Floor to ceiling windows gave it a lovely, light, delicate feel, and the room had been divided into a sitting space on one side and an area for formal dining on the other. There were large plain white armchairs and sofas, and one piece of 'art' furniture, a strange green and black chair with a round, stuffed base and padded back, which looked to Lorraine like a cartoon-style tea-cup or a fairground waltzer.

Cindy Nathan sat in the tea-cup, curled up like a child with a glass of orange juice cupped in her hands, rolling a clear plastic beach ball back and forth over the same six inches of floor with a tiny, tanned foot, drying the varnish on her toenails. 'Oh, hi, have you come to give me a massage?' she said brightly, getting up. Today she had her hair in Dutch-girl braids, high on her head, and had made up her eyes in a defiantly garish blue, her lips with raspberry frosting. She wore a yellow top with peasant-style embroidery and blue and yellow windowpane check pants.

Cindy's acting – as she pretended Lorraine was a masseuse – was as bad as it had been in her TV roles. She gestured for Lorraine to follow her into an adjoining room. It was a gym, very professional with weights, sit-up bars, medicine balls and leg stretchers. Close to a boxing punch-bag, in the centre of the space, was a row of different-sized gloves in bright red leather. 'I always used to call this Harry's toy cupboard. He was always in here when he was home, working out.'

'He must have been fit.'

'Yes, he was. Well, so he should have been. He spent enough time looking after his body.' She giggled, and covered her mouth. 'I reckon the reason he was so obsessive was . . .' she held up her little finger and waggled it '. . . he was kind of small. Some parts of the body you can never build up.'

Lorraine perched on one of the black leather-covered benches, irritated by the girl's innuendo. 'Did you kill him, Cindy?' she asked.

'No, I did not. I did not.'

Lorraine smiled encouragingly at her. 'Good. Now, can we talk in here or not?'

'Yes, it's safe.'

'Safe?'

'Ah . . . yes. Harry used to record stuff,' Cindy said, colouring slightly, and Lorraine had the impression that the girl had said something she hadn't meant to. 'But down here was his private place. Nobody came down here but him,' she chattered on. 'I used to have to go out to my classes – he wouldn't let me work out down here.'

'What kind of thing did Harry record?' Lorraine asked.

'Oh . . . just conversations. He taped phone calls, and there were cameras in all the rooms in the house. For security, you know, the art.'

'You knew about that, though.'

'Oh, yes, I knew.'

Again Lorraine felt that Cindy wasn't telling the full truth, and she wondered whether the presence of a pornographer, an ex-actress and a large number of cameras under the same roof had had the inevitable consequence. 'He didn't make any other sort of recordings?'

'No,' Cindy said, a shade too quickly. 'He was just paranoid, even about personal things. I mean, he hated anyone to know he'd had a face-lift, and he dyed his hair – plus he took his drugs down here.' It was a titbit thrown out to shift the conversation away from a subject Cindy clearly didn't want to discuss.

Lorraine asked, 'What drugs did he use?'

'Oh, stuff for body-building mostly. Sometimes he'd have a few lines of cocaine, but mostly it was steroids, or speed – he was a real speed freak. But he was careful. He'd never over-indulge – he always knew exactly what he was taking.'

'Did you take drugs?'

'Me?' Cindy gave a goofy grin, suddenly the little girl again, as if it were all a game. 'Oh, yeah, I'd do anything that was going, mostly cocaine. But I haven't touched

43

anything since I knew about the baby. I've got to take care of myself. You have to when you're pregnant.'

Cindy gazed at her reflection in the mirrors, and Lorraine considered how to question her. She would like access to the tape recordings Cindy had mentioned. 'Can I just take you through the events up to your arrest?' she said.

'Sure. Do you want a drink?'

The girl's butterfly mind digressed into trivia – either she didn't realize the seriousness of her situation, or she was trying to hold on to some kind of normality. She wandered off to a small kitchen area, tucked away at one side of the gym by the showers.

'Just water for me,' Lorraine said, following her.

Cindy opened the fridge and selected a can of Diet Coke for herself. She opened a cupboard and took out a glass. Having forgotten, it seemed, Lorraine's water, she opened the can and poured out the contents.

'Where exactly were you on that morning?' Lorraine asked, sitting down on a work bench and taking out her notepad.

'I was lying on the balcony, over there.' Cindy waved her hand. 'I fell asleep.'

'Would that be at the front of the house?' Lorraine asked.

'Sort of. There's balconies all over the house, but I kind of move around with the sun, you know, so I was on that one.' She pointed to indicate which side of the house she meant.

'And the swimming pool is where exactly?'

'Behind you,' Cindy said.

'Is there access from here to the pool?'

'Of course. Behind the mirrors, they slide back.'

44

'Right. So what time were you sunbathing?'

'Oh, the usual time.' She took a slug of her Coke, draining the glass.

'Yes, but I don't know your usual routine, so if you would just take me through it.' Lorraine tried not to sound irritated.

'Okay. I get up usually about nine, sometimes earlier, sometimes a lot later, shower, then work on my tan for a couple of hours – just my body, I don't do my face.'

'Do the servants all know your routine?'

'Of course, I've been doing it since I got married – get up, shower, sunbathe, swim, get dressed for lunch.'

Cindy started doing half-hearted t'ai chi exercises in front of the mirror.

'So on the day you discovered your husband's body, you were sunbathing as usual and you fell asleep. A loud noise woke you – about what time would that have been?'

Cindy wrinkled her nose. 'Maybe eleven. I was asleep the first time, then I heard it again. At first I thought it was a car backfiring. It was just one loud bang. Then I saw all these birds flying up, from the garden by the shrubbery. You can't see the pool from the balcony, just the edge of the garden, so I called Harry, wondering if he was messing about.'

'Messing about?'

'Yeah. Sometimes he'd take pot-shots at the birds. It used to make me mad as hell, because once he killed one.'

Lorraine doodled on her pad as Cindy went into a long monologue on how she loved all of nature's creatures. Finally she interrupted, 'You know, Cindy, if you're found guilty of murdering your husband, you'll be locked up in a prison and you'll be hard pushed to hear a single tweet. Now I know it may be tedious, but I have to ask all these questions so I know exactly what I should—'

'I never killed him,' the girl said, red-faced with anger.

'I know you didn't, but you're to stand trial for it, unless—'

'I never killed him. I found him, that's all.'

'So, will you close your eyes and tell me exactly what you did, from the time the noise woke you to the moment you discovered your husband's body?'

Cindy covered her eyes with her hands. 'You mean, like creatively visualize?' Clearly this was something she was familiar with.

'Just tell me what happened.'

'After the bang, I called out his name,' Cindy began. 'When I got no reply, I picked up my towel, and my sun creams and my straw hat. I went into the bedroom and decided I'd have a swim. I didn't have anything on – I sunbathe naked – so I put my swimsuit on and got a big outdoor towel. Then I heard another bang – I was pretty sure it was a gun this time, so I put on my mules and went downstairs . . .' She withdrew her hands from her face, and her big blue eyes stared ahead. 'I went to the pool and put my towel on the chair by the table. I saw Harry's towel, his sandals, and his cigarette packet. I looked around because one cigarette was smoked down – there was a long line of ash on it.'

Cindy blinked, and Lorraine noticed that she was looking at herself in the mirrors again as she spoke.

'I was about to dive in so I went to the deep end. First thing I noticed was the water was kind of pink, and then I saw him. I called out his name – he was lying face down, arms outstretched – but I knew something bad had happened, and I started to scream. I screamed and screamed.'

'How long was it before someone came out to you?'

Cindy stared at herself and Lorraine had to repeat the question.

'I don't know, it seemed a very long time. Then Juana came out, with Jose just behind her, and she said to me, she said . . .'

For the first time since they had come into the gym Lorraine saw some emotion. 'She said to me, "Holy Mother, Mrs Nathan, what have you done?"'

Lorraine waited, watching Cindy closely. The girl's breathing had become irregular, and she was swallowing rapidly. 'Go on, Cindy. Then what happened?'

'Jose jumped into the pool, and he said, "She's shot him! She's shot him!"' She gulped air into her lungs, her chest heaving. 'They dragged him to the shallow end. I could see white bone . . . and they couldn't lift him out.' She shuddered.

Lorraine tapped her notebook. 'Go on.'

'They called the police, I guess.'

Lorraine looked up. 'But Cindy, you told me you called the police.'

Cindy blinked. 'Oh, yes, that's right. I did.'

Lorraine made a note that the call to her office had come in at just after eleven o'clock. If Cindy couldn't recall contacting the police, maybe she couldn't remember calling Lorraine either.

Cindy continued, 'I called Mr Feinstein, because the next thing the garden was full of people and someone brought me some brandy. I was still by the pool, but sitting on one of the wooden chairs, and all I could think of was that he'd been sitting where I was sitting, smoking that cigarette. Then Mr Feinstein said to me, "Cindy, they want to take you into the station to ask you some questions," and that it would be best if I got dressed.' Cindy began to twist a strand of her blonde hair through her fingers. 'I got dressed, I got my purse and my sunglasses, just like I was going out shopping or something, but I didn't put any make-up on, and then they took me to the station.'

'Do you recall the name of the officer who questioned you?'

'No.'

'Did Mr Feinstein come with you?'

'No, he came on later.'

'So you had no lawyer with you?'

'No, I was on my own.'

Lorraine jotted some notes, then looked up sharply as Cindy began to cry. 'They said they found my gun, they said I did it, but I kept on saying over and over that I couldn't have done it, that I wouldn't have done something that bad even if I said I would.'

Lorraine repeated, ' "Said I would"?'

'Well, I told you, I was always threatening him.' Cindy's voice steadied a little, and her chin lifted. 'I was always saying I'd kill him, because he used to get me so mad. He could be so mean to me, I'd get mad as hell. I'd scream and shout and try to hit him, but he would just laugh, and that got me even madder, but I never meant what I said. It was just I was upset.' She dissolved into real tears again – more at the memory of her anger and humiliation, Lorraine thought, than out of grief at her husband's death.

'I need a tissue,' Cindy said, sniffing, her dark blue mascara beginning to run.

Lorraine crossed to the shower area and headed for one of the toilets to get some tissue. She dragged off a length of paper and hurried back to the gym.

'I didn't do it. I wouldn't kill him, even though he got me madder than hell!' Cindy mopped her face, then blew her nose. 'I didn't kill him, did I? Please tell me I didn't do it.'

Lorraine bent down to her, in an almost motherly fashion. 'But you didn't do it, did you?'

Cindy wiped her face and blew her nose again, her voice a hoarse whisper. 'I don't know. You see, it's all blurred. I mean, I'd know, wouldn't I? I'd know if I *had* done it. That's what you got to help me with, because I'm all confused.'

Lorraine straightened up. One moment Cindy had given her a detailed description of what she had done leading up to the discovery of the body, the next she was asking if she could have been the one to pull the trigger. It didn't make sense.

'You've just told me how you found the body, Cindy, so why are you thinking now you might have killed him?'

Cindy rocked forward, head in her hands. ''Cos I can only remember going to the pool and seeing him in the water. Nothing before that. I do the same thing every day – I mean, I could be just filling in the gaps.'

'But you said you heard the gunshot?'

'Yes, I know. *I know I said that.*'

'Are you telling me now that you didn't hear it?'

'*Yes.* No, I heard it, I'm not lying to you. I heard that one, but . . .'

'But what?'

Cindy twisted the damp tissue in her fingers. 'Maybe it didn't happen when I think it happened.'

'I don't understand.'

'What if I'd done it before?'

'You'll have to help me, Cindy, I can't follow what you're saying. How do you mean before?'

'Earlier.'

Lorraine sighed. 'You mean before you went to the balcony to sunbathe?'

'No. I mean the first shot. When I was sleeping. I mean, I could have done it half asleep. Like in an altered state of consciousness – you know, the way people remember past lives, and sometimes they just act them out? I mean, I could have been a murderess or anything. Maybe I just couldn't help myself.'

Lorraine rolled her eyes as Cindy sprang to her feet, thinking that her client had been watching too many of her husband's killer-bimbo fantasies. She watched the girl dive at the punch-bag and hit it, her face a mask of anger. Lorraine let her go until she tired herself out and eventually put her arms around the punch-bag, hugging it tightly.

'Sometimes he didn't come home,' she said softly. Lorraine kept silent. 'Often he stayed out all night, and I knew about the other women. I knew he was never faithful, he always said that to me, said he could never be faithful to one woman and that I'd just have to accept that. The day before I found him, he'd been really mean to me. We argued at breakfast, and then he came down here. I came after him and he was furious, but I wouldn't go. I said to him that if he carried on this way I'd leave him, and he said he didn't care what I did and he laughed at me, kept on punching this thing, laughing and ignoring me. So I went and got the gun, and when I came back he was on that weight machine, and I went right up to him and I pointed it at his head, and I said that was the last time he was ever going to laugh at me.'

Lorraine still said nothing, but was interested to note that Cindy was calm now, her mind focused on what she was saying.

'He looked at me, then he reached out and pulled the gun over so it was almost in his mouth and he told me to fire it.'

'And?'

Cindy sighed. 'I did. I pulled the trigger, but it wasn't loaded.' She pushed away the punch-bag, which began to swing slowly. 'He got up from the bench and hit me in the stomach. I fell backwards onto the floor and he kept on coming towards me, but he stepped right over me and walked into the showers. I screamed at him that I would get him the next time. Next time the gun would be loaded.' She rubbed her belly. 'Punched me right in the baby, and it hurt so bad I was sick, but he made me get dressed and go out for dinner at Morton's, and he told everyone what I'd done, and they all laughed. He kept on fooling around at dinner with this baby zucchini as the gun, shoving it into his mouth, and everyone laughed, and I got so upset I was crying, but I wasn't going to stay and be made a fool of. So I got up and I shouted it out. I said the next time he wouldn't live to tell anybody anything because the next time I'd make sure I killed him.'

Cindy went to fetch another Diet Coke. This time she drank it from the can. 'He didn't come home. I waited and waited, and it was six o'clock in the morning when he came back. He was in his dressing room, taking his clothes off, when I went in to see him. He just told me to get out, but I wouldn't. I said he shouldn't make a fool of me in front of people like he had done, but he just kept on choosing which shirt he was going to wear, ignoring me again.'

Lorraine waited while Cindy sipped the Coke.

'I went into the bedroom to get the gun. I meant it, I was going to kill him, and I'd just figured out how to load it, but I couldn't remember where it was, or if I'd taken it from the gym. I was looking all over the room for it when he strolled in all dressed up and Jose knocked on the door.' Cindy frowned as she tried to recall the details.

'Jose said that the car needed to be serviced, and did Harry need it after his breakfast meeting at seven. Harry said he didn't. He'd had a long, hard night and he'd just sit by the pool reading scripts after his meeting. Then . . . he started laughing and he told Jose that I'd threatened to kill him again and that Jose was his witness that I was a real flake, a psychiatric case. He knows how upset I get about him saying things like that because I've had, you know, some problems.'

Lorraine shifted her weight. 'Problems?' she said gently.

'Mmmm, I have these . . . kind of bad days, you know. I get depressed, uptight about things, angry.'

'Can you go back to what you were saying about when your husband and Jose were talking in the bedroom? What happened then?'

'Oh, yeah. Well, Harry left. And I went back to bed. I'd had such a bad night I told Juana not to disturb me. I couldn't sleep, so I got up and went out on the balcony

52

to lie in the sun, and I guess I must have gone to sleep there. I had a nightmare, me shooting Harry, like I'd threatened to do, and something woke me up – well, I think it was me woke myself up because I pulled the trigger. I fired the gun. But I'm sure it was in my dream and then I'm not sure. That's what terrifies me. Did I do it or was I dreaming?'

'How long do you think there was between the two shots, or the one shot and what might have been a car backfiring?'

'Er . . . maybe ten minutes.'

'About how long does it take to get from the balcony to the pool, Cindy?'

Cindy drew open the sliding door. 'Oh, four, maybe five minutes, but it would depend on how fast you were moving.'

Lorraine picked up her purse and followed Cindy out. 'Do you think you're going to be all right here alone?'

'If I'm not there's Jose and Juana, but they don't like me.'

'When you said I had to pretend to be a masseuse you seemed worried someone would find out that I was investigating the case.'

'I am. I don't want Jose or that bitch Juana to know. I don't want anyone knowing my business because they all believe I killed Harry, and so they won't say nice things about me in the court. But if they saw this, maybe they would change their minds.' Cindy pulled up her top. There was a nightmare bruise across her belly, a virtual imprint of a fist. 'This is nothin'. He was always knocking me around, just not my face.'

'Does anyone know he did this to you?'

'Maybe his ex-wives or his girlfriends – my mother

53

always used to say once a wife-beater always one – but they won't lift a finger for me, will they? Nor will my mother come to think of it.' Lorraine lit a cigarette. She asked Cindy for the names of the people who had been at the dinner the night before Nathan was killed, the addresses and names of girlfriends and ex-wives, business associates, anyone who would benefit from his death, anyone who had a grudge against him. Eventually she said, 'Let's leave it there for the present, Cindy,' and got up to go. 'I'll start checking some of this stuff out.'

'Sure.' Cindy shrugged. 'But I'll see you tomorrow anyway, won't I?'

'What?' Lorraine was surprised.

'Harry's funeral. The coroner's office released the body last night. I just called Forest Lawn and told them to take care of everything – they said they'd put a notice in the papers and all that stuff. I'd kind of like it if you came. I mean, my folks aren't going to be there, and I never liked his that much.'

'I'd be glad to,' Lorraine said, thinking that a chance to get a closer look at Harry Nathan's friends and relatives would be welcome. 'What time?'

'Eleven,' Cindy said. 'It's in that fake New England church they have there. Match all his phoney friends.' She gave a wry smile, but Lorraine saw the flicker of pain in her eyes. She could see too that having become Mrs Nathan III at the age of nineteen hadn't landed this isolated, mixed-up girl in any bed of roses.

'Okay,' Lorraine said. 'Just one last thing. Can I have access to some of these recordings Harry made?'

Once again it was clear that Cindy was uncomfortable, but she said, 'Oh, sure. I'll have Jose send them over.'

'Couldn't I have them now?'

'It might take a while to find them. He kept them in weird places.'

She was evidently preparing the ground for some of the tapes to become conveniently untraceable, Lorraine noted. 'Didn't the police ask for them?' she asked.

'Well, I didn't tell them about them. I figured, I pay my taxes, let them do their job!' Cindy said with another touch of defiance. But then the fight went out of her. 'Besides, they're so fucking sure it's me that they aren't going to bother listening to ten million hours of Harry talking about all the ginseng he stuck up his ass.'

'I see,' Lorraine said evenly. 'Well, *I*'d be interested to hear about it, if you could send over any tapes you have. See you tomorrow.'

By the time Lorraine returned to the office, she felt drained and Decker looked at her with his head on one side. 'Go well, did it?'

Lorraine tossed her purse down. 'You try interviewing Cindy Nathan. The porch light's on, but there's nobody home. She's not sure that she didn't do it, because she dreamed that she'd just pulled the trigger when she heard a gunshot, or as she told me repeatedly, it might have been a car backfiring!'

'What's your gut feeling?'

Lorraine leaned back in her chair. 'I don't think she did it, but I'd better find something fast to prove that she didn't because, pushed by any decent prosecutor, she'll admit that she did. She's that dumb.'

'Why would someone like Harry Nathan marry such a flake?'

Lorraine sipped her coffee. 'Because she's twenty and

55

he was a fifty-year-old guy dyeing his hair and having face-lifts, and she's got a body like a fourteen-year-old Venus, and an angel's face. He also had quite a line-up of women as well as Cindy, plus remained friendly with his ex-wife, who still, by the way, runs his art gallery. I'd say Cindy was the classic babe armpiece for a man with a small dick.'

'Oh, he had one of those, did he?' Decker said, camp.

'According to Little Miss Bimbo he did, but she's having his baby. Not that he seemed all that interested – almost punched it through her backbone. I saw the bruise.'

'So,' Decker said, leaning on the doorframe, 'what's the next move?'

'I think she's hiding something about tapes Nathan made at the house – phone conversations, security videos. She didn't tell the police and she kind of let it slip to me, but she said she'd send the tapes over. We'll just have to wait and see what we get.'

Cindy Nathan brought the boxes upstairs from the gym herself and stacked them in the hall. She had listened to some of the conversations again and again, just to hear his voice, but they had agreed a code and stuck to it and there was nothing to make Harry or anyone else suspicious: even the police could have listened to them, if they'd found them. She dialled a cab company, said she wanted some items delivered, and sat down to wait for the driver to come. It would have been easier, of course, to send Jose, but she was sick of Harry's housekeepers knowing all her comings and goings, the pair of them always watching her. They had been surprised when she had given them the rest of the day off, but within half an hour they had been on their way to Juana's sister.

When the cab driver showed up, Cindy gave him the boxes of tapes with Lorraine's address and twenty-five dollars. Good riddance, she thought. Mrs Page was welcome to listen to all the rambling rubbish Harry recorded. There was nothing to find.

The videos, though, they were something else – but where the fuck were they? Harry had kept all the recordings together in the safe under the floor in his dressing room but the videotapes, both the ones from the security cameras and the . . . the other ones, were gone. Cindy tried to tell herself that if she couldn't find them, nobody else was likely to, but the possibility that they might be circulating somewhere out there tormented her.

It was more likely that the tapes had never left the house, she told herself. Harry had just moved them again, the mistrustful, suspicious-minded bastard. She set off for the stairs to have another look in the gym, where there was certainly no visible hiding place for the substantial stack of videos. She deduced he must have had a new cavity let into the floor or the wall.

The noise of Cindy's tapping on what she considered various likely spots on the walls masked the sound of the doors opening to the pool area. At first she didn't notice the man's presence, and for over a minute he watched her in silence before he spoke.

'Cindy,' he said, his voice curiously cold and flat.

She froze.

'Cindy,' he said again.

'Jesus, Raymond, you gave me such a fucking scare! Don't ever do that to me again! How did you get in here?'

In front of her was a tall man with thinning silver-grey hair, and an extraordinarily handsome face. When he began to speak, it became clear that behind the distinguished façade was a vapid, unstable personality. There was only one thing Raymond Vallance could ever have been, and that is what he was: an actor.

'Through the pool doors. I still have the key to this fairy bower, Rapunzel, remember?' He had the mannered and over-emphasized diction of the lifelong performer, and shook the key at Cindy before he put it back in his pocket.

'Well, long time, no see,' Cindy said, trying to ignore his apparent *froideur* and assuming a coquettish air as she moved across to him. She made to slide her arms round his waist, but Vallance stepped away immediately. Close to, she could see that he was grey in the face, haggard, as though he hadn't slept in days, and his clothes were creased and dirty. Not that that was necessarily anything new with Raymond, she thought, but he was clearly in no mood for fun and games.

'Cindy,' he said, 'we have to be very careful now, you know that.'

'For Chrissakes, Raymond. Harry's being pickled in brine at Forest Lawn right this minute!' Cindy cried. 'We don't have to hide anything.'

'Don't talk that way about him, you tacky little piece of trash,' Vallance snapped, and Cindy recoiled from the cold anger in his voice. For a moment she had the impression that he was genuinely in the grip of strong emotion, almost as though he were fighting back tears – but if Raymond was so crazy about Harry, what had he been doing fucking the ass off Harry's wife every time his back was turned?

'Raymond, I haven't seen you in weeks. I'm, like, totally strung out and I'm *pregnant*, Raymond. Doesn't that mean anything to you?' she began, her voice trembling.

'Not particularly,' Vallance said, in the same odd, cold tone she had never heard from him before. 'Other people's children have never interested me much.'

'Raymond—' Cindy wailed.

Vallance cut her short. 'I came here to ask you only two things, Cindy,' he said. 'First, what happened to the tapes?'

'I don't know,' she said, her eyes sliding away from his.

'Did the police take them?'

'I can't find them – I mean the videos. They were in the safe and now they're gone. I took the tapes from the phone out and—'

He interrupted her again. 'And where are they?'

Cindy squirmed. 'I . . . put 'em somewhere safe.'

'Cindy,' Vallance said, grabbing the girl by her upper arms, 'tell me where the fucking tapes are right now or I'll break your arm.' He shook her hard, and she saw a darkness in his eyes she had not seen before. It chilled her to the bone.

'I – I hired a PI to, like, look after us,' Cindy stammered, beginning to cry. 'I gave them to her. I had to, Raymond, it would've looked worse if I hadn't, and I checked 'em all.'

Vallance thrust her violently away from him. She stumbled in the high, unwieldy shoes and fell backwards onto the floor. 'You sent those tapes to a private investigator?' he said, now white with rage. 'Tell me her name.'

'Page,' Cindy sobbed. 'Lorraine Page. On . . . West Pico.'

'Well, I'll take care of that,' he said. He stood looking at the girl's huddled body on the floor, listening to her cry. He turned to go, but then bent down beside her.

'Cindy?' His voice was oddly gentle. 'Just one last thing I need to know, Cindy.' She lifted her head and wiped her eyes with the back of her hand, smearing the blue eye-shadow in streaks across her face.

'You killed Harry, didn't you, Cindy?'

She sensed danger immediately and tried to roll away from him, but in one movement Vallance caught her by the hip, turned her onto her back and sat astride her. 'Did you kill him, Cindy?' he asked, as though they were exchanging pleasantries at a party.

'Raymond,' she wept, almost hysterical, 'you're hurting me! You'll hurt the baby!'

'Answer me, Cindy,' Vallance demanded, and banged her head hard on the floor. 'Did you kill him or not?'

'I didn't! I swear it! I swear it on my kid's life, Raymond – it's Harry's kid.' She did not know what prompted her to add the last words, but she felt the high tension in Vallance's body slacken.

'Well,' he said, releasing her and giving her a look almost of disgust, 'maybe it is.'

He rocked back onto his heels with a peculiarly graceful movement, and got to his feet, looking down at her as dispassionately as though she were a drunk he had to step over in the street. 'See you at Forest Lawn,' he said, and was gone.

Decker's phone rang. It was the doorman: there had been a delivery, in three cardboard boxes. He'd bring them up.

The boxes were stiff-sided packing cases, thickly Sellotaped across the opening flaps, and numbered one to three. Decker and Lorraine ripped open case one.

'Harry Nathan's private recordings of phone calls and anyone who called at the house,' Lorraine said.

'Dear God, this'll take weeks to plough through.' Decker looked over the rows and rows of tapes, marked with dates.

Lorraine pointed to case three. 'Start with the most recent and work backwards. See you tomorrow after I've held Cindy's hand at Forest Lawn.' She bent down and clipped on Tiger's lead. The big dog immediately began to drag her towards the door.

Decker checked his watch – almost six fifteen. He packed twenty of the tapes for the last three months into his car tape case, stuck it in his gym bag and decided that he would start playing them as he drove home.

Raymond Vallance sat in the downstairs lobby of Lorraine's building and observed Decker carefully through the iridescent blue lenses of his last season's Calvin Klein sunglasses. He had been just in time to see three packing cases go in, and one lady, a big dog and now quite a cute little fag come out. No boxes.

He gave the doorman a pleasant smile, folded his newspaper and walked out onto the street. He leaned back against the wall, as Decker went to the entrance to the motor court, and took a slim leather address book from an inside pocket.

No numbers were ever deleted from Raymond Vallance's little black book: you never knew when you might want to look up an old friend, perhaps for a favour or, even better, suggest something that might be mutually beneficial. Not that this party was a friend exactly, but he had been useful to both Harry and himself on a number of occasions in the past with respect to little matters of entertainment – company or chemicals. But this was more serious. He dialled the number and the young man picked up almost at once.

'Yo, bro,' Vallance began in the slangy sing-song voice and Brooklyn accent he adopted when talking to black people. 'You busy tonight? Got a little job for you . . .'

CHAPTER 3

NEXT DAY when Decker walked into the building he noticed that the door to Page Investigations was a fraction open and assumed that Lorraine must have called in on her way to the funeral. He extended his hand to open the door further and his nostrils burned with the smell of acid. Decker stepped back and kicked it open instead.

The packing cases remained where he had stacked them on the floor, but the cardboard was sodden, and the tapes still smouldered as the acid destroyed even their plastic surrounds. Not one was salvageable – yet nothing else seemed to have been disturbed. He entered Lorraine's office with trepidation – had she disturbed the intruder?

The desk drawers were open and a few papers littered the floor. At first sight nothing else seemed to have been damaged except for a photograph of Lorraine, which lay behind the desk, acid eating into the face, burning and twisting the features grotesquely.

'Jesus,' he said quietly, and picked up the phone, about to call the police department, then hesitated. Even after working for Lorraine for such a short time, he knew that she would want any decision to involve the police to be hers alone. Instead he dialled Reception and asked casually if there had been any security problems during the night. The doorman assured him that there had not. Decker hung up and dialled Lorraine's mobile number. He swore as an electronic voice advised him that the phone was switched off.

Lorraine drove past the fountains and through the gates of Forest Lawn. She had never been to the exclusive cemetery before and found herself in what looked like a cross between the park of an eccentric nobleman and an outdoor department store of death. All tastes were clearly catered for, she observed, as she passed birdhouses, replicas of classical temples and 'dignified' churches. It had an air of frivolity and consumerism rather than reverence or repose.

The Nathan funeral was clearly taking place in the 'Bostonian' church, from which a long line of parked cars tailed back. As Lorraine got closer, she observed a number of people standing about outside. Most were pretending not to notice that they were being photo-graphed by a little knot of journalists, but some were unashamedly smiling and posing. She tried not to stare at the wannabe actresses who had been unable to resist the chance to wear the shortest of short skirts, evening sandals, nipple-skimming necklines and elaborate hats.

The men had mostly confined themselves to dark jackets and ties, but Lorraine noted one with a straggling ponytail in a black Nehru jacket over dirty black jeans and Birkenstock sandals – a sort of ageing rock star ensemble completed by little round John Lennon sun-glasses. As he turned his head to speak to the older woman beside him, his resemblance in profile to Harry Nathan was striking. They must be the family, Lorraine thought, an impression confirmed when she saw that Kendall Nathan was standing in front of the pair making exaggerated expressions of sympathy and grief.

She, too, was dressed like a Christmas tree, in a fussy black evening dress with chiffon yoke and sleeves, and dowdy pleated skirt. Apart from Lorraine, Harry Nathan's mother, in a conventional dress and coat in black wool crêpe, was the only person whose appearance had been influenced by the sombreness of the occasion. She also seemed to be the only person genuinely distressed by Harry Nathan's death.

Lorraine turned to watch as a limousine drew up, followed by an ordinary taxi-cab. The cab disgorged its occupants first, the middle-aged Mexican woman who had let Lorraine into the Nathan house and a Hispanic man, evidently her husband, who made their way straight into the church, ignored by everyone. As soon as the staff were out of the way, the limousine door opened to reveal Cindy Nathan in a long black sleeveless dress – Empire line to accommodate her undetectable pregnancy – and black velvet platform boots. Her blonde hair was elaborately dressed into a plaited coronet on top of her head, her wrists laden with pearl and jet. A silver snake bracelet encircled one of her slim upper arms, perfectly matching the black cobra tattooed around the other. She looked like a young pagan goddess, and all the nearby long lenses were immediately trained on her.

The girl stood motionless in front of the crowd. No one approached or spoke to her – in fact, Nathan's family and Kendall looked away pointedly. My God, she must have been crying all night, Lorraine thought, as she

65

observed the deep shadows around Cindy's eyes. But as she got near enough to the girl to smile and greet her, she realized that the effect was deliberate: Cindy's startling blue eyes and full, flower-like mouth had both been expertly made up in fashionable metallic pink.

Cindy did not speak, but gave Lorraine a strange, controlled smile, like that of a beautiful alien, and carefully arranged a black lace mantilla over her head. With a gesture bizarrely reminiscent of a wedding, she took Lorraine's arm and the crowd parted in front of them as they made their way into the church, leaving a wake of exquisite lily scent and audible hisses of outrage.

'Fuck 'em,' Cindy said, under her breath, as they reached the porch. Her lovely face remained immobile as she spoke. 'Fuck the whole damn lot of them.'

They made their way up the aisle towards the front pew, and the clergyman approached, rearranging his amazed stare into an expression of sympathy. Lorraine also noticed a tall, grey-haired man give the young widow an icy glance and immediately move way.

'Who was that?' Lorraine asked, when they had sat down.

'Raymond Vallance,' Cindy said coolly, staring straight ahead at the enormous wreath on her husband's coffin.

The rest of the mourners began to file in, the Nathan family occupying the front pew on the other side of the church from Cindy.

Once everyone was settled, the minister announced a hymn, which no one bothered to sing. Most of those present were more interested in craning their necks to see who else was there. They were eventually brought back to the purpose of the gathering by the clergyman's invitation to remember Harry in silence for a few minutes while they listened to one of his favourite songs, a rendition of 'Light My Fire', arranged as elaborately as an oratorio and played like a dirge on an electronic organ.

Then the minister paid tribute to Nathan's personal charm, energy and talent. As he moved on to talk about his civic virtues and unstinting support for many good causes, Lorraine was conscious of a stir at the back of the church. She turned to see a tall woman with strangely white hair, elegant as a borzoi, who had walked in alone. She came slowly up to the front of the church, her high heels clicking on the stone floor, and sat down with great dignity in the front pew, some six feet away from Cindy. She inclined her head, smiled slightly at the girl, and Lorraine caught a glimpse of a pair of remote, unnerving eyes.

She immediately recognized Sonja Sorenson, the first Mrs Nathan, and tried to study the older woman unobtrusively. She was about fifty, Lorraine guessed, and although her immaculately cut, jaw-length hair was white, her lashes and brows were still dark. Her clothes were formal and elegant, a military-style black wool suit worn with black gloves, hose and shoes, and no visible jewellery. She stared straight ahead, ignoring the congregation's scrutiny.

When the service ended, Vallance, Nathan's brother and four other men advanced to lift the coffin and carry it out. The congregation filed after them, to form a group around the grave. Lorraine dropped back to let Cindy and Sonja stand at the front, noticing that, the minute they got outside, the older woman had put on a pair of dark glasses. Kendall, determined not to be outdone, elbowed her way up to stand between Nathan's other two wives, clutching a single white rose. She beckoned to Mrs Nathan senior to follow her, but the old lady shook her head as though in distaste.

The minister read in a sonorous voice from scripture while the pall-bearers pushed the coffin carefully into the space in the wall and stepped back. As soon as the reading was over, Kendall moved forward to thrust her flower into the tomb, wailing theatrically, then stepped back as though challenging the other women to cap her performance. Sonja did not move, but Lorraine froze as Cindy took a step forward, calmly removed her wedding ring and laid it on the end of the coffin. There was an audible gasp as people wondered how to interpret the gesture: did Cindy mean that her heart was buried in the grave with Harry, or that she wanted her last remaining tie to her husband to be severed in the most public way?

The tomb door was closed and people turned away. Lorraine scanned the crowd for Raymond Vallance and saw that he was in surprisingly heated conversation with Jose and Juana. He was certainly making a point of keeping his distance from Cindy, Lorraine thought, to whom he had not addressed a word. But as his exchange with the two Mexicans came to an end and they drifted away, she saw him glance in the girl's direction. Sonja, she noted, was still beside the tomb.

Cindy was looking bored by whatever the minister was saying to her and Kendall, and Lorraine decided to rescue her. 'Cindy, I wonder if I could speak to you for a second,' she said, with a smile. 'Sorry to interrupt, but I'm just going.'

Cindy left Kendall with the clergyman. 'You and me both,' she said. 'Jesus – I can't stand to listen to Kendall saying she hasn't eaten a thing since he died when all I can think about is how soon I can get a tuna melt. It's the baby,' she said, and Lorraine saw her eyes lock momentarily with Raymond Vallance's. 'It makes you crave weird things.' Lorraine wondered whether it was just food she was talking about, but the girl said nothing more.

Lorraine breezed into the office just before lunchtime to find Decker showing out two men in overalls. Half the beige carpet had been taken up in the reception area.

Decker's expression was uncharacteristically grim. 'Lorraine,' he said, 'there's been a . . . problem. Sit down for a moment. Somebody broke in and sprayed fucking acid over the tapes.' He decided not to tell her about the photograph yet.

'I see,' Lorraine said, pushing her hand through her hair. 'Well, that's interesting. Cindy said no one else knew about them.'

'Well, maybe she changed her mind about letting you listen to them,' Decker said.

'Maybe,' Lorraine said, meditatively. 'I can't quite imagine her going to these lengths, though.'

'Perhaps she has some more . . . extreme friends,' Decker suggested. 'Who was she with at the funeral?'

'Nobody. Though she was breaking her neck not to be seen looking at Mr Ageing Romeo himself, Raymond Vallance. Pouting and glowering on both sides, though – sexual tension you could cut with a knife.'

'Raymond Vallance?' Decker pulled a face. 'I thought he was already planted out there. He must be about two hundred – the oldest living really terrible actor.'

'Looks every day of it,' Lorraine said. 'Though perhaps the shock of losing his close friend Mr Nathan was affecting his looks. He and the mother were the only people to shed a tear.'

'Actually,' Decker began, serious now, 'something else happened in the break-in.' He picked up the photograph. 'They did this.' Lorraine's face remained expressionless as she registered the damage. 'It looks like a get-the-fuck-off-this-case message, wouldn't you say?'

Lorraine shrugged. 'Maybe.'

'Maybe something else. Maybe somebody who knows you,' Decker went on. 'It's a really creepy thing to do, Lorraine. I knew you wouldn't want me to call the police until you got back, but I really think you should. I mean, it's like a threat.'

'Well, thanks for the concern, Decker, but there's no way I want the police knowing about either me or the tapes or that Cindy sent them here. I wish we'd got to listen to them, though. There must have been something on them that somebody didn't want us to find.'

'Well, we still have some . . .' Decker said. 'I took twenty home last night. But there's nothing on any of the ones I've listened to so far.'

'Sit down, boy wonder, I'll make you some coffee – you deserve it.' She smiled broadly. Clearly, as far as Lorraine was concerned, the subject of any personal danger was closed.

But the knowledge that Cindy Nathan had lied to her burned at the back of Lorraine's mind, and as soon as the office was back in shape she called her, only to be informed by Jose that Mrs Nathan was lying down after the stress of the funeral and could not come to the phone. He suggested she call again the following day.

Decker assembled the tapes in date order as far as he could, but some had only a number. 'How do we want to start – backwards, or at the beginning?' he asked.

Lorraine pursed her lips. 'In whatever order we can. We'll list any names mentioned, anything that may be useful. There's nothing else to do, apart from searching Harry Nathan's garden, and we'll have to do that at night.'

'Wouldn't it be easier in daylight?'

'Of course, but we'd be seen doing it. The police won't be there at night.'

'How do you know?'

'I was a cop, Decker, just take my word for it.' She pressed Play and sat on the cherry-coloured sofa, Tiger's perch. She could smell him on it.

'Hi, how you doing?' The voice was warm, easy-going, with a nice smoker's edge. It was Harry Nathan.

Lorraine leaned forward to catch the low volume. Decker turned up the sound.

'I've been better. I didn't get the fucking part.'

'I'm sorry, I thought it was in the bag.'

'So did I, pal, so did I, but they said they felt they needed a name. I said, "I have one," and this kid, no more than twenty years old, says to me, "I meant a name anyone under forty has heard of." I wanted to say, "Go fuck yourself," but what can you do? They need a fucking name to sell toothpaste nowadays. That's what I hate about this industry, no respect.'

'Mm, yeah. So, you on for tonight?'

'I guess so. I'm going down to Hollywood Spa this afternoon.'

'You spend more time in the sauna than you do in your own home.'

Their conversation droned on but, to Lorraine's irritation, Nathan never once used the caller's name.

The rest of the tape consisted of equally boring calls, as Nathan arranged his day between his masseur, his personal trainer and his yoga guru, and had a long discussion with someone about colonic irrigation. Four further tapes were just as mind-numbingly dull, but Nathan's personality was emerging clearly: he seemed to have little interest in work as every call was of a personal nature, ranging from haircuts to manicures and massage – even an eyelash tint.

'Jesus, is this guy for real?' Decker asked.

'You're listening to him, darlin',' Lorraine answered, as bored as Decker.

Decker inserted another tape and leaned back, doodling on his pad as the tape whirred and scratched before the connection was made.

'Hi, it's Raymond.'

Lorraine and Decker looked at each other – it was the sauna and steam-bath caller, Mr Raymond Vallance.

'Listen, I've just met this chick – she's beautiful. I was having lunch and she was at the next table, man. She is *stunning*. She has a body you'd cream yourself over, and she's got this blonde hair, like, man, it's down to her waist, and she's got to be five eight, maybe even taller. She's cover-of-*Vogue* class, so I won't be coming over.'

'What's her name?'

'Trudie. And she was giving me the real come-on. I mean, man, I could *feel* her looking at me. I'm seeing her tonight.'

They continued discussing the nubile blonde, their conversation more like that of two teenage boys than middle-aged men. That Nathan even bothered to record the entire tedious conversation was extraordinary. Decker saw that Lorraine was fast asleep, so he rewound the tape, put on some fresh coffee and inserted the next one. He would wake her if anything of interest came up. He listened to more of Nathan's grooming arrangements and more of Vallance's lectures about diet. Then a female voice, enquiring nervously if Mr Nathan wanted to see the dailies, to which Nathan replied that he wanted them sent over, that he would look at them in the evening. No date or time was stated, but Decker listed the call: it suggested that Nathan did occasionally do some work and that some movie was being shot. The next call made him listen intently.

'Harry? It's me, and I'm pissed – you got a fucking nerve. You don't like the dailies, well, fuck you. If you could spare a second to come on the set you'd know we got a fucking brain-dead male lead. I warned you the script sucked, but this is puerile shit and I'm walking.'

Nathan's angry voice retorted that he didn't give a shit if he walked or not, and there was an angry alter-cation between the two men that resulted in Nathan screaming that the man could sue him, but as he was broke he'd never get a cent.

Lorraine woke with a start.

'Listen to this. Seems Nathan wasn't the rich man we think he was.'

Decker replayed the tape.

'You're a piece of shit, Harry.'

'Yeah, so tell me somethin' new.'

'I'm telling you straight, an' no amount of fucking blackmail and threats will make me stay on this garbage.'

Nathan laughed. 'You threatening me?'

'No, but you do whatever your dirt-bag mentality wants. I am through making second-rate porno shit.'

From then on, the tape was all business, one call after another from the studio as the film was halted. The director had walked and the cast and crew were threatening to quit unless they got paid. Then came a series of calls made by Nathan as he replaced the director, raised further finances to cover the production costs, and another when he suggested that certain incriminating photographs of Julian Cole be released to the gutter press, to teach the son-of-a-bitch a lesson – that nobody messed with Harry Nathan. The astonishing thing throughout the flurry of calls was how relaxed and easy Nathan sounded as he cajoled and bullied everyone he spoke to. Last on the tape came a pitiful call from Julian Cole, the director who had walked off the set, begging Nathan not to release the photos.

'Listen, my friend, you owed me a favour. You quit on me and caused a lot of aggravation. I warned you . . .' Nathan said airily.

There was a deep intake of breath on the line and then the weeping man hissed, 'You bastard! I'll make you sorry.'

'Try it. Many have before, Jules, but they've always failed. Screwing under-age kids'll make headlines. You're finished. You'll never get a gig in this town again.'

The tape ended and Lorraine looked at Decker. 'You ever heard of this Julian Cole?'

Decker nodded. 'He made some movie about a whale and a mermaid – Oscar nomination years ago – but I think he's got one hell of a habit. Disappeared, or his later movies did.'

Lorraine got up and stretched her arms above her head. 'Maybe he could be a suspect – maybe half the callers we just listened to could be. Seems a lot of people wanted Harry Nathan dead.'

Decker agreed. 'What a sleaze-bag. I'll run a check on all the callers we got.'

'Mm, yes, but first run a check on Nathan's finances – let's see how broke he was. Something tells me he's the kind of man that has stashes of cash but won't touch a cent of his own money if he can blackmail, or whatever else, to make some other poor schmuck pay up.'

Decker rewound the tape and reached for the next. By tape five they had Raymond again, still talking about his latest nubile love. The calls were as tedious as the rest, until the last one on the tape when Nathan suggested that, as Raymond's career was going nowhere, he should do a small favour for him.

'You must be joking, I haven't reached that level.'

Nathan laughed. 'I'm talking private tapes, man.'

'What?'

'You heard me.'

'I don't follow, Harry,' Raymond said, fear audible in his voice.

'Yes, you do. You know about my wires, my little personal kicks.'

'Jesus Christ, are you serious?'

''Fraid so. I need money, and . . .'

'But you wouldn't, I mean . . . They're just between you and me.'

'They were. But, like I said, I need cash. I got a studio to run, a movie about to go down, which will cost me, so—'

'I can't – you know, I can't.'

There was a long pause.

'Harry? You still there?'

'Yeah, man.'

'Don't do this to me.'

'Then you do somethin' for me.'

'I can't. Jesus Christ, I can't. I've got my career to think of.'

Nathan sighed, and his voice changed. 'What career, Raymond? You are dead meat in this town – both you and your career, if you get my meaning.'

'I thought you were my friend,' came the plaintive response.

'Raymondo, nobody is my friend when I'm tight for cash, and right now I'm tight. So, friendship apart, I need you to star in *Likely Ladies*. And I'll release my private films if you don't agree to wave your flaccid dick around in it. Now, you got that?'

'If I refuse?'

'Then I just release the private videos.'

The call cut off, and Lorraine looked at Decker. 'My God, all those calls we listened to – he was just waitin' to pounce.'

Decker nodded. 'We got another suspect, right?'

Lorraine reached for the next tape. 'Yes, sir, we do. And now it's understandable.'

'What is?'

'The acid bath. Any one of the callers we just listed wouldn't want these tapes released, and Raymond Vallance is moving up the list.'

Decker looked at his notes. A lot of people wanted, or might have wanted, Harry Nathan dead and for good reason: blackmail.

The next tape was disappointing, but just before it ended, Decker and Lorraine pricked up their ears.

'Cindy, it's me.' It was Vallance's voice.

'Oh, hi. Harry's not at home.'

'Oh, really?' There was an artificial brightness in Vallance's voice. 'When would be a good time to call?'

'Oh – I'd say if you were to call . . . Harry, between three and four, that would be a good time.' As usual, Cindy's acting wasn't up to much, and she suddenly dropped back into more natural tones. 'Though I'm real sick. I think I got flu.'

'It's important.'

'But I'm feeling real sick.'

'I have to call *Harry*, Cindy.'

'Well, OK. Between three and four. I'll tell him you called,' Cindy said, in the arch voice of the chambermaid in *Paradise Motel*.

Vallance hung up, and Lorraine made a note, looking at Decker. 'Bit of a code going on there, wouldn't you say?'

'Mm, let's play it again.'

They did so, and came to the conclusion that Raymond Vallance and Cindy Nathan were using a code to arrange meetings of their own. The last tape they played recorded Nathan talking about the reshoot of his film, with Raymond Vallance now as the 'star attraction'. Finances were in place, and the film could continue shooting. At the end of the tape Nathan laughed. 'I'm out of the shit,' he said to an unknown caller, 'and I have pre-sales that'll keep me out of it. We're back on schedule.'

'I sincerely hope so, Harry,' said a low, clipped male voice.

Lorraine rewound the tape. 'That's his lawyer, Fein-stein. I recognize his voice,' she said.

'Shall I put him on this ever-growing list?' Decker asked, pen poised.

'No, lawyers don't get involved in the dirt. They just get their clients out of it.'

Decker held up the last tape. 'Ready for one more?' He inserted it and pressed Play.

'Harry, this is Kendall.'

'Hi, honey, how you doing?'

'I'm doing fine, but we need some publicity for the gallery. How's Cindy, by the way?'

'Got flu,' Nathan replied.

'I'm really sorry.' Kendall seemed to be laughing.

'I bet you are.'

'No, I really am.' There was a slight lisp in the woman's voice.

'I'd better come over and see you.'

'I'll be expecting you.' There was an almost mocking note in the sexy voice. The phone went dead.

'Put her on the list,' Lorraine said, then looked at her notes. On paper, it still looked like a Raymond/Cindy inside job, but there was something about both ex-wives that had made her suspicious at the funeral. 'I want to see Kendall Nathan and maybe I should speak to Sonja Sorenson, too. They're the ones we know least about,' she said.

'I don't follow. Shouldn't you be seeing all these other names?'

'Right. I do want to see them, especially Raymond Vallance. Blackmailers' victims don't usually murder, but—'

'But?' Decker butted in.

'I think Harry Nathan was killed by one of his ex-wives. Question is, which one?'

Decker smiled. 'Well, darling, I've heard all the tapes, and I'd say my main suspect would be Raymond Vallance.'

Lorraine grinned back at him. 'That's because you're a man. I think Harry Nathan blackmailed or screwed everyone he ever came across. We could have endless lists of possible suspects, but he was killed – murdered – by someone close to him. Call it female intuition. It was either Cindy, Kendall or . . .'

'Sonja,' Decker interjected.

'Yes. The murder was carefully premeditated by someone who knew his routine. Nathan lived by blackmail, he got what he wanted by fear and intimidation, so he would have been wary of strangers. Therefore, whoever killed Harry Nathan had to be someone he trusted.'

The office phone rang, and Decker picked it up. 'Page Investigations,' he said curtly. Then he covered the mouthpiece. 'It's Cindy Nathan, and she sounds hysterical. You want me to put her through to your office?' he asked.

Lorraine hurried to her desk. 'Tape it,' she said, but he'd already switched the phone on to record.

'Mrs Page, it's me, Cindy Nathan. Can you come over, and hurry – you got to come over here.' She was crying.

'Cindy? Are you all right?'

Lorraine signalled to Decker, who looked over. 'You want your car brought round?'

Lorraine nodded and returned her attention to the phone. 'Cindy, I can't hear you. Tell me what's happened.'

79

'I was only out for ten minutes. Somebody's been here. I don't know what to do, I'm all by myself and I'm scared.'

Cindy eventually calmed down enough to explain that the house had been broken into. The housekeeper and her husband were out and Cindy had not called the police, but when Lorraine suggested that she do so, she became even more hysterical, shouting that she had to see Lorraine first.

'I'll be right over.'

It took Lorraine no more than twenty minutes to get to the house. The gates were wide open, as was the front door, and Lorraine ran from the car into the house.

'Cindy?' she called, and her voice echoed round the vast hallway. There was no reply. First she went downstairs into the basement, then made her way up the wide open-tread staircase to the first floor. 'Cindy?'

All the bedroom doors were closed, the polished wooden floor giving way to white thick-pile carpet, which bore the marks of painstaking vacuuming. On a white marble plinth against one wall a massive pre-Columbian ceramic piece was balanced precariously, as if it had been knocked or pushed to one side.

'Cindy?' Lorraine called again, but still there was no response. Lorraine hesitated, and chose a door at random. Without a sound, she turned the glass handle of one of a pair of ten-foot-high polished pine double doors, and stepped tentatively into the room.

The bedroom was a sea of white: white carpet, white walls. The only colour in the room was in the centre of the bed – where there was a dark red pool of blood.

Lorraine almost had heart failure as Jose appeared from behind her. 'What are you doing in here?'

Lorraine whipped round. 'I got a call from Cindy—'

'She's not here.'

'What's happened?'

'Who are you?'

Lorraine opened her purse and handed the man her card. He glanced at it, then looked back to the landing at his wife. 'She's a private investigator.'

The woman gave Lorraine a hard stare. 'I thought you said you came to give her a massage?'

'Cindy asked me to say that,' Lorraine said, silently cursing the girl for making her go through the silly charade. 'She wanted to consult with me in private and was . . . feeling insecure.'

There was a pause, while the housekeepers registered that they were clearly the source of Cindy's mistrust. Then Lorraine asked, 'Where is she?'

Juana came closer. 'Hospital. We had to call an ambulance.'

'What happened? Was she attacked?' Lorraine said impatiently. They looked at each other. 'For God's sake, answer me. She was hysterical when she called me and now . . .' Lorraine looked at the bed as Juana went to remove the stained cover. 'Leave that and tell me what happened.'

'Mrs Nathan started to have a miscarriage. We found her in here, and dialled 911.'

'Didn't you go with her?'

'She didn't want us to,' Juana said, pulling the coverlet from the bed and bundling it up with a look of disgust.

'I think you should leave,' said Jose.

Lorraine studied him: he was very nervous, his dark, thick-lashed eyes constantly straying to his wife's. It was obvious to Lorraine that the pair knew more than they

81

were prepared to admit about the sequence of bizarre events in the house.

'What about the police?' Lorraine said flatly. 'Mrs Nathan told me the house had been broken into.'

'What?'

Lorraine sighed. 'When she called me, she said someone had been in the house, that she'd only been out ten minutes.'

Jose shook his head. 'No, we have been here all afternoon. We only left to do some shopping earlier. Nobody has been here.'

'Are you sure?'

There was yet another furtive exchange of glances. 'Have you looked around the house?' Lorraine asked. 'Because if you haven't, I suggest you do.'

Juana crossed to the doors with her bloody bundle, calling back, 'You show her round, Jose.'

Lorraine turned back to Jose. 'Is this the master bedroom?'

'No, this is a guest suite.'

She asked to see Cindy's bedroom, and Jose indicated that it was the next room along the corridor. According to him, it was Mrs Nathan's own suite. When Lorraine asked if Cindy had slept alone or with her husband he shrugged. 'I think it depended on how Mr Nathan felt.'

There were no photographs or knick-knacks in the ice-blue bedroom, but Cindy's wardrobe made Lorraine gasp. She had never seen so many designer labels, not even in the smartest department store, row upon row of evening gowns, daywear, a whole closet of beach and casual wear, and racks of shoes. The walk-in wardrobe was more like a room, the size of her own bedroom, and from the sales tickets still attached it was obvious that many of the items had never been worn.

'Mrs Nathan likes to shop,' Jose said, with humour.

'Obviously,' Lorraine murmured, and looked around. 'She's surprisingly neat and tidy.'

Jose raised an eyebrow. 'Tell that to my wife and she'd split.' He gestured to her to follow him from the dressing room. 'My wife spends hours every day just tidying up after her.'

Lorraine looked back at the pale blue room. It felt cold, empty and unused. It was hard to imagine Cindy sleeping in there, let alone dressing and . . . 'What about her bathroom?'

Jose paused, already at the door. 'Through the mirrored wall beyond the bed.' He moved soundlessly across the thick blue carpet, passed his hand across a certain area of the mirror and the door slid back electronically to reveal yet more ice-blue, this time stained floor-to-ceiling marble. Again, the room was obsessively neat. The only thing that seemed out of place was a single toothbrush left beside one of the washbasins. Jose opened one of the cupboards underneath, took out a spray of glass polish and a cloth, cleaned carefully around the washbasin, replaced the cleaning fluid and cloth and put the toothbrush neatly into a pale blue glass holder.

He caught Lorraine watching him. 'Mr Nathan hated anything out of place. He checked every room every day.'

'You mean she couldn't even leave a toothbrush out?'

'Water stains the marble. He even used to check under the taps. He was quite obsessive about cleanliness.'

Jose ushered Lorraine back across Cindy's bedroom.

'He showered sometimes six, seven times a day, and changed his clothes as often. But he worked out a lot, and he would need clean clothes to work out in, clean clothes to change into, and then he would start the whole process again.'

Lorraine followed him across the landing. 'Must have been tough to work for him.'

'Not really, you got into his routine. This is his room – the master bedroom.'

Lorraine waited as the pine doors opened, then said softly, 'Well, I think you'll have quite a job in here, Jose. I'm sure Mr Nathan never left his room in this state.'

'Oh, my God!' Jose whispered.

The lurid orange linen had been torn from the twelve-foot-square bed and strewn over the floor. The rugs had been drawn up in places and pulled into the centre of the room, throwing a tall metal chair onto its side. A glass coffee table had been broken, as had a lighting fitting. A canvas had been dragged from the wall and the drapes on the lower windows had been torn down. A marble plinth lay on its side, and what had been a Chinese *famille rose* peach vase lay shattered in tiny fragments.

'Well, Cindy was right. Somebody *has* been here, and this must have taken quite a while,' Lorraine said, watching Jose carefully. He seemed genuinely shocked by the destruction in the huge room.

There was a dressing room similar to that of the guest suite, Lorraine noticed. Its electronic door was ajar. 'Can I go in here?' she asked, and the man nodded without speaking. At first sight, Harry Nathan's dressing room was untouched, the clothes neatly stored.

'I think I should check the entire house, Mrs Page,' Jose said, 'if you would care to come downstairs with me.' Lorraine wondered if there was some reason why he wanted her out of the room. 'Could I just see his bathroom?' she asked.

Jose pointed towards it as he surveyed the bedroom. 'I just don't see when this was done. My wife and I left the house for such a short while.'

Lorraine glanced into the bathroom, another room with the charm of a meat safe, then did a double-take. 'Oh, my God . . .'

The blood was in pools, not even dried, and there was a heap of blood-sodden towels in the centre of the otherwise spotless bathroom. Jose stepped past her, bent down to the towels, then recoiled. He leaped to the washbasin and retched. That reaction clearly wasn't faked, Lorraine noted. He had not been with Cindy when she had lost her child.

'Let's take a look round the rest of the house,' she said, already heading out, not turning back when she heard Jose vomiting. The wreckage in the bedroom made her wonder if Cindy herself had caused the damage – perhaps that was what had made her miscarry, unless she had walked in on someone else and been attacked. Lorraine was still deep in thought as she crossed the landing towards the stairs. Suddenly she paused. Had she seen all the rooms on this floor?

'What's that room?' She indicated a closed door.

'No one is allowed in there. Mr Nathan never let anyone in even to clean it.'

'Mr Nathan is dead now, so let me see in there, Jose, would you?'

'It's always locked.'

But Lorraine had turned the handle as he spoke and the door opened.

This was Nathan's office: here, at least, the walls were still intact, though covered with two-foot-square wood tiles stained red and black in an ugly checkerboard effect. There was the usual office equipment, a photocopier, fax machine, computers and telephones, and a bank of four television sets, like monitors, was recessed into the wall. Two shelves that had previously contained videotapes were now empty, the tapes removed from their cases and thrown on the floor. Lorraine saw that they were labelled with the names of Nathan's films and of TV shows he had appeared in – someone had clearly gone through them to check that the contents of the boxes matched the labels outside.

There was something in this house for which someone had been searching desperately, that much was obvious to Lorraine. The fact that the phone tapes had been destroyed suggested that it might have been a recording, but it hadn't been on any of the tapes she had listened to or, presumably, the ones that had been destroyed, or the burglar wouldn't have bothered looking any further. Nor could it have been on any of the videotapes in front of her, or they, too, would have been destroyed or removed. There was, however, a cache of tapes from the security cameras, which Cindy had mentioned but which had never been found, and these must be the object of the search.

'What did Mr Nathan do with the tapes he recorded on the security cameras?' Lorraine asked.

'He took care of all that himself,' Jose said. 'I thought he kept them in here, or just used them over and over.'

'When was all the security put in the house?'

'A couple of years ago. The same firm did some of the decorating.'

'Oh, really?' Lorraine asked casually. 'Any work on the walls or floors?'

'Wall panels. Like in here,' he said.

What a surprise, she thought, scanning the checker-board walls. 'Jose,' she said, with her sweetest smile, 'could you get me something with a flat blade – like a big knife or a chisel?' She had a good idea that she would not need any implement to open the hidden compartment she was sure was in the wall, but she wanted him out of the room. He nodded and disappeared.

As soon as he was gone, she began to scan the rows of large wooden tiles on the walls, then spotted a row of metal bandstand chairs in dolly-mixture colours folded flat against one of the walls. She examined the floor in front of them, which, thanks to Harry Nathan's secrecy, did not benefit from daily vacuuming. She could make out the marks where a chair's sharp metal legs had indented the thick pile – deeper than one would have expected if someone had been merely sitting on it, but not if they had stood on it, particularly a tall and heavy man . . .

She pulled out a chair, set it up with its feet on the same marks, then climbed up on it. She pressed carefully along the vertical edges of the two large wooden tiles within easy reach, and swore under her breath when they remained still. Then she tried the horizontal axis. One of the tiles gave, just a quarter of an inch. It seemed to be spring-loaded on the other side to prevent it opening too easily and to keep it flush with the rest of the wall. She had to press hard but finally a wooden door opened. Behind it were pile after pile of tapes. Lorraine pulled one out. There was no title, only a date and the name 'Cindy'.

'What are you doing?' Jose spoke suddenly behind her, and she almost fell off the chair. The man was standing in the doorway with what looked like a carving knife, Juana beside him.

Lorraine looked coolly at them. She had no idea what their intentions towards her were, but she had to try to face them out. 'I was looking for evidence relevant to my client's case, and it seems like I found it. My assistant and I are working closely with the police, and I will naturally be informing them as soon as possible. I imagine they will want to talk to you about how the house came to be torn apart today, and how this evidence came to be concealed.' She willed her voice to remain calm.

'We have nothing to do with this,' Juana said immediately, angry and defensive, and Jose shot her a warning glance. 'We were going to go to the police ourselves – tell her, Jose.'

'Be quiet,' he ordered. 'There is nothing to tell.'

The woman's eyes flashed. 'How much longer are you going to hide that man's dirt, Jose?'

'Be quiet, woman!' he repeated, but his wife stood her ground.

'He is dead. We have nothing. Tell her the truth.'

The man sighed. 'Perhaps it is better. Perhaps we should go downstairs.'

Lorraine relaxed. 'I'd certainly be more comfortable. But I'd like to take the tapes. They become Mrs Nathan's property, I believe, under the terms of Mr Nathan's will, and as I just said, she has asked me to gather any evidence relevant to her case.'

Jose looked at Juana again. 'Let her take them. I want them gone.' There was a note of resignation in her voice.

Lorraine scooped into her arms as many of the tapes as she could hold and climbed down from the chair. 'I'll lock these in the trunk of my car before we talk.'

Juana nodded, a look of relief crossing her face. 'I will make some tea.'

Lorraine made two journeys out to the Mercedes, doing her best to appear unconcerned, but prepared for any attempt the two servants might make to stop her. Neither approached her, though, and she could hear them talking in Spanish in the kitchen, Juana's voice much more prominent than Jose's. She locked the trunk before returning to the house.

Lorraine walked back into the hall and through to where she could hear Jose and Juana's voices. The kitchen, which had the air of an operating theatre, was in monochrome black and white, and the table was set with crockery of almost transparent white porcelain in a variety of deliberately irregular shapes. 'Mr Nathan certainly seemed to like the minimalist look,' Lorraine said.

'Mr Nathan was a criminal,' Juana said, tight-lipped. 'He was a thief.' Jose said nothing: his wife had clearly convinced him that their interests no longer lay in loyalty to their former employer.

She poured Lorraine a cup of slightly perfumed tea, and pushed a plate of home-made crinkle cookies towards her.

'What makes you say that?' Lorraine said, as she bit into a cookie, but before the woman could answer, the telephone rang.

Jose picked it up. 'No, Mrs Nathan, I have no authority . . .' he said mechanically.

Lorraine looked up at the mention of her client's

name. 'Can I speak to her?' she asked, but the man shook his head.

'It is not Cindy,' Juana said. 'It is Kendall. She has been calling every day since Mr Nathan died. Cindy won't let her in the house.'

Jose continued to say yes and no to a clearly pushy caller, and told her that Cindy had suffered a miscarriage and been taken to Cedars-Sinai.

When he hung up, Lorraine asked, 'What did she want?'

'What she always wants. She says there's some property here of hers. Mr Feinstein has given instructions that she is not to be allowed to remove anything – I think it's some of the paintings.'

Or maybe some tapes, Lorraine thought, wondering when Harry Nathan's interest in home movies had started.

'What were you about to say, Juana, about Mr Nathan's having stolen something?' she asked.

Juana looked at Jose, indicating that he should speak. He pulled at his tie. 'Mr Nathan owed us a lot of money, Mrs Page. Our life savings, plus back salary. We were only here because we wanted to get paid. Six, seven years ago, he said he would invest it for us.'

Juana folded her arms. 'For the first few years we didn't question it. He said he had invested it for us and even paid us dividends, so it seemed our money had doubled, then trebled and then . . .' She went on to describe how when Nathan had married Kendall, they had wanted to leave. 'She was an evil woman, but when we went to him and asked for our money, told him we couldn't stay, he . . . he told us that he'd had some bad news about his stocks and shares. He said he hadn't been able to tell us because he was so upset about it – that he had lost everything as well.'

'But that obviously wasn't true,' Lorraine said, jerking her head towards the rest of the house.

'He said the house was remortgaged and he made us all these promises about selling his art collection. We stayed on here because we had no place else to go and no money to go anywhere with. At least by being here we could see if he did make any money and then we'd get paid. He promised us we would. He owed everybody he ever met,' Jose said flatly. 'Now we just hope that we'll get something if his estate is sold.'

'Does Cindy know about this?'

Juana shook her head. 'That silly child knows nothing, and he'd made her so crazy anyway. We think he was going to leave her, find a woman with money, probably.'

'Do you think she killed him?'

There was another exchange of looks, and then Juana sighed. 'Yes, we do. She threatened it more than once.'

'You were here in the house, though, weren't you, the morning Mr Nathan was shot?'

'Yes, but I was working in the laundry, and Jose was out back near the garages. We didn't hear anything at all, not until Mrs Nathan started screaming.'

Jose went on to describe how he and Juana had tried to get Nathan's body out of the pool, but it was so heavy they couldn't lift it.

'What was Cindy doing then?'

Jose thought for a moment. 'She was sitting by the pool, and I shouted at her to help us. She just kept saying over and over that she didn't do it – no, what she said was she didn't *think* that she had done it. That's a strange thing to say, isn't it?'

91

'But you think that she did?'

'Yes, I do,' said Juana.

'She had reasons,' Jose agreed. 'I think she knew he was going to kick her out. They did nothing but argue, and she was drinking heavily, and—'

'Tell her,' Juana said. 'Tell her everything.'

Jose looked shifty, and wouldn't meet Lorraine's eyes. Then he said, 'She was having an affair with Raymond Vallance, Mr Nathan's closest friend.'

Juana looked at Jose as if she expected him to say more: when he remained silent she spoke up herself. 'And *he* has offered us money – to keep our mouths shut and give him the tapes.' Juana met Lorraine's eyes squarely. 'I would have taken his money with pleasure, but we did not know where the tapes were.'

'Did you tell him that yesterday at the funeral?' Lorraine asked.

'I have told him many times.' She noted that Juana did not confirm what her conversation with Vallance had been about.

'Did you know what was on the tapes?'

'I can guess. Mr Nathan used to take drugs and party in the basement on the weekends. He would tell us to take time off. When we went in to clean, you could smell the . . . sex in the air.'

'Do you think Raymond Vallance could have been here this afternoon?' Lorraine asked.

'He has a key,' Jose put in. 'She gave it to him.'

'I see. Well, thank you both very much. If you think of anything else that might be important, I'd appreciate it if you'd call me – here's my card.' She placed it on the kitchen table. 'I'll go see Cindy tonight.'

92

'What about the jeep?' Juana said hesitantly to her husband.

He shrugged.

'What was that?' Lorraine asked.

Jose chewed his lip. 'Well, it's probably nothing, but I saw it very early, parked down the road. It was odd – most residents around here never park on the street, there's no need.'

Juana added, 'But it wasn't there when you looked later. Tell Mrs Page, tell her whose car you thought it was.'

'It was the same colour, maybe even the same type, as the jeep Mrs Kendall Nathan drives,' Jose said.

Lorraine could hardly contain herself. She asked when Jose had seen it and when he thought it had been driven away. He was unsure of the exact time, only that it had been there early that morning and had gone after the murder.

'You won't tell her what we've said, will you?' Jose said nervously.

'No, of course not. Whatever we have discussed remains private,' Lorraine lied, setting off down the steps. 'Goodnight.'

The couple stood in the doorway for a moment until the security lights came on, then closed the front door. Lorraine waited until she thought they must be back in the kitchen, then hurried across the lawn, stepped into the shrubbery and, under cover of the thick bushes, began to examine the ground. She got down on her hands and knees and inched her way on all fours, scratched by the bushes, feeling in front of her. She searched for ten minutes until the security lights went out and she could no longer see anything. She decided to come back the following day and continue. She was still kneeling, as she turned to make her way out of the shrubbery, when she felt something digging into her knee. When she looked down, the object glinted faintly. She picked it up: a large, snub-nosed bullet. She'd found it. At least Cindy Nathan had been telling the truth about one thing: that two gunshots had been fired the morning of the murder.

CHAPTER 4

LATER, LORRAINE realized that the discovery of the bullet might mean nothing, because Nathan had been known to shoot at birds. It was quite possible that there would be a number of bullets in the grounds. But if this one fitted the murder weapon, Cindy had told the truth. The question still remained as to whether or not Cindy had fired the gun.

Lorraine showered, changed, and put some disinfectant on the scratches that covered her arms and legs, and the two on her face. Tiger had been disgruntled – he'd been left alone most of the day – but Lorraine had fed and walked him now. He had perked up when she decided he could ride with her to the hospital. It was after ten by the time she turned off San Vincente Boulevard and drove between the imposing towers of Cedars-Sinai Medical Centre, lit up like a liner at night. She went to the emergency rooms to enquire about Cindy Nathan, and was told that Cindy had been admitted to a medical ward on the eighth floor.

When Lorraine asked at the nurses' station if she could see Mrs Nathan, they refused. Cindy had been sedated and was not allowed visitors. 'If you would like to leave your number, Mrs Page, I will tell her you came to see her when she wakes,' the night nurse said authoritatively, a challenging look in her eyes. The unit was frequently used by celebrities and their families, and it was clear that the staff were well versed in keeping unwanted attention away from them. Lorraine checked her watch, thought about waiting around, but decided to go home. She had a lot of new developments to get on top of, and she was tired.

'What time can I see her in the morning?'

'That will depend on the doctor and the patient. She's in a private room with a phone, so I'm sure she'll call you if she wants to. Now, if you will excuse me . . .' and the nurse set off down the corridor.

Two clerical staff were behind their desks at the administration station, and Lorraine moved closer. 'Excuse me, do you know if Mrs Cindy Nathan has had any visitors since she was admitted?'

One woman, with permed hair, looked over her half-moon glasses, apparently irritated to be distracted from her copy of the *National Enquirer*. 'Are you a relative?'

'No, I spoke to you earlier.'

'I'm sorry, we're not allowed to give any personal details to anyone not related to the patient.'

'What if I said I was her sister?'

'But you just said you weren't related,' the woman snapped.

Lorraine threw up her hands. 'I'm a close friend, and she's just miscarried her baby. At a time like this she'll need a lot of comfort and, above all, the support of her friends, right? And I would like to contact—'

'No visitors,' the perm said.

'Thank you for your co-operation,' Lorraine replied sarcastically, and walked out. She was, she thought, probably the only person who did care about poor little Cindy, for she felt genuinely sorry for her, but at the same time, she was relieved to be going home again.

Back at the car, Tiger had eaten his leather lead, and Lorraine was so absorbed in scolding him that she didn't see the two-toned Mitsubishi jeep pull into a space just a short distance away. She was still berating Tiger as a woman got out, carrying grapes and a bunch of flowers. But Kendall Nathan had seen Lorraine and stood in the shadows, keeping well out of view, watching her drive out.

Kendall did not get such short shrift from the receptionist: as she had the same surname as Cindy, the perm presumed she was a relative and allowed her to talk to the night nurse monitoring Cindy. She was told that Cindy was still sleeping, and, although not critically ill, in a deeply depressed state. Kendall was about to leave her gifts and go, when the nurse offered to check if Cindy was awake.

She showed Kendall into the plush private room, with its dimmed lights, controlled atmosphere and television mounted on a bracket on the wall. Kendall leaned over and smiled: Cindy was awake, but very drowsy.

'I came as soon as I heard. I talked to Jose and he told me – I'm so sorry.'

Slowly Cindy turned away her face. 'I bet you are,' she whispered, so softly as to be barely audible.

Kendall turned and smiled sweetly at the nurse. 'I'll just sit with her for a few moments.'

The nurse hesitated, but Kendall looked hard at her, and she nodded. 'I'll check on the other patients and come back, but you mustn't stay long.'

'Thank you so much,' Kendall said softly. As soon as

the door closed the sickening smile froze on her mouth. She moved to stand at the end of the bed, unhooked the notes attached to the foot and flicked through them before she spoke.

'How are you, darling? I was so sorry to hear you lost the baby.' She put the clipboard back. 'You must really regret the abortions now.'

Cindy glared at her. 'I never had any abortions.'

'Oh,' Kendall smiled, 'it must be a mistake. I'll tell the nurse to alter this "previous pregnancies" thing on my way out.'

Cindy said nothing.

'I didn't even think it was true, the baby,' Kendall continued. 'Whose was it?'

Cindy closed her eyes.

'It wasn't likely to be Harry's, you little whore. You screwed anything in pants.'

Cindy opened her eyes again. 'You mean like you did to get yourself pregnant? That was why he married you, wasn't it?'

Kendall's eyes slanted like a snake's as she cocked her head to one side. 'If you hadn't shot him he'd have kicked you out, and you know it.'

'The way he kicked you out?'

'You're a poisonous little bitch, aren't you?'

'Takes one to know one.'

'My, my, that was quite a fast retort – unusual for you. That chemical garbage you stuff yourself with usually makes you totally fucking off the wall. But I'm sorry, really I am. It won't be quite so heart-rending now, will it? "Pregnant wife on trial for her husband's murder" would have been quite a sexy angle.'

'Go away. Leave me alone.'

Kendall pursed her lips. 'Was it Harry's?'

'Yes. And that must have really pissed you off.'

Kendall recomposed her features into what she hoped was a pleasant smile. 'Look, Cindy, that's all water under the bridge. I'm sorry for . . . teasing you – I guess I'm just jealous, you know, about you and the baby and all.' She gave a sigh, as though of sorrow at the realization of her own human weakness, and her expression grew still more saccharine-sweet. 'Let's you and me not fight,' she went on. 'I mean, we've both suffered such a terrible loss and we're both in the same boat about a lot of things – Harry, and the will, and . . . well, you know there's just a few little videotapes out at the house I think both of us would rather not watch with our moms.'

'What?' Cindy said weakly. 'Harry . . . did stuff with you too?'

'Harry did stuff with the Koi carp and the juice extractor, darling.' Kendall's voice was more businesslike now. 'Did you get the key to the office?'

'No. But somebody else did. Somebody broke in – there were tapes all over the floor, but just his movies and stuff, they didn't take any. I can't find the private ones. I looked all over.'

'They must be still at the house, and Feinstein's in charge now while you're lying here, Cindy. You don't want him finding them and sitting around whacking off to them, now do you?'

'I guess not.'

'Well, then, call Jose and Juana and tell them to let me in to collect them. I won't take anything else.'

'Like fuck you won't, Kendall.' Even Cindy was not

too dumb to be taken in by that ploy. 'I know you'd walk out with a couple of Jackson de Koonings, or whatever they are, tucked in your tights.'

'Cindy, I don't intend to discuss this with you at this time,' Kendall said prissily. 'You got my attorney's letter and you know that the collection of art works at the house, which Harry and I built up, was jointly owned. My paintings do not form part of the contents of the house, and I can prove it because I paid the insurance premiums – which shows Harry acknowledged before he died that I had a proprietary interest. And what the fuck would you do with a lot of Jackson *Pollocks*?'

'Sell them, Kendall, same as you. And I have news for you. If you're banking on that premium business to set up your case, you're in a whole lot of trouble because he never paid the insurance. I just found that out.'

'What?' Kendall said, her expression reverting to its former undisguised anger and greed. 'How do you know?'

'I found the letters telling him that the policy had expired, last chance to renew kind of thing. He never paid a penny in insurance in the last two years.'

Kendall was speechless with rage and shock. 'But I gave him about two million fucking dollars in that time. What did he do with it?'

'The usual things, I guess,' Cindy said succinctly. 'His dick or his nose. And I have something else to tell you—'

'What?' Kendall snapped.

'I'm kind of tired now, Kendall,' Cindy said, with a yawn. 'Maybe I'll tell you some other time.'

Kendall jolted the bed. 'You straighten out with me right now, Cindy, or I'll slap your face!'

Cindy struggled to sit up. 'You lay one finger on me and I'll scream the place down. I just lost my fucking baby, for Chrissakes.'

Kendall returned with an effort to sweet-reason mode. 'Look, Cindy, we're just playing into the lawyers' hands by fighting each other. If there's some other problems with the art, I think you should tell me. Otherwise it will just go to Feinstein and he'll make ten billion dollars while we get zip.'

Cindy could never stand up to a more aggressive person for long. 'Well,' she said, sinking back on her pillows, 'you know that Chinese vase? The family of roses or whatever? In his bedroom? It fell off its perch.'

'*You broke it?*'

'Not on purpose, but . . . how old did you say it was? Only, for something so old, how come it's got a sticker inside?'

Cindy enjoying seeing Kendall froth at the mouth. 'Yeah, a sticker with a dealer's name on it, right inside the thing. Some company called Classic something or other.'

'Classic Reproductions,' Kendall said, between gritted teeth.

'Oh, that's it.' Cindy faked surprise with all her *Paradise Motel* skill. 'I knew you'd have heard of them.'

Kendall picked up her purse. 'Look, there's no point in us talking any more now, I have to go. I'll check things out with the insurance brokers tomorrow and call you.'

As the other woman turned away Cindy said, 'I didn't kill him, Kendall. I don't think I did, an' that's the truth. I even thought that maybe . . .'

'Maybe what?' Kendall was heading for the door.

'Maybe you did. Where were you when he got shot?'

'I was at home.'

'Oh, yeah?' Cindy said quietly. 'Got a witness, have you?' She turned back to her pillow and closed her eyes. Before Kendall could reply the nurse walked in, hurried to Cindy's bedside, and turned in surprise at the sound of the door slamming shut.

Cindy gave a weak smile. 'If Mrs Nathan comes again tell her I'm too tired to see her – she drains my energy centres. Can you get me something to help me sleep?'

'I'll check with the doctor. Oh, you had another visitor, a Mrs Lorraine Page. She left her card.' The nurse handed it to Cindy and went to see about sedation.

Kendall Nathan sat in her jeep, gripping the steering wheel. She was sure Cindy was lying about the vase, but the only way to be certain was to go to the house and see for herself. She knew Harry was a thief and a con-man, but would he have conned her, too, after all she had done for him? She had a terrible, sinking feeling that he just might have.

Half an hour later she was still shaking as she sipped hot water and lemon juice, and paced the black Astroturf with which she had carpeted her bedroom; the building's beautifully preserved thirties exterior had not deterred Kendall from filling her apartment with screamingly modern design as near to the décor of the Nathan house as she could afford. The sight of all these things now, which had previously given her such satisfaction, filled her with fury as the possibility of Harry Nathan's treachery sank in.

She wanted to scream, wanted to get back into the

jeep and get over to the Nathans' house, but she knew she had to be calm. If the *famille rose* vase was a fake, what had happened to the original, worth three quarters of a million dollars? She had to find out without betraying how important it was to her. And it *was* important: the vase represented part of an art collection worth twenty million dollars, half of which she knew was hers. Eventually she slumped onto her bed, and nausea swept over her.

Lorraine was in her bathrobe, eating chicken with spinach and walnut salad. She had just settled down in front of the video recorder to play some of Harry Nathan's tapes when the phone rang. She looked at the clock – it was almost eleven, and she wondered who was calling so late.

'Lorraine? It's me, Cindy Nathan.'

'Oh, hello. I came by the hospital earlier – how are you?'

'I'm okay. They give me somethin' for the pain, but it's the one in my heart that hurts more. I lost my baby.'

'Yes, I know, I'm so sorry.'

'So am I, and I would have liked to talk to you.'

'I'll come by tomorrow – I need to talk to you too.'

'There's a reason I called, but I don't want to talk about it over the phone. It's just I know something about, well, I think I know somebody with a motive for shooting Harry. I think it might be Kendall.'

Lorraine reached for her cigarette pack. 'Can you just answer me one thing? You know the telephone tapes, the ones you sent over to my office? Who else did you tell that you were sending them to me?'

'I didn't tell anyone else – well, not exactly. You see, there's a locked room, Harry's office, and I couldn't find the key. It's one of those plastic card things, you know – some hotels use them. I couldn't find it, an' I didn't know how to get into the room.'

'Did Jose and Juana know?'

'Hell, no. I wouldn't tell those two nothin'. I called Harry's wife, Sonja, and she said she didn't even know there was a locked room. Well, she wouldn't have, she hadn't been living there for a long time, so then I called Kendall.'

'Did you mention the telephone recordings to either of them?'

'Yes, well, maybe I did, I can't remember.'

Lorraine wondered if this was true, or whether the girl was trying to throw suspicion on the other two wives – she had seemed certain before that nobody else knew about the tapes. 'I'm sorry, I got to go now. I'm too tired to talk. They give me something to help me sleep.'

'Well, I'll come by in the morning. You sure only Mr Nathan's ex-wives knew about the tapes?'

'Yeah. I didn't tell anyone else. G'night now.'

The phone went dead. Lorraine moved back to her new white sofa, which Tiger was now occupying. 'Get off.' He gave a low growl. 'Hey, man, cut that out. You've moved in on the office and don't try it here. Get off.' He got up and padded into the bedroom. 'Not on the bed either, Tiger,' but he had already disappeared.

She pressed Play on the remote control and settled back, only noticing as she lifted the fork to eat her supper that the chicken leg had been removed. She was about to go after Tiger when the tape started, a shot clearly set up in Nathan's bedroom. Cindy was spreadeagled naked and face down on the bed, and Nathan was working her over.

Lorraine felt sick as she watched three more videos, two showing explicit sex acts with Cindy, one with Kendall, each more violent and degrading than the last. Cindy was made to beg on all fours, while Nathan beat her with a thonged leather strap. He was into S and M in a big way, screwing her so violently, every muscle straining, that the sweat dripped from his body and matted his dark hair. He had tied Kendall over the back of a chair in a way that enabled him, with a jerk of the rope, to splay her legs wide apart, then insert a selection of objects, animal, mineral and vegetable, into various orifices, while some unknown female friend shrieked in the background with hyena-like laughter.

Worse was to come. Threesomes featuring not only Cindy but other very young girls were next on the tape, then a sickening sequence starring Raymond Vallance. In this session, Nathan sat watching, grinning and jerking off as the girls strapped on black, studded dildoes and forced Vallance down on all fours. Lorraine couldn't watch another minute of it and went to bed. What she had seen might provide Cindy with a provocation defence, or at least a position from which to bargain down the charge, but it also gave both her and Kendall Nathan a motive and a half: both women had been subjected to the grossest abuse.

Tiger lay sprawled across one side of the bed and didn't move an inch when Lorraine got under the duvet. He sighed with contentment when he realized that she wasn't going to push him off.

It was the first time in her life that Lorraine had owned a dog, and she understood now what it meant to have something that asked nothing from her but a half-share of her bed. Tiger had the love she found so difficult to give elsewhere, but he could not fill the void inside her – and it was a void. Lorraine was more lonely than she had ever been, and although she was financially secure, it frightened her to think about her future. Only Tiger heard her fears, and only he saw the vulnerable side of Lorraine that she showed to no one else – so in need of love, and so afraid she would never find it.

Decker had swept up the nightly shower of ficus leaves, had placed a fresh vase of lilies in Reception, and a jug of coffee was percolating. He had already sorted the office mail, mostly bills and circulars, when Lorraine arrived at eight thirty.

'Morning. Another lovely sunny day,' he said brightly, watching Tiger set off in search of a blue rubber boxing glove Decker had bought him, which he adored chewing and flinging about. 'He seems fit and well.'

'Yeah, so he should. He had a good two miles' walk this morning, ate half my supper last night *and* demolished his own.' She threw her hands up. 'Shit! What is happening to me? He's a goddamned dog! He's taking up too much of my life!' The boxing glove was hurled across the room, and Lorraine laughed.

'You know, Mrs Page, you have a wonderful laugh,' Decker said.

'Yeah, just not a lot to laugh about. You want to come in with the coffee and I'll give you an update, before I go to see Cindy. She's in hospital.'

'What's the matter with her?'

'Get the coffee and I'll tell you.'

The curtains had been pulled back from the windows that formed one whole wall of Cindy Nathan's hospital room, giving her a beautiful view of the early-morning haze clearing from the Hollywood Hills. In daylight, the room looked even more like a luxury hotel to Lorraine, and the breakfast on the tray table could certainly have come straight from room service.

Cindy was sitting up, a bed-jacket draped round her shoulders, eating orange and date muffins and fruit compote.

Lorraine drew a chair close to the bed. 'Right, tell me about Kendall Nathan.'

'She's a vicious bitch for a start-off. She claims she owns half of Harry's art collection, so I don't get it along with the house.'

'Has Feinstein told you the value of the estate?' Lorraine asked.

'Well, there's not nearly as much money in the company as anyone thought – Harry hadn't made a film that did any business since *Mutant Au-Pairs*, so the art's likely to be the big thing.' Lorraine waited, noting that the girl seemed much recovered and even quite cheerful. 'Means I don't have as much of a motive, do I?' she said cheerfully. 'Assuming I knew he was pretty broke, which I didn't, of course.' Cindy was a prosecuting attorney's wet dream.

Lorraine waited as she carried on with her breakfast, pouring some juice and drinking it thirstily before she lay back on the pillows.

'Harry was a con merchant, and anythin' he could steal he did. He used everybody – that's how he got his kicks, right?'

Lorraine remembered the videos – he had got his kicks in a lot of other ways as well.

'The gallery was real expensive – I mean, it's on Beverly Drive, right? Clients got a lot of money, and they paid through the nose. But I think he and Kendall were up to something crooked.'

Lorraine sat back. 'Go on.'

'Well, all those paintings at the house, they had to be insured. Lot of dough for the premiums, which is why we got such high security – all the stuff in there is the real thing, unlike what those other poor schmucks have got. Harry got the lot – that's including pre-Columbian stuff, and there's a Giaca—' She hesitated. 'A Giacaroni and stuff like that. You with me?'

'Yes.'

'Okay. Now, Kendall was paying Harry the money for the insurance premiums, which she says is because they had agreed that half the art was hers – like, in her dreams.' Cindy licked up the wheatgerm still adhering to the rim of the juice glass with a practised flick of her tongue. 'Still with me?'

'Yes.' Lorraine sighed – it wasn't too taxing to keep up with Cindy's thought process.

'She asked me to find the insurance certificates. I didn't know then it was for some scheme that she and her lawyer have cooked up to show she owns the stuff, so I got 'em out. But the only ones I could find were out of date, which means he hadn't been paying the cover. So ask yourself why.'

'Perhaps you'd tell me.'

'Well, look at the security at the house. The place is jam-full of lasers – you move one of them things off the wall and it's the full orchestra, you know what I mean?' Lorraine nodded.

'Well, I checked the dates when he stopped paying the insurance – it was when he got all the security in and started taping all the phone calls. I only checked because I knocked this vase off its stand. This is some Chinese rose vase supposed to be worth three quarters of a million dollars.'

Lorraine smiled encouragingly.

'It fell off the plinth, an' I got real worried. I thought the fucking alarms would start screaming, but nothing happened. It just broke.'

'Yes, I saw it.' Lorraine was wondering where all this was leading.

'Broke into lots of pieces,' Cindy said.

'I noticed. Go on.'

Cindy held up her hand. 'One: no alarms. Two: I find a sticker inside it, a modern sticker like a price thing – the vase had this long, thin neck so that normally you would never see inside. There was a name scrawled on it – Classic Reproductions. I dunno who they are, but what's their name doing inside some piece of porcelain that's supposed to be a billion years old?'

'It's a fake.'

'Right. Which brings me to Kendall Nathan.'

Lorraine waited while Cindy licked her lips.

'She thinks she owns half the so-called art stuff, and she thinks it's all legit, but if it's not it means Harry sold the real art on, took the money and didn't tell her. Now if she found that out, it's one hell of a motive to kill somebody, wouldn't you say? It's called being fucked

109

over twice. He ditched her for me, then ripped off all her money. She was paying him to cover the insurance and he took that as well. You see what I mean, Lorraine?'

'Do the police know this?'

'Hell, no. I only just worked it out myself when the vase fell off its perch. I started to put it all together and then—'

'Then?'

'I lost my baby.'

Lorraine's mind worked furiously. Having seen the videos, and learned that Cindy and Raymond Vallance had been having an affair under Nathan's nose, the possibility that either Cindy or her lover had shot him seemed, as Decker had said, the obvious conclusion. She wondered if Cindy was dragging out all these ideas about art in an effort to throw her off the scent. She said, 'Cindy, I won't press you if you're feeling low, but when you called me, you said somebody was at the house. I saw the rooms were wrecked.'

Cindy nodded. 'I thought I saw someone, like a young black guy, going down the stairs to the gym. Then I went upstairs and saw the place had been trashed. It really freaked me out.'

Another convenient mystery burglar, Lorraine thought sceptically, but it wasn't out of the question that the same person who had destroyed the tapes in her office could have broken into the Nathan house. 'You didn't mention that when you called me.'

Cindy plucked a tissue from the box at her bedside. 'Didn't I? I guess I wasn't that together – I mean, it was just before . . .' She gestured weakly at her belly. She blew her nose, then turned her gaze back to Lorraine. 'I know things look bad, but I swear I think somebody's framing me, because I'm sure now I didn't kill Harry, I know I didn't.' Cindy lay back again, and put her hand over her eyes.

'Cindy, there's a couple of things I need to ask you about,' Lorraine said quietly.

'Sure,' Cindy said, blinking back tears.

'I found some videotapes, hidden in a wall in Harry's office.' There was a pause: Cindy wouldn't look at her. 'I'm sure you know the ones I'm talking about. I think your lawyers should see them, plus—'

'No way,' Cindy said, crumpling the tissue in her hand. 'I won't allow anyone to see them, especially not those fuckin' lawyers. I hate 'em.'

'But you were subjected to extreme violence and a lot of sexual abuse.'

'Yeah, I sure as hell was.' Lorraine watched the girl pluck at the tissue. 'Me and God knows how many more.'

'Like Kendall Nathan and Raymond Vallance, for example,' Lorraine said casually. 'Jose and Juana seem to think that you and Mr Vallance were . . . close. Is that true?'

Cindy said nothing for ten, twenty seconds, then, 'Yeah, we had a thing. Lasted all of five minutes and then he pissed on me too. It's like I have a sign round my neck, which only guys like him and Harry can see, that says, "Fuck Me and Dump Me" – oh, and "Beat Up on Me While You're There."' She began to cry in earnest.

Lorraine was surprised that Cindy had admitted the affair so readily – it made things look even blacker against her. Vallance had a key to the house, and he could easily have been responsible for the damage, particularly since there was no sign of forced entry, but Cindy seemed determined to cast suspicion elsewhere, first by the sudden mention of an unknown black youth – and now she was back to Nathan's ex-wife.

'What's gonna happen to me, Lorraine?' she wept. 'I know it looks like I had more reason than anyone to kill him, but I swear I didn't do it. It's Kendall Nathan who's pulling all the strings here, I just know it. She has no alibi for the time Harry was shot, and if the art thing's true, she's got a motive as well.'

'I'll go to the gallery just as soon as I can and see if I can talk to her,' Lorraine said soothingly, reaching out to give Cindy's hand a squeeze. 'Did the hospital have anyone photograph your bruises, by the way?'

Cindy nodded.

'Well, when you next see your lawyers, at least mention it to them, and also that Nathan had been violent to you on many previous occasions. I take it you haven't told the police any of this?'

'No, nothin'. A cop, a real bastard, asked me a lot of questions, but I told him nothin'.'

'You don't recall his name, by any chance?'

'Yeah, Sharkey.'

So he was still on the case. Lorraine walked to the door. 'I'll be in touch. You try to get some rest, and call me when you're discharged. Do you know how long you'll be here?'

'Depends on the doctor – could be out later today.'

Just as Lorraine opened the door, Cindy spoke again. 'I did love him at the beginning. I was only eighteen, he was so nice and he made me all these promises, about being in one of his movies. But they were as fucking sick as he was – he was just making porn.' She pulled herself

112

up on her elbows to look Lorraine in the eye. 'You think I killed him now, don't you?'

Lorraine met the girl's gaze before she replied, 'No, Cindy, I don't believe I do. Take care now.'

She went out and closed the door quietly after her. She had made no mention of the bullet she had found, or Jose's revelation about the parked jeep that could have been Kendall's. She didn't want to raise Cindy's hopes, because unless Lorraine could clear her name, Cindy Nathan would have to stand trial for the murder of her husband.

As soon as Lorraine got back to the office she asked Decker to check out Jose's story about the jeep. 'Find out if anyone else saw it there. Talk to any residents close to where he said it was parked.'

'Anything else?'

'Yeah, can you get me any newspaper coverage of fine art auctions or galleries selling top quality paintings?'

'Sure.'

'Maybe come on as a buyer. Don't act up the investigator.'

'As if I would,' he said, with a camp flick of the wrist.

Lorraine grinned at him. 'Get out of here – go on.'

'On my way,' and he left with a prancing swagger.

Lorraine began to thumb through notes of her last interview with Cindy, in which she had underlined the name of Detective Sharkey.

Jim Sharkey, the officer she had worked with on her first case in Pasadena. She was sure she'd be able to get some inside info on the police inquiry – if she paid for it.

She called the police department, asked for Sharkey. It was a while before he came to the phone.

'Sharkey,' he said abruptly.

'Lorraine Page,' she replied politely.

'Yeah, they said.'

She could tell he was smoking as she could hear him inhale, then hiss the smoke out from his lungs. 'Can we meet?'

'Not right now, I'm busy.'

'So am I – but I think we should meet. I may have some information for you in regard to the Nathan inquiry,' she said, still keeping her voice over-polite, almost coaxing. 'What about lunch? I'd prefer to discuss it away from the station.'

'Like I said, I'm busy.' His voice sounded tense and irritated. 'Mrs Page, if you have anything relevant to my present investigation, then you should come in and talk to my lieutenant.'

'I'd prefer to discuss it with you. Surely you don't want me to spell it out.'

'Spell what out, Mrs Page?'

'Oh, come on. Stop playing games with me. You know I'm working for Cindy Nathan, I know you're on the case. Now, if you don't want to meet, then you can go fuck yourself. If, on the other hand, you want to have a cup of coffee with me, I'll be at the Silver Spoon, corner of Santa Monica and Havenhurst, about two.' She put the phone down. Detective Jim Sharkey had been given a lot of backhanders by Rooney, and now he was coming on all pompous and squeaky clean. It infuriated her, as she knew just how much money Rooney had palmed the man in return for access to police files for the last murder case she had worked on.

The phone rang and, still angry, she snatched it up to hear the bleeps of a payphone. 'Mrs Page?' It was Sharkey again.

'Speaking.'

'Don't ring the fuckin' office – I got the Captain at my fucking elbow listening in on every word you said.'

'All I said was I wanted a meet.'

'Yeah, yeah. I'm gonna give you my mobile number. You want me in future you call that, not the station, and I'll see you at two at the Silver Spoon.' He dictated the number and hung up. Lorraine checked the time. Still only eleven – she would have time to see Kendall Nathan first.

CHAPTER 5

LORRAINE WALKED up Beverly Drive, looking for Kendall Nathan's gallery. Although the location was a notch below the premier sites on Rodeo Drive, the smell of wealth and luxurious living was everywhere in the air. Lorraine passed store after store selling designer clothing, shoes and leather goods.

The neighbourhood was also full of art-related retailing – jewellery and antique stores, and Gallery One was next door to a shop selling antique Oriental kelims. The gallery itself had a plain white store-front, with its name in hammered metal letters, and large, plain plate-glass windows behind which were displayed a sculpture and a couple of star attractions from the latest exhibit.

Lorraine walked a hundred yards down the block and turned up the back alley between Beverly Drive and Canon to have a quiet look at the back of the premises before Kendall Nathan was aware of her presence. The parking area belonging to the gallery had been walled off behind high wooden gates. There was, however, a gap of about half an inch between gate and post, and, squinting through it, Lorraine could make out the paintwork of a parked vehicle: it was cream and black, the same colours as the jeep Jose had seen parked near the house on the day Nathan died. As she stepped back, she noticed a young black guy walking towards her up the alley. He was looking right at her, almost as though he thought he knew her, but he dropped his eyes as soon as she met them and passed her without a word.

Lorraine walked back to the front of the gallery and in at the door, triggering an entry buzzer. She stood in the centre of the large, light, virtually square room. The ceiling had rows of spotlights positioned to show off the paintings, hung strategically around the walls. The canvases were mostly unframed, and one wall displayed the works of only one artist, landscapes in bright acrylics. On another wall were oblong canvases, all of block colours, deep crimson, dark blue, black and walnut, all with an identical white and silver flash of lightning in the right-hand corner.

The only furniture was a desk made of what seemed to be aluminium, with riveted legs, and an uncomfortable-looking chair to match. There was a leather visitors' book – open – a Mont Blanc pen and a leather-bound blotter, all neatly laid out next to a telephone.

'Can I help you?'

Lorraine turned, and for a moment her eyes were unable to distinguish anyone: the cross-beams of the spotlights made it difficult to see after coming in from daylight. She couldn't work out where the voice had come from.

'Or would you prefer to be left alone?'

Lorraine smiled, her hand shading her eyes. 'No, not at all. I wanted to speak to Mrs Kendall Nathan.'

'You already are.'

Kendall Nathan was wearing a simple black almost ankle-length cotton dress with a scoop neckline and long sleeves. Her right wrist was covered in gold bangles, and she wore a gilt chain-link belt, and a large amethyst ring on her third finger. She held out long, thin fingers, which were bony to the touch, but her grip was strong.

'Lorraine Page.' They shook hands.

'Did someone recommend that you . . . ?'

'No, I'm not here with regard to your paintings.' She laughed lightly, feeling slightly embarrassed, partly because as Kendall was standing in the shadow she couldn't see her face clearly. Kendall Nathan walked back into the main gallery and Lorraine went after her.

'I'm afraid you won't find much to interest you here in that case,' Kendall said mockingly, moving lightly round the desk like a dancer. Now Lorraine could see Harry Nathan's second wife well. She was different from how Lorraine had remembered her at the funeral. There was something simpering in her manner, and the narrowness of her body was accentuated by one of the longest faces Lorraine had ever seen.

Kendall had a wild mop of frizzy, curly hair down to her shoulders, hennaed a reddish colour, which made her olive skin tones slightly yellow. Her eyes were dark, almost black, sly and hooded, and although large, were set too close together on either side of a long, pointed, Aztec-looking nose. Her small mouth was tight and thin-lipped and, even in repose, bore the hint of a snarl.

She smiled. 'What can I do for you, Mrs Page? I'm rather busy.' Kendall obviously did not recognize Lorraine from the funeral: she had been far too concerned with her own performance to take note of who had attended. She eased into her uncomfortable chair and crossed her legs.

Lorraine looked down – even the woman's feet, in

leather sandals, were long and thin. Lorraine perched on the edge of the desk. This annoyed Kendall, who recoiled, angling her body away.

'I'm working for Mrs Nathan.'

The eyes flicked up, then down.

'Mrs Cindy Nathan,' Lorraine explained. She had noticed that the woman didn't like hearing the words 'Mrs Nathan' unless they referred to herself. 'Mrs Nathan, as you are aware, was arrested for the murder of her husband, your ex-husband.'

'Yes, I knew that,' Kendall said briskly. 'Are you a lawyer?'

'No,' Lorraine said. 'I'm a private investigator.' She took out her card and handed it to the other woman, who looked carefully at it, then set it down on the desk.

'Well, I'm so sorry, I really can't help you,' Kendall said, with a quick, false smile.

'You haven't really heard what I'd like to discuss,' Lorraine pointed out.

Kendall pushed up her sleeve and looked at her Rolex. 'I have an appointment shortly, Mrs Page. This will have to be brief.'

'Would you mind telling me where you were on the morning Mr Nathan was shot?' Lorraine asked. 'Cindy says you told her you were at home.'

'I was at home,' Kendall said, her eyes scanning Lorraine as she wondered what else Cindy had told her.

'Was anyone with you?'

'No – not unless you count my cats. I had nothing whatsoever to do with Harry's death, though, so if that's what you're getting at, I'm afraid you're wasting your time.'

'Though I understand you do benefit under Harry

119

Nathan's will,' Lorraine went on casually. 'He retained an interest in the gallery, which now passes to you, is that right?'

'Cindy gets a damn sight more than anyone else,' Kendall said, and Lorraine could hear the bitterness in her voice. 'And Sonja Nathan gets something too – you'll be treating her as a suspect too, of course?' she sneered.

'Do you think she should be treated as one?' Lorraine asked, almost matching Kendall's sarcastic tone.

'Why not? East Hampton's not that great a distance. Maybe she flew in for the day from New York, killed Harry, then flew home.'

Here we go again, Lorraine thought. Wife three says it was wife two, and wife two says it was wife one. Presumably Sonja would say Harry's mother had killed him. Still, Sonja Nathan had remained something of a shadowy figure so far, and Lorraine was interested to hear more about her. She made a mental note to check out her address in East Hampton.

'You and Sonja didn't get along?'

Kendall gave a light, brittle laugh. 'Well, considering Harry left her for me, we weren't best friends. But before Harry and I married we were . . . business associates.' This was clearly an edited version of events, and Lorraine made another mental note to check out the facts. 'I know Sonja quite well. She is not a normal person, I would say, an unbalanced woman, and cold at the core. She never got over Harry's leaving her for me – never. Of everyone around Harry, the two people I would say most capable of murder are Sonja and Harry's good friend Raymond Vallance.'

'Really?' Lorraine said, sceptical as ever of information

120

so readily volunteered, and attempts to throw suspicion on others. 'So you don't think Cindy killed him?'

Kendall shrugged. 'I don't know.'

'How did you and Harry get along after you were divorced?'

Kendall's eyes hardened like stones. 'We had a mutually beneficial relationship. We were business partners in this gallery, and I relied a great deal on Harry's knowledge and judgement of art.' She paused, as though flicking channels on a television, to give Lorraine a quick flash of the downcast, heartbroken friend, then clicked smartly back to business. 'We also collected together privately, and it was agreed between us that what we bought should be jointly owned. We decided to keep it at Harry's house so that we wouldn't have to install a lot of security at two locations, but I paid the insurance premiums. Half the collection is therefore mine,' she declared, as though speaking from the Supreme Court. 'And that, Mrs Page, is not any kind of an advantage I have derived under Harry's will. It was my property, whether he was living or dead. In fact it is to my detriment that Harry died when he did, before we had . . . clarified the arrangements about the collection.'

Arrangements Kendall Nathan had probably made up the moment her ex-husband was dead, Lorraine thought. 'I see,' she said, with a bright, fake smile of her own. 'Well, let's leave that one for the lawyers to fight out. I was really wondering about your personal relationship with Harry.'

'Our relations were cordial,' Kendall said curtly.

'Did you see one another socially, as well as in a business capacity?'

'We had lunch or dinner from time to time. Sometimes we went to art markets or sales. We did not travel together. We did not continue a marital-type relationship, if that's what you're trying to suggest.'

'Oh, no, of course not,' Lorraine said, with another false smile. 'But while we're on that subject, Harry used to record, well, a lot of things that happened at the house, didn't he?'

'Cindy mentioned there were telephone recordings,' Kendall said guardedly.

'I believe he also recorded some ... fairly private activities, while you were married.'

In an instant Kendall knew that Lorraine had seen the tapes, and rose nervously from her desk. She walked a few paces towards the window and looked out into the street. 'Harry liked to go to the edge – a lot of film people do. I was very young at the time' – Lorraine stifled a smile: Kendall Nathan had married Harry in her mid-thirties, and must now be at least forty – 'and I went along with some things which, of course, I wouldn't have any involvement with now. Harry did make some tapes,' she admitted. 'I assume Cindy has told you about them too.'

'We've discussed them.' Lorraine was deliberately evasive.

'Mrs Page, I won't waste your time or mine,' Kendall continued, cutting straight to the chase. 'I realize you've seen these tapes and I'm concerned about what is going to happen to them now. You haven't shown them to any of your associates?' Her dark eyes bored into Lorraine's.

'Of course not,' Lorraine said, and saw the light of calculation enter Kendall's eyes.

'I'd be prepared to compensate you, naturally, if some

of those tapes happened to go missing,' Kendall said, moving back to her desk and apparently studying some notes on her phone pad.

'I'm sorry, but any evidence relevant to the case will have to be passed on to the police,' Lorraine responded. 'The tapes aren't mine to dispose of, and they may form an important part of Cindy Nathan's defence.'

'I see.' Kendall Nathan gave Lorraine a look that would have cut sheet steel.

'What are your relations with Cindy like?' Lorraine said, as much to change the subject as anything else.

Kendall shrugged. 'Our paths crossed, obviously, but I'd call her just an acquaintance, and one I wouldn't go out of my way to see.'

'So you don't like her?'

'I didn't say that. I have no feelings with regard to her.' That was a lie: Kendall was clearly as burned at being left by Nathan as she claimed Sonja had been.

'Well, thank you for your time,' Lorraine said, and smiled. Kendall nodded, already starting to move to the archway. 'Oh, just one thing,' Lorraine went on, 'I know you said you were at home the morning Mr Nathan was shot. What time did you leave?'

'To come to work, just after ten.'

'I don't suppose you made a telephone call to my office that morning?'

'I'm sorry?'

'I asked if you called my agency, Mrs Nathan,' Lorraine repeated. 'I received a phone call on the morning of the shooting – in fact it must have been made shortly after the gun was fired.'

'Why do you ask? Did whoever it was say it was me?' Kendall came towards Lorraine, her eyes sharp and her voice rising. It suddenly sounded less modulated, almost coarse.

'No, the caller identified herself as Cindy Nathan, but Cindy says she didn't make the call.'

'Well, it certainly wasn't me. What did this person say?'

'Oh, that she needed help, just shot her husband. It didn't sound like Cindy's voice.' She smiled at Kendall. 'To be honest, I didn't think it sounded like yours – until just now. I thought there might be some similarity, but if you're sure you didn't make the call . . .'

'I have never met you or spoken to you before in my life,' Kendall said, a considerably less polished Mid-Western accent now noticeable in her voice. 'I never called you, but I'll give you some advice. Don't believe a word that dumb bitch tells you. She's a liar. And don't get sucked in by the big baby blue eyes and the tears. She can turn them on at will. I know, believe me, I know.' She paused and made an effort to regain her poise. 'Now if you'll excuse me, I have things to do.'

Lorraine started to walk to the door, then stopped. 'Can I just ask you what kind of car you drive?'

Kendall looked penetratingly at Lorraine. 'Why do you ask?'

'Just to eliminate things, you know.'

'I drive a 1996 Mitsubishi jeep. It's convenient for carrying paintings. It's two-tone and has about twenty-five thousand on the clock. Is there anything else?'

Lorraine opened the gallery door. 'No, not at the present. I appreciate your talking to me, and I'm sorry to have taken up so much of your time. Would you mind if I came back if I need to talk to you again?'

124

Kendall looked at her calculatingly. 'No, I don't suppose so, but call first.' She went back to her desk, opened a drawer and took out a business card. 'I'll give you my home number as well.' She used her Mont Blanc, bending over the desk.

'Mrs Nathan?' A young man walked in through a small rear door, not seeing Lorraine. 'I've unloaded all the canvases – you still want me?'

Lorraine looked into the rear of the shop. She could not see him clearly, but she was almost certain it was the same black youth who had walked past her out back.

'Give me a couple minutes,' Kendall snapped, but the man remained where he was. 'I've got a workshop outside in my yard – I make up the frames and things like that. You have to have a rapid turnover in a gallery to keep the public interested.'

Again Kendall turned and this time told the man to get out. He disappeared. 'He doesn't have the right attitude for customers.'

'Do you sell mostly to passing trade?' Lorraine asked.

'A few come in, but it's mostly by appointment.'

'How does that work?' Lorraine asked pleasantly.

Kendall's condescending manner earlier was now firmly re-established. 'We have a client list and I send out an invitation every time I have a new artist I want to promote. I also work with a few designers – you know, wall hangings and textiles and so on.' She smiled with sly eyes, showing a chipped tooth. Lorraine's mind was racing: why was the woman suddenly being so friendly? Had it been the reference to the phone call? Oddly enough, Lorraine preferred her cool and snide. This smiling, over-helpful act made her suspicious.

'I won't hold you up any longer,' she said. 'Thanks again.'

The meter was almost up. Lorraine bleeped the car open, got in and sat a moment. Kendall had said she hadn't made the call, but had been at home with no alibi when it was made. She was clearly jealous of Cindy Nathan, and had continued to have a close relationship with her ex-husband. To some extent she benefited from his death, and, most importantly, she had made no secret about driving a two-tone Mitsubishi jeep, as described by Nathan's housekeepers. She also employed a young black guy. Maybe Cindy hadn't made up the man she said she had seen at the house. Kendall also knew about the phone tapes, and had admitted that she wanted to recover the videos. Someone had broken into Lorraine's office and poured acid over the phone tapes and, according to Cindy, only two other people had known that they were there. Harry Nathan's ex-wives.

Lorraine slipped on her safety-belt and started the engine. She glanced behind her, indicated and pulled out into the street. As she drove, she squinted at the petrol gauge and saw that the tank was nearly empty. She pulled in at the old Union 76 gas station on Little Santa Monica, a remarkable piece of classic sixties construction, like the wingspan of a great bird. She asked the attendant to fill up the car and check the oil, while she went in to buy a pack of cigarettes. She went to the ladies' and returned to find that the station attendant had raised the bonnet of her Mercedes.

'How much?' she said.

The man turned towards her. 'How much you worth?'

He crooked his finger and motioned her closer. 'I only noticed because the top of my pen dropped into the engine when I was unscrewing the oil cap. Have a look at this. Your brake cable's been sliced almost through. Dunno how long it'd have been before . . .' He made a screeching noise and walloped the side of the car. 'You got no brakes, lady, an' this'll have to go up on the ramp because it ain't safe to drive the length of the street.'

'How long do you think they've been like this?'

He pulled a face, sticking out his bulldog jaw. 'Well, I wouldn't know, it's a clean cut – like, it's not wear and tear, and you would have known about that, honey, believe me. So, maybe recent. You got any enemies? I'd give the cops a call if I was you – this is fuckin' dangerous.'

Lorraine straightened up. 'Can you fix them?'

'Sure.'

She sat on a low wall beside the garage as the man set to work. She lit a cigarette, her hand shaking. How long had they been cut? *When* were they cut? Most importantly, who the hell had done it? Kendall Nathan? The woman had had no chance to get at the car, had been with her continuously. The black man? But Kendall had had no opportunity to tell him to do anything. Lorraine found herself smoking cigarettes down to the filter and lighting the next from the butt.

What had she unwittingly uncovered? There had to be a reason for someone to be prepared to kill her, or at the very least to want her to have a life-threatening accident.

The car wasn't going to be ready for some considerable time, so she called a cab and went to the office, where she filled in Decker about her car.

'Did you call the police?'

Lorraine shut her eyes, then hit the desk. She'd forgotten to meet Jim Sharkey. 'Shit, I gotta go. I arranged to meet the cop on the Nathan case. I'll get a cab.'

Jim Sharkey looked at his watch. He'd had two cappuccinos and had had breakfast again in lieu of lunch. Now he was getting sick of sitting outside on a hard chair on the patio waiting for Lorraine – the Silver Spoon was one of the few places left in LA where smoking was still allowed, but plush surroundings weren't their strong suit. He was just about to walk out when a cab pulled up, Lorraine got out and walked towards the diner. She was a great looker, Mrs Lorraine Page, he thought, as she eased her body between the tables – nice easy strides, tight figure, long legs . . . He was getting hard as his eyes travelled up from her crotch to her bosom – not as big as he went for, but they looked a nice handful, firm.

'Hi, sorry I'm late.'

He shook her hand, half lifting his butt from the seat as she slid into the chair opposite. 'You want a cup of coffee?'

'Diet Coke – hot out there today.'

Sharkey signalled to the waiter and ordered two Cokes, then looked back at Lorraine. She removed her dark glasses and tossed her head back. He noticed how well cut and silky her hair was – nice, like a shampoo ad. 'Looking in good shape,' he said.

'Thanks. Wish I could say the same for you.'

He laughed. 'How's old Bill?'

'He's on honeymoon.'

'What?'

'Yeah, I don't know if you remember Rosie, used to work with me. Sort of curly hair, cute face. They married after his wife died.'

The waiter brought their Cokes, and Sharkey dipped his straw in. 'Dunno why I asked for this, I hate the stuff, but I'm not drinking.'

'Makes two of us.'

Sharkey looked at her face. He could see no signs of the dissipation, the rough ride she'd been on with the drink and drugs, just a few lines at the corners of her eyes and mouth. Lorraine was aware that he was scrutinizing her, but chose to ignore it, looking instead at the other tables under the awning, with their Formica tops and plain, functional crockery. If the place was basic, at least everything looked well-maintained and clean.

Sharkey took her matches and lit her cigarette. 'We got a new lieutenant, name of Burton, heading up the detective division – he's a real son-of-a-bitch.'

Lorraine exhaled, turning her head away so the smoke didn't blow in Sharkey's face.

'Burton, Jake Burton – you know him?'

'Nope, but then I've been out of the force a long time.'

Sharkey nodded – he knew all about it, but he said nothing.

'You want to start, or shall I?' she asked.

He shifted in his seat. 'Look, I came here because I wanted to get things straight. With this guy Burton looking over our shoulders, the days when we could trade off are gone, understand me? He's got fuckin' eyes in the back of his head.'

'Does he know you're meeting with me?'

'No, no way. Shit, I think I'll have a beer.' He signalled for a waiter and ordered a lager, Mexican light.

'Well, if he doesn't know you're here who's gonna tell him? And maybe I've got something. We could just toss a few things round.'

Sharkey sucked his teeth. 'You were hired by Cindy Nathan, right?'

Lorraine sat back as the waiter brought the beer. Sharkey waved away the glass, preferring to drink it from the bottle.

'Will you start, or shall I?' she said again softly.

He sighed, and shrugged his big shoulders. 'Well, I might as well. I mean, we've got her sewn up – the gun was hers, her fingerprints were on it, and when she was brought into the station she virtually admitted it. We got enough witnesses to sink the fucking *Titanic* who say she threatened to shoot him, plus, as far as we can make out, she's the main beneficiary of his estate – he's got quite an art collection.' Sharkey took a swig of beer and set the bottle down on the table. 'Though from what I can make out, there's not all that much in the way of liquid assets. Way I hear it, this so-called production company cum studio may go bust, which would soak up the cash from the collection.' Sharkey cocked his head to one side. 'But maybe she didn't know that.'

'Ah, but you do,' Lorraine said.

'Yeah, we checked him out. He's got a share in a gallery run by an ex-wife, but lately he'd been living from hand to mouth.'

'Blackmailing anyone he could,' Lorraine added, watching Sharkey. He didn't react.

'Yeah, we figured that one. He was a real sleazeball, but we don't have a suspect in that area.'

'You sure about that?'

Sharkey took another gulp of beer. 'Not sure of anything but the little lady. She pulled the trigger, maybe not for his money – maybe she knew he didn't have any – but she shot him. We've got a few statements from Mr Nathan's ever-loving friends that he knocked her around and that she cheated on him. These Hollywood types screw anything that moves, and Nathan certainly did his share – you see any of his movies?' Lorraine shook her head. 'Soft porn, and apparently he always roadtested his leading ladies – mind you, so would I if I had the chance.'

Lorraine's smile didn't reach her eyes. She wondered how much she should tell him, and how much he was holding back.

'You know she was pregnant?'

He nodded. 'We also know the child may not have been his – she was screwing Raymond Vallance. *He* was interviewed, shitting himself, not about the shooting – he's got an alibi, apparently—' Lorraine registered that piece of information with interest ' – but about it getting out, you know, harming his career. Someone should tell him he's been on the skids for the past ten years. The only way he's ever going to see his name in the papers again is to be up on a fucking charge.'

Lorraine gave another chilly smile. 'You know Harry Nathan made a lot of tapes? His phone calls, and people coming to the house, plus a few . . . adult material movies with Vallance and his ex-wives.'

'Oh, sure,' Sharkey lied. This was news to him. 'We're checking it out.'

'Well, some of the recordings have come my way, and I'll be sending them over – don't want to lose my PI licence for obstructing the course of justice.' She paused a moment. 'What I'm thinking is maybe someone didn't like the idea of being filmed,' she went on. 'Maybe didn't like it so much they pulled the trigger – and Cindy Nathan didn't.'

Sharkey sighed, then leaned forward. 'Look, he was garbage, but he'd been garbage for a long time. Sure he hit on everyone for money – he was a con man, he conned anyone and anything he could, it was a way of life. Once he stopped directing, he sure as hell couldn't produce a movie. He used them to score the chicks, maybe made a few bucks at the same time but he had a big lifestyle, so he hit on his friends, even his house-keepers – their wages haven't been paid for months. But nothing we've dug up, and no one we've interviewed, has changed my department's opinion. We think his wife, in a fit of jealous rage – and she could apparently throw quite a performance in that area – had had enough. She took her own gun, a weapon he had given to her and shown her how to use, and she waited until he was in the pool and popped him. Like I said, she's virtually admitted it.'

'What about his ex-wife?'

'Kendall Nathan?' he asked, and drained the last of the beer. 'She's been questioned, and she doesn't have a motive.'

Lorraine reached for another cigarette. 'She inherits half of the gallery, where I visited her today – and somebody sliced through my brake cable right after-wards.'

'Oh, yeah?' He didn't seem interested.

'Yeah. She also knew about the tapes in my office, and someone broke in and poured acid over them.'

He stared at her, waiting for more.

'I *don't* think Cindy killed him. I think somebody's fitting her up for it – maybe one of the people he was blackmailing, I dunno, and . . .' Should she tell him about the second bullet? The parked jeep? He wasn't giving her much in return.

'And?' he urged her.

'That's about it.'

'You reported the damage to your car?' He was checking his watch. 'If someone slashed my brake cable, I'd be worried. Did you report it?' he asked again.

'No, no, I didn't.' Lorraine frowned.

'Are you going to?'

'No. Guess I'll just be careful where I park.'

'You got any idea who it might have been?'

'No, absolutely none,' Lorraine said, and Sharkey checked his watch again. 'I gotta go. Sorry I couldn't be more help. If you come up with anything, you know my mobile number.'

'I'll pay the cheque,' she said, opening her purse. She took out three hundred-dollar bills and folded them. 'You settle up for me, will you?'

'Sure,' he said, as he raked the bills across the table. 'You string out your PI job, sweetheart. I would if I was in your shoes – you've got a while before the trial. Get what you can, and if anything else happens, I'd report it. You lived quite a life, didn't you? So I'd think about who might want to fuck with your car.'

Lorraine stood up. 'Thanks for the advice.'

He watched her walk out, pause at the edge of the terrace and slip on a pair of dark glasses. He wondered how much she was getting paid by Cindy Nathan, and how he'd slip in the video and phone recordings to the new lieutenant. They hadn't had a sniff of that but he'd look into it now.

It was just after three when Lorraine collected her car and drove back to the garage under the office, making sure to ask the valet to park her car close to his booth. She felt hot and tired, and the meeting with Sharkey had given her nothing new. She couldn't stop thinking about who had wanted to harm her. She wasn't frightened, exactly, just uneasy, and by the time she got into her office she was in a foul mood.

'Cops have Cindy Nathan down for it, don't even appear to be looking elsewhere,' she told Decker. He was elbow-deep in all the data they had got together so far on Cindy's case. She walked towards her own office, ignoring the thump of Tiger's tail. 'Book me a flight tomorrow for East Hampton, New York State. I want to see Sonja Nathan.' She kicked her door shut and sat down at her desk, where her mood become blacker.

Five minutes later, Decker tapped on the door. 'I've got you a flight at eight a.m. with American Airlines. Manhattan International limos will collect you and drive you to East Hampton, and you're booked into the Maidstone Arms. I have no idea what Sonja Nathan's address is – do you want me to call Cindy and check? Be a pity to go all that way and find out she may not be there.'

Lorraine muttered something, and Decker moved closer. 'Excuse me?'

'Ask Cindy Nathan for the phone number, and leave me alone – I've got a headache.'

'Fine, and when you are, so to speak, in the air, do

you want me to look after Tiger? I'm not supposed to have pets in the house, but for one night I don't see that'll be a problem.'

'Yeah, thank you,' Lorraine answered gruffly.

He shut the door quietly.

Lieutenant Jake Burton, new head of the detective division in the Beverly Hills Police Department, stood with his back to the room, noticing that the room still smelt of paint. His office had been freshly decorated, and was now as immaculate as the man himself. Burton stood six feet two with a tight, muscular body, and blond hair cut close to his head in an expensive salon style that flattered his chiselled face. His slight tan made his light blue eyes appear even bluer, and his teeth even more brilliantly white. His nickname in the Army had been 'Rake', but now that he was in the police force, and had moved up the ranks with ruthless determination, he didn't like nicknames any more. He knew that his subordinates thought he was a cold bastard, and in some ways he was, but he had been shipped in to clean up rumours of officers taking bribes and kickbacks, and it was a job he intended to do to the best of his ability.

Burton was originally from Texas, but he had travelled widely and his roots were now detectable only as a faint burr in his voice. It was in the army that he'd qualified as an attorney – he was prepared to thank Uncle Sam for that, but not for shipping him out to Vietnam with one of the last units dispatched. He had been there only two months before the conflict ended, but those two months lived on in his mind, and had marked him deeply. He never talked about it, or referred to himself as a veteran simply because he didn't think of himself as a one, having spent so little time in Vietnam and taken so little part in the war. It had been a nightmare experience which he buried deep inside, and on his return, he had left the army and enrolled in police academy. He was then only twenty-three, but older than most other recruits, and used that to his advantage. Before he had even graduated from the academy, he was earmarked as an officer to watch. He had been married for a short while and his wife, a secretary, had claimed in her divorce petition that, in fact, he was married to his job. He still was in many ways, although he was hitting the mid-forties. He had some private life now but it was mostly fraternizing with other officers, playing squash or tennis, for Burton was as obsessive about his physical fitness as he was about his job.

He had done such good work in Santa Barbara, cleaning up the department and weeding out officers who were found to be taking bribes, that he had become known for his ability and, above all, for his unimpeachable integrity. Jake Burton was as straight as they made 'em, and when the opportunity arose to move to LA, to a job with enhanced status, he had readily accepted it.

He had, at the time, been involved with a divorcée and the time had seemed right to move on from her too. Recently, he had been dating a girl from the legal department, a well-groomed, pretty brunette with intelligent brown eyes, but somehow he couldn't bring himself to make a commitment.

At the knock on his door Burton's attention snapped back to the present. 'Come in,' he said sharply, straightening the row of brand new, sharpened pencils on his pristine desk.

'You wanted to see me, Lieutenant?'

Burton nodded and opened a file of reports on the Cindy Nathan case. 'Sit down.' He gestured to a hard-backed chair in front of his desk. 'What's this about tapes?'

Sharkey cleared his throat. 'I got a tip-off. Apparently Nathan recorded everything but bowel movements.'

'And this is the first we've heard of it?'

Sharkey nodded. 'He filmed everyone coming in and out of the house on security cameras, and also some porno stuff with the wives, but I doubt if the tapes will tell us anything we don't already know. I mean, every-body in LA knew Cindy Nathan was a fucking whore.'

'Really?' Burton said coldly. 'You had access to these tapes?'

'No, sir.'

'So did this informant – whoever tipped you off – have access to them?'

'Cindy Nathan sent them to her.'

Burton turned the pages of the report, then tapped it with his index finger.

'Why would Cindy Nathan send the tapes to this informant?'

Sharkey squirmed in his seat. 'Well, she's a private dick, hired by Mrs Nathan.'

'Really?' Burton said softly. 'So how did this interac-tion come about?'

'Well, she called me . . .'

'Yes. And?' Burton waited for a reply, tapping his desk with one of the needle-sharp pencils. He neither liked nor trusted Sharkey.

'She wanted information – you know, do a trade.'

Burton waited, his eyes on Sharkey. 'A trade in what, exactly, Detective?'

'Well, you know, what I'd got – et cetera, et cetera.'

'Did you tell her anything relevant to the investigation?'

'Hell, no, nothing like that.'

'Did she pay you?'

'Of course not. Didn't give her nothing.' Sharkey grinned.

'I sincerely hope not. So what is the lady's name?'

'She used to be a cop.'

'So did most PIs. What's her name, Detective?'

Sharkey sucked in his breath. 'Lorraine Page.'

Burton opened the file again, and appeared to be devoting his full attention to it as he said quietly, 'So, tell me about this lady, this Lorraine Page.'

CHAPTER 6

CINDY NATHAN had always known something like this would happen: now that it had she found herself strangely calm, as though the fate she had always known was walking just behind her had finally taken her hand.

'Take off your clothes,' the man said, and she slowly unbuttoned the white shirt and took it off.

She began to unfasten the zip of the tight aqua jeans, then stopped. 'Will I take off my shoes?' she asked docilely, as though speaking to the nurse at school.

'Everything.' She sat on the edge of the bed and unbuckled her high ankle-strap sandals, then pulled off her jeans with her underwear still inside. She was naked now except for a choker of tiny black glass beads, strung into a fine pattern like a broad strip of lace. He did not look at her: the female body held no mystery for him.

'Now go into the bathroom,' he said. 'Take that thing off from round your neck.'

At eight fifteen that evening, Juana cooked supper at the Nathan house and pressed the number for Cindy's bedroom on the intercom. There was no answer. Juana was a little annoyed and wondered if Cindy wanted to eat in her room instead of at the dining table, where the meal had been laid. She dialled Cindy again just after eight twenty, and still received no reply from the room, although the girl had specifically ordered what she wanted to eat – a grilled swordfish steak, salad of fennel and watercress dressed with lime juice, and no wine or fruit, just a glass of sparkling water.

Juana prepared a tray and rang again at eight thirty, but still no one picked up. She wondered if Cindy could be taking a shower, waited a few minutes more, then asked Jose to go up to Cindy's room and check that she was all right. Jose went upstairs, tapped on the bedroom door and listened outside. He could hear music playing quite loudly, but there was no answer from Cindy. He tried the door, only to find it locked. Perplexed, he returned to the kitchen and he and Juana ate their own supper. At nine fifteen Jose went to Cindy's room again. This time he banged loudly on the door, and then, with Juana at his side, used his pass key to enter the room.

The room was empty, and the clothes Cindy had been wearing were strewn across the bed, her shoes discarded beside it. Jose went towards the closed bathroom door, tapped, and waited a moment. He could hear the shower running, and turned to Juana. 'She's taking a shower. I told you not to worry.'

Juana pursed her lips, put the tray down on a bedside table and closed the doors to the balcony, through which the curtains were billowing in the wind. Jose had already left the room. Juana crossed back to the bathroom and listened again: the water was still running. She knocked and called that she had left Cindy's supper tray on the bed, relocked the bedroom door and went back downstairs.

Lorraine arrived home after driving up to Santa Monica to walk Tiger on the promenade, a pretty stretch of parkland on the bluffs above the beach, just as darkness was falling at about six o'clock. She immediately checked her answerphone, to find only one message from Decker, giving Sonja Nathan's home number, which Lorraine took down. After a shower, she fixed herself some agnolotti and salad, cooked up some meat and vegetables for Tiger, and was just about to make the call to Sonja Nathan when Tiger let rip with a deep bark, then growled as footsteps became audible on the walkway up to the apartment.

Lorraine went to the window and looked down into the road. She saw the Chevvy, parked directly underneath. She didn't recognize the car and looked quickly at her watch. Just after ten. After the incident with the brakes, she was immediately tense, and Tiger was ready to pounce.

The door buzzed, and Lorraine hesitated before she picked up the entryphone. 'Who is it?'

'Lieutenant Burton, LAPD.' The voice was neither friendly nor familiar.

Lorraine looked out of her window and could see Burton standing back from the front door on the steps. He was holding his ID card up for her to see, so she pressed the door-release button and told Tiger to sit. The dog still wasn't convinced and she had to hold his collar in one hand as she opened the door to the apartment.

'Hi – can you just say hello to my dog?'

Burton smiled. 'Sure. Hi . . . Do I put out my hand or what?'

'Just stay where you are, let him have a sniff. He'll be okay soon.'

As Burton leaned forward Tiger growled deep in his throat.

'Good boy . . . good boy.'

Lorraine slowly released her hold on the dog's collar and he relaxed. 'Sorry about that. Come in.'

'No, I'm sorry, I should have called first, but . . . you want another look at my ID?'

She smiled. 'No, that's okay.'

Lorraine tried to think what the hell had brought Burton to her apartment, while smiling and offering him coffee or tea, both of which he refused.

'I suppose you're wondering why I'm here?'

'You could say that.' She sat down opposite in an easy chair. Burton was not the kind of man she found attractive – she had always preferred men with darker colouring – but she was impressed by him. He seemed quite a cool guy, though the hair was too short, and judging from the pressed pants, polished shoes and so on, he was anally retentive. She laughed at her analysis.

'Did I miss something?' he asked.

'I'm sorry. It's just you being here all spick and span, and at the same time my mind is wondering what the fuck it is you want?'

He laughed – a pleasant laugh – and she also noted he had nice, even teeth.

'You had a meeting with one of my officers.'

'Yes, Jim Sharkey.'

'Yes,' he repeated softly. 'Jim Sharkey.' Nothing Sharkey had said had given him any indication about how Lorraine Page looked. Nor had anything he had read about her. He had not expected to be bowled over by her looks.

'So, you're running that division now, are you?' she enquired. He liked the way she tilted her head when she spoke, her silky blonde hair falling forward over one side of her face.

'Yes, I hope you don't mind my calling. It's not official – just wanted to touch base.'

'Really?' she said, with a half-smile, then again offered him something to drink. This time he accepted a glass of iced water. He had strong hands with long, tapering fingers, which brushed hers for a second as he took the glass from her.

Burton drew out a hard-backed chair from the little dining nook, and brought it over to the coffee table, although there was a more comfortable chair and the sofa. He twisted the chair round and sat astride it, leaning his arms along the back.

'You want to trade information,' he said, looking at her directly. He leaned over, picked up his glass, and sipped from it, then replaced it carefully. 'As I said before, this is unofficial, but I'm new in town – new to the station. I like to get a handle on some of my officers, especially if they're taking backhanders, and I know most of them are. I'm on what you might call a clean-up campaign.'

Lorraine cocked her head to one side, and waited.

'Did you offer any payment to Detective Sharkey?'

'No, I paid for his cappuccino, that's all.'

He stared at her. It was his turn to wait, and there was a long pause. 'I see. Have you traded information with Detective Sharkey before?'

'No. I did some work on a case with a former partner who was an old buddy of Sharkey's, Bill Rooney – Captain Rooney. I think they sank a few beers together and discussed the investigation. It was the disappearance of—'

'Yes, I read the file. Girl was found murdered in New Orleans, wasn't she?' He half smiled. 'You got a bonus, so I heard, a big one.'

'Yes, I did. Not that I think it's any business of yours, but it's what I used to open up my office.'

'Did Sharkey get a cut of your bonus?'

'No, he did not. It was split between myself and my partners.'

Burton drained his glass, and held the blue goblet loosely in his hands. 'You working for Cindy Nathan?' he asked casually.

'Yes.'

'You mentioned a number of things to Detective Sharkey – some tapes, telephone and video . . .'

Lorraine stood up. 'Yes, I did, but he said you knew about them, or the investigating officers did.'

'Then he lied. It was the first we'd heard of them. You want to tell me about them?'

Lorraine was getting edgy. Burton had got up and was wandering around the room. It unnerved her, as if he was mentally sizing up both her and her apartment. 'It seems Nathan recorded all incoming calls, and had video monitors set up all over the house.'

'So what did you glean from these tapes?' he asked,

bending to look at a photograph of her father in police uniform.

'That Nathan was both vain and paranoid,' Lorraine replied. 'Most of the tapes were of him making beauty appointments. None that I had the opportunity to listen to were of much interest, and some were destroyed.' She had his full attention now. 'Someone broke into my office and poured acid over them.'

'Did you tell Sharkey this?'

'No.'

'And the videos?'

'Well, they're a little different. They are explicit recordings of Nathan's sexual exploits with his last two wives.'

Burton folded his arms. 'Is that why you wanted to see Sharkey? Trade off these videos?'

'No, though I offered them. A good defence attorney will also use them – Cindy took a lot of abuse.'

'Enough to make her kill him?'

'No, not necessarily. I know the evidence against her is pretty incriminating – maybe too incriminating – but I don't think she did it.'

'You mean she could have been set up?'

'Possibly.'

He sat on the arm of the sofa. 'By whom?'

'I don't know, it's just a theory.'

'And you are obviously being paid a good retainer to find out?'

'Again, I don't think that's any of your business. I'm doing my job, that's all.'

'Apart from the tapes and the videos, do you have anything that would cast suspicion on someone else?'

It was Lorraine's turn to pace the apartment. Should she tell him about her suspicions of Kendall Nathan, the parked jeep? She played for time, tidying a stack of magazines on the coffee table.

'You had a problem with your car?' he said. 'Sharkey told me.'

She straightened. 'Yes, brake cable had been cut, sliced in two.'

'But you didn't report it?'

'No.'

'Do you think someone was warning you off?'

'I'd say it might have been a bit more than a warning – if I'd been going at any speed and had to stop I might have been killed.' She swung round to face him. 'And this unofficial visit is beginning to get to me. Do you think I'm withholding evidence or something? Why would I? Christ, I'm hired to get my client off a murder rap. Surely anything I come up with I'd feed back to—'

'I'd like to see the tapes.'

'Fine, send someone round to my office and you can have them.'

'What else have you got?'

She glared at him, and he looked back at her with laser-like intensity.

'You don't believe Cindy Nathan killed her husband. Is it just a gut feeling, or do you have other evidence that might implicate someone else?'

Lorraine thought for a moment, then said, 'Okay, there was a jeep parked across from the Nathans' house, unidentified so far, seen by the housekeeper. He was sure it didn't belong to anyone in the neighbourhood, two-tone Mitsubishi, driven away shortly after the shooting. Kendall Nathan owns a jeep that matches that description. Kendall Nathan was also one of only two people who knew that the tapes which were destroyed at my office were in there.' Burton remained impassive. 'Cindy Nathan thinks she heard possibly two shots – the first she presumed was a car backfiring, so she didn't pay any attention to it, and the second made her get up and walk round to the pool area. That's when she found her husband.'

'He was shot only once.'

'Yes, but . . .' Lorraine decided against saying anything about the bullet she had found. 'There was also a phone call,' she went on. 'Someone called me right after Nathan was shot, said she was Cindy Nathan, but Cindy subsequently said it wasn't her. Now that I've met her, I don't think the voice was hers either. It could have been Kendall's but she denied it.'

'But Kendall Nathan doesn't have much of a motive, right? She gets half an art gallery, but Cindy's the one who stood to inherit the house and the stock and everything.'

Burton had surprised Lorraine – division heads didn't usually spend much time poring over reports and, in her experience, few had been sufficiently involved with an individual case to discuss motive. But, then, she had never had an unofficial home visit from anyone that high up either.

'Maybe the motive isn't financial,' she said. Burton gave her that penetrating look again. 'Nathan's finances, as far as I can gather, are not as healthy as one would expect – Cindy Nathan is not coming into a fortune. I'd say she might even find herself in debt after she's paid off all Nathan's creditors, so I'm in two minds about money being in the picture at all.'

147

Burton hesitated before replying. 'Maybe you're right, but even if it's not money, Cindy Nathan is still in the frame. You've said he abused her – maybe she'd taken enough. She'd threatened publicly to kill him and, according to the reports I've read, she was pretty confused when she was arrested, not saying categorically that she didn't kill him, but that she didn't *think* she did, that she couldn't have. Then she said, "Could I?"'

Lorraine sat down on the sofa. 'Yeah, I know, but she found the body. She was presumably in a state of shock.'

'Perhaps you don't know the results of the medical examination, after she was brought into the station?'

'She was pregnant. Yes, I do know, and she lost the child – in fact she's only just been released from hospital.'

'I wasn't referring to her pregnancy. Cindy Nathan is or was a cocaine addict. According to the report, your client was high as a kite on the morning of the shooting.' He looked at his watch, then extended his hand. 'Thank you very much for seeing me, Mrs Page.'

She shook his outstretched hand, trying not to show her astonishment that Cindy Nathan had been doped up when she had first spoken to her.

'I'll have someone collect the tape footage from you first thing in the morning,' he said coolly.

She walked beside him to the front door. He stood head and shoulders above her, and she was close enough to smell his aftershave, fresh, lemony, discreet. He took her by surprise again when he opened the screen door and said softly, 'You don't look anything like your photograph.'

She looked up into his face. 'My photograph?'

'Mug-shot. I read up on you, Mrs Page.'

'Did you?' she said coldly.

148

He held open the screen door with the toe of his shoe. 'But, then, that sort of photograph is never very flattering, is it?'

'No, and it was a long time ago.'

He nodded thoughtfully. 'Yes, I congratulate you. It takes a lot of personal courage to beat alcoholism – beat the demons, so to speak.' Lorraine made no reply. He had read the reports of her drunkenness and her arrest for vagrancy, no doubt he even knew she had prostituted herself, but she felt sickened above all that he knew what she had done – knew why she had been cold-shouldered out of the force. It made her flush.

'What happened to your scar?'

Lorraine jerked back her head as Burton reached out to touch her cheek with one finger. 'I had it fixed.'

'You mind if I say something to you, not as an officer, but as a friend?'

She took two steps back, avoiding his eyes.

'You haven't reported the break-in at your office, that someone tampered with the brake cable on your car. You had a tough climb out of the gutter, Mrs Page. Perhaps someone from your past, nothing to do with Cindy Nathan, is carrying a grudge. I'd take a little more care.'

'Thanks for the advice.'

'Take it, Mrs Page, and if you need to speak to me at any time, please call.' He took out his wallet, adroitly produced his card and a pen, and wrote down another number for her. 'That's my extension and my home number.' He put his wallet and pen back in his jacket, and held out the card.

Lorraine took it without looking at him, and walked back into the apartment as he let himself out and closed the door behind him. She watched from the window as he went towards his car; she knew she should have told him her suspicions of a possible art fraud, which Cindy had outlined, but he had thrown her by admitting he had seen her report sheet. She continued to watch as he drove off down the street.

He had made her feel jaded somehow – his cleanness and freshness, and his neat handwriting on the card in her hand. Plus Cindy Nathan had tested positive for drugs. That put a whole new light on their meetings, and Lorraine was angry that she had not noticed, or even suspected it from the girl's odd chatter, her chronic inability to concentrate, and failure to connect with what was happening around her. Suddenly, Lorraine doubted her judgement completely, and began to think that Cindy Nathan was probably guilty, after all. The depression deepened until she sat down, her head in her hands, feeling wretched, inadequate, unable to stop the tears.

Something else, too, had crept up on her unawares – though she hated to admit it even to herself. She had been attracted to Mr Neat and Clean, and the real pain was knowing that no one or, at least, no decent man would take a second look at her, and that anyone who knew about her past would give her a very wide berth. She was almost thirty-nine years old, and she felt older. The plastic surgery only covered the cracks; it was what was inside that counted. And Lorraine was alone, with only Tiger for company, and it was the idea of a future on her own that made her weep even more despairingly.

Tiger raised his head as she sobbed, then padded across and climbed onto the sofa beside her. She put one arm around his shoulders to draw his head close.

*

It was almost ten o'clock when Juana turned on the bath taps and discovered there was no hot water. She called to her husband, who was still downstairs, asking if he had turned off the water. He didn't hear her, so she made her way along the landing, then froze as she heard the sound of water running. She was outside Cindy Nathan's bedroom – and there was no way that the girl could still be taking a shower.

'Get up here, Jose. *Hurry*, HURRY!'

Juana and Jose went together into Cindy's bedroom. Sure enough, the shower was still running, and sounded louder than normal. Suddenly both were afraid.

'Go into the bathroom,' Juana whispered.

Jose turned the handle, calling to Cindy as he pushed open the door, one inch, then two – then let it swing wide open.

'Mrs Nathan?' he said.

The water was still running and the shower screens were so steamed up that Jose could not make out whether Cindy was inside or not. He edged further into the bathroom, calling Cindy's name, seeing towels and a delicate necklace lying on the tiles. He eased back the sliding doors, which had been drawn around the bath, and gasped. Cindy was naked, kneeling in a position of prayer, a cord wound round her throat and attached by its other end to the shower jet. Her head had slumped forward, and her wet hair covered her face.

'Oh, my God,' he whispered.

'What is it?' asked Juana.

Jose didn't want his wife to see what he had seen, so he turned quickly and pushed her out of the bedroom.

Cindy Nathan was dead. Her eyes were open and her dead gaze stared down at the bottom of the bath, as water continued to spray over her kneeling body and swirl into the drain.

Kendall Nathan sat on her orange sofa in front of the TV set with a tray on her lap. She'd made her usual salad and had just poured herself a glass of white Californian Chardonnay. When the phone rang she was irritated. She had worked late at the gallery and was so tired she was in two minds as to whether to pick it up, but the ringing persisted. When she answered, she couldn't make out what the caller was saying, and had to ask repeatedly who it was.

Jose sounded terrified, his voice breaking as he half sobbed how he had found Cindy.

Kendall almost dropped the phone, and had to breathe deeply to steady herself before speaking. 'Calm down. Tell me again – is she dead?'

'*Yes*, in the shower. What do we do? What do we do?'

Kendall closed her eyes, her mouth bone dry, but her mind racing. 'Have you called anyone else?'

'No, no, we don't know what to do,' Jose said. He had tried to call Lorraine at the office but her answerphone was on, and he didn't have her home number. He had also thought about contacting Sonja, but by this time Juana was hysterical, pointing out that Sonja couldn't do anything from East Hampton. They were afraid to call the police, afraid of any blame being attached to them. Kendall had been their last panic-stricken decision – she would know at least what they should do. They could explain to her that they could not be held responsible.

152

Kendall calmed them, forcing herself to take deep breaths so that her voice was controlled. 'I'll come right over. Just stay calm and I'll be there as soon as I can. Don't do anything until I get there, do you understand? Don't make any more calls,' Kendall repeated, not wanting to find Feinstein in occupation by the time she got to the house. 'Wait for me to get there.' This time, she was determined to get into the house before anyone else did – and get at least one of her paintings out.

She replaced the receiver with shaking hands, and took a few moments to compose herself before she grabbed her coat, car keys and purse and ran from the house. It took her no more than fifteen minutes to get to the Nathans', where she screeched up to the garage compound and slammed on the brakes.

Jose was standing, pale-faced, at the front door.

'Where is she?' Kendall snapped.

'Bedroom. I found her in the shower,' he said, as Kendall ran past him towards the staircase.

A tearful Juana was sitting on a stair and looked up, wiping her eyes on a sodden tissue. 'There's a note.' She sniffed.

Kendall looked down at the woman, then continued up the stairs and along the landing towards the master suite, Jose behind her.

'No – she's in her own room,' he said, and Kendall bit her lip before continuing more slowly along the landing. Cindy's bedroom door was slightly ajar. She took a deep breath and walked in. Jose was about to follow her, but she turned round. 'Leave me for a minute, please.' Jose stepped back and the bedroom door closed.

Juana appeared, still clutching the tissue. 'Did you show her the note?'

'I left it on the dressing table.'

Kendall picked up the single sheet of scented pink notepaper, across which Cindy's childish writing sprawled: 'I can't live like this. It's all over. By the time you read this I will be dead – Cindy.'

Kendall sighed and set down the note on the zigzag, nursery style blue and white wood unit that Cindy had used as a dressing table, then turned towards the bathroom.

She leaned over Cindy's body, bending down first to try to find a pulse at the wrist, then reached out as though to turn up the face, but recoiled: Cindy's eyes bulged and her tongue protruded, her face swollen and discoloured. Kendall shut the shower door and walked out.

She stood in the centre of the room, breathing deeply to steady her nerves. She looked at the note again: very Cindy. But that was all finished with now, in the past. She shifted her gaze to her future, hanging in front of her in the form of a large Andrew Wyeth canvas on the wall . . .

Jose heard a single cry and looked at his wife. He was about to go into the bedroom when the door opened. Kendall almost pushed him out of her way as she hurried towards the master suite, stopping halfway along the passage to stare at another painting. She was breathing hard, and cried out again before she pushed open the doors to the master suite.

'Go downstairs both of you, just go downstairs.' She slammed the door after her.

Jose looked at his wife in confusion. 'Do as she says, Jose.'

'But shouldn't we call someone? She's dead in there,' he said, pointing to Cindy's bedroom. Suddenly there was a crash, and they heard a scream, as Kendall hurtled out of her ex-husband's bedroom, her face flushed and her eyes wild.

'Who else has been in this house? You'd better tell me, Jose. I want to know who has been in this fucking house, do you hear me?'

Jose was halfway down the stairs, but looked up to see Kendall leaning over the banisters.

'Who has been here? *Tell me.*'

Juana answered from the bottom of the staircase. 'No one, Mrs Nathan. I swear to you, no one but the police and Cindy.'

'Has Feinstein been here? Any of his people?' Kendall sprang down the stairs to stand, trembling with fury, in front of Jose and gave the man a sudden shove. 'I want to know – *tell me who has been here!*'

Jose lost his footing, stumbled and clung to the rail. 'No one, Mrs Nathan, I swear to you.'

Kendall held her head between her hands, repeating, 'Oh, my God, oh, my God, *no* . . . NO!'

Juana and Jose watched as Kendall ran from room to room like a woman possessed, screaming and shouting incoherently. She smashed ornaments, knocked a piece of sculpture to the ground, dragged two canvases from the walls. The couple were so scared they ran to the kitchen and shut the door. They stood listening to

Kendall's shouts and screams, and the thumps and crashes as she continued moving through the house. Then there was silence, but at least ten minutes passed before she walked in.

'Call the police – call whoever you want, but you'd better call somebody and tell them about Cindy.' Kendall made towards the back door.

'Aren't you staying, Mrs Nathan?'

Kendall opened the back door without even turning around. 'No, I hope she rots in hell.'

The door slammed shut after her, and they heard the jeep rev up outside and roar into the road. Jose crossed to the telephone, and Juana looked at him, all distress gone from her face and her features set.

'Who's going to pay us what we're due now?'

CHAPTER 7

LORRAINE KNEW something was up as soon as she saw Decker's face.

'Cindy Nathan died last night.'

'How?' she asked, without emotion.

'Found hanged in the shower. Looks like suicide – she left a note and, according to the guy at the house, the police aren't treating it as murder, for the present at least.'

'Jose called here?'

'Yeah, about half an hour ago – phone was ringing as I walked in.'

'What else did he say?'

Decker ran a hand through his hair. 'Odd, really – I don't think he knew why he'd called here. Said his wife suggested it. They both want to talk to you. I said you'd call when you got in.'

Lorraine pursed her lips. 'I think I'll do one better – I'll go and see them. But first get me Jim Sharkey on the phone, would you?' She changed her mind. 'No. Ask if Lieutenant Burton will speak to me.'

As she closed her door, Decker knew immediately, from her lack of reaction to Cindy's death, that something was troubling her. Her mood was abnormally flat, and she had deep circles beneath her eyes.

Lorraine was thinking rapidly. Why had Cindy committed suicide, if, in fact, she had? The girl hadn't shown any signs of considering suicide, even just after her arrest when she had been under most strain, but perhaps alone, day after day at the house, the prospect of the trial had overwhelmed her. If she had killed her husband, maybe suicide had seemed like the easy way out or, at least, preferable to prison. But what about Kendall Nathan? Could she be involved in some illegal activity to do with the art market, and had killed Cindy, or had her killed, because she had found out? That seemed too far-fetched to be true, but there were the art works, which Kendall had so insistently declared were hers. Could Kendall have imagined that she would stand a better chance of claiming them, if Cindy was dead? She must have known that she would not inherit anything in Cindy's place, and the collection would now most likely be shipped off to Milwaukee – Lorraine could not stifle a smile at the prospect of millions of dollars' worth of modern art hanging on the walls at Cindy's parents' five and dime. Unless she had left it to someone else? Lorraine wrote herself an immediate memo to do three things: find out the exact terms of Harry Nathan's will, if Cindy had made any provision in respect of her property, and to check out where Kendall Nathan had been when Cindy Nathan died.

Decker walked in, put some fresh coffee and bagels down on her desk, then tilted his head to one side. 'You seem kind of low.'

'Well, maybe I am. Let's face it, we just lost a big client.'

'That's all, is it?'

She snapped, 'Yes, that's all, and stop looking at me

158

like I got two heads. Some days you don't feel so bright, and this just happened to be one of them. You call Lieutenant Burton?'

He told her that Burton's line was busy, and he would call back. 'Anything else you want me to do?'

She tried to think straight. 'What about Sonja Nathan?' She made another mental note to find out what Sonja got out of the estate.

'I cancelled the flight – since we don't have a client, there's no point in wasting either her time or your money going out there. You want me to do anything else?'

'Not right now. Oh, yeah, pack the tapes up and send them to Lieutenant Burton. The PD wants them.'

'They're welcome to them, I'll do it straight away. Did you walk Tiger?'

'YES. Now get out and leave me alone.'

Lorraine sipped the coffee: Decker could really get on her nerves. The intercom light blinked.

'Lieutenant Burton, line two,' Decker said briskly, and Lorraine picked up the phone.

'Mrs Page?' Burton enquired.

'Yes, speaking.' She assumed her most businesslike tones. 'I've asked for the Nathan tapes to be sent over to you, though I understand that may be unnecessary now.'

'Word travels fast,' he said softly.

'She was my client,' Lorraine said icily.

'So what can I do for you?'

'Excuse me?'

'I'm returning your call, Mrs Page.'

'Oh, I just wondered if you could tell me any details. I understand there are no suspicious circumstances – is that so?'

159

He paused a second before answering. 'It looks that way, but until I've read all the reports I can't say.'

'Have they done the autopsy?'

'Presumably.'

'Not giving away much, are you?'

'As I said, Mrs Page, until I have seen the reports, I can't discuss the incident.'

'You mind if I call you again in a couple of days?'

'I should have all the facts by then.'

Lorraine felt ill at ease. It was as if they had never met: he seemed cool and offhand. 'Well, thank you for returning my call,' she said lamely.

'Not at all. Goodbye.' He replaced the receiver immediately, leaving her listening to a dull buzz.

'Prick,' she muttered, and pressed the intercom. 'Can I have some fresh coffee?'

'By all means.' Two minutes later Decker walked in with the coffee pot.

He topped up her cup and she gave his sleeve a tug. 'Bad morning, sorry.'

He perched on the desk. 'You want to talk about it?'

'Not really. It's just some days, or nights, there doesn't seem much point. You know, I keep seeing that long tunnel and the future looks kind of dark, and . . .' He swirled the coffee pot, waiting for her to go on. 'Well, I sometimes wonder what the hell I'm going to do with my life – or the rest of it. I was fine when I was planning the office and the apartment, and I've got this place up and rolling. We may not be exactly snowed under with work, but I've got more money in the bank than I ever had . . .' She sipped the coffee, and looked through the open door at Tiger stretched out comatose on the sofa.

'And I got my boy out there. I mean, I've got a lot to be grateful for.'

'But you're not happy?'

She had to turn away from him because she wanted to cry. 'I should be, I know that.'

Decker knew intuitively not to say anything. She was slowly, and for the first time, opening up to him, and he valued that, because he liked her, and seeing this vulnerable side of her made him like her even more.

'I'm not complaining,' she said, fishing in her pocket for a cigarette. Decker still said nothing as she found her lighter, lit up, and inhaled deeply. She repeated, so softly he could scarcely hear her, 'I'm not complaining.' Then she swallowed and tried a small smile. 'Gonna give these up.' She was looking at the filter tip, the smile hard to hold.

'That'll be good – well, better for your health, and mine,' he said, passing her the ashtray.

'Yeah, well, who cares about my health?'

'I do,' he said, easing off the desk.

'Thank you. But apart from you, you think anyone will ever care about me? I'm so lonely, Deck, and sometimes I guess I'm frightened that this is all there's ever going to be for me.'

'Everyone needs to be loved,' he said quietly.

She nodded, still looking away. 'They sure do, and I had so much love, Deck, and I threw it all away. It's just that, having known it, I want some more but sometimes I don't think I have the right. You know what I mean?'

He put down the coffee pot, and moved round the desk. 'Come here.'

She shifted, not wanting him close, but he lifted her

161

from the chair to stand in front of him, then wrapped her in his arms. She resisted, straining away from him, but he held her tightly until she relaxed. He stroked her hair, soothing her, then patted her back as a mother would her child.

The phone rang – Jose calling from the Nathans' house – and this time Lorraine took the call. She agreed to come and see him straight away. She kissed the top of Decker's head as she left, and he could see that her mood was 100 per cent better than when she had arrived.

Lorraine drove up the gravel drive to see that curtains had been drawn behind the garden doors and the sliding timber screens on the upper floor were closed.

She had to wait a few moments before Juana came to the door, looking tired and drawn. 'Thank you for coming.'

Lorraine stepped into the cool, darkened hallway as Jose walked towards her from the kitchen. He smiled sadly. 'We just thought she was taking a shower. Juana even prepared her supper tray.'

They all walked into the kitchen and Lorraine and Jose pulled up tall metal stools to the glass counter. Lorraine said little while Jose told her how they had found Cindy.

'So, she gave no indication that she was depressed?'

Juana shook her head. 'No, she worked out in the gym for a while, then she came in here and said she wanted a light supper.'

'Nothing happened that might have upset her? Any phone calls, any visitors?'

'No, we would have heard, but the phone never rang and nobody came.'

'Did you see the note?'

Jose nodded, and Juana broke down in tears when Lorraine asked what it had said. 'Oh, just that she could not go on, that she did not want to live. I know this sounds very bad, but it was the first time I ever felt sorry for her, when I saw her . . . in the shower. She seemed so young, so small, so . . . defenceless. She looked as if she was praying.'

'Could I see the room?' Lorraine asked, and they agreed to take her upstairs. As they walked from the hall to the staircase, Lorraine registered the shattered ceramics, and the pictures that had been pulled down. One had even been slashed, while others hung at drunken angles on the walls.

The room was in shadow, the blinds pulled down, and everything had been left as Juana and Jose had found it: it didn't even seem as if the police had been there. Lorraine noticed that another painting had been taken down from the wall and left on the floor, but remained silent.

She went into the bathroom where she noted the discarded towels and the necklace still lying on the floor, then turned back to the bedroom. Cindy's shoes were still by the bed, and Lorraine crossed to the dressing table where cosmetic jars had been left open, and tissues stained with make-up remover were scattered about.

'The note was left here?' she asked.

'Just there.' Juana pointed.

Lorraine examined the dressing table more closely. 'What was it written on? Just a scrap of paper, or was it like a letter?'

'It was on her own notepaper.'

Lorraine looked round the room. 'Where does she keep it?'

Juana opened one drawer then another, then scratched her head. 'I think downstairs in the study. I don't recall seeing anything in here.'

Lorraine asked if they had seen Cindy's purse. Jose duly searched the room, and found it half under a chair, partly hidden by the ruched frill. He picked it up and handed it to Lorraine.

'I'm surprised the police didn't find this,' she said softly, opening it. She tipped the contents out onto the bed. 'Did the police take the paintings down? It looks like they made a lot of mess,' she said casually.

'No, no, they didn't touch anything. Well, not that I could see,' said Jose.

Lorraine glanced up and caught the look that passed between the two servants.

'They didn't do that,' Jose said eventually.

'Who did?' Lorraine asked, and knew again that the Mexican couple were wondering whether to give or withhold some piece of information.

'It was Kendall Nathan. Jose . . . We panicked, he called her.'

'Kendall was here last night?' Lorraine asked immediately.

'Yes.'

'She was at home when you called her? What time was that?'

'I don't know – late. I was going to take a bath before I went to bed. That's how I noticed – the water was cold,' Juana said.

'It was after ten o'clock,' Jose volunteered.

'But when was the last time you saw Cindy alive?' Lorraine asked.

'About six, I think, when she came out of the gym. The shower was running when we took her tray up at eight thirty.'

But since she was found dead in the shower, that didn't necessarily mean she had been alive at that time, Lorraine thought, then said aloud, 'What did Kendall do when she got here?'

'She was here for about an hour, and she was – she acted kind of crazy. We could hear her up here, breaking things, but we didn't know what to do,' Jose said.

What had all that been about? Lorraine wondered. Had Kendall been trying to mask her own guilt by staging a performance of grief and shock so memorable that the housekeepers would be sure to mention it to the police and, if necessary, testify to it? Had she already been at the Nathan house once that evening – or known that someone else had and that Cindy was dead before the Mexican couple told her?

'Did you tell the police this?'

'We told no one, only you. We didn't know what to do,' Jose said again.

'What happened to the note?' Lorraine asked, examining the contents of Cindy's purse as she spoke. 'Did the police take it?'

'They must have,' said Juana. 'It was gone when they left.'

Lorraine was concentrating on the contents of Cindy's purse. There were a couple of sales receipts, a compact, lipstick, a few loose tissues and a wallet. The wallet contained two thousand dollars in notes and some loose change, a driving licence, parking tickets, more clothing store receipts, and a bunch of receipts from a jewellery store, but for payments made by the shop. There was also a small silver pocket book with a pen. Lorraine opened it and flicked through lists of things to buy and appointments for massage, beauty and hairdressing, all written in childish, looped script, which Lorraine studied closely. She looked at the date on her watch: the hair-dressing appointment had been for that morning. Odd that Cindy had arranged to see people over the next few days if she had been thinking of committing suicide but, Lorraine thought, it was always possible that she had taken her own life as a result of an unexpected mood swing – the girl had admitted she had had psychiatric problems.

'The suicide note – I don't suppose you noticed what it was written with? Ink, ballpoint?' Kendall Nathan's Mont Blanc pen was in Lorraine's mind.

'In ink, I think,' Juana said, looking to her husband for confirmation, but Jose shrugged. Lorraine replaced the items in the purse, noting that the pen attached to the pocket book was a tiny silver ballpoint, and put it back where they had found it.

Juana said tentatively, 'There is something else we would like to talk with you about.'

Lorraine nodded pleasantly and followed Juana down-stairs, but she was wondering whether she could persuade Burton's office to let her see the note. In the kitchen, Jose and Juana asked her if she knew what would happen to them. They wanted her to talk to Mr Feinstein on their behalf, to see if she could get him to release the monies owed to them.

'I'll do what I can,' she said, and Juana clasped her

hand gratefully. When they reached the front door, Lorraine paused. 'Cindy Nathan had two thousand dollars in her purse, plus she wrote cheques to me on her own account. Didn't you ever think of asking her for money?'

'She said that it was nothing to do with her, and she was already selling her jewellery. That's what she told me,' Jose answered.

'Well, I'll get back to you as soon as I can.'

Lorraine was itching to contact Burton. Once outside in the car, she dialled his number but hung up almost immediately it began to ring. She didn't want to look as though she was chasing him like a teenager – yet she needed to see Cindy's note, and she knew that he was the person through whom to gain access to it. Somehow it seemed less frightening just to go to his office, say she was passing. After all, it was true, she convinced herself. Driving back east on Santa Monica, she was only a stone's throw away.

She walked coolly into Reception at the police department, produced her card and told the clerk that she was there to see Jake Burton. Annoyingly, the man insisted on calling upstairs, and suddenly the idea of just turning up didn't seem like such a good one. But, to her relief, Burton must have agreed to see her, as the desk clerk gave her directions to go on up.

She made herself rap smartly on the door: there was no answer. She raised her fist to knock again and almost hit Burton in the collar-bone as he opened it suddenly.

'Oh, hi,' she said, her voice a good octave higher than it normally was, which made her sound, she thought, about nineteen.

'Well, hello, Mrs Page,' Burton said expressionlessly. 'I wasn't expecting to hear from you again quite so soon. Won't you come in?' He opened the door wide.

She was uncertain, as yet, if she was welcome and found herself talking too fast. 'I was just up at the Nathan house, and I was just wondering whether I could have a quick look at the note Cindy left?'

'If you just swung by my office, you mean?'

Lorraine found herself blushing furiously: it was as though he really did think she was inventing excuses to see him. 'Well, since this would be unofficial, I can't ask you to send it to me Federal Express,' she said, making her voice as cool as she could.

'You know I'm not in favour of this "unofficial" traffic in information between PIs and police,' he said, his manner still betraying no warmth. 'Plus, who's paying you to do this? Your client's got no more worries now, has she?'

'She paid me a lot of money up front,' Lorraine said stiffly. 'Look, you remember what I said about Kendall Nathan? It turns out she was at the house last night. I just think it's a hell of a coincidence, and I want to know if Cindy really wrote that note, that's all.'

'Well,' he said, 'I really don't know whether I can justify spending the department's time in gratifying the wishes of . . .' he smiled for the first time and she realized he was teasing her '. . . curious bystanders. I have to account to the city for every cent.'

'Don't be so tight-assed! I pay my taxes,' Lorraine said, suddenly sure she could get away with it, and laughing. 'Besides, I gave you the tapes.'

'So, we could do a little trade, you mean?' He smiled

again with a hint of mischief – or was she imagining a little flirtatiousness?

'Well . . .' she began.

'Okay,' he said. 'One-time-only offer.' He picked up the phone and asked someone to bring in the file on Cindy Nathan. As soon as the man had left he extracted from it a sealed plastic wallet containing half a sheet of pink writing paper. 'If you'd come an hour later this would have gone to forensic,' he said. 'Don't take it out of the plastic.'

'Gee,' Lorraine said with mock-innocence, 'you mean I can't paddle my pretty little fingers all over it? I was a cop, you know.'

'Sorry,' he said, smiling again. 'There's a sample of Cindy's handwriting behind it that we got from her attorney. Obviously we'll get an expert opinion but they look pretty similar to me.'

So they did: the childishly unformed letters and the unclosed As and Os were almost identical. But it was only a couple of lines long – Kendall was plenty smart enough to imitate that much of someone else's handwriting, Lorraine reckoned, and the words were written in ink. It was interesting that the note was addressed to no one, but said, 'by the time you read this, I will be dead', as though Cindy had had a particular reader in mind. Lorraine also noticed that, though the handwriting sprawled all over the page, the gap between the two lines Cindy had written was larger than the gap between the first one and the top of the page.

'I think this has been cut from a longer letter,' she said. 'Look at the top.' Burton leaned closer, and Lorraine was conscious that he cast an almost imperceptible appraising glance over her, taking advantage of her concentration on the paper to do so. When minutely examined, it was clear that the top edge of the paper was not completely straight. 'It's been cut with a pair of scissors,' she said. 'You can see the blades were long enough to cut the whole thing in one go.'

'Jesus, you might be right,' Burton said, and Lorraine realized he was embarrassed that his own officers had failed to notice it. 'Forensic would have picked it up, of course.'

'I'm sure they would,' Lorraine said graciously – in any case, it was true.

'Kind of makes your theory about the other Mrs Nathan a little more credible – though I don't suppose she killed both of them.'

'Wouldn't surprise me,' Lorraine said. 'She's that kind of a girl.'

She was now certain that the killer was Kendall Nathan, and found the desire to see the woman again, to take the investigation on just one more stage, almost uncontrollable. It was true that there was no reason to do so now that Cindy was dead, but loyalty to her former client, the pathos of her death, so wasteful, sordid, at only twenty years old, made Lorraine feel that she could at least spare half an hour to ask Kendall where she had been the previous night. She promised herself that she would do nothing more, that if anything made her suspicious, she would hand it straight over to Burton. After all, if Cindy had been murdered, it was his job to find out who had done it.

'I won't take up any more of your time,' she said. 'I'm sorry for bursting in on you like that.'

'It's been a pleasure – and very instructive,' he said

with a genuine smile, and she felt his eyes flick over her again.

'Well,' Lorraine said, knowing she sounded ridiculous, but forcing herself to carry on, 'you know where my office is on West Pico. Stop by any time.'

'I might just do that,' he said, still looking at her.

Oh, yeah, she thought, sure you will. 'Well, I'd better get going.' She set off down the stairs.

Gallery One was virtually on her way back to the office, she told herself, getting into her car – and she would only be inside for five minutes. She turned left into Beverly Drive, and as she pulled up outside she could see Kendall Nathan sitting at her desk, talking to the young black man.

Both of them looked round as soon as the door buzzer sounded, and Lorraine noticed at once how exhausted and haggard Kendall looked – like someone, in fact, who hadn't slept all night.

'What are you doing here?' she said immediately, with no attempt at politeness.

'I wondered if you'd heard Cindy Nathan was dead,' Lorraine said. The pair in front of her were looking intently at her, Kendall's strange eyes darker than ever, it seemed, clouded with pain.

'Yes, I heard,' Kendall said curtly. 'That terminates your involvement in other people's affairs, I think.'

'Were you here last night, Mrs Nathan?' Lorraine asked, not so much expecting an answer as wanting to observe Kendall's reaction to the question.

'What is this?' Kendall snapped. Her nerves seemed at breaking point. 'You have no business whatsoever to come around harassing me, insinuating—'

'So you weren't here last night?' Lorraine cut in,

noting how quick Kendall was to think she was being accused.

'Yes, as it happens, I was,' Kendall retorted angrily. 'And Eric was with me. We left at nine thirty, and I went home – all of which Eric will confirm.' She looked pointedly at him.

'That's right,' he said. 'We were both here.' Much weight you could give to *his* assertions, Lorraine thought cynically. If he didn't back up his employer he would lose his job. He was still staring at her, she thought, with anger, almost hate in his eyes. Had he done Kendall's dirty work for her?

'I see. I'm sorry to have troubled you.' She turned on her heel.

'See you don't come around here again, Mrs Page,' Kendall called after her. 'If you do, you'll have reason to regret it.'

Lorraine turned round and looked the other woman directly in the eye. 'Was that a threat, Mrs Nathan?'

'Just a warning,' Kendall said. 'Now get off my property and stay off.'

'Glad to,' Lorraine said. 'Good afternoon, Mrs Nathan.' She walked out, not bothering to close the door behind her, leaving the buzzer whining loudly.

She was excited as she drove to her office, eager to discuss the new developments with Decker. She roared up to the building, and handed her keys to the valet parking attendant, who now had strict instructions always to keep his eye on her Mercedes.

He drove it into the underground motor court, and pulled up next to an immaculate, gleaming Rolls Corniche. He hadn't recognized Raymond Vallance, and had only realized who the owner of the Rolls was when he'd parked the car and seen the name on some mail on the front seat. He would have liked to sneak a look at the letters, but he'd been summoned by Reception on his mobile, so hadn't had time. As he locked Lorraine's car, he leaned towards the Corniche again, thinking how amazing it was that people left such personal things in their cars and tossed the keys to valet parking boys, unaware that they always had a good sniff around. He knew of some cases where guys had been paid nice regular sums for information – not that he would ever stoop to that, but some folks were so dumb they deserved to be ripped off. House keys attached to their car keys was an open invitation for a quick impression to be taken, making access to their homes as easy as taking candy from a baby – even more so if you got a couple of hours clear when they were dining out. He wouldn't co-operate in *that* kind of crooked deal, but he allowed himself a good snoop around, and often found a few dollars tucked down the back of expensive limo seats. He never thought that was stealing – that was just getting lucky.

Raymond Vallance's mail wasn't that interesting, and the Corniche wasn't his. It belonged to some woman. The parking attendant smiled as he saw that Mr Vallance also had a nasty letter from his bank. His financial situation was even shakier than the attendant's. He put the letter back in the envelope, had a good feel around the seats and opened the glove compartment, whistling as he saw it was jammed with parking tickets and CDs. There was a powder compact too, with lipstick attached, a pair of sunglasses, and a number of pieces of folded pink writing paper. He looked around to see if anyone was watching, and opened out the top sheet. It was a note, childish handwriting in brown ink, from some woman, by the looks of it, rambling on about how no one understood her or cared about her. God, he thought, glancing quickly over the pages of appeals and complaints. He got enough of that at home. He refolded the pieces of paper, stuffed them back among the other contents of the glove compartment, and had another quick feel behind the seats before he was satisfied that there was nothing of interest, not even a few coins. So much for the movie star. He wouldn't waste his time asking Vallance for an autograph.

CHAPTER 8

LORRAINE BURST into the office, and Decker got up immediately. 'You have a . . .' he said quietly, nodding towards the other side of the room.

Raymond Vallance turned from the window, removing his Gucci shades. Well, Lorraine thought, look who it is.

'Mrs Page? Raymond Vallance.'

He stowed the glasses in a pocket and held out his hand. Lorraine crossed the room and shook it: it was limp, clammy, unpleasant to the touch. He was taller than she would have expected, at least six foot one, and he was certainly making a serious effort to charm, but Lorraine thought she detected a touch of strain behind the ingratiating manner.

'I'm sorry, I should have made an appointment – if this is not convenient . . .'

'No, no, please come into my office.' She gestured to him to go ahead then turned back to Decker. 'What does he want?' she whispered.

'I don't know, but he's been waiting half an hour.'

Lorraine followed Vallance into her office and closed the door. 'Sorry to keep you waiting.' She smiled, as she moved round her desk and sat down. 'Do you mind if I smoke?' she said, already taking a cigarette out of a pack.

Vallance's hand reached her lighter a moment before hers did, and struck a flame. He stared hypnotically at her with his wide-set, ice-blue eyes, a half smile playing on his slightly feminine lips. There was also something effeminate about his hands: the long fingers were tipped with carefully shaped and buffed nails.

'Not at all,' he said, his voice overtly sexual, then clicked off the lighter and put it back on the desk, folding his hands in his lap. He was wearing a navy Armani suit, a pristine shirt in the palest powder pink, and a tie in such a severely 'tasteful' muted shade that it must have set him back two hundred dollars at least. His hair was silver-white, and much thinner than she would have expected, especially in Hollywood where most actors used weaves or spider hairpieces to disguise their hair loss. He had a broad face with a slight dimple in the chin, but his profile was superb, as he clearly knew – his nose was perfect, from both right and left sides, and his high cheekbones looked as if they were carved.

It was a wonderful face, but the man behind it was so conscious of his beauty that he seemed constantly to be turning from one side to the other to display his features to their best advantage.

'So, Mr Vallance, what can I do for you?'

'It's rather a delicate subject,' he said softly, plucking at his trouser crease, and crossing his legs.

'Best just to come straight out with it, then, isn't it?'

'Mm, yes. You, ah, may or may not know that I was a friend of Harry Nathan.'

'Yes, I am aware of that.'

'And of Cindy Nathan,' he said, his manner just a fraction too casual.

'Yes,' Lorraine said, smoking. When he flashed her

that penetrating look, she met and held it unflinchingly, his eyes slid away. She wondered if he knew that Cindy was dead, but decided she would bide her time before mentioning it.

'You were retained by Cindy to . . . investigate Harry's death, weren't you?' he went on.

'Yes, I was.'

'And I understand that you received some . . .' He coughed slightly. 'I find this very difficult.' Lorraine did not help him. She found the ageing man somehow faintly repulsive, but the opportunity to find out what he knew about Harry and Cindy was too good to miss. 'I understand that you received some videotapes from Cindy.'

'Some tapes did come into my possession, yes,' Lorraine said, deciding not to reveal that she no longer had them until he had told her just a little more.

He knew, just as Kendall had known, that she had seen them. 'I'm afraid that sort of thing is quite common in Hollywood,' he said. 'Though those tapes were, of course, recorded without my knowledge.'

Well, that was a lie, Lorraine thought, but decided to let it ride.

'I've been approached about a leading role in what will undoubtedly be one of the most important films made in this decade,' he continued pompously, and Lorraine permitted herself a sceptical lift of one eyebrow. 'Very sensitive political material. The director's name I'm sure you can guess . . .' he gave her a meaningful look '. . . and I happen to know that some of our . . . ah, friendly government agencies would just as soon I didn't get past first base. Anything negative attaching to an artist's image, and an offer can be immediately withdrawn, and, of course, they don't hesitate fabricating material if nothing genuine can be found. For those reasons, Mrs Page, I have to say that I need to recover those tapes.'

Lorraine had heard all this before. 'I'm sorry, Mr Vallance, those tapes aren't mine to dispose of.'

'I want them,' Vallance said sharply. Lorraine stubbed out her cigarette. 'Obviously, a man in my position cannot have that kind of—'

'Pornography,' she interrupted.

It was delightful: he was flushing under his tan.

'I am willing to pay you for them,' he said.

'Really?' she said, almost mockingly.

He adjusted his tie. 'They are not something I am particularly proud of.'

'I'm not surprised, but it is possible, Mr Vallance, that they may be required as evidence.'

'Evidence?' he said nervously. 'But why? I can't see why anyone would want them – they're private, were recorded without even my knowledge. In fact, I could sue.'

Listening to him, Lorraine wondered if he knew about the phone tapes, also recorded without his knowledge, and if he did, had he wanted them badly enough to hire someone to break in and pour acid over them? 'I am sure you could if they were to be offered for sale,' she said. 'I understand there's quite a black market in pornographic tapes of that kind, especially featuring – or should I say starring? – someone like yourself.'

Vallance stood up, hands clenched at his sides. 'How much do you want?'

Lorraine turned up her palms innocently. 'I can't sell them, Mr Vallance.'

He leaned forward, his face distorted with anger. 'So what do you intend doing with them, Mrs Page?'

'As I have said, they might be required as evidence, Mr Vallance, and I cannot simply hand them over to you. They are not my property in any case. They belonged to my client.'

'Cindy?' he snapped.

'Yes, Cindy Nathan,' she said firmly. Vallance turned away, his hands still clenched. 'You were involved in what I would describe as quite brutal sexual games – she was young, she was innocent . . .'

'Like fuck she was! She's a tough little whore.'

'Cindy died last night, Mr Vallance,' Lorraine said, watching him closely. 'Suicide, it seems.'

For a moment, Vallance did not react. Then he said, looking straight at her, 'I'm . . . sorry to hear that.' His eyes were curiously shuttered, and Lorraine's skin crawled. Cindy's death had not been news to him, whatever he wanted her to believe.

'You and Cindy had a close friendship, I believe,' Lorraine said.

'You could say that.' He was guarded.

'Was it your child, by the way?' Lorraine asked casually. 'The baby she lost?'

'No,' Vallance said curtly. 'It could have been any number of people's, but it was not mine – that I can be sure of.'

'Really? But I have seen you in action, Mr Vallance, so to speak.'

He turned those wide eyes on her and they were beautiful, a wonderful, dazzling blue that flashed like lightning. If only he could have brought that look, or the strength of feeling behind it, to his performances, he might perhaps have reignited his dying career.

'You didn't answer me, Mr Vallance. I have seen you in the videos that Harry Nathan made and, as far as I could tell, you . . .' She gestured eloquently with her hand. 'You were very aroused. Oh, of course, I'd forgotten.' She touched her forehead, feigning surprise at her absent-mindedness. 'There was the one where you strapped on a—'

He leaned forward, almost spat at her, 'I want those fucking tapes, you hard-nosed bitch.'

'They most certainly are fucking tapes.' Lorraine laughed, and then leaned forward. 'Perhaps you'd be happier if it really was your own hard prick, and not some plastic strap-on number. You might get a whole new career for yourself. What's the matter, Mr Vallance, can't you get a hard-on? Is that the—'

He slapped her across the face. She took the blow and paused a moment before she swung her right fist and caught him full on his perfect nose. He flopped back into the chair, one hand to his face while he fumbled with the other for a handkerchief. She watched him feeling the bridge of his nose gingerly, afraid she'd broken it, staring at the fine trickle of blood on his hand before he put the handkerchief to his face.

'I'm sorry, Mr Vallance. I only just heard about Cindy and . . .'

She looked carefully at him: his head was bowed and he was weeping, covering his face with the white cloth. Lorraine picked up the glass of water and held it out to him, but he shook his head and turned away from her. It was about three minutes before he composed himself, checked his nose again and looked at the spots of blood

180

on the handkerchief before he put it back in his pocket. He reached for the glass of water and raised it to his lips, his hand shaking badly. He sipped carefully, then slowly replaced the glass on the desk.

'How did she do it?' he asked flatly.

'She took some cord, wrapped it round the shower head and then round her throat – only a short distance, but enough. She was kneeling, as if she was praying, according to the servants.'

He sighed, and reached for the water again, drained it and held the empty glass in his hands. 'I'm sorry. Maybe she wasn't as tough as I thought.'

'Nobody ever is,' she said, and he looked up. 'Can I ask you frankly, Mr Vallance, do you think Cindy killed Harry Nathan?'

There was a moment's silence, and Lorraine had the impression of a curtain falling at the back of the man's eyes. 'Yes,' he said finally. 'Yes, I do. She would never have been convicted, of course. Harry should have kept right away from women – he just wasn't himself with them, they made him dirty, sucked him dry. I used to tell him that he ought to regard women as liquor to an alcoholic, that they were something he would have to cut right out of his life, just accept that they brought out negative things in him, things he didn't need.'

'Harry was different then, away from female company?'

Vallance gave a strange, bitter-sweet smile. 'He was such a prince when he could cut loose from all that, the kindest, funniest, most generous guy you could meet, and so damn talented . . .' God, Lorraine thought, he sounded like some high-school girl gushing over her first beau. 'Cindy never gave a damn about Harry,' Vallance went on. 'She never gave a damn about anyone but herself. She wanted his money, and she thought . . . I guess she thought she'd got it.' His quick correction didn't escape Lorraine. Could Vallance have had anything to do with Cindy's death? Was it possible that he and Kendall had acted together?

'But, Mr Vallance, although you say you and Harry were such good friends, I have to say that I know he was blackmailing you.'

He laughed softly. 'That's what I mean. The women changed him, made him dirty, selfish. That's not the way he started out, but it was sure as hell the way he finished up. Once Harry stopped making money, I doubt if there was anyone he knew that he didn't put the squeeze on. He wouldn't think of it as blackmail, though – he would probably have been shocked if you called him a blackmailer. Conman might be a better description.'

'Did you pay him?'

He stared at a point on the wall. 'I guess so. I paid Harry in women, but he also paid me his way – sometimes my rent, phone bills or whatever. He liked me to have to ask him for hand-outs, but he could be generous.'

Lorraine waited. Vallance was digging deep inside himself, and she knew from his body language that it hurt: he seemed to have shrivelled, as if he was ageing in front of her.

'So why did you put up with it?'

His shoulders lifted. 'It didn't happen overnight, darling. Our sort of relationship goes back a long way.' Again there was a pause, and Vallance sat back, as though watching a movie playing on her office wall.

'I knew Harry before any of them – we used to share an apartment.' What a surprise, Lorraine thought. 'We used to work out together – this is before anybody worked out. Harry always kept himself in shape. We'd pick up these little girls and bring them home, and we'd both come on with the heavy romance, and they'd think they'd met these two really great guys.' Vallance almost chuckled. 'And then, after a while, of course, we'd get them in bed and give them all the I-never-met-anyone-like-you-before crap, and then as soon as we'd fucked them, Harry used to put on this crazy voice and yell, "Grand Central Station, ladies and gentlemen!"' Vallance produced an odd, caterwauling yodel like an Appalachian railway porter. '"All change!" And then, of course, I'd fuck his and he'd fuck mine. Sometimes the girls'd kick up a fuss, and Harry'd say,' Vallance's face contorted with amusement, '"A fuck is only a fuck, my dear, but a friend is a good cigar."' He laughed, slapping his thighs. 'That was when Harry started all the goofy kind of comedy he used to do later on. All that came right out of that apartment we used to have, I swear it.'

Jesus, Lorraine thought: Vallance imagined he was not only Harry Nathan's heroic friend, ideal lover, but also his muse. The reality, however, was painfully clear: Vallance couldn't get sex with Harry, so the next best thing was sex with the women who did, and preferably thirty seconds after Harry had pulled out.

'Presumably all this fun and games had to stop when Harry got married?'

'You bet it did,' Vallance said bitterly. 'What he ever saw in that fucking Swedish bitch, God knows. She was great-looking, of course, but, Christ, they all were.'

'So, you didn't see so much of Harry after that?'

'Oh, I saw him okay,' Vallance said. 'Harry was innocent, and he just assumed we'd all be friends. He started making a lot of money with his movies, but Sonja just pissed on all that too. I used to go out to the house most weekends, watch her spending Harry's money doing the place up like fucking Versailles. Then when she finished the house, she started saying how bored she was, so Harry bought her the gallery. Anyone else would have got down on their knees in gratitude, but Sonja said Harry did it to stifle her talent, to make her play shopkeeper when she wanted to be alone, to create . . .'

'But she must have had talent of some sort,' Lorraine said. 'I mean, she has quite a reputation now.'

'You can sell just about anything on the modern art market, Mrs Page, provided it's full of enough neurosis, sickness and self-possession, and Sonja Sorenson had all those things to burn.'

'So what happened? Why did they get divorced?'

'Well, Sonja was miserable. Nothing was ever right for her, and first it was Harry's fault, and then it was *my* fault,' Vallance said, and something in his voice told Lorraine that he was about to embark on another pack of lies. 'She started blaming me for everything, trying to turn Harry against me, saying I was at the house too much, saying I was just taking money off him. Sonja got more and more up her own ass, and then they couldn't have kids, and by the time they finished up she was in her forties and she looked pretty terrible.'

'She didn't look so bad at Forest Lawn,' Lorraine said, thinking of the elegant woman she had seen at the funeral.

'That's just clothes,' Vallance said dismissively, turning round to lean against the sill.

When Vallance was lying, an airy nastiness entered his voice, and Lorraine knew he was lying now. She was

184

quite certain that his account of the Nathan marriage was as biased, distorted and selective as it was possible to get.

'So, did you encourage him to leave her?' she asked.

Vallance sat down again, brushed at his immaculate suit and adjusted his perfectly knotted tie. 'Let's just say I helped along what was going to happen anyway. Kendall was on the scene by then, and she was digging Sonja's grave from the minute she walked through the door.'

Lorraine pricked up her ears.

'So you and Kendall helped things along together?' she suggested. 'Did you get along well with Kendall?'

Vallance fell silent. He got up again and straightened one of her prints without looking at her. 'Not really. Kendall didn't get along with anyone.' He seemed disinclined to say any more. The changes in his mood were rapid: sometimes he seemed to want to talk, then something he didn't like would come up and he would sink into silence.

'But would you say she was another of those self-absorbed, selfish sort of women Harry seemed to go for?' Lorraine asked, pretending sympathy with Vallance's point of view.

'Was she ever,' Vallance said, with a scornful laugh, rising to the bait. 'Have you seen Kendall lately? All set up in her fancy art gallery, with her fancy friends and her fancy clothes and her fancy voice? Kendall was her maiden name before she married Harry. Her real first name is Darleen. Doesn't play quite so well, does it? She came to LA as just another little piece of white trash and got a job as a secretary to some decorator, and then it was an antique dealer, and the next thing Sonja – God, she was dumb – gave her a job in the gallery. I guess she thought Harry would never look twice at her – she wasn't his type and she looked like shit. Big hair and big shoulders and these terrible tacky little suits, but my, that little lady was quite some operator.'

Clearly there was no love lost between the two of them, and Lorraine rapidly revised her theory of Kendall and Vallance acting together to get rid of Nathan and Cindy. 'You mean in a business sense?' she asked, deliberately misunderstanding him.

'You could say that. Kendall has been in business since she was in diapers – the business of promoting Darleen Kendall Nathan. She acted at first like she worshipped Sonja, studied her clothes, copied the way she talked, and, of course, she changed her name just as soon as she could, said it was because Sonja used to call her by her surname, like as a pet name, when they were working together. Kendall started to play up all this great artist garbage too, and Sonja'd lost the plot anyway, by this stage – her hormones had curdled, I reckon, over this whole no-kids stuff.' He gave a sigh of irritation with these unsavoury feminine preoccupations.

'Sonja said she had to start working again so she locked herself in the studio for about a year and Kendall just waved her hankie and said bye-bye. She took over the gallery, of course, and worked her ass off there until she was running it. Gradually she took over Harry too.' Clearly this turn of events had not suited Vallance.

'Of course, Harry's mother,' Vallance continued, well into his stride now – Lorraine had been waiting for them to get to old Mrs Nathan – 'hated Sonja's guts, and she rammed Kendall down his throat. Kendall started sweet-talking the old lady, and Abigail thought she was just the sweetest girl, and so maternal. Every time Sonja went out of town, Kendall would just suggest to Harry that he invite his mother, so diplomatic.'

'How long did this go on?' Lorraine asked.

'Well, they had a thing behind Sonja's back for a long time, but Harry wouldn't leave Sonja until Kendall announced she was pregnant. He had to tell her then.'

'How did she take it?'

Vallance dug his hands into his trouser pockets. 'I don't know. She just left. All I knew was she flew to New York, and she never came back. She tried to claim some share in the gallery, but his lawyers made such a fucking production out of the whole thing that she backed down. That was the way Sonja was. If she didn't get what she wanted immediately she just walked away.'

A full two minutes passed. Then Lorraine asked, 'So he remained at the house, Sonja went to New York, and they started divorce proceedings?'

'Yes. Harry and Kendall got married and had their kid, but the kid died and Harry was losing money. He changed. He was never the same again.'

'Why did you hang on?' Lorraine asked.

'Jesus Christ . . . you want me to spell it out?'

'I guess so.'

He sighed and looked at a point above Lorraine's head, then back to her. His wide-set eyes were like a sick dog's.

'I loved him, and when he didn't need me any more I let him use me. When he ditched Kendall for Cindy, I went through it all again. He used me, just as much as he used Cindy, used everyone he ever knew. But I still loved him.'

Loved him enough not to want anyone else to have

187

him? Lorraine wondered suddenly whether Vallance could have killed Harry. In a way, he had loved Nathan longer than anyone else, had been obsessed by him and, in his own mind, been betrayed by him too.

'Anyway,' Vallance said, seeming to drag himself with an effort back into the present, 'I guess I'd better go.' Lorraine stood up to walk to the door with him, sorry for him in spite of her revulsion. He had walked in like a movie star, and was walking out so weak and jaded.

'Can I just ask you one final thing?' she said, as she opened the door and Vallance fumbled with his shades. 'Were you at home last night?'

He knew at once that she was asking him if he had an alibi for the time at which Cindy Nathan had died, and he was not so emotionally battered that he could not reply at once.

'Yes, I was,' he said. 'A number of my friends called, as it happens.'

He had put on the dark glasses now, and Lorraine could not see his eyes. 'Okay,' she said. She walked with him past Decker's desk, and showed him out. He left without a smile or a handshake, and without looking back.

Lorraine raised one eyebrow at Decker. 'Well, guess who the most beautiful man in the world wanted to shove his dick up?'

'Jesus Christ, you can be so fucking crude,' Decker said huffily.

Lorraine leaned on his desk, and grinned. 'He was in love with Harry Nathan himself.' Then she gestured towards her office. 'Come in and chat to me. I want to discuss a few things that came up this morning.'

Decker collected his notebook, and asked her whether

188

she was doing all this work *pro bono* or if they were going to be paid.

Lorraine sighed. 'Oh, shit, I forgot. I have to go talk to Feinstein.'

Vallance drove out of the garage, unaware that the smiling, bowing valet had given his car a thorough going-over. He was on his way now to play Prince Charming to Verna Montgomery, to get his rent money out of her. She had to be sixty years old, though she insisted she was no more than forty-four. He hadn't even bothered to rearrange the white wisps of his hair because he knew that if Nathan's videos ever got out any last shred of hope he had of resurrecting his career was gone. As he drove onto Sunset he was crying, his white hair blowing in the wind – Raymond Vallance, the most beautiful man in the world.

CHAPTER 9

DECKER GOT Lorraine an appointment with Feinstein almost immediately. His address in Century City was certainly impressive, on one of the smartest blocks of the Avenue of the Stars. The building had only recently been opened, and Lorraine had to concede that it was a truly handsome piece of modern architecture, a soaring tower of golden granite and blue glass that seemed to cut the sky.

Lorraine went up the steps and into a lobby whose sheer moneyed lustre exceeded anything she had seen, even in Los Angeles. The commissionaire directed her to the forty-third floor, and she made her way to the bank of elevators.

She emerged from the elevator car into another lobby bathed in light, streaming in through semi-transparent blinds of fine white cloth. Feinstein's receptionist was a beautiful, long-limbed girl, wearing a straight tunic dress in mint green crêpe-de-chine and a pair of transparent plastic court shoes, whose four-inch heels made her well over six feet tall. She introduced herself as Pamela, with a charming smile, and asked her if she would mind waiting a moment. Lorraine sat down in one of four low armchairs with curving black backs and white leather upholstery ranged round a table of quaking-leaf fern.

Feinstein kept Lorraine waiting only a minute, then she was shown into an enormous office carpeted in a smooth silver grey like whaleskin, full of beautifully crafted wooden furniture whose dignity and majestic scale jarred with the bald, weasel-like lawyer. He only bothered to rise a couple of inches from his chair and motioned Lorraine to a lower seat placed in front of his huge desk. She began to thank him for seeing her, but his intercom blinked and his voice rasped loudly, making her jump: she had not noticed the transparent plastic speaker plugged into his right ear or the mouthpiece at the corner of his lips.

'Just tell her I'm in conference, Pamela, and that goes for the rest of the week!' He listened to whatever Pamela said in reply, then snapped, 'I am not talking to her, Pamela!' and detached the headset. He began to shuffle files on his desk, avoiding Lorraine's eye as he asked what she wanted to see him about and reminded her that he was a busy man. He opened a drawer and took out a foot-long cigar, sniffed it before unwrapping it, then sniffed again and clipped the end.

'I'm a private investigator,' Lorraine began, and Feinstein sighed, sucking on the unlit cigar end.

'Yes, Mrs Page, I know who you are.' He patted his pockets, looking for his lighter.

'I was acting for Mrs Nathan,' she said. He ran his lips around the fat cigar and puffed it alight, the smoke forming a blue halo round his head.

'Just get to the point. I'm inundated with calls from Kendall Nathan, and so I'll tell you what I've told her – and keep on telling her. Until I've had time to assess the

Nathan estate, I can't give any personal or financial information to anyone.'

'I wanted to discuss Cindy Nathan's—'

Feinstein cut her off. 'Suicide? Well, I'm sorry, obviously. Is that why you wanted to see me? Or – don't tell me – you, like everyone else concerned with Nathan, want a pay-off? Worried you won't get your fee, is that it?'

'I wanted to ask you for some details about the art gallery, and specifically Mr Nathan's art collection,' Lorraine said, controlling her temper – she would have liked to punch the cigar down his throat.

'I'm not prepared to discuss anything with you, Mrs Page. Like I said, I'm sorry about Cindy, but it doesn't come as a shock. I mean, you threaten to do something often enough, kinda takes away the element of surprise.' He gestured in the air, one hand clutching the cigar.

'Cindy had threatened suicide before?'

Feinstein looked at his watch. 'She made it public knowledge often enough, and I got enough faxes and notes from her, threatening the same thing, to paper the walls with. She was . . .' He twisted his finger at the side of his temple.

'Would it be possible for me to see them?'

'No, it would not. If however, the police require them, that is a different matter.'

'And I suppose Harry Nathan had nothing to do with Cindy's previous suicide attempts?'

'Maybe, maybe not. I don't know the ins and outs of my clients' domestic set-ups – it's tough enough getting the business side of their lives sorted out.' He sighed. 'I know she was young, but she'd been around and, to be honest, I couldn't stand the girl. Never could understand why my client put up with her hysterics, but then, once a man gets involved with these bimbos, what can you expect? Money's all they're after. I see a lot of greed in my profession. I've even got Harry's goddamned domestics calling, plus his entire family, all like vultures, all wanting to know how much. I have to protect my clients.'

'But not all your clients are murdered, I hope,' Lorraine said quietly.

Feinstein examined his manicured hands. The cigar stuck in his wet lips as he dragged heavily on it and blew a wide ring of smoke behind his head, his voice halting with false emotion. 'Harry Nathan was my client, and he was also a man I admired and respected. Whatever he did in his private life was none of my concern. If you submit your account to my assistant, I will endeavour to see that it's paid. Now, as I said, I'm a very busy man, Mrs Page, so if there's nothing else . . .'

'What will Kendall Nathan inherit now under the will?' Lorraine asked.

Feinstein started at her, his gaze studiedly blank. 'I don't see that that is any concern of yours, Mrs Page. Do I have to repeat myself about client confidentiality?'

Lorraine persisted, 'Does she get anything now that might have gone to Cindy – like the art or anything?'

Feinstein wagged his finger. 'Listen, honey, you just lost one client, so this, I presume, is a fishing trip for another. You wanna work for Kendall Nathan, go talk to her. Now, please, I'd like you to leave.'

Lorraine got up and picked up her briefcase, smoothing down her skirt. 'Is that one of the Nathan gallery paintings?' She indicated a massive canvas on the wall, and Feinstein moved round his desk, impatient to show her out. 'I notice you had one similar in Reception.'

The lawyer was now opening the office door. 'Mrs Page,' he said curtly, sweeping one hand in a mock-gallant gesture towards the door, but Lorraine had moved closer to the painting, a huge composition of brightly coloured, but somehow warlike shapes, and saw a small gold plaque on the wall underneath that named Frank Stella as the artist.

'Very impressive,' Lorraine murmured, then walked towards him. 'Are you a collector?'

Feinstein turned away from her as Pamela appeared outside the open door. 'Kendall Nathan has called again – she's on the phone now,' she said in a low voice. 'She says it's very urgent, Mr Feinstein.'

'Get rid of her, and show Mrs Page out.'

Lorraine was now close to the attorney, who reached to just below her shoulder. What little hair he had left was dyed black and slicked backwards, making his weasel's eyes, under arched – and, if Lorraine was not mistaken, plucked – brows, seem even smaller and beadier. With his silk suit and Gucci shoes, Feinstein smelt of money as strongly as of his overpowering cologne, but no amount of polish could disguise the coarseness of the personality underneath.

'Is it an original?' she asked sweetly.

'What?' He blinked.

'The painting. Did you buy it from Nathan's gallery? It's just that the real reason I came to see you was that I had a conversation with Cindy, shortly before she died, and she seemed to think that her husband, and probably his ex-wife, Kendall Nathan, were involved in some sort of art fraud.' Feinstein frowned, and looked past her to the painting as Lorraine continued in the same saccharine tone. 'But, then, as you're a collector, I'm sure you would have had any work you purchased properly authenticated.' The false sweetness of her smile matched her voice as she walked past him out into Reception.

Feinstein followed. 'Cindy Nathan told you about a fraud. What fraud?'

Lorraine paused at a canvas that covered most of one wall, and tapped the frame. 'Well, it appears that a lot of the paintings, not only in Nathan's house but also sold through the gallery, were probably only copies. This must have cost a fortune, it's a . . .' She leaned to read another small gold plaque. 'Ah, a de Kooning. I mean, I'm no connoisseur, but I know his work is sought after and commands a high price – if it's an original, that is.'

Feinstein continued to follow in Lorraine's wake, glancing at the painting as he passed it. 'What else did Mrs Nathan tell you?' he asked nervously.

Lorraine had her hand on the door to the lobby, and tilted her head to one side. 'Well, Mr Feinstein, my client Mrs Nathan may, sadly, no longer be with us, but nevertheless she is still my client, and as you have pointed out, I must continue to respect the confidentiality of her affairs. Thank you for your time, and if you should wish to see me again, please call.' She proffered one of her cards, then breezed out of the door, which swung closed behind her.

Feinstein glanced at her card, then hurried into the boardroom. There were two canvases at either end of the twenty-five-foot room, and he almost ran to the one further away, then stopped in his tracks and turned to look at the other. He had nothing like the expertise necessary to tell whether his so-called investments were genuine or not, and panic began to rise like bile in his gullet. Then he yelled at the top of his voice. 'PAMELA! PAMELA!'

The girl hurried into the room, notebook at the ready, to find Feinstein sitting at the centre of the boardroom table. 'Your next appointment is here, Mr Feinstein. Mr . . . are you all right?'

He was pulling at his collar, loosening his tie. 'I need a glass of water, an' get that guy, the art historian, the one who went with me to Harry Nathan's gallery.'

'Yes, Mr Feinstein. Do you want him to meet you there, as usual?'

'No.' His voice was harsh. 'Get him here. I want him fucking here.'

Pamela scuttled out. As Harry Nathan's lawyer, Feinstein knew not only what a mess the Nathan estate was in, but that the outstanding claims against it far exceeded its worth. The only thing Feinstein had been sure about was Nathan's private art collection, whose value had yet to be assessed, but he had been depending on it to cover the majority of the debts and, most importantly, his own fees. He was sure Harry wouldn't have pulled a fast one on him. He was his lawyer, for Chrissakes. He'd been his friend, hadn't he? But as he calculated how much he had paid for the canvases, a sinking feeling engulfed him. He had always known that Harry Nathan was a thieving, conniving, two-faced bastard. It took one to know one.

Kendall hung up the telephone, shaking with impotent rage, as Feinstein's secretary informed her yet again that her boss was in conference. She had been calling him every half an hour since she had spoken to the insurance company and disovered that Cindy had indeed been telling the truth – Nathan hadn't paid the premiums on the art collection for two years.

In an effort to calm her nerves, she'd had three brandies, but they hadn't helped. If anything they had made her feel worse. Part of her was still refusing to believe what had happened, sure there was some mistake – but it was pretty clear what the explanation was: Harry had not bothered to insure the paintings because they were worthless. As soon as she had got a closer look at them she had known that they were fakes. She and Harry had had the brilliant idea of selling valuable original paintings to various ditzy members of the film community, arranging for copies to be painted, and then, after the buyers had had their purchases authenticated, delivering the fakes. No one had noticed; no one had bothered to get the paintings checked a second time.

Now, however, it seemed that Harry had pulled the same scam on her, and switched the originals hanging at the house for a second set of copies. The reason, too, was obvious: he was cutting her out of the proceeds of the fraud and intended to keep the approximately twenty million dollars they had reckoned on netting. Harry wouldn't have done that to *her*, would he?

She was almost panting with hysteria, and her outrage rose the more she thought about it: her role in the whole thing had required months of preparation, negotiation and unremitting stress.

Kendall poured herself more brandy, forced herself to try to think logically: what if Harry Nathan hadn't been shot? It had happened only weeks before they had intended to move all the paintings. What if he had carried into effect what they had so carefully arranged, that the paintings would be moved one by one to private buyers in Europe? Harry had even been in Germany arranging the deals. Kendall's head throbbed with trying to think straight. She had paid good money for two false passports for him, covered his periods away from LA by saying he was filming, and made calls on his behalf to ensure that no one, not even Feinstein, knew where he was. Maybe Feinstein didn't know about their scam. But what had happened to the original paintings and sculptures?

She had yet another drink, calmer now, her thin face pinched as she tried to piece together the events of the last weeks, thinking about what Cindy had told her. There was no other explanation, other than that Harry had been concealing the treasures somewhere outside the house for two years. She started to shake: he had been lying to her for two years and had intended to cut her out.

'You shit,' she screamed, crying with anger now. He had known she couldn't report him to the police because she would have been charged for her part in it. He had screwed her into the ground. The fact that he was dead made no difference – he had betrayed her, as he had betrayed Sonja before her, and what a fool she had been, trusting him, a blind, trusting fool . . . just like Sonja.

As soon as she had seen Harry, she had wanted him and she had told herself at the time that it was love. But it had been something darker and more complex. All her life she had wanted to get out from under, to belong, to be on the inside, and she had known that she had the potential to do that, to lead a life that her parents in Kansas had never dreamed of. Harry Nathan was the most attractive and dynamic man Kendall had ever met:

198

when Sonja had hired her he had been making movies that did reasonable business, still had some respectable friends in the industry. He was charm itself when Sonja brought Kendall out to the house to introduce her, talked to her easily, naturally, as though she was his equal, and over the coming weeks she felt that he took a special interest in her – used to chat to her for a few minutes on the phone if he called the gallery to speak to his wife.

Kendall had soon come to feel that she was like Sonja – her clothes became more elegant, her movements more graceful, the inflections of her voice smoother – but also that, as she herself became more attractive, Sonja was deteriorating. She had never been as beautiful as Sonja, about that she had no illusions, but she was twelve years younger, and she was prepared to make Harry the project of her life in a way that Sonja could not. It was not difficult to get him into bed, though the whole business felt rather perfunctory, almost tawdry, the first time a quick fuck at her apartment, after which he had immediately said he had a meeting and had to go. Kendall had wondered whether perhaps there was some truth in a few remarks Sonja had made, hinting that her husband was selfish and unaccomplished in bed.

Harry had been reluctant either to tell Sonja about their affair or to contemplate leaving her. Some deep, sick, neurotic bond held them to one another, Kendall decided, particularly since Sonja said she had almost finished some major project which she planned on exhibiting. Harry seemed to have bought into all that garbage about disturbing her creativity. That was fine, Kendall reckoned, as she visited her gynaecologist for shots to enhance her fertility – she gets her baby, I get mine.

Sonja produced a remarkable piece of work: a huge construction of a series of storefronts, not unlike the block where the gallery was on Beverly Drive, in which the stones in the sidewalk, the trash cans, the merchandise in the stores seemed to be living, watching the parade of humanity with strange, childlike faces.

At the opening Kendall was quiet. She was wondering whether the quick fuck Harry had given her on just the right day two weekends ago, while Sonja was working at the studio, had done the trick.

She received confirmation of her pregnancy a week later, and served this information on Harry like a writ. She intimated, too, suitably indirectly, that if he didn't leave Sonja and marry her he would indeed receive a writ in the form of a paternity suit. Harry had no option now but to tell Sonja, as Kendall would soon start to swell, and she could see, too, that the idea of a child had worked its old magic, primitive but effective, on his vanity as a man. So that was settled. Sonja received the news as silently as a dagger slid expertly under her ribs, packed her bags and went.

While Kendall was pregnant things hadn't been too bad – the prospect of the child had interested Harry more than its mother – but after she had her daughter the marriage went downhill fast. Now that Kendall was preoccupied with the baby, clucking endlessly about the contents of bottles and diapers, she bored Harry and got on his nerves.

She was baffled by the deterioration of their relationship, as though they had fast-forwarded, somehow, through what was meant to be the honeymoon period and had settled down into the stress, irritation and distance that longer-term marriages seemed to wallow in.

Then their little girl died suddenly, inexplicably, at seventeen months old, and neither of them was ever the same again. Kendall never forgave Harry for his insensitivity to her at the funeral, spending more time with that low-life closet case Vallance than with her, and he became embittered, his humour blacker and sicker, his lifestyle tackier and more decadent by the hour. Kendall knew they were in trouble now, but when she tried to talk to her husband on the odd occasions that she saw him, he said his actions were fuelled by anger at the child's death.

It was in the weeks following the funeral that Harry had developed his interest in adult parlour games. Kendall hung on grimly, no matter what she had to go along with and how much of a blind eye she had to turn to his other playmates. She refused to become a member of the army of divorced and discarded women the city was thronged with. Vallance's revenge for Kendall's hostility had been to introduce Harry to Cindy and – after they had been married a little less than four years – Kendall knew she had lost him.

As her divorce settlement, he gave her a half share in the gallery and although she thought maybe she could have got more, she was glad to have the link of a business partnership with him, just to retain some contact. Devoid of sexuality herself, she had never been able to understand its power over others, and she was certain that the Harry–Cindy alliance would last no longer than her own marriage.

On the other hand, Kendall had always had a keen business mind, and unencumbered by the tasks of parenthood, she soon put her mind to making money again. The gallery did well enough, but she figured that to make serious money, you had to bend the rules a little. Harry had jumped at the idea of the forgeries, and if it was his money that financed the scam, it had been her brains that set it up.

Everything had gone sweetly up until now, and as Harry grew predictably disenchanted with Cindy and stories of the couple's rows and public slanging matches circulated around the city, Kendall permitted herself to fantasize that he would realize what an asset she had been to him – how transitory the delights of the flesh, how enduring the joys of bank accounts containing seven-, even eight-figure sums. Kendall had convinced herself that when the fraud came to fruition and the paintings were sold on elsewhere, Cindy would be kicked out in the cold and she would be reinstalled as Harry Nathan's wife.

All those dreams were now in ruins around her. She had nothing: he'd cleaned her out, just as he had Sonja, and he had dumped her for good, just as he had Sonja.

Kendall took another swig from the bottle, but she didn't feel drunk. Harry had used her and lied to her, but she knew him well enough to be sure he wouldn't have been able to arrange this latest deal alone – hadn't had the intelligence. He must have had someone assisting him. Vallance? Cindy was out of the question, and she wondered if Sonja could have played any part in it. She began to pace up and down the room, drinking and stumbling around over the floral parterre rugs, which were meant to make the green carpet look like a garden, a witty allusion to the black Astroturf beyond. Sonja was the obvious person: she knew more about art than either Kendall or Harry. Was it possible that she had come back into Harry's life?

202

Kendall wouldn't allow herself to believe it. What about Harry's brother Nick? He was an artist, he could have been behind it, and there was Harry's mother – she had a considerable interest in art and antiques.

Abigail Nathan had been so friendly when Harry and Kendall were married, so pleased that Harry had got rid of Sonja, and overjoyed about her first grandchild. But Kendall had known in her heart that Abigail cared only about her sons. In her eyes they could do no wrong, and Kendall wondered if the whole Nathan family had ganged up against her. She remembered Cindy saying that someone had broken into the house and Abigail had keys, so the family could have taken the paintings, but how could she prove it without implicating herself?

Kendall began to search her desk drawers: Harry might not have kept up the house insurance premiums, but she had always paid the insurance of the gallery personally. Now it was all she had, and she knew what she would do: torch it, and claim the insurance. At least she would come out with something, and the more she thought about it, the better she felt. It could be done easily enough – the workshop was full of inflammable spirits, canvases and wooden frames and would catch fire quickly. As it was attached to the gallery, the whole site would go up.

She hurled everything out of the desk drawers, until she found the documents: the gallery was well insured, and the stock valued at two million dollars. She checked the insurance papers, just to make sure that, in the event of fire, she was fully covered, then crammed the rest of the documents, including the mass of crazy notes she had received from Cindy Nathan, back into the drawer. Those were certainly best out of circulation – she didn't want anyone thinking she had had anything to do with that fucked-up bimbo's death.

Kendall hurried out of her apartment to her Mitsubishi jeep. She loaded the cans of white spirit she kept in her garage into the back of it, muttering drunkenly that nobody was ever going to treat her like a doormat again. She would show that bastard and his family, and she was laughing as she drove out past Lorraine Page, who had parked a few yards from her front door, and whom she did not see. She was too intent on planning her revenge. Kendall wouldn't be left penniless like Sonja, wouldn't walk away without a fight.

Lorraine adjusted her driving mirror and watched the two-toned Mitsubishi jeep career down the road. She had hoped to challenge Kendall about Jose's statement that he had seen her car on the morning of Harry Nathan's death as well as Cindy's suggestion of some fraud to do with the paintings, and her subsequent mysterious death. She tried to follow the jeep, but lost it after a few minutes. Kendall was going somewhere and fast: Lorraine wondered if Feinstein had already called her.

Lorraine returned to her office and tossed the car keys to the valet parking attendant, who gave her a wide grin. 'Hi there. Nice day. You having one?'

'Yep. How about you?'

'Could be better,' he said, getting into the Mercedes.

She rode the elevator up to her floor, headed for her office, and was about to enter when she heard voices.

Decker was serving coffee and chocolate madeleines,

which he must have rushed out and bought, to Lieutenant Jake Burton. Lorraine hesitated, then smiled. 'Hello.'

Burton stood up with a smile. 'Off duty. Wondered if I could have a few moments?'

'Sure, go into my office. I'll just get rid of my coat.'

Decker ushered Burton into Lorraine's office and closed the door behind him. 'He just called in. Been here a few minutes,' he whispered. 'Single white male his age – don't pass him up. I'd pull him.'

Lorraine made a face and walked into her office. She went behind her desk and sat down. After what Decker had just said she found it hard to look at Burton.

'Off the record, Mrs Page, I called to say thank you for sending over the videos and for your ... other assistance, and to tell you that as yet we've had no news from the county morgue on the Cindy Nathan autopsy.'

He kept staring at her, then added, 'That's all really. Thank you.'

He walked to the door. 'Is your dog a cross between a German shepherd and ...'

'I'm not sure – I kind of inherited him, but he's got malamute or maybe wolfhound somewhere.'

'I used to have a Dobermann,' he said. 'Miss them when they go – especially the walks. Kind of clears your head, or it did with me. Anyway, thank you again.'

He was about to open the door when Lorraine said, 'Whenever you feel like walking, just call me – he's always available.'

He gave a shy smile. 'I will. I'd like it even better if there was some company too. Anyway, I'd better make tracks. Thank you again.'

'Let me give you my home number,' she said suddenly. She wrote on one of her cards, and passed it to him.

'I'll take you up on that.'

She followed him out, and he asked where she usually walked. 'Oh, sometimes the park, but on nice evenings I drive to the promenade. He loves the beach.'

Decker was listening, but pretending to be busy. Tiger raised his head as they passed and Burton patted him, then nodded to Lorraine, and grinned at Decker. 'Nice meeting you again – goodbye.'

Lorraine watched him leave, and Decker rolled his eyes. 'My God, you are so *slow*. He was *begging* you for a date – when a guy talks about taking your dog for a walk, you know, sweetheart, it's you he wants to go walkies with.'

'Oh, shut up,' she said, returning to her office.

'So what *did* he want?'

Lorraine shrugged. 'Nothing, really, just to thank me for sending the videos over.'

'Oh, really?' Decker said, raising his eyebrows. 'He had to come and see you to do that? So he *is* after your ass.'

'Oh, for God's sake,' Lorraine said dismissively.

He laughed. 'Sweetie, trust me, you'll have to make the running. He's all male, all testosterone and incapable of coming out with the line "I suppose a fuck is out of the question", *but* he has major hot pants for you, trust me.'

'Not in a blue moon, Decker. I wouldn't trust you as far as I could throw you.'

'If you could see your face – ' he giggled ' – go take a look!'

She slammed her office door, and scurried to look at

herself in the make-up mirror she kept in a filing cabinet. She was flushed, and she did have the hots for Burton. Decker was just a sex-obsessed fag – but intuitive.

Kendall turned into the alley that ran along the back of the gallery, overlooked by barred windows and full of huge commercial garbage bins. Most businesses left their back yards open to use as a parking area, but Kendall had enclosed all the space that belonged to her to construct a workroom, and she pulled up now in front of the high iron gates she had installed. On the other side of the alley were the backs of the shops and other properties that fronted Canon Drive. One was a men's accessories shop, run by a guy called Greg Jordan. Now she saw him standing at the back door of his shop. She waved across to him, making sure he saw her, not wanting to appear furtive. 'Hi, how's business?' she called loudly.

He walked out into the alley. 'Slow. How is it with you?'

'Not so bad. Got a client coming in – 'bye now.' She waved again, and pushed open the big double gates.

Eric was in the yard, stacking a delivery of old frames they would repair in the shop. She tossed him the keys of the jeep, a little irritated that he was there: she had forgotten about him. 'Eric, there's a delivery of white spirits in the jeep – bring them in for me, will you?'

'Sure, Mrs Nathan, but we've got plenty in stock,' he said, heaving an old gilded plaster frame up to lean against the wall of the workshop.

'I know, but I don't want it cluttering up the garage.'

Eric wandered out to the alley, unobserved by Greg Jordan, now busy with a customer. 'Where do you want

207

them?' he asked Kendall, as he carried the crate of spirit into the workshop.

'Just leave them by the door,' she said nonchalantly, bumping into the big trestle table covered with paints and pots.

'You all right, Mrs Nathan?' he asked.

'I'm fine. We do any business today?' she asked, trying to appear casual, and he said there had been just a few customers, but no sales.

'Well, I might close up early,' she said, then had to hold onto the ledge of the table as the room was spinning. 'Got a headache, actually,' she muttered, and he looked at her but said nothing. It was obvious she had been drinking.

'You want me in the morning?' he asked.

'Of course. Maybe come in a bit early as I want to shift some of these paintings into the main space.'

'I can do it now, if you want.'

'No, tomorrow will be fine. I'm going out to dinner, so I won't be here long. I'll just lock up and then I'll be leaving.'

'Okay.' He stared at her again: she was dragging some wooden frames from behind a screen.

'You sure you don't want me to stay an' help out?'

'No, just go. See you tomorrow.'

Eric hovered by the door, watching her stumble against a wall. He'd never seen her like this in the two years he'd worked there. 'You sure you're okay, Mrs Nathan?'

She turned on him angrily. 'I'm fine. Now just go, go on, get out.'

'On my way,' he said, picking up his jacket. He didn't give a shit either way – he'd never liked her or her hawk face. 'See you tomorrow,' he said, as the door shut after him.

Alone, Kendall did not move until she had heard the yard gates clang shut. Then she heaved more and more wooden frames into the centre of the room, laughing softly, knowing they would catch light fast.

Lorraine was clearing her desk, getting ready to leave for home, when the phone rang. She checked the time – five thirty. Decker buzzed her office. 'Call for you, Mrs Page, line two. Lieutenant Gorgeous. Okay if I leave?'

'Sure. See you tomorrow.' She hesitated, then switched to line two. 'Lorraine Page speaking.'

'Hi . . . er, I was just wondering . . . I'm off duty early this evening, and it's a . . . well, it's a nice night, and I was wondering . . . if you were going for a walk. Or if you were busy I could take your dog out for you.'

She smiled. 'I'm just leaving the office.'

'Oh, well, another time.'

'No, no, I meant that I'd go home, change, and I'd like . . . we could walk together.'

'Oh, yes, fine.'

She gave him her home address again – just to make sure – and they arranged to meet at seven thirty. She couldn't stop smiling. She had a date! Well, she *and* Tiger had one.

Usually, when she got home, Lorraine tore off her clothes, pulled on an old track suit and sneakers, then walked to the nearest park, ran for almost two miles and went home. Tonight she washed her hair, redid her make-up, and put on a pale blue track suit with a white T-shirt that she wore only for the gym on Saturdays – it was an expensive designer label, and she knew the colour suited her. Then she tidied the apartment, arranged some fresh flowers and sprayed air freshener, while Tiger padded after her, wondering what the hell was going on. He even dragged his lead from the hook by the door and sat there waiting, afraid that she would go out without walking him.

On the dot of seven thirty, she heard Burton's car outside. She cast a quick glance round the room and tossed a magazine onto the sofa as the entry phone buzzed.

When she let Burton in, Tiger hurled himself, barking, at the door, and Lorrane grabbed his collar and yelled at him. 'It's okay, Tiger, stop it. Good boy . . . *Tiger!*'

Burton wore an old pair of torn jeans, sneakers and a T-shirt, and concealed his shyness by making a fuss of Tiger. 'Hello there . . . Who's a good house-dog, then, eh? Hello, good boy, good boy.'

Tiger allowed Burton to ruffle his ears, then tried to squeeze between his legs to get out of the half-open door.

'*Wait!*' Lorraine yelled, but Burton grabbed his collar.

'It's all right, I've got him. He seems pretty eager to go.'

Lorraine agreed, saying that she had only just arrived home, and he was used to his routine. 'I just throw on a track suit and we run.'

Burton looked at her, flushing. 'Well, you look lovely, that colour suits you.'

'Oh, thanks. I'll get my keys.'

He clipped Tiger's lead on, and went ahead of her down the stairs to the street. He hadn't had a chance to notice how she had cleaned the apartment: all he had been looking at was her, and he liked what he saw – but, then, he had thought the same when he'd first met her.

They used her jeep to drive the short distance to Santa Monica beach. Burton drove, and Lorraine liked the way he asked if she'd like him to drive, not too pushy, easy and relaxed. She tossed him the car keys, and as he got in he pushed the seat back to accommodate the length of his legs. Tiger was stationed in the back seat, his head almost resting on Burton's shoulder. She liked the way Jake had checked the gear shift and made sure he knew where everything was before they drove off. Out of his working clothes he looked younger, and she noticed he was well built, and had strong, tanned arms. He asked if she had any special route or if he should just take her the way he knew. She said she'd leave it to him, but started to direct him down the avenue anyway. He laughed, and didn't seem to care that Tiger was drooling on his shoulder. When they stopped at lights he tilted his head to one side to run it against the big dog's muzzle, and Tiger licked his face in reply.

He was relaxed, at ease, and as he drove, Lorraine was able to sneak glances at his profile. He was, as Decker had said, a very handsome man, and seemed even more so this evening than when she had first seen him. He was not exactly drop-dead gorgeous, but he had strong features: his nose was aquiline, and he had high cheekbones, and a deep cleft in his chin. His eyes were deep-set, and although she knew they could be cold and unfriendly, now they were teasing.

He knew she was scrutinizing him, but didn't mind. He would have been a bit suspicious of someone who pushed their way into his life, and would have been sure, as he presumed she was, that the walk with the dog was just a pretext.

'So, this was unexpected,' she said.

'Don't you trust me? Do you think I have some ulterior motive?'

'Possibly,' she said lightly.

He half turned towards her, then back to concentrate on driving. 'I used to have a dog, I told you. I like . . . taking walks, and I prefer some company, not all the time, but occasionally.'

Lorraine stared out of the window. It had been so long since she had had company, and not just for walking Tiger. 'Yes, me too,' she said softly.

Kendall arranged the frames, not obviously, but stacked at the side of a long trestle table, draped a length of muslin over them and soaked it in white spirit. She poured a trail of the liquid across the bare floorboards, which were splattered with paint and spirit spilt over a period of years. She brought more finished canvases out of their slats in the storage area, again not making an obvious bonfire but resting them against the walls, leaving space for air to circulate under them to feed the flames. She worked for almost an hour, sweating with the effort, and soaking rags from the bins in yet more spirit. Then she carried out more old canvases and laid them along the walls of the short passage between the workshop and the gallery, to encourage the fire to spread into the gallery itself. She was still drunk but so intent on what she was doing that she wasn't aware of it.

At seven thirty she entered the gallery, turned on all

the lights, and opened all the doors. She made four phone calls arranging for artists to meet her the next morning, opened her desk diary and entered the appointments, plus notes of possible sales – all to create the impression that she had no financial problems and had been planning normal business for the next day. She spread more papers and anything that would catch light quickly on the floor, and started to make her way back to the workshop. Half-way there, she crossed to the big gates to look out – then swore. Heading towards her was Greg.

'Hi – that you, Kendall?' he called, and she opened the gate. 'You got any fresh coffee? It's just that I'm stock-taking, and I've run out and can't be bothered to go to the store.'

'Sure, come on in. I'm working late myself – I've just got a new artist and I'm planning the show for him, so I'm moving things around to make space.'

She kept calm, walked into the little kitchen area in the warehouse with Greg, and passed him a half-used packet of coffee.

'So, business is good, is it?' he asked.

'Yep, well, I hope it'll be even better. I am always looking for new talent. You know – eye-catching stuff.' She smiled, wanting to get rid of him, but then realized he would make a good witness, and elaborated on her new deals, even gestured towards the warehouse. 'You can see it's kind of cluttered in here, so I've got plenty to keep me busy this evening.'

'Well, I'll leave you to it. Thanks for the coffee – I'll repay you in kind tomorrow, okay?'

'Oh, it's on the house.'

He thanked her again. She smelt of alcohol, and he

213

was sure she was tipsy. She didn't offer him a drink, though, and he hadn't really wanted the coffee – he'd wanted a chat with Eric, from whom he scored a variety of recreational chemicals.

Kendall watched him leave, and not until he was back inside his shop did she return to the warehouse.

The beach was almost deserted, and Lorraine and Burton had walked a fair distance. Tiger was having the time of his life running after sticks, chasing stray dogs, hurling backwards and forwards, and barking and diving around them.

'He's a great dog,' Burton said, throwing a stick as far as he could.

'I never thought I'd get so attached to him, but he kind of grows on you.'

They walked side by side, and then, as if it was the most natural thing in the world, Burton caught her hand. The touch of his, warm and strong, made her heart pound, and she curled her fingers tightly around it, trying to calculate just how long it had been since someone, anyone, had taken her hand and walked with her the way they were walking now.

'So, Mrs Page, do you want to start first, or shall I?' he said casually.

'Start with what?'

'Well, I want to know about you . . . I want to know you.'

'Ah, well, that might take more than a walk on the beach, Lieutenant Burton.'

'But it's a start,' he said, and released her hand to pick up the stick Tiger had dropped at his feet. After he had thrown it again, he didn't take her hand, but rested his arm loosely around her shoulders.

'I'm forty-five years of age, and I've been married once, to my childhood sweetheart. I was nineteen and it lasted four years. I joined the army and she and I grew apart, she left me, and married another childhood friend – my best buddy, as a matter of fact, and they live very happily in Seattle, two kids . . .'

She loved his arm around her. 'I'm thirty-eight, divorced, and my ex-husband lives not far from here with my two daughters. He's married again to a very beautiful lady called Sissy. I don't have any contact with my daughters because . . .' She trailed off as Tiger arrived back, exhausted, with the gnarled stick. This time she picked it up and threw it, and he hurtled after it like a greyhound on the track after a mechanical hare. 'He'll sleep tonight,' she said. She wanted Burton's arm around her again.

'You were a cop,' he said, and slipped his arm around her again to draw her closer. 'I pulled your report sheet.'

'Yes, you told me,' she said coldly.

'I know I did. Do you mind?'

'Why should I? It's public knowledge.'

'Not quite, but I wanted to know about you.'

'Yes, well, there are some things that don't make it into reports,' she snapped.

'Hey, I'm just being honest. Don't get all uptight on me.'

'I'm not uptight, but I'm amazed you still wanted to take a walk with me. Most men would have run a mile.'

'Yeah, maybe, but everyone has a past – nobody's perfect.'

She wanted to break away from him, but didn't. She

stopped walking. 'Maybe, Lieutenant, but not everybody has a past quite as colourful as mine, or as seedy, or as dramatic or as—'

'Sad?' he suggested, gently.

She glared at him. 'What is this? Yeah, I've had my problems, and I admit to them, but I don't want anyone feeling sorry for me. What do you want from me?'

'I don't want anything, or not the way you think. I wanted you to know that I knew, that's all.'

'So?'

'It doesn't bother me what the fuck you were, or whatever you did.'

'Thank you, I'm grateful, but we are just walking my dog. I know what I did, I live with it. I know what I was and I live with that too. So take your pity and screw it.'

He grabbed hold of her. 'What's with you? Pity? You think I pity you? Jesus Christ, woman, I don't pity you. I'm out of practice with these things. All I know is I wanted to see you so badly, from the first moment I set eyes on you. I wanted to be with you, so I pulled your file from records. I'm sorry – all I wanted you to know was that.'

'Well, I want you to know that I'm not some charity case, and I'm not so desperate that I'd hide anything I've done. I killed a kid when I was drunk on duty. I was a drunk for eight years. Well, I'm sober now and I'm not prepared to be anyone's lame duck. Thanks for the walk – you can get a cab ride back.'

She marched off down the beach, stopped and yelled for Tiger, but Burton was throwing a stick in the opposite direction. She turned and yelled again for the dog, but he was already galloping away.

216

Burton turned to face her. 'Okay, that was your turn. You mind if I have mine now?'

'What?' she yelled back at him.

He strolled towards her, and said nothing until he was within a foot of her. 'I said, it's my turn now to fill in a few things about me.'

'You think I want to know?'

He tilted his head to one side. 'I sincerely hope so. Now where was I? Oh, yeah, forty-five, been married and divorced, joined the army at eighteen, educated by them, qualified as a lawyer and . . . of uniform, couldn't make it out, so joined the cops. This of any interest at all?'

'No – should it be?'

He came a fraction closer. 'You free for dinner?'

'No.'

'Tomorrow?' He reached out and drew her close to him.

'No.'

'I suppose a fuck is also out of the question?'

She turned away. 'Very funny.'

He moved behind her and put his arms around her, pressing her close to him. 'You sure?'

'Don't play games,' she said quietly.

'I'm not. I just don't know what I should say that'll make whatever I said before you told me to get a cab back okay. It's a hell of a long way, and my car's at your place.'

She turned in his arms, tried to break free from him, but he held her tightly. Her body was rigid, her face set, but he wouldn't release her, and gradually she let her body relax against him.

She rested her head against his shoulder, loved the

smell of him mixed with the sea air. He rubbed his chin against her fine, silky blonde hair. 'You smell so good,' he said, and she eased her face round, inch by inch until their lips met. His kiss was so sweet. Then he cupped her face in his hands. 'I've wanted to do this . . .'

He never finished as they kissed passionately, and slowly sank to their knees. He pulled her down beside him, until they lay side by side, Lorraine caught in the crook of his arm, her body pressed against his. He moaned softly, and she nestled against him: there was no need for words, no need to know anything more about each other. Lorraine was filled with rushes of emotion and couldn't talk.

Tiger bounded up and dropped the stick on Burton's chest: keeping one arm around Lorraine, he picked it up with the other hand, and held it high for a moment before he threw it towards the sea.

'You free for dinner, Mrs Page?' he asked.

'I guess so.'

He rolled over to lean on his elbow, looking down into her face. 'Then let's go eat.'

She traced his face with her hand. 'Sounds good to me.'

He bent his head, and gave her another sweet kiss. She could feel that he was aroused, and her whole body ached – a fuck was not out of the question, not at all out of the question, but he was one guy she knew not to treat like a one-night stand. This man, Jake Burton, she knew she wanted more from, more than she had believed she would ever want again. She was falling in love, but had so little confidence in herself that she couldn't accept that he was attracted to her, and just might want commitment from her too. It was too much to hope for, so she made herself play cool. 'There's a great Chinese near the apartment,' she said huskily, not able to be quite as offhand as she would have liked.

'I could handle that,' he said, then sprang to his feet and whistled for Tiger, who was further down the beach where he appeared to be digging his way to Australia. Lorraine sat up, shading her eyes against the evening sun, to watch Jake bend forward as Tiger loped towards him and clip on the lead. She liked everything she saw, and it scared her.

Kendall was ready, everything was set. She struck the match and let it drop to her feet. She expected things to happen as she had seen in movies, a thin blue tongue of flame, spreading and building steadily before bursting into an inferno, and began to panic that it wasn't catching. She didn't want the smoke alarms to go off before the fire took hold, so she bent down, fanning it with her hands, but still only a single, pale blue flame spluttered weakly. She bent down further, and used the hem of her skirt to create a draught. The flame still seemed about to go out. She leaned even further forward, struck another match to throw towards the spirit-soaked rags she had stuffed into the trash can and padded around it.

'Burn, you bastard, burn,' she muttered. She hated Harry Nathan with such venom. She would beat the bastard at his own game by claiming the insurance money – she was going to be all right. Now she was leaning further towards the fire, flapping her skirt furiously, and then the flames suddenly shot upwards so fast that she stumbled backwards and fell on her side. Her skirt was alight, and she was trying frantically to beat out the flames. Next moment she screamed in terror – her hair was on fire, and she could smell it burning. No matter how much she shook her head, or hit it, it kept burning. Her hands were still covered in white spirit – they were burning too, and then she was engulfed in flames as the alarms began to scream their warning. The fire roared forwards, spreading fast now, moving in every direction, and surrounding Kendall. She turned this way and that, screaming in terror as the flames leaped higher and higher, and the thick, dense smoke burned her eyes, blinding her.

Greg heard the alarms ringing, and looked out of his shop window, to see smoke spiralling upwards across the street, from inside the Nathan gallery's yard. He rang for the fire brigade and then took off across the alley as fast as he could, flung open the gates and burst into the yard as the fire erupted skyward, like a bomb, through the workshop roof. He could hear terrible screaming from inside, and ran to try to wrench open the workshop door, but was at first forced back by the billowing smoke. The horrific, high-pitched shrieks went on and on.

At last he got the door open, but smoke and flames obscured his vision as he shouted Kendall's name.

Suddenly she seemed to launch herself towards him, her mouth wide in terror: she was burning alive, her clothes, hair, her entire body alight.

Greg dragged her into the yard, wrapping his coat over her head in an effort to suffocate the flames, then to the gate to get them both out of the reach of the fire. The flames were now shooting out of the workshop, spreading, as she had intended, towards the gallery itself.

She was curled up beneath his jacket, which covered

her face and the top part of her body, but he could see the terrible burns to her legs. As he lifted away the coat from her, he felt a rush of hysteria – his coat was smouldering, on fire from her body, but the sight of her face made him catch his breath. Her hair was burned to the scalp, and her face was a gruesome mass of burned flesh and blisters. But she was alive, and her eyes pleaded with him. She was trying to say something, her fingers plucking at his arm. Greg didn't know what to do: his panic made him scream for her, and once he had started screaming he couldn't stop, his cries drowning her awful, low moans of agony. Behind them, the fire reached the main gallery and even though the sprinklers had come on automatically, nothing could hold it back.

Within minutes the fire engines and the ambulance had arrived. Greg watched, shaken and distraught, as the paramedics gently lifted Kendall onto the stretcher. He asked if she was alive and one of the men looked down at her and nodded. She was alive, but she had already inhaled so much smoke that he knew there was little hope of survival.

The gallery alarms were ringing, police and fire sirens wailing, and the sound of the plate-glass windows cracking and shattering made it impossible to hear what her last words were. Kendall died, painfully moving her burned lips and using the last breath in her smoke-filled lungs to whisper the word, 'Bastard.'

CHAPTER 10

THEY HAD ordered too much food by far, choosing every dish they had wanted to try but never ordered before, so that half-empty cartons of Chinese takeaway littered the kitchen counter and the coffee table. An exhausted Tiger lay flat out, his head almost resting on Burton's foot. Jake stroked his head just behind his right ear, and the dog growled contentedly, wanting more.

'You've won him over,' Lorraine said, leaning back. There was about a foot between them on the sofa, but she wanted to be closer, wanted to feel his arms around her again.

'Good, that makes life easier,' Jake said, then gestured towards the cartons. 'Will he eat the rest?'

'*Will* he?' she laughed, but fell silent as he reached for her hand.

'So?' he said softly, his fingers laced with hers.

'So,' she repeated. The gap was still between them.

'So,' he said again, then loosened his hold on her hand to turn towards her. 'Can I stay?'

Lorraine said nothing, and he began to stroke her arm, circling her slender wrist with his fingers. Then he drew her towards him until she rested against him. 'Yes,

I want you to stay,' she whispered, nestling against his shoulder. She could smell Chinese takeaway, and sand, and sea, and him, and his chin rested against the top of her head as she slipped one arm around him. He reached down and drew her leg across his lap, gently stroking her calf as he eased off her shoe. It fell onto Tiger, still at their feet, who grunted and got up sleepily to walk a few feet away before he sighed loudly and slumped down, head on his paws, watching them intently with his pale blue eyes.

Lorraine sighed as Burton massaged her leg, his hand slowly moving higher, inching up her thigh. He continued to caress her, running his hand under the high-cut leg of her silk panties to find her with his fingers and feel she was wet for him, her legs parting. He slid from the sofa and began to ease her panties down. She made no effort to stop him, wanting him to do what he was doing and more. She rested her head back against the sofa as he knelt in front of her, opening her wider, and then began to kiss first the inside of one thigh then the other, kissing closer and closer to her until he bent his head and she felt his tongue inside her. Lorraine moaned and lifted her pelvis a fraction, wanting him deeper, and he continued to lick and suck her, pulling her shirt out from the waistband of her skirt so that he could slip his hand over her ribs and under her bra to feel her breasts and her hard, aroused nipples. She came quickly, her body shuddering and her thighs tightening around his head until at last he moved upwards, dragging her underwear off her body, and taking her breasts in his mouth as she moaned with pleasure.

They kissed with passion, he lifted her from the sofa, carried her to the bedroom, kicked open the door, stumbling slightly in the darkness, and laid her on her bed. He stripped off his clothes in front of her, unself-conscious about his nakedness, and he noticed the rows of slender candles at her bedside. He asked where she kept the matches. She watched his lean, muscular body bend forward as he lit each candle in turn. She was about to undress when he turned and knelt on the bed. 'No. Let me do that.'

He allowed her to do nothing to help him as he took her clothes off, kissing her as he removed each garment, until she lay naked, smiling up at him. He held up his hand and disappeared, returned with her cigarettes and put them on the bedside table before he lay down beside her. He continued to caress her, tracing the scars on her arms with his fingers, and turning her over to see the uneven white tissue of the other scars on her back. He didn't ask about them, but kissed each one, becoming more and more aroused as he touched her until he eased himself on top and into her with a long, low moan of pleasure.

He made love to her first, a sweetness to his fucking, waiting for her to climax with him, and then they had sex, roughly, but he was an experienced lover, never losing her. There was no fear between them, and no questions asked as they whispered endearments to one another, enjoying the heated sex, their mutual lust. When Jake moved Lorraine to sit astride him, she moaned, arching her body back to bring him deeper inside her, and when she lay beside him he was able to arouse her again, until they lay curled side by side against one another, her back pressing into his chest, their legs entwined. Lorraine was tired, not wanting to speak, and eventually she felt the rhythm of Jake's breathing change.

He was asleep, one arm round her, and she felt cocooned by his presence, lulled by his steady breathing, until her own matched it and she drifted into the perfect sleep of physical exhaustion.

'Jesus Christ,' Jake murmured, fully awake as Lorraine stirred, his arm tightening around her.

Tiger had inched his way onto the bed, and Jake turned round as the massive dog pushed him slightly out of the way and rested his head on the pillow.

'I told you he liked you,' Lorraine said drowsily, falling back to sleep almost instantly. Jake wasn't so sure about Tiger's presence, as the dog's hot breath on his neck meant that his fangs, too, were close, but he was too tired to argue, and just moved closer to Lorraine. He listened to her soft rhythmic breathing as she had listened to his, and noticed that Tiger's was now audible too. He had already taken more than his share of the bed, and yet Jake somehow liked the warmth of the big dog beside him, and in fact, he was liking everything about this night – especially the woman cradled in his arms.

He woke with a start to the smell of fresh coffee and the chink of china. The duvet had been carefully tucked around him and he looked at the clock on the bedside table, then relaxed – it was only five. There was plenty of time to take a shower, get dressed and go back to his place to change into fresh clothes. He didn't look much like a division commander as he joined Lorraine in the kitchen, swathed in a sheet, and she looked up and smiled shyly, indicating the coffee. He liked the fact that she was wearing only a towel, and that her face was devoid of make-up, her cheeks rosy. He went to her and put his arms around her, kissing her neck.

'Good morning.'

He felt something thump against his bare foot, and looked down to see Tiger wagging his tail. 'Morning to you.' He scratched the dog's ear. 'Does he always sleep in your bed?'

'I'm afraid so. I've tried to kick him out, but he creeps back in during the night. He's pretty good – I mean he doesn't take up too much space, he knows which bit's his.'

She fetched cups, and cream from the fridge.

Jake washed his hands at the sink, and she was surprised to see him pick up the empty takeaway containers and put them in the trash, then collect the empty cans and all the cartons that were still half full.

'He had a feast in the night,' she said, nodding at Tiger. A few noodles were scattered on the carpet, and she picked them up before she tidied the coffee table and carried the dirty ashtray to the bin.

'You should give that up,' Jake said, as he ran water into the sink.

'Yeah, I know.' She liked standing close to him, liked him being in her tiny kitchen – liked everything about him. She slipped her arm around his waist. 'You want some toast?'

They sat at either end of the sofa, Lorraine with her legs curled under her, eating thick slices of toast with blueberry jam and drinking a mug of coffee. 'What time do you have to go to the station?' she asked.

'Nine, which means . . .' He looked at the clock. 'I'll have to leave in an hour or so, unless you want me to go now.'

'No.' She leaned towards him, and he reached out with one finger and traced her lips. Their eyes met, and she put down her mug and crawled along the sofa until

226

she was able to rest against him. 'You feel good,' she said softly. She eased around to sit between his legs, and he passed her her coffee. As she reached up to take the cup, the sleeve of her robe fell back, revealing the scars on her arm again.

'You were in the wars at one time,' he said gently, kissing her.

'Yeah, I was.' She felt her stomach tighten, and his hand massaged the nape of her neck. 'You should know, you read my sheet.' She began to slide away from him, murmuring she wanted more coffee, but she lit a cigarette, and was angry to see her hand shaking. 'Suppose you want to know how much I charge, these days.' It came out tougher than she had meant it to sound.

'Don't be so defensive,' he said lightly, then laughed. 'Besides, the takeaway cleaned me out of cash.'

'Yeah, well, I was pretty cheap – price of a drink.'

'Stop it,' he said firmly, watching her fall apart in front of him, her hands shaking as she sucked at her cigarette, her whole body tense with anger.

'You started it,' she snapped, and he raised his arms.

'All I said was—'

She stood in front of him, shoving her arm under his nose, showing him the old scars and cigarette burns. 'You missed these.'

He reached out and gripped her wrists tightly. 'No, I didn't. Like I said, I read your sheet, I know all about your self-mutilation, kind of goes with drugs, booze and . . .'

Lorraine tried to twist free of him, but he got to his feet, refusing to let go of her, then suddenly pinched her cheek, staring into her face. 'Your mug-shot's not up to date – where's the scar on your cheek, Mrs Page?'

227

Now she wrestled free of him and glared. 'I told you – plastic surgery. Gimme time and I'll get round to all the others. Now, why don't you get out of here and leave me alone?'

'Why don't you simmer down?'

She walked towards the bedroom. 'I've got things to do. You know the way out.'

He moved fast enough to reach the bedroom door before her, and dragged her inside, pushing her down on the bed.

'What's this? Gonna try some rough stuff on me now, are you? That on my report sheet, is it?'

He slapped her face, and she took it, laughing at him. He stepped back. 'I'm sorry . . . sorry.'

'Don't be, I'm used to it, I can take it. Come on, you want it again, take it.'

She opened the towel, lying naked in front of him, and he bent forward. For a moment she thought he was going to punch her, but instead he pulled the sheet from under her, so that she rolled sideways, then wrapped her inside it. Her arms were trapped and he held her so that she couldn't move. 'Don't do this, Lorraine . . .'

'Give me one good reason.' She pushed her face close to his, and then the look of hurt in his eyes made her anger evaporate. She couldn't keep up the act, and she rested against him again, a low sob shaking her body.

'Sssh,' he said softly, rocking her in his arms.

'I'm sorry, I didn't mean what I said. I'm sorry, it's just . . . It's just . . .' She couldn't continue.

'Just what?' he asked, after a long pause.

'Just that I am scared.'

'Not of me?'

She shook her head, then bit her lip and nodded. 'Yeah. I am scared of you, or of what you make me feel.'

'What's that?'

She sighed. 'Oh, please, don't do this.'

'Okay. What if I tell you that I am ... I'm only interested in this woman I've got in my arms right now. I don't give a fuck about her past, what she did or didn't do. I'm not dumb enough to think it won't come up, or that we won't have to talk about it, but for no other reason than I want to know you, all of you, the good, the bad ...'

'And the ugly,' Lorraine said, her eyes filled with tears.

'Sure, yeah, all of it. Anything to do with you I want to know about.'

She didn't know what to say to him, she just felt like weeping.

'You're supposed to say that you want to know everything there is to know about me,' he said, feeling her begin to relax in his arms.

They made love again, then showered together. Afterwards Lorraine made fresh coffee while Jake scrambled some eggs, and they ate breakfast again side by side on the sofa.

'Will you get the autopsy report on Cindy Nathan today?' she asked, trying to sound nonchalant.

Jake slipped on his jacket. 'Yes, well, it was supposed to come in today.' He crossed to her and leaned on the alcove. 'I think we might have a little talk to Mrs Kendall Nathan this morning too.'

Lorraine nodded. 'Yeah,' she said, pretending a keen interest. 'I'd check her out.' She looked at the clock. 'I should get dressed.' There was an awkward pause, while

Jake hesitated a moment, then walked to the door. She didn't want him to go, but if he had no intention of seeing her again, she didn't want him to stay either. 'I'll see you,' she said, hurrying towards her bedroom.

'Okay. 'Bye, Tiger, look after her for me.' He opened the door, and was half-way through it when he turned round. 'I'll be off at about four – you want to take in a movie?'

She felt like a kid, knew she was blushing. 'Yep, I'd like that.'

'Okay, I'll call you at your office. Are you going in today?'

'Yes. I've got a few odds and ends to sort out.'

'You're not still working on the Nathan case?'

'Well, not really – there isn't a case to work on.'

He grinned. 'You'll be touting for work.'

'Yes.'

'Okay, see you later.' He went out, and she stayed in the bedroom doorway, listening to his footsteps going down the stairs. She crossed to the window and looked out, wanting to see him walking to his car, wanting just to watch him as he unlocked it. He turned, as if he knew she was there, and smiled up at her, stood for a few moments, just looking, before he got in and drove away.

'Right, Tiger, soon as I'm dressed we go walkies,' she said, and couldn't keep the smile off her face.

Lorraine was singing as she walked into the office. Decker was sitting at his desk as she breezed past him with a loud 'Good morning.'

'It's better than you think,' he said, picking up his notebook.

'You can say that again, it's a . . .' She was about to say something silly, but instead burst out laughing.

'My, my, you got out of bed the right side.'

'I did, I most certainly did.' She sat in her chair and swung from side to side as he put a memo in front of her. 'Mr Feinstein . . . urgent, three messages on the answerphone. I called him back, but he insisted that he could only speak directly to you, and would you call him as soon as you got in.'

'Maybe they've got the autopsy results,' she said, dialling Feinstein's number.

'I doubt it. Two of the calls came in last night, and one at eight this morning.'

Decker went into his section to get coffee for Lorraine, and some bagels with cream cheese, which he had also bought. As he came back with them, Lorraine was tapping her desk with a pen. 'He won't discuss it on the phone, wants me to go round to his office. When I asked if it had anything to do with Cindy Nathan's death, he said it was an entirely different matter.'

'You want breakfast before you go?'

'No, thanks, I had scrambled eggs.' She was already collecting her purse and running a comb through her hair.

'You're looking very . . . relaxed,' Decker said, cocking his head appraisingly to one side.

'I am, and I might take off early this afternoon. Can you book me a hairdressing appointment and a manicure?'

'Got a date?' he asked jokingly.

'Yes, as a matter of fact, I have.'

'Ohhh.' Decker scuttled after her. 'So I was right!' Lorraine bit her lip and giggled, more feminine, girlish even, than he had ever seen her.

Lorraine was half out of the door. 'You just might be,' she tossed over her shoulder, and then she was gone.

Decker chucked her bagel to Tiger, who caught it and wolfed it down in two gulps. 'She got laid last night, didn't she?' he asked the dog, whose jaws chomped in reply. 'Well, well, well . . . I thought he was a pretty hot number myself.'

Clearly today was not one of Feinstein's good days. He was dishevelled, his tie askew, and he was sweating as he paced up and down the sea of carpet. 'I've had another art expert in, just to make sure, and he confirmed it. They *are* fakes, every single fucking one of them.'

'I'm sorry,' Lorraine said lamely, glancing behind him at a large painting on the wall. A letter-opener, made from the top ten inches of a narwhal tusk, protruded from the middle of it, stabbed through the canvas.

'Not as sorry as I am. Have you any idea how much money I've lost? My life savings were in those fucking paintings.' His voice cracked, and he almost broke down. Then a fit of rage seized him as with a sudden sweep of his arm he dashed pens, blotter, designer candy-dispenser and executive toys off his heroically proportioned desk. 'That shit Harry Nathan, that two-faced bastard! When I think of everything I did for that son-of-a-bitch, I'm telling you, if he was to walk in right now I'd shoot him – I'd kill the bastard.'

'What does Harry Nathan have to do with all this?' Lorraine asked, as Feinstein seized the letter opener from the canvas and slashed at it, using all his strength in an effort to rip the thing apart.

'I bought all my art through the Nathan gallery.

These are fakes, right? So somebody, somewhere, has *my paintings*, and Harry Nathan has *my money* stashed somewhere, because I've been through every fucking bank account he had and the cheque I gave him never showed up in any of them!'

Feinstein began to hurl pages of bank statements across to her. So much for client confidentiality – as soon as he was personally affected, all he cared about was himself. 'You trace those paintings, you trace his fucking secret accounts – I'm talking about millions, *millions*.'

Lorraine watched as Feinstein threw more files across the room, and waited until at last he sat down in his throne-like swivel chair. 'I will need to ask you some particulars, Mr Feinstein, and we will also have to discuss my fees.'

'I'll pay you whatever you want – just get me my paintings. *My wife will divorce me!*' He sank his head in his hands.

'I'll need to take some notes,' she said, opening her briefcase and taking out her pad.

Feinstein flicked a switch on his intercom, which had been flashing on and off since Lorraine had arrived. 'No calls, Pamela – period.' He flicked the switch off again, and patted his pockets for his cigar case. He found it, chose one, and ripped off the wrapper. 'Fucking start with Harry Nathan.' He snapped on a lighter.

'That might be a little difficult,' Lorraine said, smiling.

'You think this is funny, Mrs Page? I'm down two and half million and it's fucking destroying me.' He huffed and puffed at his cigar, then bit off the end and spat it across the room. 'Find out anything you can on Nathan's bank accounts. I can tell you some aliases I know Harry used – I want them checked out.'

'So Harry Nathan actually sold you the paintings?' Lorraine enquired innocently.

Feinstein looked at her, then at the ceiling. 'Who the fuck did you think sold me them? Sure, Kendall Nathan handled it, arranged delivery and stuff. Check her out – she wouldn't take a leak without his permission. The two of them pulled this off together and I want the slimy bitch fucking charged. I bought them through the gallery, right? I had them authenticated there, and Kendall – or somebody who worked for her – hung them for me here. So start with her.'

'Did Kendall benefit significantly under Harry Nathan's will?' Lorraine asked, knowing it wasn't strictly relevant to the art fraud but unable to resist the temptation to take advantage of Feinstein's temporarily uncontrolled state to try to find out what he had refused to tell her before.

'Well, she got the other half of the gallery,' Feinstein answered. 'Little pay-off for services rendered, by the looks of things.'

'But what about the art collection at the house?' Lorraine went on. 'Does that come to Kendall now that Cindy's dead?'

Feinstein was off on another tack. 'The police asked me for a specimen of her handwriting. I could have given them ten fucking specimens of suicide notes if they had wanted them, but they didn't ask. Cindy was always threatenin' to kill herself. She used to write letters to practically anyone she knew about how fucking miserable she was with Harry. What the fuck she thought I was going to do about it is beyond me.'

Lorraine felt another pang of grief for the tormented girl, calling out for help to everyone around her, only to meet with indifference and rejection. But it was interesting that she had apparently written letters mentioning suicide to quite a number of people. Lorraine couldn't see Feinstein killing her himself, but the idea of him perhaps selling a letter that might help in getting rid of Cindy didn't seem beyond the bounds of credibility. Or if Cindy had written to Harry's lawyer for advice on her emotional problems with him, it was not impossible that she had written to one or both of his ex-wives . . .

'Does Cindy's death benefit Kendall?' she asked again, casually.

'No way. That's not the way it works.' Feinstein had got more of a grip on himself now, had become the lawyer again. 'Anything Cindy owned when she died will form part of her own estate.'

'Will that go to her parents? They're out in Milwaukee somewhere, aren't they?'

'They may well be, but as far as Cindy was concerned they could stay and rot there. I have the last will and testament of Mrs Cindy Nancy Robyn Nathan right here in the office, and her family are not mentioned at all.'

Feinstein leaned back in his chair, sensing Lorraine's acute interest in what he was saying. He permitted himself a leisurely pause and a further pull on his cigar. 'She left everything to the House of Nirvana Spiritual Center, some fucking bunch of freaks. ' God, Lorraine thought, that was unexpected. 'Fortunately,' Feinstein said, with a self-satisfied smile, 'the tax-saving clause prevents them getting more than her pantyhose. They won't get a cent of Harry's estate.'

'What do you mean?' Lorraine said. 'Cindy didn't tell me anything about the Nathans' tax affairs.'

'It's a pretty standard thing on a large estate that will

attract a lot of taxes, particularly when the beneficiaries are all relatively young and in good shape. All of Harry Nathan's beneficiaries had to survive him by sixty days before the various gifts to them took effect. Otherwise, in the situation we have here, for example, we would be paying tax once on the estate when it passed to Cindy, then again virtually immediately when it passed to her heirs.'

The intercom buzzed again, and Feinstein screamed into it, 'Pamela, I said no calls – I MEAN NO CALLS.'

'Since Cindy didn't live for sixty days, it doesn't go to her heirs,' Lorraine said. 'So who gets it?'

'The residuary legatee,' Feinstein said.

'Who is?' Lorraine said, wanting to slap him. Lawyers: what a fucking pompous self-important bunch of creeps, she thought. Feinstein got up, turned aside to relight the thick cigar, then turned back to her as he drew on it, surrounding himself in a swirl of blue smoke.

'Sonja Nathan.'

'Sonja?' Lorraine said. 'She'll do a bit better now than the couple of keepsakes Cindy said she was going to get.'

'That would indeed have been pretty much the position if Cindy hadn't died,' Feinstein went on, in professorial mode. 'Nathan's big assets were the house, his holding in Maximedia, his art collection and his half of the art gallery. There were no substantial cash assets at all – or, at least, not in any accounts I knew about.' His eyes narrowed with rage at this reminder of Harry Nathan's perfidy. 'The will disposed of all of those to Cindy and Kendall, and Sonja would have got anything else not specifically mentioned. He had a substantial film library, for example, at his office, which would have gone to her.'

Lorraine's mind was racing: she had largely discounted the possibility of Sonja Nathan's involvement in her husband's death, but this certainly gave her a motive. True, she had had to kill two people to collect under Harry's will, but if she had been prepared to kill once, why not twice? She had certainly been expert in covering her tracks – maybe used a professional hitman – as Lorraine had found nothing to connect Sonja with either of the two deaths. However, none of that was Feinstein's business, and she tried to disguise what she was thinking by changing the subject to more mundane matters.

'By the way, I promised Jose and Juana I would mention this matter of the savings Nathan took off them and their back salary. It looks like they should contact Sonja,' she said, but the phone on the desk blinked again, and this time Feinstein, still on his feet, marched to the door and yanked it open.

'Pamela, what the fuck are you doing out there?' he shouted.

Lorraine heard whispers passing between Feinstein and his secretary before the attorney walked out, leaving the door ajar. He returned almost immediately. 'She's dead.'

Lorraine stood up.

'Kendall Nathan's dead.'

Burton looked up from reading the file on Lorraine Page to see Jim Sharkey outside the office door.

'Is it the autopsy on Cindy Nathan?' Burton asked.

Sharkey came in with some photographs and put them down on the lieutenant's desk. 'These are morgue shots. Hard to tell who it is, but it's Kendall Nathan. Last night. Initial view is she was trying to torch the gallery and it backfired. Her hair caught light and . . .'

'Dear God,' Burton said, looking at the charred form. If Kendall had killed Cindy as, he had to admit, Lorraine had largely convinced him was likely, and possibly Nathan too, she had certainly got her just deserts.

'Yeah, pretty horrific way to die. Place went up like a bonfire – lot of white spirit, plus all the canvases, the wooden frames . . . No one could do anything.' Sharkey went on to tell Burton that there was an eyewitness, the owner of a shop that shared a back alley with the gallery workshop, who had seen Kendall enter the building and had raised the alarm when he saw the smoke.

Burton's phone rang, and he picked it up; the receptionist told him that a Mrs Page was on the line. He asked the girl to take a message as he was in a meeting. He replaced the phone. 'What about Cindy Nathan?' he asked again.

Sharkey shrugged. It was still only nine thirty and nothing had come in as yet. Burton rocked back in his chair, and told Sharkey to see what he could do to hurry things up, while his eyes moved back involuntarily to the grotesque photographs of Kendall Nathan's corpse. Well, he figured, there was no more potent motive force to set off a chain of destruction than the cocktail of greed, hatred and lust that had seemed to surround Harry Nathan. Either Cindy or Kendall had killed Nathan, Kendall had killed Cindy, and now Kendall, too, was dead. The nest of vipers had consumed itself, and he was glad to close the Nathan case for good. The evidence could go back to the family now, he thought, recalling the hours of sickening videotapes he had made sure that no one but himself saw, and made a mental note to call

Feinstein to find out who was now the legal owner of Harry Nathan's estate.

Decker jumped as Lorraine banged into the office. 'Do I have a lot to tell you, darling,' she said, tossing a rustling deli bag full of wrapped packages onto his desk. 'Did you eat?'

'No,' he said. 'I was waiting for you. God, I'm hungry. What did Feinstein want?' He went into the kitchen for plates.

When he came back, she said, 'Cindy was right about the art scam. Feinstein bought over two million dollars' worth of paintings from Harry Nathan and Kendall and they've turned out to be fakes. He wants us to try to trace either the original paintings or the proceeds of sale.' Lorraine opened a tub of artichoke salad and scooped some into her mouth before continuing. 'Cindy also wrote stuff about killing herself to Feinstein and a whole bunch of other people – which fits in with what I thought about the note. I had Kendall pretty much down for having killed her, but – you won't believe this – Kendall Nathan died too last night.'

'Ding dong, the witch is dead,' Decker said ironically, arranging bread, bresaola and salad on a serving platter. 'What happened to her?'

'The gallery caught fire and she went up in smoke. That's all Feinstein's assistant knew.' Lorraine tore off another hunk of bread, assembled herself a rapid sandwich and began to eat.

'I'm sure Lieutenant Burton will be able to let you have a few more details,' Decker said, with mock innocence, and Lorraine flushed scarlet. 'Remember to ask him when he's scrambling eggs for you – I mean, next time he calls.'

'Did he call?' Lorraine asked, giving up the pretence that her association with Burton was purely professional.

'Nope, not yet. You want me to call him?'

Lorraine nodded, then changed her mind. 'No, I'll call him later. Anyway, two things. Feinstein figures that he bought the real thing from Nathan's gallery, as he got it properly authenticated there, but what was packed and delivered were fakes. Cindy told me she thought Kendall and Harry were pulling something like that, but to tell you the truth, I didn't believe her.' Lorraine shook her head. 'Poor kid. Nobody took her seriously her whole life.'

'It's not your fault she died,' Decker said gently. 'Don't beat yourself up about it.'

'Yeah, I know – part of the job,' Lorraine said with a wintry smile. 'But she told me she'd found out that some of the art at the house was fake too. Some Chinese porcelain she thought was antique was apparently knocked out by some company called Classic Reproductions. Check them out for a start.' She finished her sandwich as Decker made notes of what she had said.

'I also think we need to trace a guy who worked for Kendall Nathan, a sort of gofer who brought the paintings round and hung them for Feinstein,' she continued. 'He's a young kid – Feinstein couldn't recall his name, but I remember seeing someone when I was at the gallery so chase him up too.'

'Will do,' Decker said, making another note.

'These are pretty spectacular pieces that have gone missing, so we contact galleries in the US and in Europe and all the big art auction houses. They're all signed works by well-known modern painters, and all had price tags from three hundred thousand dollars to over two million. Poor old Feinstein really got stung.'

'I'll make some enquiries in London,' Decker said, writing furiously. 'I think they have a register of hot art works you can have searched.' He was going to enjoy doing the legwork on this case, he reckoned, schmoozing through galleries, and looking up art-world friends.

Lorraine dug into her briefcase and brought out some loose pages. 'These are the names of the people Kendall employed. Feinstein paid the wages so the list should be legit – just three people. He said they were hired to remodel frames, do repairs and so on, but they might also have been painting the fakes, so check them out. There's also a list of regular buyers – get each of them to give you the name of their art adviser. It may mean a lot of people have been stung.'

Decker nodded, excited.

'Clever bastards,' Lorraine mused, leaning forward. 'You can see by the list – all movie people. They rarely sold to a dealer or old money, because they'd recognize a fake so fast. Most of the people they sold to were just rich trash and wouldn't know if they'd bought a Lichtenstein or a fried egg. They hung up what they'd bought, put up the gold plaque to say what it was, while the original stayed with Nathan's gallery. He and Kendall were pulling the scam together.'

'And a very lucrative one,' Decker remarked.

Lorraine nodded. She frowned, and leaned back in her chair. 'You know . . . everything Cindy Nathan said is starting to make sense. I mean about the high-tech security at Nathan's – I'd say he kept the originals on his own walls.' Lorraine leafed through the pile of pages of information from Feinstein. 'There's also sculpture, ceramics, and some statues that were worth over a million dollars.'

Decker waited, pen poised, as Lorraine thumbed through the pages. 'According to Cindy, Nathan hadn't paid the insurance for the contents at the house for quite a while. Why do you think that was?'

'It's certainly a weird thing to do,' Decker said meditatively. 'Particularly since he wasn't lax about security.'

'That's what I thought. He was paranoid about it, monitored every phone call, every visitor,' Lorraine said. 'Supposing what he was worried about wasn't the paintings being ripped off out of the house, but certain people getting *into* it – like the people who thought they had the same painting hanging in the guest bath at home? I bet he was careful never to sell to anyone too close to his own social circle.'

'That's certainly one explanation,' Decker said. 'But what about Kendall getting in and trashing the stuff?'

'I've been trying to figure that one out since the housekeepers told me about it. The only thing I can think is that she discovered then that those paintings weren't the ones she and Nathan had bought.'

'What do you mean – he'd sold them again?' Decker interjected.

'Wouldn't surprise me. I reckon Nathan got two sets of fakes painted. Then he switched the originals again to cut Kendall out.'

'He was doing a double whammy?'

'Right. And Kendall found out when she went to the house the night Cindy Nathan killed herself.'

'But why the hell would she set light to the gallery?'

Decker asked. 'That was her own stock – she must have known that was genuine, at least.'

'She's going to have lost a fucking fortune on the scam – I'd say she torched it for the insurance. Which is why Feinstein wants me to look for secret banks accounts. If Nathan sold half of those paintings he's got to have millions stashed somewhere.'

'I'll start calling round and see if any of them have turned up.' Decker dangled the last piece of bresaola above his mouth and finished it with an elegant snap.

'Let me tell you the second thing first,' Lorraine said. 'Feinstein told me the exact terms of Harry Nathan's will.' And she explained how Sonja Nathan now stood to inherit not only Cindy's share of Harry Nathan's estate, but also Kendall's.

'Just so long as she lives another . . .' Decker glanced at the calendar '. . . four days. East Hampton next stop, right?'

'Yes, get me another flight. I doubt if Sonja has anything to do with it as she's been out of the picture a long time . . .' She smiled at the pun. 'But I'd like to talk to her, and besides, Mr Feinstein is paying us top dollar, so we can afford it. All fraud cases take a long time to check out too, so we don't take on anything else – well, not for a while.'

Decker rubbed two fingers together. 'Do I get a rise?'

Lorraine shooed him with her hand. 'Oh, get out of here. But if you come up with something, yes, we'll split if fifty-fifty because I'll need you to do a lot of legwork.'

'Thank you.' He bowed out, eager to make a start.

Lorraine glanced at her phone, then checked the time. It was after two, and Jake had not returned her call.

Suddenly, she felt the depression descend. It was odd, she thought, she'd got a new and interesting investigation, but a date for the movies was more important.

She spent the rest of the afternoon sifting through Feinstein's papers. When it got to four o'clock and Jake still hadn't called, she rang and cancelled her hair appointment. Much as she wanted to, she couldn't pick up the phone to Jake himself, and hard as she tried to concentrate on work, she kept thinking about him until she had convinced herself he would never call again.

It was almost six when Decker returned. 'So far none of the well-known galleries have seen any of the paintings listed, and none have been sold recently at auction. Next I'll try England, the art-loss register, and then the rest of Europe – and you've missed your hairdresser.'

Lorraine attempted nonchalance. 'This is more important. Now get out, leave me alone.'

'He didn't call, huh?' he said, hovering at the door.

'No, Deck, he didn't call. So I'll take Tiger out, and if you need me, I'll be at home. Okay?'

'Okay – but if you need me, I'm around.'

'Thanks.' She turned away from him. 'I really liked him, Deck, but I couldn't keep my big mouth shut. I just had to tell him about my past – well, some of it . . .'

Decker leaned on her desk. 'Listen, if he's put off you because of that he's not worth the effort, period. It's what you are now that counts, and I'm telling you, you're lovely.' He watched her fetch Tiger's lead and leave the office, while he stayed on to make his overseas calls to a list of major galleries that might have sold art works worth over a quarter of a million dollars. The paintings listed didn't seem to appear on anyone's records, and the case intrigued him more and more.

Burton was still in his office, wading through investigation reports and trial files. The autopsy report on Cindy Nathan wasn't passed to him until after five. The cause of death was suffocation by hanging, but she had also tested positive for alcohol and drugs. It was impossible to tell whether she had hanged herself voluntarily or whether someone else had done it.

By the time Burton called Lorraine's office, the answerphone was picking up calls. Her mobile was switched off and when he tried to call her at home he got another recording. He decided not to leave a message but to go round to the apartment on the off-chance she was there, and he continued to work, clearing his desk. Just as he was finishing, the file on Lorraine caught his eye again. He drew it towards him and leafed through it, rereading everything he had read that morning, then pushed it away. There was something that connected with the Nathan case, something that he had read or been told, that hung like a warning, but he just couldn't put the pieces together. All he knew was that it had a direct connection to Lorraine.

Lorraine sat on her sofa. She'd made herself an elaborate salad of goat's cheese and marinated vegetables, but seemed to have no appetite. She'd walked Tiger, fed him, done everything to occupy herself, even played her answerphone messages twice in case she had somehow rewound the first time and missed his call. But there was no call, and no amount of staring at the machine would make a message appear. He hadn't called, he wasn't going to call, and she had been dumb to think he ever would call. She thought back to what he had said as he had left that morning: she wasn't kidding herself, he had asked her if she wanted to see a movie – he must just have decided to skip it. She could easily call him tomorrow, it hadn't been a firm date, just a casual suggestion, but by the time it got to nine o'clock, she felt worse than depressed, telling herself that no decent guy would want to start anything with her – she wasn't worth it. She should never have thought he would want to see her again, so she took the phone off the hook, to stop herself staring at it.

It was almost nine thirty when Tiger began to bark frantically. Lorraine, wrapped in a bathrobe, yelled at him to shut up, sure he had only heard the neighbours below, but then the entryphone buzzed. 'I tried to call you at the office, and here . . .' Jake's voice said.

'Oh, yeah, sorry. I've been really busy.'

'Is it okay if I come in?'

She pressed the button to release the street door. 'Sure.'

He seemed embarrassed when she opened the door to the apartment, and paid more attention to Tiger than to her, while she wished she'd kept the appointment with the hairdresser and hadn't taken off her make-up.

'Have you eaten?'

'Yeah, I got a hamburger at the station, but I wouldn't mind a cup of coffee.'

Lorraine busied herself with the percolator, while Jake continued to mess around with Tiger. Then, suddenly, he was close and his arms slipped around her. 'I missed you,' he said quietly, and she turned towards him, putting out a hand to touch his face, feeling that he needed a shave.

'You did?' she said softly.

'Yeah, all day.'

She heard a voice inside her head telling her to say it, admit that she had missed him too, but she broke away to fetch the cups and take the cream from the fridge. 'I'd given up on you,' she said flippantly, setting out a tray.

'I'm sorry.' He ruffled his hair.

'Well, you say something about a movie, and then when you didn't return my call . . .' She reached for the cookies, and realized as she turned to him that she was holding the jar tightly. 'I did call you. Some secretary said you were in a meeting.'

'I was. I'm sorry – it was crazy all day. But when I called you back, there was just the answerphone.'

'Hell, you don't have to explain anything, I'm not interrogating you. It was just . . .' She couldn't keep up the pretence. Her voice sounded strangled. 'I didn't think you wanted to see me again, not after, you know . . .'

He took the jar away from her, and held her close. She clung to him, feeling his heart beating. 'You are wrenching feelings from me that I never thought I would have again, and I'm scared, so scared . . .'

He kissed the top of her head and the nape of her neck, then opened the palm of her hand and kissed that too, holding it to his lips. He wanted to say there and then that he loved her, but somehow the words just wouldn't come. Instead he heard himself asking her if it would be all right if he had a shower.

'Only if you stay the night,' she said, wanting to say something more loving, but she was as tongue-tied as he was.

It was not until he was beside her, lying on her bed with just a towel wrapped around his waist and a cup of coffee in his hand that they began to relax with each other. Neither said that they felt totally at ease with one another, that they loved the way their bodies fitted together when Lorraine slipped into Jake's arms and curled up beside him. They didn't need words, and she was unprepared for what he said when he spoke.

'Will you marry me?'

She didn't think twice, but agreed without hesitation. Then they were stunned by the enormity of what they had just agreed, and there was a pause before they laughed. Lorraine covered her face with her hands.

'Oh, my God, I should at least have hesitated a moment.' She rolled away from him, in disbelief at what had just happened.

'No,' he said, drawing her closer, as if she belonged with him.

'But it might take a bit of getting used to,' she whispered.

CHAPTER 11

LORRAINE MADE breakfast while Jake showered. Just setting two places felt good. She had lain awake beside him for a long time, replaying over and over in her mind the moment he had asked if she would marry him, half afraid she had dreamed it.

'Hi,' he said, as he came into the kitchen buttoning up his shirt and rubbing his chin. 'You've got one hell of a blunt razor in there.'

They were at ease with each other, and Jake ate yoghurt and cereal, poured coffee for them both, and even put his dirty dishes in the sink. He made no mention, though, of having asked her to marry him.

'Somebody house-trained you,' she said, watching him squirt washing-up liquid into the sink.

Tiger took up his position at the front door, waiting for his morning walk, and Jake offered to take him out while Lorraine showered. It was as if he had known her for months, not just days, and his presence didn't seem intrusive, just got better and better every moment he was with her.

Jake might have been well-trained in the dish-washing department, but he had left the shower steamed up, sopping towels and puddles on the floor and wet footprints on her carpet. Lorraine liked even that because it stopped him being too perfect. She remembered her ex-husband Mike, and the arguments they had had over his bathroom habits: she could never understand how he could take a shower and leave wet footprints everywhere but on the bath mat – and here she was liking it that the new man in her life was behaving in the same way. The new man in her life! She stared at her reflection in the mirror. In just two days her life had changed course, and from feeling depressed and alone, she knew now that a future was waiting for her.

Lorraine finished dressing, made the bed, vacuumed the living room and even plumped up the soft cushions, a small smile playing on her lips as she did the chores at top speed. She wished Rosie could see her now – she wouldn't believe it! Being loved, even if just for two days, had made her domesticated! Lorraine crossed to the window to see if Jake and Tiger were on their way back, and seeing them both coming up the street below, she opened the window and called down. Jake looked up and waved, while Tiger almost pulled him off his feet. He unclipped the dog's lead, still looking up at Lorraine. 'I'm going to be late, I'll call you.'

She was disappointed – she had wanted him to see how she had cleaned the house. Then suddenly she felt stupid, and a dark spiral of emotions started rushing through her mind. Why hadn't he mentioned their marriage? Why hadn't he come back to kiss her goodbye? Would she see him again? Tiger scratched at the front door, and Lorraine let him in. He went straight to his bowl, and began to gobble his food noisily. 'Hey, you! I just washed that floor!'

It was while she was driving into the office, accelerating along Rose Avenue, that she began to run through the case. The light at Walgrave and Rose was broken, blinking a steady red that permitted one car at a time to cross the intersection. Seeing the line of vehicles jammed bumper to bumper, Lorraine looked at the memos she'd scrawled to herself. Why *had* Harry Nathan been killed? Somehow she didn't think it was to stop the porn tapes being released – if someone was desperate enough to kill him for that reason, they would have ensured that they knew where the tapes were. But if that were the case, the suspects were Cindy, Kendall and Raymond Vallance, with Kendall and Vallance having the most to lose by the tapes becoming public. However, Lorraine thought, Nathan's involvement in a multi-million-dollar art fraud seemed a much more likely motive for his murder. It was almost impossible that he had been killed by one of the victims of the scam – or of his other blackmailing activities: the tight security at the house would have kept strangers out. No. Nathan had been killed by someone who knew him well, which meant his wives or his friends. Yet again Kendall seemed the most likely killer – especially since what was probably her jeep had been seen near Nathan's house on the day he died. Against that, though, she had given a convincing appearance of not having known that she had been ripped off in the scam until weeks later when Cindy died. The phone tapes indicated that she had been on warm terms with her ex-husband.

At last it was Lorraine's turn to cross the intersection and she speeded up along Airport and Centinela to make up the lost time, but the ten-minute delay meant that she hit another major jam on Pico Boulevard. Lorraine turned back to her notes, and considered other reasons why anyone might have wanted Harry Nathan dead.

Assuming that no one else had had any inkling that the paintings weren't genuine, Nathan had been perceived as a rich man; perhaps he, and the women, had been killed for his money by the person who would eventually inherit it – Sonja Nathan. Lorraine had never established who had made the telephone call to her office on the morning of Nathan's murder, which lent a shred of support to that hypothesis. It had certainly been a woman, she thought – though perhaps Raymond Vallance could have imitated a woman's voice.

The traffic was at a dead stop. Lorraine tapped her teeth with her pen, and continued to think about Sonja Nathan. If she was primarily motivated by financial greed, why had she let Nathan rip her off so spectacularly after their divorce? She had surrendered the gallery she had built up, her only means of earning a living – and which a court would almost certainly have awarded to her – because, Vallance had said, she was too proud to soil her hands. But soiling one's hands with petty squabbles over money might be a very different matter to Sonja Nathan from soiling them with an enemy's blood.

The impatient driver behind blasted Lorraine with his horn. She indicated in the mirror that there was nothing she could do, and glanced back at her notes, where she had written the words paintings, new partner. Had it been Nathan's own idea to sell the paintings without Kendall's knowledge, or had he been working with someone else? Someone who had decided to cut him permanently out of the picture – and out of the proceeds of the sale – just as ruthlessly as he had cut out his second ex-wife?

Lorraine ignored another toot from the driver behind her, and went back to her notes. Any new accomplice in the fraud would still have to be someone in Nathan's circle of intimates, or they could not have got past the security – or known that Nathan would have to be killed outside, away from the recording devices in the house. That brought her back to Vallance and Sonja again: Sonja was the one with the specialist knowledge of the art world but Vallance was the one most desperate about the porn tapes . . .

Lorraine felt that she was going round in circles, but at last the traffic began to move. She put away her notes.

When she got to the office Decker was at his desk, calling galleries and auction houses. 'I still haven't turned up any gallery selling the paintings on the list, but there's hundreds of 'em,' he said.

Lorraine told him to concentrate next on private dealers: they were more likely to have buyers who did not necessarily want their purchases made public. She also asked him to check out known buyers from Japan and the former Soviet republics, especially the latter, who had a lot of illegal dollars to spend, and not to forget the buyers on record as having purchased art works from Kendall Nathan's gallery.

'I'm compiling a list from the papers Feinstein gave you, but it'd be better if I could get access to the gallery books,' Decker said.

'I doubt if sales like this went into any official ledger, but there might be a record of them at the Nathan house.'

'Good thinking – you want me to go there?'

'No, I'm going to go out there myself and try to get Feinstein's art expert to confirm whether those paintings are real or fakes before we go any further,' Lorraine said. 'I'll call Jose now.' She dialled the Nathan house, and

Jose said she could come straight over – he and Juana would be there, and they wanted to speak to her in any case: they had been given a formal letter from Feinstein terminating their employment. 'We have to leave the property by the end of this week,' he said angrily. They still had not been paid any back salary. Next call was to Feinstein. When she told him that she thought Nathan had been keeping the original canvases at his own house, he agreed readily to call the man who had authenticated the paintings for him. Within two minutes he was back on the line and said that Wendell Dulane would join her at Nathan's house in half an hour.

'Okay, Decker, I'll be out until lunchtime, possibly,' Lorraine said, picking up her purse.

'Don't you even want a cup of coffee, dear?' he said in his best mom voice.

'We had breakfast.' She couldn't resist using the plural, and Decker laughed.

Jose opened the door when Lorraine arrived at Harry Nathan's house, but she said she would wait outside in the sun for Dulane to show up. Within a few minutes someone buzzed at the gate and a low-slung sports car drew up on the gravel. An elegant individual, dressed in a green linen suit, got out and introduced himself as Wendell Dulane.

She and Jose showed him where the paintings were hung, both on the ground floor and upstairs.

'I've seen a number of these pictures before – one or two on Joel Feinstein's behalf,' Dulane said at once. 'If they aren't the originals, they aren't crassly detectable fakes.'

'We were hoping you could tell us the difference,' Lorraine said. 'They all look the same to me.'

The man nodded. 'Certainly. I'll call you when I'm through.'

Jose was evidently itching to talk to her about the letter he had received from Feinstein, and sure enough, when he ushered Lorraine into the kitchen, a small pile of correspondence had been set out on a black and white laminated table.

Juana came across to greet her. 'Mrs Page, I'm so glad you have come. Did Jose tell you we have been told to leave?'

'Have you been able to find any other employment?' Lorraine asked, sitting down at the table to read Feinstein's note and his brief apology for being unable to settle any outstanding accounts until the Nathan estate was in order.

Jose shrugged, and Juana pulled out a chair. 'We have no references. We asked Mr Feinstein to provide some for us, but he doesn't mention it in his letter and it is difficult to get decent employment here in LA without them. We have a few things we are looking into, but nothing definite. We were wondering if you could help us.'

'I would if I could,' Lorraine said. She didn't know many people who could afford live-in help, but there were always movie people needing housekeepers.

'But not without good references. We have worked for Mr Nathan for so many years . . .'

Lorraine knew what they wanted, and didn't mind their rather obvious way around asking her for it directly. She said that she could give them some kind of reference and would speak to Feinstein again about their back salary and proper references. And then she had an idea. 'Perhaps Sonja Nathan could give you a reference,' she suggested, and saw a look pass between the couple.

'We have written to her,' Juana said, looking at her husband.

'She hired you, didn't she?' Lorraine said, fishing for more information about Harry Nathan's enigmatic first wife. 'Was she easy to work for?'

'Very easy,' Juana said. 'She was a lady. The rest were whores.' There was a fierce look in her eyes, and a note of finality in her voice. Lorraine glanced at Jose.

'Harry Nathan robbed her,' he said slowly, 'as he robbed us.'

A polite cough sounded behind her. Dulane had appeared in the doorway, Lorraine got up and motioned him into the hall where they could speak more privately.

'It's bad news, I'm afraid,' he said. 'They're fakes, all right – carefully executed, but I don't think there can be any doubt. Just as well, I suppose, considering the damage some of them have sustained. Tell Feinstein I'll call him later. Nice meeting you, Mrs Page,' he said.

As Jose appeared to show Dulane to the door, something suddenly occurred to Lorraine. She walked back into the kitchen and asked Juana if the police had taken Nathan's diary. 'They took a lot of things from here. He had personal things like that in his briefcase, and they took that away, but there was an appointment book – it was stacked with the magazines.'

Lorraine followed her out to the main living area and across the large light room to a glass-topped table on which a number of upmarket glossies were spread out. Juana moved them aside, brought out a leather appointments book and handed it to Lorraine. She riffled through it: there were weeks without anything written in at all, then a few scrawled appointments. 'Can I make a few notes?' she asked, and Juana nodded, then withdrew. Lorraine took out her notebook and jotted down any name she came across – there was none she had heard mentioned before, and she wondered if they were art dealers, which Decker could check out. She turned page after mostly blank page. Some had a single line drawn through them and, she almost missed it, just the single letter S printed right at the top. The Ss were more frequent in the weeks leading up to the murder, but there was never more than one in a week. Lorraine noted each date, and wondered if the letter stood for 'Sale'. Or could it refer to the first Mrs Nathan?

Juana returned with a sandwich of smoked chicken and salad leaves, in sun-dried tomato bread, neatly laid out on a tray with a napkin and some iced water. 'Juana, if I run through some dates with you, can you see if you can recall them for any reason? Visitors, or even Kendall Nathan being here?'

Lorraine listed date after date but Juana shook her head, so Lorraine asked her to send in Jose. He, too, was unable to recall anything specific regarding the dates. 'How about two days *before* the murder? Can you remember anyone coming here?'

Jose shook his head, but then he came closer and asked for more dates. 'You remember somebody?' Lorraine asked.

'No, but I think . . . I am sure most of the dates are . . . wait. Let me talk to Juana.' He hurried out and a minute later returned with her. This time Juana carried a small cardboard-backed diary, and Lorraine read the dates again.

'Ah! I may be wrong, but most of the dates you want to know about are our days off. They weren't usually on the same day every week, Mr Nathan would just tell us we could have the day off.'

Nathan must have made sure that his domestics were not in the house so they wouldn't know who came or went, what paintings were exchanged or hung or, most importantly, who was taking items away.

'Did you ever notice anything unusual going on with the paintings?' Lorraine asked.

Juana raised her hands in an uncomprehending gesture. 'They were changed so many times. Mr Nathan was always asking if anyone had been to the house, if anyone had seen them – he acted like he never wanted anyone to see them.'

'Was there anyone in particular who used to come to look at the paintings?'

The couple looked at Lorraine. 'No one in particular.'

'Did Kendall Nathan still come to the house after the divorce?'

'Many times,' Juana answered. 'She used to bring paintings out here and say where they were to be hung. Sometimes the new ones looked identical to the old ones.'

'Did anyone ever come with her to help hang the paintings?'

Lorraine waited as they thought about it. 'Sometimes she had a black kid who was her odd-job man. They were big canvases, and she couldn't carry them in and out of the house on her own.'

Lorraine pushed back her chair and stood up. 'During the last few days or weeks before Harry Nathan was shot, did anyone come and take away paintings? Or replace paintings?'

Jose said, 'Yes, once, but we didn't see him – it was our afternoon off. Mr Nathan said it was a man from the insurance company checking on them.'

'Where was Cindy when this went on?'

'I don't remember, she never paid any attention to the paintings.'

'Can you give me the date the insurance broker was here?'

'It was a Monday, a week or two before the murder. I remember because Mr Nathan gave me three thousand dollars for household expenses, and to pay the gardener. I remember the day, too, because later in the evening, we had just served dinner and he called us into the dining room. He poured us glasses of champagne, said he was going to be a father, that Cindy was pregnant, just a few days, but pregnant.'

'I see,' Lorraine said. 'Well, thank you for all your information. I'd better get myself back to my office.' She got up to go, having deliberately held back the question she most wanted to ask until last.

'I don't suppose Sonja ever came here after she and Harry Nathan split up?' she asked casually, as the couple walked out into the hall with her.

'Sonja, never,' Juana said, without hesitation, her eyes meeting Lorraine's. 'She never came here again.'

Decker was just hanging up the phone when Lorraine arrived at the office, and seemed very upbeat. 'I just got an address from the welfare department for the kid who worked for Kendall Nathan,' he said. 'The one on Feinstein's payroll was out of date.'

'Well, check him out,' Lorraine said. 'Feinstein's art guy said all the paintings at the house are fakes.'

'I'll get over to his home right now.'

'Ask him if he ever met Sonja Nathan,' Lorraine added. 'Did you fix me up a flight to New York?'

'I'll get on to it as soon as I get back,' he said.

Almost as soon as Decker had closed the door the phone rang and she picked it up: 'Page Investigations.'

'Hi! It's me.' It was Jake. She pushed away her notes and leaned back in her chair.

'I was wondering if you'd like dinner at my place tonight.'

'Yes.' She laughed, and said she knew she was supposed to play hard to get, but . . .

'Pick you up from your office at about six thirty?' he suggested.

'Yep. Oh, just one thing – the Cindy Nathan autopsy. Did it come in?'

Jake told her the results. Then Lorraine said, 'I don't think the note was genuine. Or, at least, she didn't write it that day.'

'Well, it's possible she wrote it on a piece of paper she cut in two herself, for some reason,' Burton replied. 'I'm not going to push an investigation unless another suspect emerges besides Kendall Nathan.'

Lorraine said nothing, having decided not to mention her suspicions that either Raymond Vallance or Sonja Nathan might have some connection to Cindy's death until after she had seen Sonja.

Burton went on, 'The forensic team are still sifting through the debris of the gallery workroom, but they seem to think Kendall died accidentally, possibly while trying to start a fire. Wouldn't surprise me if she was trying to burn the place down for the insurance – the business was in debt, and she couldn't afford to renew the lease.'

'Anyone else involved?' Lorraine asked, and Burton said that, according to the witness, Kendall had been alone.

'When did you know about her death?' she asked.

He had been told the previous day. Lorraine wanted to ask him why he hadn't mentioned it, but she didn't because she wanted to avoid any awkwardness between them. At the same time she thought perhaps he should have told her, and, as if reading her mind, he said, 'I was going to tell you about it last night, but . . . I got a little sidetracked, if you remember.' He laughed, in a low, intimate fashion, then had to cut short the call as there was another waiting. He reminded her that he would pick her up later, then hung up.

The light on the answerphone was blinking. Feinstein wanted Lorraine to come over to his office at her earliest convenience.

Lorraine sighed. Now that the attorney was paying her, she had no choice but to do as he asked, and by just before four she was in his reception in Century City.

Dulane had informed Feinstein that further fake copies of his paintings had been found at Harry Nathan's house, and Feinstein demanded to know what the hell was going on.

'Well,' Lorraine said, 'it looks like Nathan did to Kendall what she did to you and swapped the paintings again.'

'Jesus,' Feinstein swore. 'Crooked fucking bastard.

261

Where the fuck are the paintings now?' He glared at Lorraine as though she must know the answer.

'It looks to me like they've either been sold on to other buyers, probably outside the US, or he had another partner who's got them stashed somewhere,' she said.

'Find them,' Feinstein said, rubbing his eye sockets wearily. 'Just fucking find them.'

'Right now my assistant is checking out the man who worked for Kendall Nathan,' Lorraine said smoothly, 'and when I have his report, I will give you a further update. We're still checking out auction-houses, galleries and other possible outlets for the paintings.' Feinstein pursed his lips. 'You know, Mr Feinstein,' Lorraine went on, 'you could report this to the police. You have been used in a serious fraud.'

'No,' he snapped.

'May I ask why not?'

Feinstein pinched the bridge of his nose, then leaned back in his chair. 'One, I do not wish to appear like a total asshole and, believe me, if the media get a hold of this, you think anyone is going to want me to represent them? The schmuck that didn't even know when he was being ripped off? I have my reputation to think of and . . .' he spread his hands on his desk '. . . like I said, sometimes clients, like Nathan, do certain deals in cash . . .'

'Did you benefit from cash payments, Mr Feinstein?' Lorraine enquired.

Feinstein half sighed, half hissed his reply. 'Not cash, exactly. I thought I made that clear.'

'Not quite. If you weren't paid in cash, how were you paid?'

Feinstein steepled the fingers of his sweaty hands. 'An

early de Kooning like the one I bought costs maybe a few thousand dollars more than I paid. It was a good deal – one for the future if you understand me, not to be sold on until a few years had gone by. It wasn't hot, just an exceptional deal – in lieu of fees, you understand.'

'I see,' Lorraine said, loathing the man, who continued to play with his fingers.

'So this stays a private investigation. You find who stitched me up, then I'll deal with it my way. That's what you're hired to do so no more talk about reporting the fakes to the cops. Is that clear?'

'Absolutely, if that's what you want.'

He stood up, and began to move round his desk.

'Did you also handle Sonja Nathan's business?' Lorraine asked.

Feinstein turned. 'No, I didn't. I was introduced to Nathan by Raymond Vallance, the movie star. Most of my clients are in the industry, which is another reason why I need confidentiality.'

Lorraine headed for the door, then turned back to him. 'Do you know if Sonja Nathan and her husband were still in contact after they divorced?'

Feinstein blinked hard. 'One of my partners handled the settlement. I met her during the meetings – they both had to be here.'

'And Sonja Nathan is now the main beneficiary of the estate, correct?'

Feinstein nodded. 'Yes – considering the other two wives conveniently dropped dead.'

'Now that we know the art at the house isn't genuine, what sort of sum would Harry Nathan's heir be expecting to receive?'

Feinstein stuffed his hands into his pockets. 'I don't

know. The house is worth about three million, the corporate stock not a lot in the present climate, and the gallery nothing – Harry and Kendall didn't own the freehold on the site.'

'And if his secret bank accounts are traced, would whatever money is in them also belong to Sonja Nathan?'

'I will certainly be instituting a claim to trace the value of my property into those funds,' Feinstein said, with emphasis, 'but I can't say what anyone else ripped off by Harry Nathan will be doing. Basically if nobody else claims it, it's hers.'

It was five thirty by the time Lorraine got back to the office. She had expected Decker to be there, but he hadn't even called. She cleared up some correspondence, tidied the office, took the garbage down to the incinerator, and had almost got everything in order when the doorman called to say someone was in reception to see her.

It was Jake – wearing a casual sweater, old cord trousers and sneakers. 'Hi. Maybe thought we'd do the walk before we went to my place – you all set?'

Tiger hurled himself at his friend, tail like a windmill, then pranced around barking.

Lorraine made a last-minute check before they left. Her car stayed in the garage, as Burton had the roof down on his rather beaten-up Suzuki jeep. 'This is for going to the beach,' he said, excusing the state of the jeep, but Lorraine liked it, and so did Tiger. He had jumped in and sat on the back seat before Burton had the door half open. Lorraine patted his head, remembering Tiger's previous owner – as perhaps the big dog was too. All that seemed a long, long time ago, and she thought about her old partners, Rose and Rooney, wondering how they were, and when they would be returning from their honeymoon.

Jake looked sideways at her, then reached over and took her hand. 'You're miles away,' he said.

She squeezed his hand. 'Yes – I was just thinking about a couple of friends of mine I want you to meet. They're on their honeymoon.'

He released her hand, and suddenly she wished she hadn't said honeymoon, because the word made her think about the proposal he'd made to her. He'd made no further mention of it, and she didn't want him to think she was trying to drop hints or remind him of it, so she started talking about Rosie and Rooney instead. She wasn't aware of where they were going, just chatted about how she had first met Rosie and that Bill Rooney had once been her boss when she was a cop. Jake listened, but seemed to be paying more attention to the road as he drove out towards Pacific Palisades. Tiger stuck his head out of the window, his ears blowing upright, then rested his head on Jake's shoulder. The atmosphere was relaxed and easy, and Lorraine began to unwind from the day. She stopped thinking about Harry Nathan, Kendall, Cindy, and the repellent Feinstein, and by the time they were walking beside the ocean, and Jake took her hand in his, all she could think about was the man she was with, and how good it felt to be with him again.

'So, you're back from wherever you've been,' he said softly.

'Sorry, sometimes it takes me a while to relax.' She moved closer to him, and he put his arm around her shoulder.

'I understand – I was a bit wound up myself.'

'Had a bad day?' she asked.

'Hell no – I was nervous about seeing you, worried you might have changed your mind.' They stopped and faced each other. 'I meant what I said last night, Lorraine. It may have been jumping the gun a bit – we hardly know each other, and I'm not . . . I mean, I don't want to hold you to anything said in the heat of the moment, but if you want to just let things run as they are, then that's okay by me.'

The pain in her stomach almost made Lorraine gasp. 'Do you mean *you* want to . . . er . . . you know, let things run?' She could hardly speak with nervousness.

He cupped her face in his hands and kissed her, then looked into her upturned face. 'Thing is, I feel like I've been hit by a truck. It was tough working today because I kept on wanting to call you, just to hear your voice. I can't hide my feelings, maybe because I've never felt this way before, so if I'm behaving like a kid, then you'll just have to wait for me to calm down. I want to go to bed with you right now, I want to wake up beside you, and not just one night here or there, *I want you*.'

She felt a small twinge of guilt because he hadn't been on her mind all day – in many of her thoughts, maybe, but not all of them. But being with him now, she forgot everything else. The words came out as naturally as breathing, three words she never thought she would say to anyone again. 'I love you.'

He closed his eyes and whispered, 'Oh, thank God.'

CHAPTER 12

D ECKER HAD checked out the Museum of Contemporary Art and driven from one gallery to another, sitting in the back rooms discussing auctions and buyers. He'd asked everyone about Kendall Nathan's gallery, and had prowled Rodeo, Beverly, Melrose Place and sections of La Cienega looking for other exclusive galleries that relied on private clients. He had palmed money to porters at auction houses and, dressed in his best gear, exploiting his good looks and acting experience to the full, he had posed as a buyer or a dealer.

He took one real dealer to lunch at the Ivy, and by four o'clock he was exhausted, but he felt he now knew conclusively that none of Harry Nathan's pieces had been on the market during the past two years. He had records of sales past, or forthcoming; catalogues from European auctions and a thick stack of literature from the English art houses, Sotheby's and Christie's, from both their London and New York centres of business.

He decided now to talk to the kid who had worked for Kendall. He was a little wary as he followed Washington Boulevard into east Los Angeles, more than aware that he was crossing the divide into gangland territory.

Signs of poverty became visible in the form of discount marts and Spanish-language churches, bars appeared on every building's doors and windows, and gang signatures, often half obliterated by rivals then resprayed, were noticeable among the graffiti on walls and metal shop shutters.

He made sure the doors to his car were locked as he drove, and that he knew exactly where he was going, not wanting to look lost or vulnerable as he turned south on La Brea to hit Adams Boulevard. Decker slowed down as he turned into a smaller side-street of mainly single-storey bungalows, little more than flat-roofed boxes in dingy white or ochre shades, with here or there a pantiled porch, canopy or new garage as the residents attempted to improve their homes or give them some individual character. Most of the tiny front yards were clean and neat, and only a few had old furniture and other junk piled around the back door or resting against the walls. Bars and chain-link fences were, however, everywhere and Decker reckoned astutely that the parents who lived there were probably solid enough citizens but were losing their authority over the kids, grown and half-grown, who were running with gangs.

Decker found he had overshot his target, and stopped and reversed. Number 5467 was a small two-storey frame house, one of the less run-down properties, with roses and elephant's ear fern on each side of the door and the drive clear enough for him to park in. He locked his car and looked around before heading towards the porch, carrying his portable phone.

The front door had thick safety glass, made opaque with strips of masking tape on the inside. Decker knocked and waited, then rapped a little harder. He knew someone was at home because he could hear the sound of a blaring television.

'Who is it?' a distant voice called.

Decker knocked again, then called out that he was from the art gallery. He listened while the volume of the television was lowered. 'I'm coming,' said a hoarse female voice.

It was a few minutes more before the woman inched the door open on the chain.

'Good afternoon, I'm here about Kendall Nathan's gallery, and I wondered if I could speak to . . . your son, would it be? Eric? Mr Lee Judd?'

'He's my son,' came the asthmatic reply.

'Is he home?' Decker enquired.

'No, he ain't here.'

'I just want to ask him a few questions. I'm from the insurance company, and as Mr Lee Judd was employed by Mrs Nathan . . .'

'She got burned real bad,' Mrs Lee Judd said, but made no effort to open the door. 'My boy's real cut up about it. He got no job now. That's what he's doing, looking for work.'

'Could I just speak to you?'

'You *are* speakin' to me. I ain't opening this door for nobody, I don't know nothin'.'

Decker gave up in frustration and headed back towards his car. He was about to unlock it when he looked back at the house. The curtains moved on one of the downstairs windows. The figure behind them was that of a young man. Decker hurried back towards the door and pounded on it. 'Mr Lee Judd, I know you're in there, I just saw you at the window. Please, I'm not the police, this is just an insurance enquiry. Can you just open the door for a few minutes? Hello?'

There was no sound at all now, not even the television. Decker waited, then whipped round as he heard the sounds of running feet in the next-door yard. The young man had run out the back of the house, leaped over the fence and headed into the street.

Decker started to run after him, then returned to his car. The man had set off at high speed along the sidewalk, but he kept him in sight. Decker backed out into the road and followed him: his bright red windcheater and sneakers made him easy to spot, and although he was moving fast, he didn't duck into any of the driveways but headed for Adams Boulevard.

Decker still had Lee Judd in his sights as he stopped at traffic-lights. He saw the boy cross the main drag and turn into an alley about twenty yards up ahead on the left, between a dance rehearsal studio, exhibiting all the thinly cheerful signs of an attempt at urban renewal, and a boarded-up building, which still bore the ominous smoke stains of the riots. As soon as the lights changed, he pulled over and indicated left, turned into the alley and slowed down. It ran along the back of the other stores that fronted the boulevard – a liquor store, an exotic-looking hair-and-beauty salon and a Mexican music outlet. Piles of garbage overflowed from huge battered plastic bins, and a number of abandoned-looking vehicles and a couple of narrow passages led to any number of places for the youth to hide. Decker slowed to walking pace, but he knew he had lost him.

The alley ran straight through to a side street off Adams, so Decker had to drive on through. He was swinging out of the alley, preparing to head back the way he had come, when out of the corner of his eye he saw Lee Judd again. He was walking now, shoulders hunched and head bent low, keeping close to the façade of run-down shops. Decker had to drive on: the traffic was so heavy that there was no way he could stop quickly.

He was just dialling the office to see if Lorraine was there when he noticed a green pick-up truck career out of a side street, and slot into the traffic close behind him as he turned onto La Brea. He accelerated, but the pick-up came even closer, almost hitting his bumper. He accelerated again, tossing the phone onto the passenger seat. He was about to put his foot down when the pick-up rammed him so hard that his car spun through a hundred and eighty degrees, almost into the path of an oncoming vehicle. The driver screamed and blasted the horn as Decker righted the car and now hit the gas pedal hard. His heart was thumping. These guys behind were trying to run him off the road, and his mind raced as he tried to remember when the next set of traffic lights came up. He checked that his door was locked, and overtook a car in front, but the truck did the same, its cabin so high above its customized, extended wheel-base that Decker couldn't get a clear look at the driver. All he knew for certain was that this was for real, and he started to sweat with fear, wondering whether he should take a side turning. He decided against it, hoping he would have more opportunity to outrun the truck when they had passed under the Santa Monica freeway. He hoped and prayed that there were no signals ahead, because he would be forced to jump the lights or stop.

The truck edged out to his right, and Decker was sweating freely. His hands clutched the wheel and his back arched with fear, then terror, as the truck swiped his car from the side. He screeched over to the kerb but managed to turn out of the tail spin. Now, his accelerator pressed flat to the floor, he screamed forward, burning rubber, the needle of the speedometer moving higher and higher. He was nudging eighty, with the truck still close on his tail. Suddenly up ahead were the traffic lights on Washington, at yellow turning to red. There was no way Decker could pull up in time. He gritted his teeth, accelerated harder, and crossed the traffic lights at eighty-five miles per hour.

The garbage truck had only just moved out from the left-turn lane at the intersection as Decker's car shot the lights. It was impossible to avoid collision. Decker's car left the ground and somersaulted in the air before landing on its crushed bonnet in the centre of the junction. The pick-up truck did a U-turn, and disappeared as the garbage collectors ran to Decker's crushed, smouldering car. Blood smothered the windscreen, but they could see Decker's lifeless body still strapped into his safety belt, hanging upside down as glossy art brochures tumbled around it.

Jake's condominium was in a quiet street near Pico, within ten minutes' drive of the police department, a late seventies Cape-Cod-style construction with a lot of shingled-wood facings, gables and white-painted wood on the exterior. It was simple, neat and orderly inside. A small kitchen led off the dining room, which in turn led off an equally compact lounge. There was one bedroom with bathroom en suite, and the entire apartment was carpeted in a drab grey, with featureless furnishing and bland landscape prints on the walls.

'It's rented,' he said apologetically.

'I should hope so. It's – well, a bit characterless,' Lorraine said.

'Yeah, I guess it is, but I never intended staying here. At least not permanently.'

Tiger sniffed around the room, and lay down on a white rug in front of a fireplace containing a gas fire burning round fake logs.

Burton went into the kitchen: he'd already bought the groceries, which were still in their bags on the kitchen table. 'You watch TV, or whatever, and I'll cook.' Jake began to unpack the food and set out the things he would need, and Lorraine noticed a number of small deli items – exotic mushrooms, purple basil and an hors d'oeuvre of ready-cooked stone crab, which Jake had clearly picked up to impress her.

'You want me to set the table or anything?' Lorraine asked.

'Nope, I'll do it. It's just crab, steak and salad,' he said, opening one cupboard after the next as he searched for plates and bowls.

Lorraine opened her briefcase and called the office on her mobile to replay her messages, but there were none. She called her apartment next, but there were no messages there either. She looked at her watch. After eight o'clock. She took out her notebook and looked for Decker's home number, only to find she hadn't brought it with her. 'It's odd he hasn't checked in,' Lorraine said, crossing to the kitchen. Oil was burning in a pan, and a bluish pall of smoke spiralled to the air-conditioner.

'Oil's a bit hot,' she remarked, and Jake whipped round to take the pan off. He had assembled the salad and was now rubbing garlic over the steaks.

'He usually calls in, or leaves a message for me at home.' Lorraine picked up a carrot and munched it.

'Who you talking about?' Jake asked.

'Decker – he's been out all day, checking art galleries.' Lorraine reached for another carrot, as the steaks sizzled and spat in the pan. 'I don't have his home number with me, or I'd call.'

'Is he in the directory?' He pointed with a fork to a side table. Lorraine walked over to it. Then she frowned – she couldn't remember Decker's boyfriend's name, so she looked up Decker. She knew the phone wouldn't be in his name and shut the book. 'I'll do it later when I get home.'

Jake carried out glasses, wine and a corkscrew, and set them down on the table with a clatter. He opened the wine, filled a glass and drank, then dived back into the kitchen. A few moments later he reappeared. 'I got some of that alcohol-free lager for you. It's on the side table.'

He leaped back into the kitchen, and she could hear him cursing. Then there was a hissing sound as he immersed the burning pan in water.

'Do you want me to make a dressing?' Lorraine asked, carrying the bottle of lager into the kitchen.

'No, I'm almost ready. I made it earlier.' He was pouring a sachet of raspberry vinegar dressing over the salad.

'I need a bottle opener,' she said, crossing to one of the drawers. Burton passed her, carrying the platter of crab, the steaks on their plates and balancing the bowl of salad on his arm.

'Okay, it's ready.'

Lorraine brought the bottle-opener to the table and sat in the place Burton indicated. Tiger lifted his head, sniffed and inched over to sit beside her, knowing he might be in line for a titbit.

Decker was dead on arrival at the emergency room of Midway Hospital. Adam Elliot, his boyfriend, was contacted at nine thirty-five, and drove straight to the hospital, unable to take in that Decker was dead.

By the time he was led to the chapel area to identify the body, he was in a state of such distress that he had to be assisted into an ante-room. Decker, who rarely exceeded the speed limit, Decker who always nagged him about wearing his safety belt and warned him never to take risks, who said that life wasn't worth an extra twenty miles an hour, had been killed outright travelling at eighty-five miles an hour in a built-up area of downtown Los Angeles. It didn't make sense. Nothing made sense. The loss of his beloved partner was more than he could comprehend.

Lorraine sat watching a movie, her feet resting on Jake's knees and Tiger at their feet. Jake had consumed his bottle of wine, and Tiger the charred steaks, though at least the crab and the salad had been delicious.

'I got another job today,' Lorraine said. 'It's sort of connected to the Nathan case.'

'How come?' He stroked her legs.

'Well, apparently Nathan sold original paintings, then switched them when they were hung.' She explained the complex scam she believed Nathan had pulled, and that his attorney, her new client, had been one of its victims.

'How much were they worth?' Jake asked, draining his glass.

'That depends. I'm still trying to get to the bottom of it all, but Feinstein's down maybe two million.'

'And do you think this fake stuff had something to do with Nathan's murder?'

'I don't know. To be honest, all I do know is that somebody, somewhere, has a cache of art work worth a mint – or else the mint. Maybe that was the motive for killing him, but with Cindy and Kendall both dead, it'll be hard to find out. Another odd thing is that there was a survivorship clause in the will, some tax-saving scam, Feinstein says, which meant that both Cindy and Kendall had to survive Nathan by sixty days before the gifts to them took effect. Since neither of them made it, everything, or whatever is left of Nathan's estate minus the art, goes to his first wife, Sonja Nathan. The house will be the main asset, as any cash Nathan got from the fraud he had stashed in secret accounts.'

'How will you go about tracing hidden bank accounts?' Jake asked, and Lorraine grinned and pushed him. 'No, I'm serious,' he said. 'How do you do that? If different names have been used, how do you trace them to Nathan?'

'Well, you start with his papers,' Lorraine said, tilting her head to one side. 'Nobody ever has anything *that* well hidden – there's always some kind of documentation somewhere. Then you look into travel, abroad or otherwise, and start checking – you know, do you know this man, et cetera. It's a long, slow process.'

'So it'll be a nice cash cow for you?' he said.

She nodded. 'It'll also mean a lot of painstaking enquiries.' Lorraine's face clouded as she thought about Decker. 'Maybe I should call home, see if he's left a message.'

Burton poured the dregs of the wine bottle into his glass and studied it for a moment. 'Have you ever thought about . . .' He stopped, and sipped the wine.

Lorraine had the phone in her hand. 'Thought about what?'

'Well, I know you have two daughters.'

She replaced the phone. 'Yes, Julia and Sally.'

He leaned against the back of the sofa, looking at her. 'You want any more kids?'

'What?'

He turned away. 'I'd like a family. I just wondered if you . . .'

'With you?'

'No, with Burt Lancaster. Who the hell do you think?'

She crossed to him and slipped her arms around his shoulders. 'You're serious about us getting married?'

'Okay, I have to admit that when I said it, I kinda had heart failure. I'd not even thought about it and it must have sounded crazy. But I've had time to think and maybe why I did say it was because I was feeling like a kid on acid! That was the way you made me feel. Now I'm calmer, I've had time to think and I wouldn't change that moment for the world. I know it's what I want, so, if you want me to ask you again, I will. You want me to ask you again?' He took her hand and drew her down to sit beside him, and she nestled into his arms, curling her legs onto the sofa.

'It's all moving so fast. Don't get me wrong – I like it this way, but . . .' She closed her eyes, and he rested his chin against her head. 'First we have to find a nice place, move in, get settled, but . . .'

'You okay?' Jake whispered.

Lorraine couldn't stop the tears from streaming down her face.

'I'm sorry if what I said upset you but we do need to talk about our future.'

She couldn't speak. The tears kept on coming, and every time she tried to say something she felt as if her throat was being squeezed.

'Maybe I've moved things on too fast. It's just that, now I've found you, I don't want to waste any time. But you can tell me to put the breaks on. All you've got to do is tell me, but we have to talk, Lorraine.'

She broke away, wiping her cheek with the back of her hand, and her words came out in spluttering gasps as her chest heaved. 'I want to talk to you too, I want—' She started to sob, and he made no effort to stop her, as if he knew she had to let her feelings out before she could calm down. She gasped for breath, determined to get it out, to tell him that she wanted his child more than anything else in the world. The thought of carrying Jake's baby made her heart swell. She would be a part of him, have a future with him and be protected by him. Knowing for sure that he really loved her, that what had seemed too good to be true was not fantasy but reality, made the terrible darkness she lived with roll away. She felt as if a burden had been lifted from her soul, and that she was forgiven, cleansed. 'I want your child . . . I never want to lose you, I love you.'

They embraced, broke away from each other, laughed, kissed and kissed again. For the first time in years, she was truly happy, and it was a blissful state, a feeling she had believed she would never be allowed to know or enjoy. Leaning back against him, curled beside him, she whispered, 'I am so happy . . .'

Lorraine left at seven, having stayed the night with Burton, and as she walked Tiger in the early morning, the smile never left her lips. She went home, fed the dog, showered and changed for the office. Just as she was leaving she noticed the light on her answerphone blinking. She pressed the button, but could hardly make out what the caller was saying. He was sobbing. She knew, though, that something terrible had happened. As the message continued, and it became clear what it was, she had to sit down.

Lorraine drove to Decker's home in Ashcroft Avenue as though on automatic pilot. The neat bungalow was in a row of equally well-kept small houses, and was painted a smart navy blue with the windows, doors and eaves picked out in white. Lorraine parked on San Vincente, fed the meter, and walked, in a mechanical, non-aware state, up the hand-laid brick steps to the house. The door opened. 'Come in.' Adam Elliot was wearing a terrycloth robe, and his face was ashen, his eyes red from weeping. Lorraine said nothing as he led her down the hallway, every inch of wall space filled with paintings, prints, photographs and pieces of tribal and primitive art, which, she guessed, had been picked up on travels abroad. She could feel the woven coir matting beneath her shoes, and noticed that it was strangely dark. All the blinds and shutters in the house were drawn.

The kitchen was a blaze of colour, or would have been in normal light, as tangerine paint had been added in a vibrant drag effect over yellow walls. Well-tended ferns of all sizes and shapes and a little lemon tree were displayed in polished copper planters, which Lorraine recognized with a pang as the same as the one Decker had bought for the office. She sat at a table and Elliot poured her coffee. Her hand shook as she lifted the china cup to her lips. He sat opposite, lighting a cigarette, then looked at the stub. 'I gave up two years ago but I've smoked two packs since last night.'

The coffee tasted bitter, but stirred Lorraine into life.

'How did it happen?'

There was a long pause, then Elliot explained what had happened. 'I'm so sorry,' she said quietly.

There was another terrible pause. Elliot made no effort to check the tears that ran down the dark stubble on his face. 'I loved him so much.' The words were barely audible. 'I just don't see how I can go on without him.'

Lorraine stayed for almost an hour with Decker's lover, saying little, but listening to him and looking at the photo albums he showed her of how they had met and their life together. She remained calm, saying what she hoped were the right things, but Adam wasn't really listening – he just needed to talk. He said the same things over and over again. Eventually he gave her three plastic carrier bags of things he had taken from the car, including Decker's notebook and the catalogues of paintings.

She sat in her car, still in a state of shock, then drove to her office. Everything seemed unnaturally clear and bright – the doorman, the bell-boy, the décor in the lobby, the elevator. It was as if she was seeing everything for the first time, as if she had never been there before. She placed the plastic bags Adam had given her on

Decker's desk and walked into her own office, shut the door and hung up her jacket.

It was deathly quiet, and there was no smell of fresh coffee. Lorraine bowed her head.

'Oh, Deck, I'm going to miss you so much.'

The coroner determined that death had been accidental, a conclusion consistent with the medical evidence. The speedometer of Decker's car had remained stuck at the speed he had been doing – eighty-five miles per hour. The body was cremated at Forest Lawn, and the ashes placed in a niche after a short ceremony attended by many of Decker's relatives and friends. Lorraine stood at the back of the crowd, not knowing anyone, and she, too, wept.

On the way home she bought herself a bunch of exuberant red gladioli to remember Decker, and sat with Tiger, finding him a comfort. She knew the dog would miss Decker too – the walks, and the special dinners concocted from leftovers that Decker had brought to the office. It never even occurred to Lorraine that Decker's death might have been connected to her or to the line of enquiry he was working on when he died.

In the early afternoon, Jake called to ask about the funeral, and to check that Lorraine was all right. They arranged to meet after eight as he had a lot of work to catch up on. She took Tiger for a walk, but it was still only four thirty when she returned. She tidied the sitting room and arranged her flowers but time seemed to stand still. She turned on the TV but was restless and couldn't concentrate. She began to think over the Feinstein case. She started a list of relevant facts – the art fraud, the secret bank accounts, then wrote 'Sonja Nathan', and underlined the name.

Sonja Nathan was now the main beneficiary under Harry Nathan's will: should Lorraine still make the trip to see her?

Without her notes and files, Lorraine tried to recall all the intricacies of the case. No one else had been charged with Nathan's murder and the police investigation was closed. What if someone had engineered everything so things would end up that way? Could Raymond Vallance have been that clever? How could he have planned to get access to the large sums of money Feinstein was sure Nathan had to have stashed somewhere? She wrote down his name on the list. Before she could make any real progress on suspects, though, she had to trace Nathan's missing haul. Then she could work backwards.

The entryphone buzzer made her heart pound, but Tiger barked furiously, then wagged his tail. It was Jake, and just seeing him put the investigation into the background.

'Hi, I'm sorry. I'm later than I said. There's been a double homicide over at Burbank.' He looked tired, and Lorraine took his jacket from him, told him to sit on the sofa and put his feet up. 'This bastard broke into an apartment, held the woman hostage, demanded details of the safe and their cash cards, then beat the hell out of her when she said she couldn't remember. Then her husband came home with their daughter, and he shot them both at point blank range.' He scratched his head, and gave a helpless gesture. 'Kid was only fifteen years old. I mean, how the hell do you live with that, seeing it? And there was nothing in the safe, just papers – her husband never kept any valuables at the house.' He sighed and leaned back on the cushions. 'Sorry to lay it on you, but . . . it hasn't been a good day.'

'That's okay. You want me to get some wine? I can run down to the liquor store. Or maybe some whisky. What do you feel like?'

He reached out for her, and drew her close. 'I feel like lying next to my woman.'

She kissed him, and told him to take a shower, then get into bed. He looked at her, and traced her face with his hand. 'I'd like that . . .'

By the time she joined him in the bedroom he was fast asleep. He was naked, vulnerable, hadn't even pulled the duvet over himself, and she loved him. The fact that he had come to her, in a way needing her, touched her deeply.

'I love you,' she whispered.

Lorraine couldn't stop thinking about Decker. She had lain awake beside Jake for a while, then slipped from the bed to return to her notes, only getting to bed after midnight. Tiger was already flat out nose to nose with Jake, and he grunted when she got into bed. Jake stirred and lifted his arm for her to snuggle close, and then went back to sleep.

She had begun to work out the next stage of the Feinstein inquiry. She would need someone to take care of Tiger for a night, as she had decided that the next day she would fly to New York, get the Jitney bus to East Hampton, and stay overnight, as Decker had suggested, at the Maidstone Arms. She would then arrange to talk to Sonja Nathan, and could be back in LA the following afternoon. There was something else she wanted to talk about with Jake, and she was going to do it first thing in the morning before she left. She was going to tell him that when this Feinstein case was finished, so was Page Investigations. Not that he had asked her to contemplate giving up her business – it was something *she* wanted. It might look like a fast U-turn on her part – one moment striving to make the agency work, the next letting go of it – but she knew she was getting her priorities right. More than anything else, she wanted to marry Jake, and to have his child. She felt that a new phase of her life had begun.

The alarm clock rang shrilly, and Jake shot up, while Tiger hurled himself off the bed, barking. Lorraine felt as if a heavy weight was pressing her head onto the pillow.

'What time is it?' she groaned.

'Seven, and I'll have to get going.' He was already stepping into the shower.

Lorraine pulled on a robe and went into the kitchen. She had a terrible headache, the kind that hung just behind the eyes, so she took two aspirin and felt them lodge firmly in her gut; now she had indigestion too, and Tiger's constant barking at the clattering of neighbours made her head worse.

She squeezed some fresh orange juice, and brought out muesli and cereal. Jake was shaved, dressed and ready to leave. He drank only the juice, saying he'd send someone out for a sandwich. He kept looking at his watch, checking his pockets for car keys and wallet, and then bent down to kiss her. 'I'll call you.'

She hurried after him. 'Is there any way you could take care of Tiger, just for today and tomorrow?'

'What?'

'I need someone to look after him, I've got to go to New York.'

He stopped at the front door, sighed and looked at his watch. 'Will you be back this evening? I can come by later and walk him and feed him.'

'Well, I'd planned on staying over.'

'Why didn't you mention this last night?'

'You were flat out. Look, forget it, I'll find someone else. No problem.'

'You sure?'

'Yes, I'm sure. Go on – you don't want to be late.'

He stared at her, then looked away with a sigh. 'No, I don't, and I can't take him to the station with me, can I? Look, I'll call you. What time will you be leaving?'

'That depends. I might not go until later. I haven't arranged my flight or anything.'

'Who are you going to see?'

'Mrs Nathan,' she said, pouring coffee and turning to him with the cup in her hand. 'There's one left, the first wife.'

He looked at his watch again and Lorraine could see him hesitate before he crossed to her. 'I love you, and I'm sorry about not taking Tiger off your hands. Next time, huh?'

'Yep, next time. Talk to you later.'

Lorraine had showered, changed and washed her hair, but her head still throbbed, and the aspirin refused to be dislodged from her gullet. When she got to the office she took some antacid and gulped down some water.

She had considered the Hispanic family in the apartment below hers – and rejected it – as a temporary home for Tiger, and she felt depressed. She had so few friends, and without Rosie and Bill Rooney around, there had only been Decker left. She started thinking that maybe there was no reason to rush off to the Hamptons – Sonja Nathan might not even be there. But when Lorraine called, someone with rather a nice deep voice said he would ask Mrs Nathan to return her call. Soon afterwards her phone rang and Sonja Nathan was on the line.

Lorraine explained that she would like to meet Sonja to discuss a few things in connection with her former husband's estate.

'Are you with the insurance companies?' Sonja asked.

Lorraine told her that she was working for Feinstein and Sonja suggested, without asking any more questions, that Lorraine had better come to the Hamptons right away as she was planning to go to Europe. 'I can be with you Thursday morning,' Lorraine said, in two days' time.

'Fine, I'll see you then, about ten o'clock. You have the address?'

'Yes, I look forward to seeing you.'

Lorraine arranged a flight for noon the next day, booked into the hotel, and was just about to sort through all the art catalogues that Decker's boyfriend had left when Tiger barked. Lorraine walked out into the reception area.

'It's me,' said a high-pitched voice.

'Tiger, sit. Who?'

'It's Rosie, for Chrissakes. Who the hell do you think it is?'

286

Lorraine ran to the door, shrieking, 'Rosie, *Rosie,* ROSIE!'

Rosie was plumper, but tanned and sporting a new hairstyle. The frizzy curls had been 'straightened', and the colour had also been toned down and was no longer quite such a vivid red. For a moment neither could speak, they were so pleased to see each other. Lorraine had missed her one true friend, and burst into tears. Rosie already had tears streaming down her cheeks. They had climbed together out of a dark past and now Rosie had found the love she craved, found a future. She wished all that she had for Lorraine too; then her happiness would be complete.

'You look fabulous,' Lorraine said, holding her friend at arm's length. She sniffed back the tears and wiped her cheeks with the palm of her hand. 'I dunno why I'm crying.'

Rosie kissed her again. She had an array of gifts for Lorraine in carrier bags and boxes that she had dropped as soon as the door had opened.

'Any chance of some coffee? I'm dying for a cup,' Rosie said, collecting her things and stacking them on the coffee table, before she went over to a rather bemused Tiger. He sat as she rubbed his big head. He didn't like many people to fondle him but as Lorraine joined in he accepted it.

'He's changed so much, Rosie. I don't know what I'd do without him now.' Lorraine nuzzled him and he rolled over legs in the air as she scratched his belly.

'My God, he's enormous,' Rosie said. 'He looks like a different dog altogether!' Tiger's coat looked glossy and clean and as he grunted with satisfaction, he looked as if he was smiling. 'Nick'd be happy to see him like this,' she said softly.

'Yeah, Nick would be proud of him – well, most of the time.' She gave Tiger a last tickle and stood up.

'So, this is the workplace huh?' Rosie said.

Lorraine opened her arms wide. 'This is Page Investigations, Rosie.'

They went on a tour of the office. Rosie said all the right things, then watched as Lorraine opened her presents like a child – scarves, beads and hair-bands, a watch and bracelet, souvenir tea towels, baseball caps and cut glass.

Then the two women decided to have lunch together at a small local bistro, where Rosie, as usual, ate ravenously, ordering a supposedly healthy sauté of zucchini and mushrooms dripping with olive oil. Lorraine had a small portion of fettuccini. She was regaled with stories about the trip and there were six wallets of photographs, showing the honeymooners arm in arm and hand in hand in all the various countries they had visited.

Rosie insisted she see the new apartment next, so they collected Tiger, closed the office and piled into Lorraine's jeep. Rosie was impressed with it and even more so when she heard about the Mercedes. 'Well, it's your money and you could always get run over by a car tomorrow, so live for today,' but she sounded worried, or maybe a little envious.

After the tour of the apartment, where Rosie enthused about every curtain, every piece of furniture, they settled back to more gossip. Rosie's happiness shone in her face, and through the affectionate, funny stories she kept telling about big Bill. It made Lorraine reach over and clasp her hand. 'I'm so glad it's worked out for you two, you seem so well suited.'

Rosie folded her hands over her tummy. 'Now, you've heard all my news – you start now.'

'I'm going to get married.'

Rosie's jaw dropped and then the tears started. She hugged Lorraine and wanted to call Bill and tell him, but Lorraine said she wanted to tell him herself. He might even know her new boyfriend, Lieutenant Jake Burton. Rosie's jaw dropped still further. 'A cop?'

'A chief of detectives, Rosie!'

'Jesus. That is incredible!'

Lorraine smiled. 'Yes, it is. I guess I'm happy too. But I'm also scared to death – that it might all blow up in my face. So, please don't say anything to Bill, not yet, and . . . you mind if we change the subject?'

'Sure,' Rosie said, aching to know every single detail. But Lorraine had that set expression on her face so she asked instead what her friend was working on. She listened as Lorraine, trying not to sound too emotional, told her first about Decker. Then she moved on to her case. 'It's the Harry Nathan murder. I was hired by his wife, Cindy, but she committed suicide.' Lorraine explained briefly how Cindy had contacted her, then lit a cigarette, inhaled deeply and her mood changed. Rosie could feel her tension but she said nothing, just waited, like in the old days. She had learned never to push for information from Lorraine – she'd tell you what she wanted you to know and nothing more.

Lorraine took another deep drag of the cigarette, letting the smoke drift from her mouth. 'You ever heard of a movie star called Raymond Vallance?'

'Yeah, you know me and movies. He used to be fantastic-looking. Is he involved in your investigation?'

They both jumped when the entryphone buzzed and it took Lorraine a while to drag Tiger away from the front door. Standing on the step was a sheepish Bill Rooney, holding a faded bunch of flowers.

'Hi, how you doing, eh?' he said, and squeezed Lorraine so hard against his expansive chest that she gasped for breath.

Lorraine gave him a tour of the apartment while Rosie made a fresh pot of coffee. Rooney nodded and congratulated Lorraine on her taste but she knew he must have had a few drinks because he muttered to himself as he followed her from room to room, telling her that now he liked putting his feet up and watching football on the TV and the best part was Rosie bringing him his dinner on a tray. 'I've done enough travelling, for a while,' he said, and then nudged Lorraine like a naughty schoolboy. 'Don't repeat that. God knows where she's planning on going next, but me, I've gone soft. TV, football, a home-cooked meal and fast asleep by eleven. Lovely!'

Lorraine found it sad that he seemed to need to repeat himself. He had got even fatter and his bulk made the wide four-seater sofa in the lounge seem small. He seemed ill at ease, knowing that Rosie was annoyed with him for intruding on her evening.

Rosie had the coffee ready and waiting now. She'd even found some biscuits and laid them out on a silver plate – solid silver, she had noticed. As she poured the coffee, there was a strange, uneasy silence that continued until Rosie banged down the coffee pot and nudged Rooney. 'Before you barged in and interrupted us, Lorraine was just telling me about this case she's working on. Do you remember a movie star called Raymond Vallance?'

'No,' Rooney said, selecting a biscuit.

'Tell him, Lorraine,' Rosie said, settling back on the sofa beside her husband. The pair sat riveted as Lorraine filled them in on the case. She was concise but made sure she left nothing out – except the threats on her life. She didn't want to worry her friends. When the silence fell again, it was like old times. Rooney was leaning back, eyes closed, but not sleeping even though it was way past eleven. He was 'thinking', and so was Rosie, twisting a strand of hair round and round in her fingers.

'Well, you got all the facts, almost.' Lorraine looked at Rooney, wanting him to give her the answer she couldn't put her finger on. His eyes opened, but he shook his head, pulled himself onto his feet and stuffed his hands into his pockets.

Rosie broke the silence. 'I think it's Vallance. He, out of everyone, had the most to lose, am I right? Do you think it's him, Bill?' Rosie was excited, her cheeks flushed: from what Lorraine had told them, everything pointed to the actor.

Rooney still said nothing. Lorraine was fascinated because he had suddenly become his old self: Rooney the cop. He was acting the way he used to, not wanting to give away too much, not wanting to make a mistake by jumping the gun, staring at the wall, not meeting Lorraine's eyes. Finally, his hands digging deeper into his pockets, the loose change jangling as he turned a coin in his fingers, he said, 'I think there's a hidden agenda. Christ only knows what it is, but there's something. It may even be staring you in the face, sweetheart.'

'Is that it?' Rosie blurted out.

Rooney's eyes now met Lorraine's, a steady rather unnerving gaze. He touched her hand. 'I'll call you, all right? Let me sleep on this.' Then he caught Rosie's hand. 'We should go, darlin', it's late.' There was a firmness in his voice and Rosie didn't argue. They said their goodbyes, waving from the car, blowing kisses to Lorraine by the open window, watching them drive away. She didn't wave, she just stood, arms folded.

Rosie took a sidelong look at her husband. She had been about to tell him about the new man in Lorraine's life when he swerved to the side of the road and pulled on the handbrake like his life depended on it.

'What happened? I didn't see anything,' Rosie said, looking back to the road.

'I just needed to think,' he said in a gruff voice that made him sound like a stranger. He had known Lorraine for a long, long time. He knew her heartbreak and had witnessed her pain. He had been disgusted by her spiral into the gutter and would never have believed she would climb back, just as he would have laughed if someone had said he would end up not only working alongside her, but admiring and loving her.

'I know her, Rosie, God help me for saying this, but I have known her when she was not worth the shit on my shoe. I have seen her humiliated and heartbroken. She's been beaten within an inch of her life and I've picked her up out of stinking, garbage-strewn gutters.'

'Is all this going someplace?' Rosie asked, staring out of the car window rather than looking at her husband. He was unapproachable, made her feel uneasy, and she almost cringed back from him when he hit the steering wheel with the flat of his hand, hit it so hard the car rocked.

'Yes, it's fucking going somewhere, for Chrissakes. I just needed to work it through, to think about it, because she was fucking hiding something. She wasn't telling us the truth.'

'Why would she lie?' Rosie said, easing round to look at him.

'I know her so well, Rosie.' He ran his finger round his collar: he was sweating.

'Yeah, you said, and so do I. We both know her pretty well, I'd say.' She rolled down the window, feeling hot herself.

'Rosie, I have never seen fear in that woman's face, no matter what she has been through, not once, not ever. I saw it tonight. She tried to hide it but I know she's in trouble and I'm afraid for her.'

CHAPTER 13

NEXT MORNING, Lorraine leaped back into action: her flight was at noon, and Rosie's visit had taken up virtually all of the previous day. Jake had called and said that as he happened to be off duty, he would like to see her and drive her to the airport, and that today he could take Tiger for her.

Lorraine had packed an overnight bag, changed and tidied the apartment, and was now becoming impatient, afraid she would miss her plane. He was late, only arriving at ten thirty. In the car, she gave him instructions about Tiger, plus Rosie and Bill's telephone number in case the dog was in the way, or she had to stay longer in the Hamptons than she expected. 'You think you might?' he asked, as they hurried through the terminal building.

'No, but you never know, just covering all the options,' Lorraine said. It had crossed her mind that the legacy to Sonja Nathan would not take effect until midnight the following night, and she wondered whether the next forty-eight hours might be more eventful than she was anticipating – but there was no point in worrying him. She handed over her ticket to a stewardess, who said that the flight was already boarding and she should go straight to the gate.

Jake kissed her, and Tiger almost choked himself on his lead as he tried to follow her into the departure lounge. Lorraine walked away, but then had an urge to turn back, so strong she couldn't resist it. Jake was still standing there, and Tiger still straining at his lead. Jake waved, mouthed that he loved her, and their eyes locked. She wanted to run back to him, stay with him, but she forced a smile and hurried out of sight.

The duration of the flight was only five hours, but with the time difference between the west coast and the east, they wouldn't arrive until almost eight thirty in the evening. Lorraine had been in such a hurry she hadn't brought any books or magazines, so she read the in-flight journal over dinner, and slept for the rest of the flight. After the plane had landed and she had retrieved her bag, she caught a taxi to Queens and waited for the last Jitney bus to the Hamptons.

It was right on time at nine fifty, and the driver smiled pleasantly as he stowed her bag in the hold, then helped her up the steps into the cool, air-conditioned interior. She chose one of the wide, comfortable seats midway up the aisle, next to the tinted windows – this was no ordinary bus, and the occupants were not ordinary people, either arty or glamorous: one woman even climbed on board with two Pekinese and a chauffeur.

Lorraine looked out of the window for a while, but then closed her eyes, not sleeping, just wrapped in daydreams about Jake, still hardly able to believe it was all true. He did love her – she had seen it at the airport. In some way if he had turned and walked away before she had said her last goodbye, it would have been a bad omen, but he had waited, and the last thing she remembered was his smile, and that he had said he loved her.

Rosie was grimly washing a mass of arugula in the little farm-style kitchen of the apartment Rooney had shared with his first wife, putting together a big salad. She and Bill had both half-heartedly decided to diet.

'I hate this job,' Rooney moaned, emptying the dishwasher.

'So does everybody,' Rosie answered.

'Anyway,' he said, clattering the plates into the glass-fronted dresser, 'Jim Sharkey couldn't believe his ears. He kept on saying I had to have it wrong, it couldn't be Burton. Are you sure you got the name right?'

'How many Lieutenant Jake Burtons are there, for Chrissakes?' Rosie said, tossing the salad.

'They don't like him,' Rooney said, stacking more dishes.

'You mean Jim Sharkey doesn't,' Rosie said.

'No, Jim said the boys don't like him, said he's a real bastard. Everyone knows there's a bit of a trade that goes on with information – you know, a backhander here and there. Everybody knows that. We even dish dough out of our own pockets to some informers. I've done it, we've all done it, but he's watching them like a hawk.'

Rosie started to set the table. 'Well, that Jim Sharkey certainly had his hand out when we worked with him, didn't he? You remember, when we needed the lists of statements taken in connection with the Anna-Louise Caley murder. And he got a four-course dinner, beer, wine, and five hundred dollars on top of it.'

Rooney took the plastic cutlery basket out of the machine and banged the knives and forks into the dresser drawer. 'All I said was they think he's a tight ass.'

'You shouldn't have been asking questions, I never told you to do that. I said find out what he looks like. That's not the same as rapping with Jim Sharkey, is it?'

Rooney slammed the cupboard door shut, replaced the basket and closed the dishwasher.

'So, what does he look like?' she asked, hands on hips.

'I dunno. I never saw him, did I?'

Rosie pushed past Rooney to the fridge.

'Young? Old? Good-looking? Short? Tall? What kind of cop were you?'

Rooney slapped her behind. 'He's about fifty-five, five feet seven with a paunch, red face and bulbous nose, but . . . a lot of women think he's sexy.'

Rosie laughed at his description of himself, kissed his plump cheek, and they settled to their meal.

The Jitney bus made its way through Southampton, then Bridgehampton, with few passengers getting off and none getting on. The street-lights were turned on, and the little towns looked like some magical place that time had passed by, with old-world shops selling antiques and pine furniture on every corner, along with street markets and traders offering logs for sale.

They eventually arrived at East Hampton, and the bus drew up outside the Palm Hotel. Lorraine waited as the driver fetched her bag, and pointed out the Maidstone Arms Hotel, which was just across the street.

By the time she had unpacked and taken a shower it

was after one o'clock in the morning, and even though she felt hungry, she decided to go straight to bed.

Next morning, breakfast was served in the dining room, and Lorraine, dressed in a smart tan skirt, cream silk blouse, oyster tights and court shoes with a low Cuban heel, came down and sat in one of the Queen Anne chairs. She ordered scrambled eggs, brown toast and coffee, which was served promptly by an attractive blonde girl, who also presented Lorraine with the *New York Times*. When she had finished, Lorraine took a brisk walk along the main street. The shops were all elegant, and what prices she could see were expensive. Sight-seeing over, she returned to the hotel and ordered a taxi to take her to Sonja Nathan's address in an area known as the Springs. The same pretty blonde girl who had served breakfast was now acting as a receptionist. She handed Lorraine a street map and said she would order the taxi straight away.

Lorraine returned to her room, and put in a call to Jake. He wasn't at home, but when she called his office, she was told that he hadn't got in yet, so she went downstairs to wait for her cab. She watched some of the rather elderly guests coming down for late breakfast, everyone apparently talking about the weather – it had, as Lorraine heard a number of people say, turned into a lovely clear day.

'Mrs Page,' the blonde girl called, 'your taxi is here.'

Lorraine went out of Reception and turned down a narrow path that led into the car park, expecting a yellow cab but finding a gleaming limo. 'Mrs Page?' the driver enquired, doffing his cap.

Lorraine nodded, and gave Sonja Nathan's address. 'Is it far?' she asked.

'No, ma'am, nothing's too far round here. Be there in ten minutes.' They drove on in silence for four or five. 'Turned out a real nice day,' the driver said, smiling at Lorraine via the driving mirror. 'You from New York?'

'California.'

He spent the rest of the drive listing which movie star had bought which local residence, and was very proud to have driven Barbara Streisand, Paul Simon and Faye Dunaway. Suddenly he screeched to a halt, peered at a narrow gateway, marked with only a red mailbox, checked the number, then reversed about two hundred yards, stopped again, reversed again and turned into a narrow dirt-track drive.

'This is it,' he said, now concentrating on his driving, as the track was narrow, overhung with high hedges and brambles. He made his way slowly past yellow notices nailed to the trees stating NO SHOOTING and TRESPASSERS WILL BE PROSECUTED. The tall fir trees became more dense, and now there were big red notices: DRIVE SLOW – DEER. The driveway began to curve to the right, and there was yet another notice: TURTLES CROSSING.

They were crawling along now and Lorraine was finding the drive, which, she calculated, was at least two miles long, spookier by the minute.

'Does all this land belong to Mrs Nathan?'

'I guess so, but it's protected round here. This is an animal sanctuary.' He swerved to avoid a lump of rock. Suddenly the wilderness began to appear more cultivated, and the drive widened into a tree-lined circle. Lorraine got out of the car to see a huge outdoor swimming pool, surrounded by a fence built of thick timber slabs, its margins ablaze with brilliantly coloured flowers.

The sun beat down, giving a clean dry heat, completely different from the fug of LA. She paid the driver, who asked if she would be needing him later. She said she would call.

The shingled, wood-frame house looked small, vulnerable and unoccupied, with both garage doors shut. Lorraine looked again at the garden and knew, by the flourishing, sweet-scented borders and beautiful conifers, that the garden was lovingly cared for. She tilted her head to the sun, her eyes still closed, then opened them rapidly as she thought she heard someone call. She listened, but hearing nothing more, she set off up the front steps, whose shallow treads were made of slabs of wood like stone.

The screen door was shut, as was the inner door. The bell did not work, so she tapped and waited, then knocked a little louder. The gravel crunched at the side of the house, and Lorraine turned sharply to see a tall, suntanned man with pepper and salt hair, who seemed almost as shocked to see Lorraine as she was to see him. 'I'm looking for Mrs Nathan,' she said.

'Ah! She's out in the studio. Wait a second, this'll rouse her. It's at the back of the house.' He disappeared, and Lorraine heard what sounded like a ship's bell being rung.

'She'll be right with you.'

Lorraine smiled.

'When she starts working, she's in a world of her own. We're meant to be going to a deer meeting in town tonight if I can drag her away.'

The main door of the house opened, and the tall

woman Lorraine had seen at the funeral appeared, raising one of her hands, deeply tanned with long, strong fingers and blunt-cut nails, to pull her strange white hair loose from a band which held it scraped back. She was less glamorously dressed today, in an old pair of chino pants and a deep blue linen shirt, but her intense, slightly cool presence was just as arresting.

'Mrs Page?'

'Yes, I'm sorry if I disturbed you. Were you working?'

'Oh, that's okay. I was just packing something,' Sonja Nathan said, with a taut smile.

Lorraine walked up the steps and extended her hand. 'It's very nice to meet you properly. Thank you for agreeing to see me and, by the way, it's Lorraine.'

'It's a pleasure,' the older woman said, with the same quick smile, no more than a social reflex. Her eyes, Lorraine saw at close quarters, were grey-green and her gaze had a curious quality of restless abstraction, like a sea, Lorraine thought, a cold northern sea. She noticed, too, that Sonja Nathan did not invite her to call her by her first name, though perhaps that was down to pre-occupation rather than hauteur.

'Do come in,' Sonja Nathan said, standing back to usher Lorraine into the house.

As she walked inside Lorraine gasped: nothing could have prepared her for the view. The house had floor-to-ceiling windows on all four sides, like complete walls of glass, and outside, drawing her in like a glorious living painting, was a vista of the most breathtaking seascape. 'A woman from LA came here a few days ago. She called it awesome. Tiresome word, but it does describe it.'

Sonja led Lorraine down a flight of stairs and into a spacious kitchen with a wood and brick fireplace. The view seemed less spectacular from here than it did from upstairs, but still drew attention.

'Now, what would you like to drink?' Sonja said, opening the fridge.

'Anything cool, really – water, juice, Coke.'

Sonja produced a can of Coke, a tall glass and ice from the dispenser. She poured some coffee from a percolator for herself, not seeming to notice that it looked cold, tarry and unappetizing.

'You're working for Mr Feinstein, did you say?' Sonja said, moving towards the doors. 'Let's sit outside.' Lorraine followed her out onto the veranda. 'I must say, I never much cared for Feinstein,' she continued.

'Well, I imagine he'll be becoming something of a fixture in your life for the next few months at least – the estate is complex, he says.'

Sonja Nathan immediately detected Lorraine's attempt to work the conversation round to her having inherited all her ex-husband's property, and clearly was not disposed to play ball. 'So it is. What exactly did Feinstein tell you to ask me?'

'Oh, he didn't send me here, exactly. He's retained me to investigate an art fraud, which it seems Harry and Kendall were pulling.' Sonja Nathan did not react, but the restless movements of her green eyes stopped, and her gaze became opaque. 'It seems they sold genuine canvases then delivered fakes. Feinstein got stung – as did a lot of other people who haven't tumbled to it yet.'

'That is an extraordinarily audacious piece of dishonesty,' Sonja said. 'They might be found out at any time if the owner had the painting valued or sold it again, or if someone who could tell wheat from chaff just happened to come to the house.'

'I was wondering, Mrs Nathan, whether you might have fallen into that category,' Lorraine said. 'Did you go to Harry Nathan's house recently? I don't suppose you noticed anything about the paintings at any time? If I were to give you a list of the paintings, would you tell me if you ever recall seeing them at the house?'

Lorraine went back inside to find her briefcase, which she had left in the hallway. She took a quick look around the room as she picked it up: there were a number of large canvases, some carvings, wonderful pottery and antique tables. Nothing matched, but as an ensemble they worked well.

When she returned to Sonja she gave her the list, which Sonja glanced at and handed back. 'I never went there,' she said evenly. 'I haven't set foot in the house since I left LA seven years ago.'

'Do you ever go back to LA?' Lorraine asked.

'Oh, yes,' Sonja said lightly. 'I still have friends there. And the city, of course, was important to me at one time.' She got up, looking out over the woods and water.

'I've seen pictures of the work you did there – it's very powerful,' Lorraine said. 'Have you been back recently except for Harry's funeral?'

Sonja looked her straight in the eye. 'I haven't been there other than then for a year, and I wasn't in LA the day Harry was killed, if that's what you mean.' There was a moment's pause, and Lorraine felt that it was almost as if the other woman were defying her to prove anything different.

'Feinstein is concerned only to make good his own losses, but it affects you too, of course,' Lorraine went on, resisting the other woman's efforts to close the subject. 'I mean financially. Harry Nathan apparently pulled the same scam twice. He had the originals in the house, then switched them again, we think to cut out Kendall. The original art at the house was Nathan's major asset. If we can't recover it, the value of the estate, which I believe now comes to you, is greatly reduced.'

Sonja shrugged, pushing back with her arms to propel herself off the rails of the verandah. 'I never expected to inherit a penny of Harry's and I couldn't care less if I don't.'

'Sonja.' A deep voice spoke suddenly from inside the kitchen, and Lorraine thought she detected in it a note of warning. The man she had met earlier came out to them; he had clearly heard every word of what Sonja had just said.

'I'm going to take the kayak out for an hour,' he went on. 'I'll be back in time for lunch.'

'Fine,' Sonja said, glancing at him only briefly. 'You be careful now, Arthur dear.'

Lorraine watched the couple with interest as Arthur spoke again, apparently casually. 'You too, sweetheart.' She did not meet his eye. 'Goodbye, Mrs Page. I imagine you may be gone by the time I get back.' He spoke courteously, but both Lorraine and Sonja understood his message. Lorraine was conscious of a certain relaxation in the other woman once they heard him leave the house.

'Does Arthur . . . have a problem with Harry's having left you so much money?' Lorraine asked, with bold naturalness, assuming an intimacy with Sonja she knew didn't exist. She was surprised when Sonja answered equally directly.

'He has a problem with Harry. It's just jealousy, I guess, that I shared so much of my life with Harry, that we were something to one another that Arthur and I cannot be. It's just the way life is. One can't go back. Can I get you another drink?'

Sonja had picked up the empty glass before Lorraine had time to say anything and disappeared into the kitchen with her own untouched coffee: it was clear she wanted an excuse to absent herself for a few moments. Lorraine would have liked a closer look at the rest of the house, while Sonja clattered with the ice-dispenser in the kitchen, but it was the studio she most wanted to see, and now that she had mentioned the art fraud, she could hardly ask to see it without as good as announcing to Sonja that she suspected her. But did she suspect her? The woman didn't seem interested enough in money to commit such a crime – but, on the other hand, there was something about her that made one feel that death was near her.

However, by the time she came back with a tray, Sonja had readjusted her manner.

'How well did you know Raymond Vallance?' Lorraine ventured.

Sonja snorted with laughter as she handed Lorraine another tall glass of Coke. 'Raymond Vallance was an albatross round Harry's neck.' For all her amusement, there was venom in her voice. 'He destroyed any talent Harry might have had, convincing him that all those disgusting frat-party movies he made were worth a good goddamn. Any merit there was in that whole period of Harry's career he drew from me. That's where my own creativity went – he sucked it out of me and put it into his own work.'

'I'm sure,' Lorraine agreed. Vallance and Sonja were

305

like a pair of bookends, she thought, perfectly matched in their unshakeable belief that the other had been Nathan's evil genius and they themselves the true muse.

'Raymond never forgave Harry for marrying me, needing me more than he needed him,' Sonja went on, well into her stride now in ripping the ageing matinée idol apart. 'He hated both of us, in a way, though he tried to get me into bed, of course. I thought, talk about obvious, darling, if you can't be with the one you love, love the one *he*'s with.'

Lorraine smiled: Sonja was no slouch in the bitching department. She said, 'He had something similar going with Cindy, it seems.'

'Doesn't surprise me,' Sonja said. 'Poor kid – I never met her except at the funeral, though, of course, I saw pictures.'

'I don't suppose she ever wrote to you,' Lorraine asked casually.

Sonja looked at her with interest. 'Yes, she did – pages and pages. I knew why she wrote – she was embarrassed about calling, never thought she was entitled to five minutes of anybody's time. Sometimes I wish I'd given her a little more . . . I don't know, time, assistance.' There was real sadness and self-blame in Sonja's voice.

'You never felt jealous of Cindy?' Lorraine asked gently.

'Not really,' Sonja said. 'Harry wasn't the same person I had known by the time he married her. Vallance and . . . and Kendall had carved him up between them by the time Cindy got him. He was no longer a man . . . but, then, Kendall was never a person at all.'

'What do you mean?' Lorraine had now dropped all pretence of confining her questions to the art fraud: she was trying to find out who murdered Harry Nathan, and wondered whether the killer might be sitting right in front of her.

'Kendall was similar to Harry in a way. There was something central missing from both of them,' Sonja said, with some deliberation. Lorraine had the impression she was delivering verdicts she had considered for years. 'Kendall, however, was full of insecurity, or she was to start with, whereas I don't think Harry ever had a self-critical thought in his life. Kendall came into our lives when our relationship was hitting a transition. Harry had been eating me to keep himself alive and fuel his work for years. Perhaps if we had had children it would have been different, but . . . I let him do it. I suppose it took me quite a while to grow up.' Sonja gave another wry smile. 'Then I wanted to live my own life and create for myself, and Harry would have had to find some reason to be with me other than what . . . he could consume of me. Obviously that was difficult for him. Harry never liked to do anything that was difficult.'

Sonja had got up again, part of her seeming barely conscious of Lorraine, though another part of her, Lorraine somehow knew, had been waiting for years for an anonymous listener – a confessor. 'I don't really think Kendall set out to destroy our marriage. She loved me first, if you like. She had nothing, was nothing, knew how to be nothing when I met her.' She was staring out to sea, as though hypnotized, her gaze drawn to the horizon like a compass needle to the north. A moment later, though, her voice seemed more normal as she went on. 'As I said earlier, to try to repeat the past is a sort of death.'

'But Harry must have loved you, even at the end,'

Lorraine said, conscious that she was perhaps pushing the other woman into deep water. 'You were the constant in his life.'

Sonja shook her head. 'Vallance was the constant. I realize that now. He was there before me and he was there after me.'

'But Harry left Vallance nothing in the will. He must have wanted to recognize something in leaving the entire property to you.'

'It comes to me only by default,' Sonja said. 'Neither he nor I could ever have predicted that both Kendall and Cindy would drop dead.' She turned round. 'And, of course, who knows? I might drop dead. I have another day to go, don't I?' There was a strange, hunted look in the back of her cat's eyes that chilled Lorraine, as if she were waiting for an executioner to arrive, for an axe to fall.

Lorraine realized that she had been sitting very still, barely blinking. She made herself move now, swirling the ice in her glass as though to chase away ghosts with the sound. 'I think that's correct – but you're most unlikely to die.'

'Well,' Sonja said, and again Lorraine had the sense that she was listening to the expression of thoughts that had been considered and rearranged many times, 'there is life and life. Or, rather, there is life and there is existence without dignity, which one betrays oneself to endure. I used to think that there was some kind of other dignity in endurance, but it is better to be dead than betrayed, I think now.' She had been talking rapidly and fell silent just as suddenly, then turned back to the sea again.

'Who do you think killed Harry Nathan?' Lorraine found herself asking, without really meaning to do so, as though it were the only chance she would ever have.

'Harry Nathan killed himself,' Sonja said, her voice low, resonant, beautiful. 'He became a thing that someone would destroy.'

The screen door banged at the front of the house, and Sonja started and looked round. 'Arthur,' she said, with a smile. 'He doesn't trust me alone for too long.'

No wonder, Lorraine thought, glancing at her watch. He hadn't been gone long and Sonja was already circling round the subjects of killing and death.

Sonja walked back into the kitchen and called upstairs, 'We're down here, Arthur.'

Did she want to warn him that she wasn't alone? Lorraine wondered.

The big man lost no time in joining them and Lorraine saw his eyes go immediately to Sonja, as though trying to gauge her mood. 'Mrs Page, how nice you're still here,' he said, with a polite smile. 'I hope you don't mind if I join you.'

'Not at all,' she said. He sat down beside her and Sonja disappeared inside, murmuring that she would bring out some wine. 'Do you work out here?' she asked, pretending to be making small-talk but, in fact, trying to place the man, as he well knew.

'Yes,' he said. 'I do, on and off.'

'Are you a writer?' She knew she sounded pushy now but she didn't care: it was the only way she could do her job.

'No,' he said slowly. 'I'm a painter.'

Well, that was interesting, Lorraine thought.

309

'I don't suppose I'm allowed to see any of your work,' she said, with a fake, girlish laugh she suspected didn't fool him for a minute.

'I'm sorry, I've just packed virtually all of what I have out here for a show,' he said evenly, as Sonja came back with glasses and a bottle. What a surprise, Lorraine thought, but decided to have one last try at getting into the studio.

'I'd love to see any of your work before I go, Mrs Nathan,' she said, 'Though, of course, I know all artists are very private.'

'I'm afraid even I wasn't allowed to see the last thing Sonja did,' Arthur said. 'She kept me right out of the studio for a month. Fortunately I have another room at the top of the house.'

'Do you work mainly to commissions, or speculatively?' Lorraine asked Sonja.

'I rarely work to commission – or, at least, not to an exact commission,' Sonja answered, carefully opening the bottle. 'This last piece is to open a series of shows – a women's thing, in the new gallery in Berlin. They indicated a few months ago that they would appreciate it if I had something new, but it was up to me what it was.'

'And what will you do next?' Lorraine said, conscious that she sounded like some vapid celebrity interviewer. 'Do you have any plans, or will you just wait and see what comes?'

'I have stopped working,' Sonja said, in an odd, unnatural tone. 'That part of my life is over.' Suddenly she gave a light, sweet laugh. 'It went on far too long.'

'I'll drive you back into town, Mrs Page,' Arthur said quickly. 'I think you said you had to go.'

'Arthur!' Sonja said, now laughing as though she

hadn't a care in the world. 'That's not very hospitable –
I've just opened the wine.'

'No, I really must be getting back – and, in any case,
I'm sorry, I don't drink,' Lorraine said, getting up.
'Thank you so much for your time – and it's been
wonderful to meet you.'

'Goodbye,' Sonja said simply, with a slow, almost
childlike smile.

Arthur led Lorraine out to an old Blazer jeep, and
began to make determined small-talk as they drove the
few miles into town.

'Will you be returning to New York tomorrow or
staying over?' he said, as they pulled into the Maidstone
Arms car park.

'I haven't decided,' Lorraine said. 'I may stay another
night.'

'It's just that if you were thinking of seeing Sonja
again, we do have to pack to go to Europe and Sonja
needs to prepare for Berlin – she's expected to make a
speech and she needs to concentrate on that.' It was
more than apparent that he was trying to deter Lorraine
from making any further visits.

'She's a very unusual woman,' Lorraine said, unable
to resist the temptation to fish just a little.

'She certainly is,' Arthur said carefully, pulling up.
'I'm sorry if I seemed rude, hustling you away, Mrs Page,
but the truth is, Sonja is not quite . . . herself at the
moment. You know that she and Harry parted on bad
terms, and she pretends that his death didn't touch her –
but, of course, that's not true. She has been very shaken.
She cared deeply about him, and, God knows, sometimes
I think he was the only man she ever loved.'

Lorraine was surprised at this personal and clearly

311

heartfelt revelation. She realized that Arthur did not dislike her, he was merely trying to protect Sonja.

'For that reason she is blocked in her work and she imagines she will never work again. As her work is everything to Sonja, she is in a low state of mind at the moment. So, please, if I can ask you a favour, she needs to avoid strain. Going over all this stuff about Harry is just about the most painful thing there is for her. If you've asked her everything you need to know I'd be grateful if you'd just leave her be.'

'I don't think there's anything else,' Lorraine said, preparing to get out of the jeep. 'Goodbye – it's been nice meeting you.' She smiled and waved as she watched him drive out, wondering what exactly he and Sonja Nathan had to hide.

Sonja was still sitting at the table when he returned. 'I'm tired. I think I'll go and lie down for a while.'

He looked at her, saying nothing, though he hated the hours Sonja spent locked alone in her room. Then he reached over and touched her face lovingly. 'If you should see Mrs Page again, don't talk too much.'

'I won't,' she said, tilting her head like a little girl making a promise, suddenly seeming young, vulnerable.

'I love you,' he said softly, and she smiled. He adored the way she smiled, and it always made his heart lift, even though he knew that though she was with him and was caring and loving towards him, he was not her true love. Arthur envied Harry Nathan even though he was dead, envied that he had shared Sonja's youth, that the mere mention of his name made Sonja's face fill with darkness and grief.

'You know, I think I'm too tired to go to the deer meeting tonight,' she said. 'I don't really feel like going into town.' Arthur's heart sank: sometimes Sonja would not leave the house for weeks, withdrawing into her private shadowlands in a way that frightened and excluded him. He had been counting on the deer, a cause she cared about, to get her into town: social interactions with neighbours would do her good. 'You go, though,' she said, with a smile, already moving towards the stairs. 'One of us should.'

Arthur knew, too, what that meant: she wanted to be alone, and if he didn't leave the house she would go and range about alone outside, or take the car and drive. She was gone increasingly often, sometimes disappearing for a couple of days at a time.

'Sonja,' he called after her, 'did you say you'd finished packing your thing for Berlin? If you have I'll call the freight company – the paintings are ready to go.'

'Yes,' she said, with a smile. 'Take it.'

She disappeared from sight and he heard the door of her bedroom close.

She stood at her windows, which overlooked the bay, where she watched the sun rise each morning. Another bedroom had windows that captured the sunsets and the moon's rising: to see the beginning and end of the day made each day special, each one different. She tried to convince herself that that ought to be enough for her – just to enjoy the beauty of the seasons, to drift along with the current of time instead of trying to hold it back.

Certainly she had no intention of taking any more steps to reverse the physical signs of ageing, and booking into the clinic had been an act of folly induced by Harry's leaving her for Kendall. She had fought the impulse to recapture physical youth for some time but finally she had chosen a surgeon and clinic with care, had known exactly what she needed doing. She had wanted a complete face-lift but with a small implant in her chin, and her nose lifted.

The clinic had been discreet, but Sonja was confident anyway that no one knew she was there because, under heavy bandages and dark glasses, she had been unrecognizable. However, the name of one patient had stuck in her memory. She had discovered that the woman was a private investigator and although she never spoke to her, she had heard a good deal of a conversation the woman had had with someone else. When she had come across the advert in *Variety* for Page Investigations, she had been amused by the coincidence.

She reached for the silver-backed mirror to check her profile. She was fifty-two years old and should be content to spend her time surrounded by this beautiful calm. She should be glad that the compulsion to work fifteen or sixteen hours a day was now gone, that the long torment was over. Odd that she had never realized she would miss it so much. She would go down to the studio later in the day and see if perhaps she couldn't do something about that.

CHAPTER 14

LORRAINE WALKED back into the hotel, cold despite the warm sunlight, after the encounter with Sonja Nathan. She had been chilled by the woman and her obsession with the past. If it was a kind of death to be unable to move on from one stage of life to another then Sonja Nathan herself was dying by inches.

The woman had seemed on the verge of confessing to Harry Nathan's murder, but it was obvious, as Arthur had said, that she was also on the verge of a clinical mental illness, her talk moving in and out of reality and symbolic meanings. It was clear Sonja had hated Nathan, had seen herself as a moral guardian, saving him from his own worst self – embodied in Raymond Vallance – and that after he had left her she had considered him to be on an inexorable slide into the pit. Whether she had taken the pitchfork and pushed him in was another matter.

What about the paintings scam? Arthur was a painter, but that didn't mean anything – half the population of the Hamptons claimed to be artists of one sort or another. Sonja had seemed to have so genuine an aversion to Harry Nathan that somehow Lorraine could not see her coolly masterminding a fraud with him.

The dark world of poisonous emotion, betrayal and killing, the wrecks of lives, the semblances and fragments of people left drifting afterwards hung around Lorraine like a foul smell, and she was glad to sit in the conservatory and remind herself that there was a world elsewhere. Suddenly she could not wait to be out of the Hamptons, back home among people who loved and cared about her, with Jake and Tiger in her own apartment, and out of this whole dirty business for good. Rosie and Rooney had got it right, she thought, take the money, get out and get a life, and she had an overwhelming impulse to call Jake and say she was coming home. She would tell Feinstein his paintings were untraceable: neither work nor money was going to run her life.

Lorraine was walking across the lobby towards the stairs when she heard a voice she recognized at once, a professionally trained and pitched voice. 'My companion finds the room inadequate and we would like to move to a suite,' he was saying.

It was Raymond Vallance, looking old and eccentric in a crumpled, not entirely clean white suit, black polo-neck sweater and black Chelsea boots. He caught sight of her at once. 'Why, I see some of my friends from LA are here already – good to see you, Lorraine,' he called across the lobby, and began to advance on her. 'How're things at Fox?' The manager sidled smartly away, murmuring that he would see what he could do.

'I wouldn't know,' Lorraine said stonily. 'Why don't you call and ask?'

'Sorry about that, Lorraine.' His intrusive use of her first name irritated her and he had been drinking. He seemed madder, closer to the edge. 'Fucking bell-boys. No idea of service.'

'No, none,' Lorraine agreed, her mind racing and her previous suspicions about Sonja tumbling down like a house of cards. Vallance's presence here was virtually an admission of guilt, she thought. It could not be a coincidence that he had suddenly showed up in the Hamptons, of all places, on the last night that Sonja Nathan had to remain alive to inherit Harry Nathan's estate. Lorraine was certain that he was warped enough to want to prevent Sonja from receiving it. He had been, as Sonja had said, the constant in Harry Nathan's life, the one who had loved him most. Harry Nathan had been his life. He, Lorraine was now certain, had been Harry Nathan's death, and the death of the two women who had displaced him in Nathan's life. He had nothing more to live for – but, of course, there was one woman left . . .

'What brings you out here?' Vallance went on. There was a note of malice under the smarm. 'Not that I can't guess.'

'Well, I'm sure you guessed right.' Somehow she didn't want to mention Sonja to him. 'Excuse me, I'm just about to check out.'

'Sonja still out in the Springs?' Vallance went on, ignoring her. 'Thought I might pay her a call.' He rambled on drunkenly.

He was about to descend into maudlin reminiscence, and Lorraine cut him short. 'Well, I happen to know Mrs Nathan isn't home this evening,' she said, wondering if Vallance was deliberately playing dumb in telling her he planned to see Sonja if, in fact, he intended to kill her. Or did he just want someone to know he was going to

317

be with Sonja? Could he imagine that she might harm him? 'She and the gentleman she lives with have an engagement here in town.' She turned on her heel before he could say another word and walked rapidly upstairs. So much for calling Jake and flying home: everyone had stood aside and watched Cindy die; she was going to call Sonja Nathan and tell her to call the cops if she saw Raymond Vallance.

The sense that the final act of the drama that had centred on Harry Nathan was about to be played out, and the acrid scent of danger, cut through her.

The phone rang endlessly but at last Lorraine heard Sonja's voice.

'Mrs Nathan, it's Lorraine Page,' she began, suddenly feeling silly.

'Hello, Mrs Page, did you forget something?' Sonja said. Her voice was normal, friendly.

'Well, no. I ran into Raymond Vallance here in the hotel. He said something about coming out to see you and I thought I'd let you know. He was pretty drunk . . .' Lorraine realized she was babbling and made an effort to speak more slowly. 'I just got the idea he was planning to bother you in some way.'

Sonja laughed. 'What more can he do to me? I'd say he's done his worst by now.'

'Mrs Nathan, I know this sounds foolish,' Lorraine persisted, 'but I really feel Raymond Vallance may have some idea of harming you. He seems to feel a personal grievance towards you.'

'Tell me something new,' Sonja said, but her voice was more serious now. 'He doesn't change. I'm bigger than Vallance – I always was, that was why Harry chose me. If Raymond wants to come round, he can.'

'Well, I just thought I'd let you know. It wouldn't hurt to have the number for the police next to the phone.'

'Don't worry, Mrs Page,' Sonja said, 'we have a gun in the house. Many thanks for your concern.' She rang off.

Well, Lorraine thought, she had done her best. If Sonja shot Vallance, good riddance – perhaps she'd get a call in the morning from another of Harry Nathan's wives facing a murder rap.

She could not face hearing the disappointment in Jake's voice when she told him that she had decided to stay another night, so called Rosie instead.

'Hi, darlin'.' Rosie's familiar voice, warm as a hug. 'Where are you?'

'Still in the Hamptons. I figured I might stay another night.'

'What for?' Rosie asked. 'Didn't you get to see Sonja Nathan?'

'There's something going on. Raymond Vallance just showed up out of nowhere.'

'Well,' Rosie sniffed, 'you must be the only woman who'd hang around to see Raymond Vallance these days. Bill's been looking in on the office and he says someone's been calling and calling and hanging up after the machine kicks in. I bet it's Jake – just wants to hear your voice.'

Lorraine felt a pang of conscience – but what difference could twenty-four hours make? She'd tell Jake as soon as she got back that she was winding up the office for good, that he would be her top priority from now on. 'I'll be back as soon as I can,' she said. 'And then I'm getting right out of this business. I'll be home baking cupcakes and we'll have coffee and watch the shopping channel every day.'

'Dream on!' Rosie said, and there was sadness under the laugh that she hardly understood, as though she knew she was listening to a vision that could never become real.

'I don't suppose you'd take Tiger for tonight, would you?' Lorraine asked.

'You mean would I call Jake and tell him you're not coming back today?' Rosie said, with a sigh. 'I guess so. I don't know why I do these things, Lorraine. It must be love.'

'Thanks, Rosie – I'll see you soon.'

Sonja Nathan stood at her windows, looking out over the bay. So Vallance was in town, she thought: So what? She had the gun and nothing frightened her now: she would not be frightened to rid the world of a piece of vermin, and if he killed her, he would only have outrun her own desires by a couple of hours. She felt tranquil now, as though all things were running steadily towards their appointed conclusion, feeling her own movements acquire the languorous grace of a clock that is steadily running down.

She saw the delivery van draw up outside, and a boy get out with a cardboard box in his arms. Arthur wouldn't hear him in the studio, so she set off downstairs to let him in. 'This is for you, Mrs Nathan,' he said, handing her the form to sign. She glanced at the column marked 'consignor', and saw the letters LAPD printed in it. The police department, she thought. Some clerical officer had telephoned her about evidence gathered in

320

connection with Harry's death, which was now being returned to the family. 'Thanks,' she said, handing the form back. 'Just put it here in the hall.'

'Mrs Nathan isn't home this evening.' The words she had spoken to Vallance echoed in Lorraine's head. The temptation to go back and see if she could get a look round the studio was irresistible.

She strolled out into the street, and walked into a suitably arty-looking café, where the poster for the deer protection meeting was prominently displayed: it was at seven. That left her with the afternoon on her hands, and she walked down to the bookstore. She had originally intended to pick up some light reading, but something prompted her to ask the owner if he had anything on modern sculpture, in particular Sonja Nathan's career.

'You mean Sonja Sorenson,' he said. 'She works under her maiden name.' He produced a book devoted to three contemporary sculptresses, offering a fairly full treatment of Sonja's work, which Lorraine bought. She walked back to the hotel, flicking through it. Sonja had had two major shows since *City of Angels*, after she and Nathan had split up. The first was called *In Perpetuity*, and was a group of immensely tall structures, part-pillar, part-woman, part-tree, a cycle of strange modern caryatids in a soft, bright, reddish wood. The positions of all the figures were almost identical, but the art of the piece was in some subtlety of their overall lines and expressions: somehow one knew that the earlier figures were struggling to break free from the wood, the later ones yearning to blend back into it. Only one central figure was at rest, her face so simultaneously blank of meaning yet flooded with peace that Lorraine could not take her eyes from her: this had been Sonja's most successful show: she had then produced nothing for some time. Her latest work was a similar group, entitled *The Fall* but this time of male figures, at least eighteen or twenty, the first ten or twelve almost unchanging, but the latter ones dwindling in size and displaying a rapid degeneration into coarse, priapic, ape-like creatures. The piece was cruder and darker than its two predecessors, and you did not have to look far to see the narrative of Sonja's marriage to Nathan: it was eloquent with pain and contempt and made Lorraine speculate about what Harry Nathan had been like to inspire such intensity of feeling in the people around him. She wondered too whether, looking at the two pieces together, she could trace Sonja's attempts to liberate herself from her past and her marriage. Could she have been so tormented by him that she would contemplate killing him? Lorraine found herself wondering what Sonja's latest work would reveal, and was now even more determined to go out to Sonja Nathan's house.

It was half past six when Lorraine walked down to Reception and decided that she would sit in a coffee shop with a view of the entrance to the town hall and make sure that both Sonja and Arthur went into the meeting before she set out for the Springs.

People began to file in after about a quarter to seven. A few minutes later she saw the Blazer pull up and Arthur get out – alone. Lorraine almost groaned aloud with frustration.

Just as he walked up to the doors of the hall, Lorraine saw a couple approach him – a tall, heavy, blowsy-looking blonde woman and Raymond Vallance. They stopped and exchanged a few words with Arthur, who seemed barely inclined to give them the time of day, then continued to walk towards the hotel.

Was it Lorraine's imagination, or had Vallance suddenly quickened his own and his companion's pace? Was he now rushing back to the hotel to dump his companion and get out to the Springs? Lorraine decided she wasn't taking any chances. She flagged down a passing cab.

Sonja Nathan's house was in darkness, but all the lights were on in the studio on the far side of the garden. Approaching the studio, Lorraine stepped out of the shafts of light streaming from the windows and walked up in shadow to look inside. There were various packing materials on the floor, and it was clear that whatever work Sonja Nathan had completed was now gone. The interior was almost bare except for a row of cupboards built along one wall and a long wooden table, at which Sonja sat, staring into space, a handgun lying in front of her.

Jesus, Lorraine thought, what was the woman doing? Waiting for Vallance seemed the most likely explanation, the man who had blighted her marriage and had, if Lorraine's suspicions were correct, killed the man she had loved. The minutes passed and Sonja did not move a muscle. Something in her unnatural rigidity made Lorraine suddenly certain that Sonja Nathan intended to kill herself.

She moved noiselessly along the wall, pressed her back against the wood next to the door frame and extended her arm to its full length to rap on the door.

'Mrs Nathan,' she called, 'it's Lorraine Page.'

There was no reply.

'Mrs Nathan?' she called again. 'Can I come in for just a moment?'

Silence.

'Can I speak to you please? It's important,' she tried again, and was rewarded with the sound of the woman getting up and coming to the door. Lorraine heard a bolt being drawn, then the handle turned slowly and the door opened.

'I'm working, Mrs Page,' Sonja Nathan said. She looked deathly.

'I'm sorry. I saw Arthur on his own in town and I wondered if you were all right,' she said. It was more or less the truth, and the frank expression of concern seemed to touch Sonja.

'That's kind of you,' she said. Her eyes were turned towards Lorraine, but seemed not to see her.

'Can I come in for a minute?' Lorraine asked again.

'All right,' Sonja said. 'Just for a minute. There really are things I have to do.'

She stepped back from the door and Lorraine followed her inside. She had not bothered to conceal the gun, which lay untouched on the table.

'You see,' she said, her manner lightening, as though some oppressive third presence had left the room as soon as Lorraine had walked into it, 'if Mr Vallance comes calling, he'll find us well prepared. I've already seen a good deal of him today, as it happens.'

Lorraine raised an eyebrow quizzically. 'Did he come out here?'

'No. I received a package today from the LAPD. Videotapes of Harry's. Have you seen them?'

Lorraine nodded.

'Well, Vallance got what was coming to him. He fed all that in Harry and got bitten himself. If he walks through that door I ought to just shoot him cold,' Sonja said casually, crossing to one of the long cupboards. 'He's a destroyer.' She took out a bottle of vodka and an antique stemmed glass. She poured herself a drink.

'What were you working on?' Lorraine asked.

'Oh, nothing. What I'm always working on,' Sonja said, knocking back half of the vodka.

Lorraine sensed that she had been about to say something else, but had stopped herself. 'Well, that can't be true,' she said. 'You've produced a well-regarded body of work, haven't you?'

'A well-regarded body of work,' Sonja repeated, almost mimicking Lorraine. 'Much fucking good it does me.' She drained the rest of the glass. 'People don't live on "regard". Or on the past.' She was silent for a moment, then began to speak again, her manner now almost academically impersonal. 'What's the point of the past, do you think?'

'I don't know,' Lorraine said, 'I often wonder.'

'Well, I can tell you,' Sonja went on, bitter again. 'It's to flavour the present. In some people's lives the memory of the past is constantly present, like a sweetness, but for others it's like a poison or a mould. No matter how far you think you've got away from something, it's still always there – in every word you speak, everything you are. Every piece of work you do.' She gestured around her at the empty room.

'Are you talking about Harry?'

'Of course,' Sonja said, pouring herself another drink. 'All I ever do is talk about Harry.' She paused again. 'I can't seem to stop. I loved him, you know. Perhaps I didn't realize how much.'

'Until he died?' Lorraine said gently.

'Until he died.' Sonja fell silent. 'Something in me died too.' She looked up at Lorraine, her strange eyes bright and still, and Lorraine felt again the presence of something behind them, as though death itself were looking out.

The atmosphere was unbearable, and Lorraine felt she had to talk, to make some connection with the other woman. 'That's how I started drinking. Someone I loved died.'

'Your husband?' Sonja asked.

'No,' Lorraine said. 'He was my partner at work. I used to be a cop.' She felt a strange intimacy with Sonja, so that it didn't matter what she said. Lorraine began to talk about her own life, remembering her police training and how she had been taught to talk people back from the edge, to make them feel connected. She found that she wanted to tell it all, wanted someone to understand. She could not stop herself, as though a dam had been breached. But then, mid-flow, her voice suddenly tailed off. 'God knows why I'm telling you all this.'

'I'm sure he does,' Sonja said, taking another slug of vodka with a smile. 'Why don't you just spit it all out? You tell me your ghost stories, and then I'll tell you mine.' Life seemed to flow back into her with the current of sympathy, and she swung her feet up on the table with a lop-sided smile. 'We've got a while.'

A while till when? Lorraine was sure that it was no coincidence that Sonja Nathan had been ready to blow her brains out the day before she would become the legal owner of all of Harry Nathan's property. Did she want to show she didn't care about money – or was it something she felt she had no right to accept? She smiled to see how Sonja's problems were distracting her from her own.

Lorraine could feel the past surging up inside her again, and she had to get up and walk around. Sonja said nothing, and it was because she didn't speak, either to encourage or discourage anything, that Lorraine's pent-up emotions were able to find release. 'Drinking became my life – I refused point-blank to believe I had a problem, but I was on a downward slope.'

Lorraine put her hands over her face and started to weep. Sonja sat motionless. 'I'm sorry, I don't know what's got into me.'

'Same thing that's got into me,' Sonja said simply, swinging her legs down. She walked over to Lorraine and touched her shoulder lightly. Lorraine knew that the touch had been something Sonja felt she ought to do rather than an instinctive response: she was not a caring woman. 'Except my drug is my work. Was my work. I won't do any more now.'

'I'm sure that's not true,' Lorraine said, wiping her eyes. 'All artists get blocked from time to time.'

'Art!' Sonja said. 'It's all just fucking pain and damage. Harry damaged me. I didn't know how much.'

Until he died, Lorraine mentally filled in.

'He made me like himself – dirty, commercial, tacky,' she went on, describing a mirror image of the process Vallance had attributed to her, and Lorraine wondered what she was talking about: no one could call her own austere and disturbing work commercial, but it was clear that Sonja's standards were not those of other people. 'He made me feel things, do things, I never wanted to feel or do, filled me up with bitterness and hate. I did my best to . . . exorcize them. But I didn't succeed. They possessed me, diminished me.' She was talking slowly and deliberately. 'They caused me to lose my work. Which he gave me too. Which is myself.'

What the hell did she mean? She was raving, everything she said was a riddle.

'But you said you were working here tonight?' Lorraine said.

'On myself,' Sonja said, and the peculiar resonance was back in her voice.

'With a gun?' Lorraine asked.

'Smoothest tool of all,' Sonja said, still not looking at Lorraine, and a smile spread across her face, as though she was looking at an unseen watcher. Then she turned. 'I'm sorry,' she said, 'I sound like Raymond Vallance. I think about death a lot. Liquor makes me maudlin. But you can stop babysitting now.' She poured herself more vodka and gave Lorraine a meaningful look. 'I'll never die drunk – in case people say I didn't have the guts to do it sober.'

'I used to think that,' Lorraine said, 'that I should have died. My husband left me too, you know.' She knew somehow that, despite what Sonja had just said, she had to keep talking.

'Did you get divorced?' Sonja asked.

'Yes, I did, and he got custody of the children. Rightly so – I wasn't capable of looking after myself, never mind the kids.' She lit a cigarette, no longer feeling like weeping, no longer feeling anything except the awful, cold guilt that she would carry to her grave.

'Everyone who loves has a right to be loved, Lorraine,' Sonja said. 'Whatever happened in your past can't change that.'

The sigh was long and deep, and Sonja noticed that Lorraine's hand was shaking as she flicked the ash from her cigarette. 'You want to bet?'

'Try me,' Sonja said softly.

'OK. I was on duty, a few months after my partner had died. I had been drinking heavily. We'd been called out to what they thought was going to be a drug bust to act as backup because they said the kids were tooled up. There were four kids and they split up and ran. One ran past my patrol car, so I got out, chased him and cornered him in an alley. I gave him three warnings to stop or I would shoot. He didn't stop, and I fired all six rounds. I couldn't stop squeezing the trigger, even when he went down.'

She let the smoke drift from her pursed lips, then turned to look at Sonja. 'He wasn't armed. It was a Walkman he had in his hand, and he had earphones in so he couldn't hear me. He was just a kid, and I killed him because I was drunk. If I'd been sober I would have fired a body shot.'

'That's hard to live with,' Sonja said quietly. She seemed to be watching Lorraine with particular intensity.

Lorraine stiffened as she heard a sound outside. 'Do you hear something?' she asked.

'Yes, I do,' Sonja said evenly as she picked up the gun

329

and cocked it. God, Lorraine thought, gooseflesh breaking out all over her body: she had meant what she had said about Vallance. Now they could both hear someone's footsteps right outside the door, which still stood an inch ajar. Sonja turned round slowly, noiselessly, until the gun was aimed chest high at the door panels. After a moment they heard a knock.

'Who is it?' Sonja said. Her voice was sweet and pure as a bell, as though a longed-for visitor had finally called, and Lorraine saw the beatific calm of the central figure of her wood of women appear on her face.

'It's me, Sonja,' a voice called. A man stepped into view. Arthur.

'Jesus,' he said in surprise, finding himself looking down the barrel of a gun. 'What the hell's going on here?'

'I'm sorry, Arthur,' Sonja said, lowering the gun. 'I'm afraid Mrs Page got me rattled. Apparently Raymond's been in town making threats.'

'Not to me he hasn't,' Arthur said. 'I saw him a couple of hours ago and he was sweetness and light. We're all old friends now.'

Lorraine saw him scan the room as he spoke, and although his voice did not alter, she knew that he knew exactly why Sonja was holding the gun.

'I thought you were lying down,' he said. 'I was worried about you.'

'You're so sweet,' she said, and Lorraine saw the flicker of pain in Arthur's eyes at the lack of interest in her voice. He loved her, Lorraine could see. 'I'll go and lie down now.' She walked out into the night.

'Can we offer you a nightcap, Mrs Page?' Arthur asked as they followed Sonja out of the building. 'I guess

330

Sonja's lucky you showed up, if Vallance is roaming around out there.' She knew what he meant: if she hadn't showed up Sonja would have been dead.

'No, no, thank you,' she said quietly. 'I'll just call a cab.'

They walked out into the darkness. Lorraine could feel the urgency with which Arthur moved to catch up Sonja, to try to take her hand, knowing that he felt the same instinct she herself had experienced earlier to try to hold on to the woman. But Sonja slid away, graceful and aloof, and walked on alone.

CHAPTER 15

WHEN LORRAINE woke next morning, she was surprised to see that it was already almost nine. She had lain awake for some time after she had got back to the hotel, half expecting some call from either Arthur or Sonja, but apparently nothing had happened. She dressed and called the airline to book herself a flight to LA. All they could offer her at such short notice was a seat on an early-evening departure, so she decided to spend the afternoon in New York. She packed the few things she had brought with her and set off downstairs.

'Good morning, Carina.' She smiled at the pretty blonde girl on the desk, whose name she now knew from the plate standing in front of her.

'Good morning, Mrs Page,' said the receptionist. 'The papers are here if you'd like one to take in with you.' Lorraine picked up a *New York Times* and scanned the headlines.

'There never seems to be anything but gloom and doom in the city, does there?' she said, putting the paper down. 'I think I'll just enjoy the peace here for another day.'

That surely should have elicited any news of either a

shooting or a suicide in the locality, Lorraine thought, but Carina simply smiled again. 'Good idea,' she said. 'Save your strength for LA.'

Lorraine walked into the room where breakfast was served, and found Raymond Vallance, sitting at a table with his large lady companion. He was now wearing a tweed suit and a battered pair of brogues, and was sitting ramrod straight in the dining chair, cracking the pages of his newspaper like whipcord, wearing an expression he clearly considered aloof and patrician. He seemed almost to have absorbed a new personality, aristocratic, European from the costume, or perhaps, Lorraine thought, this was his heterosexual persona.

She walked towards their table. 'Good morning, Mr Vallance,' she said brightly. 'How're things at Fox today?'

Vallance glared at her.

'Oh, Raymond,' his companion cried, 'is this one of your Hollywood friends?'

'Mrs Page and I have met in Los Angeles,' Vallance said curtly.

'We have a lot of friends in common,' Lorraine went on smoothly. 'I saw Sonja last night, for example.'

'Oh, really?' Vallance said. 'I must try to see her today.' He looked at Lorraine with eyes like stones.

'Who is that, pumpkin?' asked the lady innocently. 'I wish you'd introduce me to more of your friends.'

'The former wife of . . . a close friend,' Vallance said. 'It's a condolence call. I'm afraid it wouldn't be appropriate for you to attend.'

'Apparently Sonja gets the whole of the estate now,' Lorraine went on, observing Vallance closely. 'The consequence of the tax-saving clause, the lawyers tell me.

The other two wives died within a survivorship period and the gifts to them never took effect. It expired last night, it seems.'

'So I suppose you and Sonja had a little celebration?' Vallance said nastily. 'Burned one of those effigies of Harry she keeps turning out, perhaps? What'll she do for art now, poor dear?'

'Well, I wouldn't say we were celebrating,' Lorraine said circumspectly.

'I really must try to call on her later,' Vallance said. 'Take my last look before she kills herself or goes up in smoke. Harry's estate doesn't seem to bring his ex-wives much luck, does it? You'll be glad to get well clear of it, I'm sure.'

Was she imagining it, or was Vallance looking at her as if he expected her to take some other meaning from his words? A coded boast about the deaths of Cindy and Kendall? A threat to Sonja – or even to herself?

'I'm still working for Harry's lawyer, actually,' she said. 'So I'll be involved for a while.'

'Well,' Vallance said, 'see you around.' He raised his newspaper again and Lorraine realized she was dismissed.

She sat down at another table and ordered breakfast, wondering whether she should bother to call Sonja and say that Vallance was still hanging around, then decided not to – she was retained to investigate the art fraud, not as minder to Harry Nathan's ex-wife, and besides, Sonja had Arthur to do that for her. Poor Arthur.

Half an hour later she was ready to check out. There was no one at the desk, so she decided to walk to the bookstore again for something to read on the bus. She was barely out of the door when she heard a car engine revving. She looked across the street to see the Blazer being wrenched backwards and forwards as the driver tried inexpertly to manoeuvre it into a parking space. Eventually, Arthur opened the door and got out, leaving the vehicle parked at an angle: it was immediately apparent that he was drunk.

Lorraine hurried across the street. 'Arthur!' she called. 'Are you OK? Did something happen?'

Arthur looked at her, his face drawn with strain, but blurred and slackened with drink too. 'Well,' he said, making an effort to talk coherently, 'not really. Nothing new.'

'Is Sonja OK?'

'She's the same as she always is.' The man's bleakness made Lorraine decide she could spare half an hour to try to sober him up.

'Give me the keys and I'll move the jeep,' she said, 'and then why don't we get a cup of coffee in the hotel? I haven't checked out yet.'

'Sure,' Arthur agreed spiritlessly. Lorraine reparked the jeep and they crossed back to the Maidstone Arms. Vallance and his companion had gone, Lorraine noticed, as they walked into the dining room, though breakfast was still being served. She ordered a pot of black coffee and a quart bottle of mineral water.

'So,' she said, when the waiter had left them, 'what happened?'

'Oh, nothing, I guess,' Arthur said, with a grimace. He took a swallow of the coffee, and seemed undisposed to say any more.

'Come on, Arthur,' Lorraine said. 'Call me naïve, but I don't have you down for someone who gets pie-eyed by ten thirty a.m. as a matter of routine. What did you do, stay up all night?'

'Pretty much,' he said.

'Celebrating Sonja's inheritance?' Lorraine probed: she had a feeling that this would hit a sore spot.

'Christ!' Arthur swore at her. 'When the fuck is she going to be free of that man? She was in a bad enough state while he was still alive, but now that he's dead she's worse.' He took another mouthful of coffee, his hands shaking.

'Drink some water,' she said quietly. 'It's better for you than that stuff.' She poured a glass for him, but Arthur did not move. 'Arthur,' she said gently, 'I could see Sonja was pretty close to the edge last night. I know you care about her but it won't do her any good if you let her drag you over too.'

'Yeah,' he said. 'She would have gone over if you hadn't been there last night. I knew that stuff about waiting with a gun for Vallance was a lot of bullshit.'

'He didn't show up, then?' Lorraine asked.

'No. I don't think he has the balls to do much of anything, though he has an ugly mouth.' He picked up the glass of water and drank. 'I didn't know she had a gun in the house,' he went on. 'She wouldn't give it to me.' He caught Lorraine's eye, and she got the message that he regarded the situation as serious.

'Did you have a fight?' she asked.

'Kind of.' He gave a low, wry laugh. 'She started watching these weird videotapes the police in California sent out to her – horrible, kinky stuff with Nathan and a bunch of other people. She kept saying how disgusting they were, how low Harry'd sunk, but she was fascinated. That's what she's like with him. That's how I ended up drinking the best part of a bottle of Bourbon and taking off.'

'Heavy,' Lorraine said.

'Oh, just the usual late-night special,' Arthur said. 'I can't take a hell of a lot more of this. She's been all over the place since Nathan's death.'

Lorraine was intrigued. 'What the hell was it Nathan had, to have all these people carrying on about him for twenty years? I'm sorry, but I've been picking my way through every detail of this guy's life and I still feel like I don't have a handle on what he was really like.'

'That was the key to Harry,' Arthur said. 'He was plastic. He was a chameleon. He was beautiful, of course. He could turn every woman's head walking down the street when he was young.'

'You knew him and Sonja then?' Lorraine asked.

'Oh, yeah. I'm the fucking jerk who introduced them,' Arthur said. 'I met her first – she was painting then.'

'I didn't know Sonja painted,' Lorraine said, registering that piece of information with interest.

'Well, it wasn't her real talent, but she was taught like everyone else in art school and she was competent. She was living with some rich old guy, but it was clear she was bored. I had a few dates with her – never really got past first base. I knew she was looking for some kind of intensity, that she thought I was pretty fucking boring, and I suppose I introduced her to Nathan and Vallance to show her, you know, that I wasn't that straight because I had these wild, crazy friends.'

'How did you first meet Harry Nathan?' Lorraine asked.

'We were at college together. He got kicked out. It was the hippie days, and he was an acid freak. He was trying to get a career together as a director, didn't have a dime, and I never thought he and Sonja'd get together in a million years. Sonja was a real ice princess in those days, always living with someone with old masters on the walls, and Harry was so tacky – picking up girls in bars and living on tacos.'

'Must have been the attraction of opposites.'

'Yeah, bang, as soon as they met. A lot of it was just physical, I think, but the big deal about Harry was that he was a kind of blank space on which other people could write whatever they wanted – the stuff he made as a director was exactly like that too, reflections, if you see what I mean, rather than anything genuinely his own. Even Sonja admits that she kind of hypnotized herself with her own illusion of what he was like.'

'But you love her anyway?' Lorraine said.

'Yeah,' he said. 'I love her – I'd walk on hot coals for her.' He spoke quietly and directly, looking Lorraine straight in the face, and she knew that his anger had passed and that he was telling her the simple truth. 'I waited fifteen years to get her back from that asshole Nathan, and I knew he still had part of her, maybe the deepest part, but I can wait another fifteen years to get that back too. It'll end. I know it will.'

Though it certainly didn't show any sign of ending any time soon, Lorraine thought privately. Another raft of speculation floated into her mind. Could Arthur have killed Nathan? Either because Sonja had asked him to, or out of a belief that while he was alive, Sonja would never get over her obsession with him?

'Were you still in contact with Sonja and Nathan when he bought the gallery?' she asked.

'No,' Arthur said, 'I couldn't stand to see her with him – couldn't stand to see her being fooled by him.

And I was damned if I was going to hang around like the bad fairy, having lunch with Sonja once a month and hoping Nathan'd get hit by a truck. The way fucking Vallance did.'

'Do you still see Vallance?'

'Not if I can avoid it.'

Lorraine changed tack. 'Did Sonja mention to you what I came out here to investigate?' she asked.

'Not really. She just said you were tracing some assets belonging to the estate.'

'Well, I am, in a way,' said Lorraine. 'She seems very detached about it all – I mean, she gets the house, and anything I can trace will go to her too.'

'She'll never live in that place again,' Arthur said. 'I don't think she cares much about the money either – she has other assets of her own.'

'You probably know that Harry Nathan's major asset was supposed to be his art collection,' Lorraine said, and thought that a trace of tension entered Arthur's manner.

'Oh, really?' he said. 'I hadn't given it a lot of thought.'

'Well, it turns out that the major pieces in the collection were acquired by fraud. He and Kendall Nathan sold various paintings to people with no experience of the art market, then delivered fakes. Kendall thought all the real stuff was hanging in Nathan's house, but it seems that he pulled the same move again on her. All his own collection was fake too.'

'Serves her right,' Arthur said.

'Did you meet her?' Lorraine asked.

'Just once or twice,' Arthur said coolly. 'So, you're trying to trace the paintings?'

Lorraine nodded. 'That or the profits of the sale. Nathan used a lot of aliases, and he must have had secret bank accounts.'

'Well, they could be anywhere by now,' Arthur said. 'People buy hot art work and keep it in a cellar for thirty years.'

'But the money must be somewhere,' Lorraine persisted.

'Well, he was a film producer, wasn't he? Surely the quickest way to make a lot of money disappear in LA is to pour it into some godawful movie. Nathan's career was in trouble, wasn't it?'

'Maybe I'll ask Feinstein to go through the books at Maximedia again,' Lorraine said. 'Though I'm sure he'll already have done so pretty thoroughly.'

'Or, of course, Nathan could have had other production companies.' Arthur seemed to be pushing this hypothesis, and though it was plausible enough, Lorraine wondered whether he might be trying to lead her down a blind alley – away from his beloved Sonja – and she moved back into the terrain where her true suspicions lay.

'Sonja didn't keep in touch with Harry after they divorced?' she asked carefully. 'I mean, she told me she didn't, but I wondered whether maybe she continued to see him from time to time – maybe didn't want you to know. Did you ever suspect anything like that was going on?'

'No, I didn't,' Arthur said evenly, and Lorraine was reminded of the housekeeper, Juana, that an unshakeable loyalty stood between her and the truth. He had already said that Sonja periodically took off, that often he did not know where she was or where she had been. 'If you're looking to trace off-record contacts of Nathan's in the art world, I'd start with his brother,' he went on.

'I saw a guy with a ponytail at the funeral, looked like Nathan. Was that him?'

'Yes, there were only the two of them, Harry and Nick. The mother had a weird relationship with them both.'

'Is Nick a dealer?' Lorraine asked.

'No,' Arthur said. 'He's a painter.'

That was interesting. Lorraine had felt she was getting nowhere with the case, but this sounded like the missing puzzle piece she had been searching for. She could have kicked herself for not investigating Nathan's family earlier – it was extraordinary how often what you were looking for was right under your nose. 'Was he any good?' she asked.

Arthur looked out of the window. 'Not bad – erratic, spoiled, a hysteric. Nick was very like Harry, you know, always in search of himself, and it showed in a sporadic, slapdash quality in his work. He was reasonably talented, but he would get into deep depressions. He wanted fame and fortune, but then he would switch styles to accommodate a buyer. He had a number of faithful collectors, but a few thousand dollars here and there couldn't keep him and the woman he always had in tow – can't recall her name.'

'Do you know where I can find him?' she said.

'Nope – he took off with the woman to Santa Fe. I don't think he and Kendall got on – she was jealous of everyone close to Harry, you know, kind of eased them out one by one.'

341

'Who do *you* think killed Harry Nathan?' Lorraine asked. She figured it was worth asking everyone who had known him. It couldn't do any harm.

Arthur turned away. 'I should have.'

'But you didn't, did you?'

'No,' he said simply.

A waiter suddenly appeared to tell Lorraine that there was a call for her. She excused herself to go and take it, knowing that the thread of the conversation had now been broken, and that she had lost Arthur.

The call was from Feinstein. Lorraine told him curtly that she now had a lead on the forger and would be following it up.

When she returned to the dining room, Arthur was on his feet. 'I have to go,' he said. 'I must get back to her. Thanks – it was nice talking to you, and I hope you have a good trip back.'

Lorraine went up to her room to collect her bag, leaving her door slightly open. Outside she heard the voice of Raymond Vallance's ladyfriend, and listened carefully.

'Did you book a table?' She must be talking about lunch: it was after twelve o'clock now, Lorraine realized.

'Sure.' That was Vallance.

'You certainly took your goddamned time. I've been sitting up here in this hideous fucking place.' She seemed very much in charge – no wonder, since presumably she was picking up the bill. 'I wanna eat and then check out. I want to stay at the America Hotel in Sag Harbor. Book us in there.'

'This is one of the best hotels in East Hampton, for God's sake. I know the people here, and there's nothing

wrong with the room, but if that's what you want . . .'
Vallance sounded bored.

'Yes, it is, and as I'm paying, there won't be any
argument, will there? Now let's go down and eat.'

'Do you mind if I just freshen up?' Vallance snapped.

'Fine, I'll see you in the dining room.'

Lorraine inched towards her door as the door to the
next room banged shut and the large blonde woman
walked past. Lorraine hesitated: should she talk to Vallance about Nathan's brother? Then she heard his voice
again: he was clearly talking on the phone.

'Sonja? Don't hang up.' His voice was cajoling. 'Just
hear me out. I'd really like for us to meet, just for old
times' sake. I mean, Harry's dead now, and that hurts
both of us. I know he'd hate to think of us being this
way with one another.' His voice was syrupy, nauseating.
'Can't we just call it all quits now he's gone? I'd just like
to see you for a few minutes.' There was a pause, during
which Vallance presumably listened to Sonja's response.
'Sure, sure – let me give you my mobile number.' He
dictated a number, then a moment later, Lorraine heard
his voice rise in surprise. 'Sonja?' She had hung up.

Lorraine felt the familiar quickening of her pulse, an
impulse to shadow Vallance and go after him if he went
after Sonja, the old thrill of the chase. She knew, though,
that she would have to put it aside: it was not what she
was paid to do, and Sonja and Arthur would find any
further contact from her an intrusion. Besides, she would
have to start resisting the urge to seek, to follow, to
know, if she intended taking up a career as a cupcake
baker and maybe . . . Well, maybe something else.

She smiled, thinking of Jake, and the home and family

she hoped they would have together: her place was back in LA. But now she was still working for Feinstein, and she had every intention of winding up the case professionally. At least it looked like coming to an end – it seemed too much of a coincidence that Nathan's brother happened to be a starving artist who perhaps wouldn't be averse to making a little money on the wrong side of the law. Arthur had had no idea how to find him, but it was worthwhile asking Vallance what he knew.

After a few more minutes she heard his door open and stepped out of her room. 'Mr Vallance?' she called. 'I thought I heard your voice.'

He stared at her, locking his door. 'Well, well, Mrs Page.'

'Could I have ten minutes of your time, Mr Vallance?'

'No, it's not convenient. I'm meeting a producer for lunch.'

'Well, can't you call down and tell them you'll be there in ten minutes? It won't take any longer.'

He glared at her, his Cupid's-bow lips pursed into a thin line of anger. 'I don't think I like your attitude, Mrs Page. Just who the hell do you think you are? I don't have to talk to you, you're not with the police, and I know the case has been closed. You have no right to question me.' He started to walk away.

'Apparently Harry Nathan had millions salted away in a secret bank account, and his lawyer has retained me to try to trace it,' Lorraine called after him. 'If you could help me in any way, I am sure that he would come to some arrangement.'

That stopped Vallance in his tracks. Lorraine leaned against the door frame, watching him thinking about what she had just said. 'I can't see how I can help you.'

'Well, why don't we just sit down for a few minutes and see? You never know, Mr Vallance, there might be something, and if there is, Mr Feinstein will be generous.'

'Ten minutes,' he agreed.

Vallance followed Lorraine into her room and she shut the door behind them. He didn't sit down, but wandered around the room, clicking keys.

'Have you any idea where Harry Nathan's brother Nick is?' she asked.

'God, no. Last I heard he went to some hippie commune in Santa Fe.'

Lorraine tapped her notebook. 'How good a painter was he?'

'I have no idea. Sonja bought some of his work, I think.'

'Do you know anything else about him – or about the rest of the family?'

'Nick was totally unstable, and Harry behaved pretty bizarrely when he and Nick were together, screaming and giggling like ten-year-olds.' Once again, Lorraine heard an unmistakable note of jealousy. 'The mother doted on both of them, wanted them to stay little kids for ever, but the father was different – he couldn't come to terms with Nick. He was a striking man, the father . . .' Vallance paused, and laid a languid finger against his brow. 'But I was never that interested in Harry's family.'

'Just him,' Lorraine said softly, and Vallance turned, a glint in the famous wide-set eyes.

'He was the only one who was worth it.'

'I'm investigating a possible art fraud Harry and Kendall seem to have been pulling out of the gallery—'

'You mean Kendall was pulling,' Vallance cut in.

'Harry would never have thought up anything like that on his own, but she was as crooked as they come.'

'What do you know about the gallery?'

Vallance turned his mouth down and lifted his shoulders. 'I went once or twice, more, I suppose, to show my face for them when they had an exhibition. Artists need press like everyone else, and I'd bring in as many faces as I could, but I didn't have the finances to buy anything from them.'

Lorraine opened her notebook and began to read out the names of some well-known film stars, part of the list of people who had bought paintings she now knew to be fakes. She flicked a glance at Vallance as he nodded at name after name. 'So you introduced buyers too?'

'Yes.'

'Were you paid a commission for doing it?'

'Yes.'

'Do you know any of these other names?' Lorraine mentioned producers, bankers and other professionals who had been approached by Feinstein with the suggestion that they have their paintings revalued. Vallance nodded only occasionally, and she ticked each name he acknowledged, but his contacts had mostly been the show-business buyers.

'Do you know who Nathan's contacts would have been in the banking world, for example?'

'No, that was Kendall's department. She made sure she knew anyone who might have the cash to cough up for her art.'

'How about any contacts in Europe?'

He twisted his keys. 'She made it her business to know foreign buyers. She was a real nose to the grindstone, in the early days I think because she could see Harry more by making the gallery her life. But she was a hustler by nature.'

'Did he ever mention any banking facilities he used, either here or in Europe?'

'No.'

'But he did travel abroad a lot. Did you go with him?'

'No, but during the past year he went away a lot. Just a week here or there, though he'd never take Cindy. Maybe Kendall went – I've no idea. But you're not much of an investigator if you haven't checked his passport – surely that'll tell you where he was sliding off to.'

'It doesn't. As he used so many aliases to open the bank accounts we've traced so far, we can only presume he also had a number of passports in different names.'

'Well, that's quite possible. Harry had picked up a few unsavoury friends along the way – I kept my distance from them.'

'Can you think of anyone in the art world who might have been working with him in the last few months before he died? Not Kendall, someone else.'

'No, I can't.'

'Thank you very much,' Lorraine said.

It was a moment before Vallance realized that she was saying the ten minutes were up. His jaw slackened. 'Oh – was that of any use?'

'Maybe. If you could give me an address where I could contact you, I'll let you know if I make headway.'

He swung his keys round a finger. 'I'm between residences at the moment.'

'What about your agent?'

The keys swivelled faster. 'Let's say I'm between agents too. Why don't I contact you, say in a couple of weeks? Just to see how you're progressing?'

Lorraine passed him her card, and he slipped it into his pocket without looking at it and walked out. Lorraine called Feinstein, who hadn't arrived at his office. She spoke to his secretary, listing what she would need on her return. 'One, can you find a recent address for Nathan's brother, Nick, plus his mother. Two, see if any passports have been issued in any of the other names Nathan used. There may be more than one. Three, will you run by Mr Feinstein that if I were to get assistance from someone, which led to either the money or the art works being recovered, it would help if I could hint at a few bucks going their way, okay?'

'Yes, Mrs Page. I will pass on those messages to Mr Feinstein as soon as he comes in,' the exquisite Pamela answered.

'Thank you.' Lorraine hung up, then went down to Reception to check out. It was now almost lunchtime. She realized she would now have to catch the three-fifteen Jitney, and might as well get lunch in East Hampton before she left. Somehow she couldn't face eating in the hotel with Vallance and his friend, so left her bag at Reception and walked out to a small seafood place down the street. She installed herself in a corner booth with the doom-laden *New York Times* and a platter of shrimp and crab, thinking of the dinner Jake had cooked for her at his apartment. It would be Thanksgiving soon, she thought. She would have him, Rosie and Rooney round for dinner at her apartment – she had never had more to be thankful for as this had turned out to be the best year of her life.

She got up, paid her bill, tossed the unread paper into a trash can and walked back to the hotel, her thoughts drifting again to the future and to images of where she and Jake would live. Her place was too small, though she loved being near the ocean, and neither of them was crazy about his apartment. They must have a proper engagement party too, she thought, suddenly wanting to do things right, to feel the warmth of tradition and ritual around her, wondering if maybe Mike and Sissy and the girls would come. She thought about her daughters every day, and it had never been lack of feeling that had kept her away from them for so long. She had been so afraid that the craziness and chaos that surrounded her would somehow enter their lives. She focused again on the idea of introducing Jake to them. She wanted him to meet them, and for them to see their mother happy and relaxed, supported and loved.

Lorraine turned into the Maidstone's driveway. A paramedics van, lights flashing, was parked in the hotel car park, with two patrol cars and a pale blue Rolls-Royce Corniche. She continued into the hotel reception, but halfway across the lobby she was stopped by an officer, who asked if she was a guest, and only allowed her to go and collect her overnight bag when she confirmed that she was. Then she saw the pretty receptionist weeping hysterically, being comforted by the barman. The blowsy blonde woman, whom she had seen earlier with Vallance, was sitting in one of the Queen Anne chairs. She screamed, sobbed and hyperventilated, and wailed the same words again and again. 'Why? Oh, dear God, why?'

Lorraine looked around more carefully. The police were keeping everyone from going upstairs, and preventing non-residents from entering the hotel. She was just about to ask one of the officers what had happened, when she overheard the pretty girl say, 'I just can't believe it, he was talking to me earlier. I got his autograph for my mother, and I served him lunch, and . . .'

Lorraine was about to go over to her, when the manager appeared. 'I'm so sorry about this, Mrs Page.'

'What happened?' she asked.

The manager's fingers were shaking as he touched his collar. 'Mr Vallance . . . Raymond Vallance committed suicide.'

Lorraine looked upstairs, and the manager clasped her elbow, lowering his voice. 'No, it didn't happen in the hotel, but in that poor woman's car.'

Lorraine glanced at Vallance's companion, whose thickly applied make-up had now smeared over her face. 'How did he do it?' she asked quietly.

'He shot himself,' the manager answered.

He had shown no suicidal intentions when she had seen him earlier. It seemed too much to believe that he had killed himself, particularly as he had been talking of going to see a woman who had said she would shoot him. Lorraine had seen Vallance just before he went downstairs, and the waitress said she had served him lunch. How could Sonja have driven into town, caused Vallance to get up from the lunch table and go and sit in someone else's car so that she could shoot him, unobserved by anyone – and then drive back to the Springs? Hadn't Arthur said he was going straight back to the house? She would have to call them and make some more enquiries in the hotel too, Lorraine thought, but she was determined not to get too far drawn into the Nathan murder again. She was going back to Jake and LA that evening. But she had time, she figured. She'd just have to catch the later bus.

CHAPTER 16

S ONJA WAS sitting quietly, looking out over the
bay, the telephone still on her lap, when she heard
a car draw up outside. Arthur, she thought, with
a pang of conscience. She would have to apologize to
him for the scenes of the night before. He did his best,
but he only irritated her with his childish insistence that
the world was really good and beautiful, that things
could change. It was like talking to a six-year-old, she
thought, and, anyway, it was pointless for anyone to talk
to her when she got into a dark state. She was the only
one who could deliver herself from it. But it was gone
now, she had acted to discharge it: she would teach
Vallance a lesson he would never forget. She felt as
peaceful as the sheet of blue water in front of her, if a
little tired . . .

To her surprise she heard someone knock loudly on
the front door. Arthur must have forgotten his keys – it
was possible, in view of the frame of mind in which he
had left the house. Glancing out of the window on her
way to the door, however, she saw not the jeep but a
police car. Her limbs weakened and trembled and her
throat constricted.

Outside was Officer Vern Muller, an old friend: she

had known him since she moved to the Hamptons, seven years ago.

'Mrs Nathan,' he said, 'I have some bad news for you, I'm afraid.' His expression was grim. Oh, God, she thought, not Arthur . . . 'Can I come in?' Muller asked.

'Certainly,' she said, standing back to let the thick-set policeman walk past her into the hall. She followed him, her stomach turning over. Arthur, oh, Arthur, she cried silently, images of his lifeless, mangled body, mingling with those of Nathan's dead body. Everything she touched she killed, she thought.

'Do you want a drink?' she said to the policeman as they reached the kitchen, wanting to put off the moment when he told her and a new phase of her life really had begun.

'No – but maybe have one yourself,' Muller said. He waited, saying nothing, while she poured herself out a measure of whisky and sat down.

'Mrs Nathan, I have something to tell you which I didn't want you to hear on the news,' he began. 'I just heard it myself from the station and I came right up. Raymond Vallance is dead. He shot himself in town. I know you were friends for many years.'

'*Vallance* is dead?' Sonja repeated.

She knew she sounded stupid and the police officer gave her a strange look.

'Yes, Raymond Vallance. He was staying at the Maidstone Arms with some woman, and . . . they're not exactly sure what happened. He just walked outside and shot himself.'

Relief raced through Sonja like a rip-tide: she felt

giddy with happiness and had to fight to keep it from blossoming in her face.

'When was this?' she managed to ask, a second realization dawning, hard on the heels of the first.

'Just minutes ago. I heard it as I was driving past the gate and I thought I'd turn in.'

God, she thought. When she had called Vallance to tell him that, if he was so keen on reliving old times, he should be delighted to hear that she intended releasing the real record of those old times – Harry Nathan's videotapes – to the press, she had not anticipated what he would do. Had he killed himself out of shame at the prospect of his own humiliation being made public, or of Harry Nathan being seen at last for what he was? She would not have been surprised if it was the latter, and it gave her a certain, almost aesthetic, pleasure to think that the sick hero-worship that had dominated Vallance's life had finally killed him.

'You're sure you don't want a drink?' she said. She didn't feel a flicker of remorse at Vallance's death but she did her best to seem saddened and shaken by what Muller had just told her. He detected, though, that the news was less of a blow to her than he had thought it would be.

'Well,' he said, 'perhaps just a small one.'

The whole thing was perfect, Sonja thought, as she got out a glass for him. She knew that both Arthur, and possibly Lorraine Page, might suspect that she had had something to do with Vallance's death – and she had a perfect alibi, a large, solid, unimpeachable policeman sitting right here in her kitchen within minutes of it.

'He was more my ex-husband's friend than mine,'

Sonja said – she needed to offer some explanation for her lack of distress at Vallance's death. 'I hadn't seen him since my divorce.'

'Yeah, I was sorry to hear about . . . your ex-husband.' Muller took the glass, looking at her, Sonja thought, just a touch too intently. Surely he could not connect her with a murder on the other side of the country. 'It was all over the papers and everything. I guess Vallance will be too – he was a pretty big star at one time.'

'At one time,' Sonja repeated. 'Poor Raymond, he hadn't worked in anything you could take seriously for years.'

'The boys are wondering whether that might have been why he shot himself – he'd been bragging all over the hotel that he had some big movie or something coming up, and apparently he got some call or other while he was eating, got up to take it, then walked out back and . . . Goodbye, cruel world.'

'He must have lost the deal, I imagine,' Sonja said, lying effortlessly, a skill she was not proud of but had had all her life.

'You can't think of anyone around here could have called him?' Muller asked.

'I'm sorry,' Sonja said, 'I can't help you. I haven't had any contact with that whole world in years.'

'Well,' Muller said, draining his glass, 'I'd better not keep you.'

'I'm sorry if I seemed a little . . . strange when you came in,' Sonja said with a charming smile. 'It's just that Arthur and I had a slight disagreement last night and I just got the idea that something might have happened to him.'

'Arthur!' the officer said, with a laugh. 'He's asleep in

354

the jeep a mile up the road. I drove past him, but I didn't have the heart to wake him up.'

The hotel was full of a mixture of shock and excitement, as people sat at tables or in the bar, discussing Raymond Vallance's career as though they had known him, waiting for the press to arrive and, Lorraine thought, secretly as thrilled as children to be caught up in events that would make news. The *East Hampton Star* had already sent a reporter, and people were talking eagerly to him. Police officers were interviewing staff in one of the conference rooms, and Reception was presently unattended. It was the manager himself who appeared and signalled to Lorraine as she stood at the door of the bar. 'Mrs Page, there's a call for you.' Lorraine was surprised, and followed him to the desk. 'You can take it here if you like. I almost said you'd checked out, but then I saw you.'

'Thank you.' She took the phone, and he backed away politely, leaving her alone. 'Lorraine Page,' she said into the receiver.

'Feinstein here.' Her heart sank. 'I got your messages,' he continued. 'You know I tried to call you earlier?' He didn't wait for an answer. 'I've located three passports – we've sent copies to your office. The brother's a bit of a fruitcake, so I've put in a call to Abigail Nathan, the mother, and she'll be calling me back. Now, about this other thing, if you get any information about missing funds or the paintings themselves, by all means agree to some payment, but discuss it with me first. Any further developments?' he demanded.

Lorraine held the phone cupped to her shoulder, as

she sat on the edge of the desk and took out her cigarettes. 'Yes, Raymond Vallance showed up here, then shot himself.'

'Good God, not at Sonja's?' Feinstein said, stunned.

'No, in the car park of this hotel.'

'I can't say I'm sorry – I never liked the man.' Feinstein was silent for a moment, then asked if Lorraine had seen Sonja. She said she had.

'How is she?' the lawyer asked.

Lorraine drew an ashtray across the desk. 'Weird. On the edge.'

'Well, she made it to the finishing tape at least. She's got the estate in her pocket now. Did you talk to her about the paintings?'

'She says she doesn't know anything about them. I don't think she gives much of a damn about the whole thing – it's her money missing as much as yours, but she just doesn't seem to care.'

'Yeah, well, if she doesn't, I do. Haven't you come up with anything else?' Feinstein pressed.

'Well, there's one other thing you might check out – the accounts of the film studio, in case that soaked the money up.'

'Jesus Christ, don't mention them. I've never seen anything like it. The company wasn't really my department – I handled Harry's personal affairs – but there was a corporate accountant, total fucking crook,' Feinstein said loftily, as though his own integrity was beyond question. 'Plus a show-business lawyer that Nathan used sometimes. We've got an auditor in. It's a mess, but I'll look into it. Did Sonja tip you off to this other movie scenario?'

'No, the guy she lives with suggested it.'

'You don't think the two of them are covering their own tracks?'

'I don't know,' said Lorraine thoughtfully. 'I just don't know.'

'How long are you planning on staying out there?' Feinstein asked, in the-meter's-running fashion.

'I'm coming back tonight,' Lorraine said, hoping that would make him happy, and thinking again of Jake. 'I just think this Vallance thing's suspicious. Everyone connected to Harry Nathan seems to drop dead. I thought I might just call Sonja again.'

'Well, quit thinking and fucking do it,' Feinstein said. 'I've got to go.'

When Arthur returned to the house there was no sign of Sonja. His head ached as the hangover kicked in. He felt tired and disoriented, and had woken in a panic, full of the compulsion to rush back to Sonja's side, make sure she was still there, still okay. Things couldn't go on this way, he thought. Either there had to be more to their relationship than this babysitting, as she called it, or it would have to end.

Both kitchen and sitting room were empty, though he noticed that the videos had vanished.

'Sonja?' he called, as he walked upstairs.

Her voice floated back. 'I'm in the bath.' That was odd, he thought. She didn't normally bathe during the day, but then, last night had hardly been a normal night.

'May I come in?' he said. The atmosphere was warm and fragrant with the citrus scent of one of Sonja's bath essences. He could tell, even before he looked at her, that her mood had lifted. She lay in the pale green water, her long limbs floating, her hair, face and neck all smothered in a layer of some rich turquoise treatment cream. She looked wonderful, he thought, like some richly decorated Egyptian idol.

She smiled at him. 'I'm sorry about last night.' Her eyes were more cat-like than ever, heavy with an expression of deep contentment. God, he thought, she didn't need him: she had positively restored herself in his absence, seemed happier than she had in weeks. 'Where did you go?' she said.

'Into town. I met Mrs Page. She kind of sobered me up. She's leaving this afternoon.'

Sonja disappeared under the water for a moment, then sat up and began to rinse the blue cream from her hair and skin. 'I hope you didn't say too much to her.'

'No more than you did yesterday, I think,' Arthur said, with a touch of irritation.

'Oh, Arthur, let's not start again,' she said, standing up in the bath to squeeze the water out of her hair. 'She has no idea that she and I've ever met before.' She swathed herself in a thick white towel and walked into the bedroom. There was some part of Sonja that he could not reach. He had no idea why one day she would be energetic and warm, the next cold and inert. Certainly he had no idea what was responsible for this sunniness, but he decided to postpone the conversation he had meant to have with her about Nathan. How many times had he decided that? he thought wryly.

The phone rang, and Sonja pulled a face, so Arthur crossed the room and picked it up.

'I'm not in,' she said, selected a comb and headed back to the bathroom.

'Speaking. Who is this?' Arthur said, gesturing to Sonja to stay in the room. 'Ah, you didn't catch the bus then . . . She's in the bath – do you want me to pass on a message?' Sonja tucked the towel more tightly around herself. 'I'm all ears.' He sat on the bed, then stood bolt upright. '*What?*' Sonja moved closer, but Arthur's attention was focused on the call. 'My God, I can't believe it.' He listened for quite a while, then thanked Lorraine for calling, and replaced the phone.

'Raymond Vallance shot himself. He's dead.' He turned to face her. 'Did you hear what I said?'

Sonja started to comb her hair. 'Yes,' she said, 'I know. Vern Muller stopped by earlier and told me.'

'Why didn't you say anything?'

'I was going to but you started in on me so quickly about talking to Mrs Page. Is that why she's still here? Vallance, I mean.'

'I dunno, I suppose so. I think she wanted to speak to you, but she didn't push it.'

'Well,' Sonja said, 'she's not the police. She has no power to make anybody answer questions.' That seemed an odd thing to say, Arthur thought, almost as though Sonja were hiding something . . . He rubbed his head, which was throbbing.

Sonja knelt on the bed close behind him and ran her arms around him, her skin still damp from the bath. 'Does your head hurt?' Her voice was gentle, almost seductive.

'Yes.'

Sonja kissed his neck, then rolled off the bed. 'I'll get you some aspirin.'

He tried to catch her arm, but missed. 'Vallance didn't come out here, did he?' he called after her. She was

359

halfway out of the room and, again, he had the impression that she was avoiding any discussion of Vallance's death.

'No,' she said, over her shoulder.

Arthur got up and followed her out of the door. 'Sonja,' he said, 'stop a minute.'

'Arthur, I'm soaking wet. I'll just get this and come right back.'

'Sonja, were you here all morning?'

'Of course I was,' she said, looking him full in the eye. Arthur said nothing. 'You can ask Muller,' Sonja continued. 'He was here within five minutes of Vallance's death. He called to tell me personally.'

'Sonja,' Arthur said, 'Mrs Page said something about Vallance getting some call at the dining table in the Maidstone Arms, just before he died. I don't suppose he called here, did he?'

He could see her hesitate between a lie and the truth.

'Well, yes, he did, but I wouldn't speak to him.'

'What did he say?'

Sonja shrugged. 'Just that he wanted to see me, said he wanted to talk about old times.'

'Is that all?'

'Yes,' Sonja said, her eyes flashing. 'That's all. Now stop the investigation, Sherlock. I'll go and put some coffee on and if your head still aches . . .'

'Yeah, aspirin urgently required.' He leaned back across the bed, feeling almost sick with the pain. Raymond Vallance was dead: he still couldn't believe it – he'd seen the man only that morning. The news shocked him, and he had hardly known Vallance – but Sonja had hardly reacted at all and she had known him for years.

He sat up, with a sense of foreboding: what if she had called Vallance? What could she have said that would have made him shoot himself?

Lorraine hung up and eased out from behind the desk. She glanced quickly round the reception area, and could see the manager deep in conversation with the journalist. Shielding with her body what she was doing, she began to flick through the accounts, looking for Vallance's name, noting that all outgoing calls appeared on the bills. She leaned closer to turn over the pages, but there was nothing under the name Vallance. Lorraine straightened up and was about to go when a computer screen caught her eye. She walked over to it. The cursor was blinking on account ledgers. She entered her own name, and her check-out time, outgoing phone calls and other items on her bill came up on room 5. She moved to room 6, and saw that it had been booked, not in Vallance's name but in that of Margaretta Forwood. The date of arrival and an intended length of stay of two days had been entered, but a cancellation typed in subsequently, with the booking fee, luncheon, wine and phone calls in a column opposite. There were four calls to LA, one to Chicago, and two local numbers, one of which she recognized immediately. Sonja Nathan's.

She heard footsteps behind her, and turned, reaching for her cigarette pack from the desk. 'Thank you so much, Mr Fischer,' she said, glancing at his name-badge. 'I'm sorry to leave my bags for so long and if it's inconvenient I'll . . .'

'Not at all. Do you know how long you'll be here, just in case anyone else should call for you?'

361

Lorraine said that she was now intending to take the six o'clock bus into New York.

'I hope you enjoyed your stay with us.'

'I did, very much. It's been a pretty terrible day for you, though, hasn't it?'

'Yes, dreadful. It's tragic, just terrible.'

'How is his companion?' Lorraine asked, assuming a look of sincere concern.

The man sucked in his breath. 'Well, the poor woman is distraught – he didn't leave a note. They had just decided not to stay over. Mrs Forwood had gone to the bar and their cases were being brought down. Mr Vallance walked past me, and I think he smiled – I know I acknowledged him, because I recall seeing him coming down the stairs. He didn't appear to be in a hurry, very casual, and he left the hotel.'

'How long after that was the body found?'

He blinked rapidly. 'I can't be too sure, not long. Mrs Forwood was just leaving, and next minute we heard this screaming.'

'You didn't hear any gunshot?'

'No, nothing. Everything's pretty confused – the shock, I suppose – but I ran out to the car park. She was hysterical, couldn't speak, just screamed and screamed, and then I saw him. The gun was in his hand, but he was sitting upright.'

He was interrupted by the telephone and excused himself to take the call. Lorraine waited, but another phone rang, and then another, lights blinking on the board. She walked out, hearing him refuse to comment on the day's events.

Lorraine made her way into the bar. The crowd had thinned, and a stool was vacant at the far side. She ordered a Coke and lit another cigarette, discreetly eavesdropping on conversations which all centred on the suicide of Raymond Vallance.

Carina, the pretty blonde, now came on duty. She no longer seemed upset, if anything rather enjoying the notoriety of having served Vallance and his lady-friend their luncheon. 'He was so charming. I was asking for an autograph for my mother – she had been such a fan of his – and he was so obliging.' Lorraine stubbed out her cigarette, unable to repress a small smile: poor Vallance – the last thing he would have wanted to hear from an attractive young girl was that she wanted an autograph for her mother. The girl went on, 'They'd finished eating and were just having a Madeira when he left the table and said he had to call his agent. He was here for a big movie – that's what he told us, wasn't it?' The barman nodded, polishing a champagne flute. 'It was going to be shot here, that's what he said.'

'Well, *he* certainly got shot,' said a man with bushy eyebrows, and there were a few guffaws, but even more murmurs of disapproval at the joke, and he apologized. Lorraine wished he would be quiet, as she was trying to hear the rest of what Carina had to say, but the girl was called out into Reception.

Lorraine followed and saw her go into the office. The phone was ringing constantly and the manager was clearly at his wit's end. He covered the receiver and told Carina to get someone to help him. Carina nodded, and turned back, almost bumping into Lorraine.

'Are you all right?' Lorraine asked, with a show of concern. 'It must have been dreadful for you. You found him, didn't you?'

The girl was clearly happy to talk. 'No, I didn't, but I served him lunch.'

Lorraine waited while she was told the entire story about how Carina had asked for his autograph for her mother. 'Did he have any calls?'

'Yes. He got up from the table either to go and call someone, or I think there was a call for him.' She sighed, and tears welled up in her wide blue eyes.

Lorraine gave a brittle smile. 'But at least your mother has his autograph, and it'll be of considerable interest now – the last one he ever gave!'

Carina blinked, aware of the sarcasm, then hurried into the bar.

Lorraine decided to screw subtlety, and went into the manager's office. 'Sorry to bother you again.'

Fischer looked up, one phone in his hand, a second off the hook in front of him. 'I'm sorry, Mrs Page, but I really am very busy. If you need—'

She interrupted, 'I do need something – I want to know who called Mr Vallance. If you don't have the name, then I would like to see the number.'

He gaped, then flushed. 'I'm sorry, that's private information.'

'I know, and I'm a private investigator.' She took out her wallet, and showed her ID.

'I'm sorry, but I've been instructed by the police not to divulge any information or discuss the incident with anyone.' Lorraine took out her wallet, and the man stood up, flushing a still deeper pink. 'Please don't even consider offering me money.'

She slipped her wallet back into her purse. Since the direct approach hadn't worked, she tried another. 'I'm sorry, I didn't mean to insult you. I'm conducting an investigation into the murder of Harry Nathan. Raymond Vallance was his closest friend. I have to report back to LA this evening, and until I have the coroner's report, I have to consider the possibility that Mr Vallance was also murdered.'

The manager's flush drained, leaving his face chalk white.

'I don't want anyone to know what I'm investigating. I have full co-operation from the East Hampton police, and I'm sure you will assist me.'

He opened a drawer and took out a sheet of computer printout.

He looked down at Mrs Forwood's account, and said that some local calls had been made when Mr Vallance arrived and some to Los Angeles during the early part of the morning. The last call, though, had been on Vallance's mobile, and the hotel had no way of knowing who or where it came from.

'So, Mr Vallance left the dining room because a call came through?'

'Yes, on the mobile. We don't allow them in the dining room so he had checked it at the desk. He was speaking to someone on the phone when he went upstairs to his room.' Lorraine watched while the man went to the computer, and typed the commands for a printout of the Forwood account.

'Has Mrs Forwood left?' Lorraine asked, as the machine printed.

Fischer turned back to her, folding the sheet. 'Yes, she ordered a helicopter to take her to New York. We're arranging for her car to be returned, after the police get through with it.'

'Did they also remove Mr Vallance's luggage? You

said you were arranging to take it to the car, so it wasn't in the car already?'

His mouth opened a fraction, and he frowned. 'Well, it must be still here, unless . . .' He walked across the room to a large double-doored cupboard, opened it and looked inside. 'It's still here.'

He took out an old-fashioned pigskin case and matching briefcase. 'I'd better contact the police. I think the confusion may have been caused by Mrs Forwood because she took hers with her.'

'Could I see it?' Lorraine asked, stepping forward. Fischer tried to open the case, but it was locked. He set it down and took the briefcase to his desk: Lorraine saw that it fastened with a zipper, had flat, beaten metal handles and two outside pockets – in one of which was a mobile telephone.

'Could I see that?' She already had her hand out. The manager hesitated, then passed her the phone. She pressed the green power button, then Recall. The telephone bleeped, and Lorraine began to scroll through the digits logged in the memory.

'Should you be doing that?' Fischer asked nervously.

'It's all right, I'm not using it to make a call, just checking something.'

She took out her notebook and jotted down number after number – none she recognized – then tried to bring up the last number dialled, but got a blank screen and a bleep. She noted the make and serial number of the phone, then turned it off. 'Thank you.' She handed it back, and the man put it back where he had taken it from.

'Perhaps there's a note inside the briefcase,' he said.

He was now very uneasy, but Lorraine moved quickly

to unzip the case. Like the locked suitcase, the briefcase was old and worn, but had been expensive. It opened into two halves and Vallance's name had been monogrammed on one corner. The compartments on one side contained writing paper and envelopes, some letters held together with a rubber band, a paperback novel, a manicure set, some hotel toiletries, and a Cartier pen. On the other side were three scripts, some flattering publicity photographs of Vallance, some postcards of India and, tucked deep inside, a worn manilla envelope.

Lorraine removed the old movie stills, and another photograph of Harry Nathan and Vallance together, arms around one another, smiling into the camera. A third person had been crudely cut out of the photo, but Lorraine could see the edge of a woman's dress and a picture hat: he had been unable to cut the section off completely because the woman's arm was resting on Nathan's shoulder. Lorraine recognized the strong hand and close-trimmed nails as Sonja Nathan's.

There was another larger, plain envelope, and Lorraine opened it to reveal several sheets of expensive, flimsy paper in a feminine pink, which she recognized at once. Her pulse speeded up as she took them out and unfolded them carefully. The bottom of the first sheet of paper was missing – it had been cut in two after the words 'Dear Raymond' and the date, some six months previously, scrawled in ink in Cindy Nathan's childish script. Lorraine flipped open the manicure set, knowing what she would find: a small pair of round-tipped scissors, the blades less than an inch long, with which Vallance had cut one of the desperate letters in half to fake a suicide note.

Poor Cindy, Lorraine thought. Her hunch had been

right. The girl hadn't committed suicide: the last of the parade of men who had entered her life, first to desire, then to abuse her, had destroyed her. Not that it mattered now: there could be no doubt as to Vallance's guilt, and now he was dead himself. That he had murdered Cindy made it more likely that he had killed Harry Nathan too. Perhaps she had the solution to the Nathan case right there in her hands, and she could leave the affair now with a clear conscience, do her best to find Feinstein's art, and go back to her own life.

But *why* had Vallance killed Cindy? Lorraine thought back to the morning he had come to her office, the night after Cindy died, with a wafer-thin veneer of normality concealing a state of considerable emotional turmoil. He had talked compulsively about Nathan and the past and, as she replayed the conversation in her mind, virtually the first words out of his mouth had been hatred and condemnation of the women around Nathan. He had raved about how they had cheapened and damaged his idol, and how he believed Cindy had been responsible for her husband's death, though she would never have been convicted of his murder. The motive that seemed most likely was a desire on Vallance's part to exact vengeance for Nathan on the woman who killed him, which made it most unlikely that Vallance had shot Nathan himself, unless he had completely lost his mind. But having spoken to him shortly before his death, Lorraine knew that that wasn't so. So who *had* killed Nathan? Would Kendall have killed him to prevent the porn tapes becoming public? Or could it somehow have been Sonja? Lorraine found it hard to believe that it was pure coincidence that Vallance shot himself in the Hamptons, within a few miles of Sonja Nathan's house, shortly after calling her . . .

Lorraine replaced everything as she had found it, and zipped up the case. She wanted to get out and was already planning a diversion to Santa Fe. She said to the manager, 'Don't let me prevent you any longer from attending to business, and thank you very much for your help. I'd pass these on to the police.' Then she hurried out to avoid any further conversation. She had found nothing relating to paintings or secret bank accounts, and no reason why Vallance had shot himself.

Lorraine sat down at a vacant table in the sun lounge and ordered a Coke and a prosciutto sandwich. She looked over the list of phone numbers she had taken down from Vallance's mobile, then circled one. She was sure the code was for Santa Fe. She was so immersed in her own thoughts that she jumped when Fischer slid down beside her, and told her in conspiratorial tones that the police were sending someone to collect Mr Vallance's luggage. She felt the man's breath on her face as he whispered that he had not mentioned that she had opened it.

'Good, and perhaps you'd better not mention that I was asking questions either – you know, there's always competition between the police in different counties.'

'Oh – well, yes, if you say so.'

'Is this a Santa Fe code?' she asked, repeating the number.

'I believe so, but I can check it out for you.'

'You could go one better and call the number for me. I'd like to know who it's registered to.' She gave him a cool smile, and he glided away. Lorraine finished her

Coke and sandwich, then walked out to Reception to collect her luggage.

A uniformed police officer was standing at the desk talking to Carina, who was handing over Vallance's cases, and Lorraine made out the same words that had been on everyone's lips all day – terrible, tragedy, unexpected – and Sonja Nathan's name.

'Of course, she'd known him more than twenty years,' she heard the officer say. 'She looked like she'd seen a ghost when I gave her the news.'

'Excuse me,' Lorraine said, glancing around quickly to make sure that Fischer was not nearby – she did not want him to see her talking to the officer and deduce that she was not, as she had said, working in association with the local police. 'Did you say you had to break the news of Raymond Vallance's death to Mrs Nathan?'

'Yes, ma'am,' Muller said, viewing her with interest.

'I know Mrs Nathan, I visited with her yesterday, and I wondered if perhaps I should call her. Was she very distressed?' Lorraine said, concern in her voice.

'Well, she was shaken,' Muller said. 'I knew she would be.'

'That's the difference between a city like LA and a place like this,' Lorraine gushed, trying to get him to say more. 'There's no way a city police department would ever have time to go and break the news of a friend's death personally to someone.'

'Well,' Muller said, 'it isn't usually part of the service here either. It's just that I was driving right past her gates when I got the news.'

'Goodness, how awful,' Lorraine went on, hoping he would not guess that she was fishing. 'So you had to tell her just a few minutes after he died?'

'Just about,' Muller said, eyeing Lorraine closely. 'You a friend of hers?'

'Not a close friend,' Lorraine said, keen now not to talk to him for too long. 'I know some connections of hers in Los Angeles and, since I was in the area, I gave her a call. I'm leaving now, actually – I'm just waiting to pick up my bags.'

She caught sight of Fischer coming towards her from the other side of the lobby with her case, and moved off to intercept him before he reached the desk. She gave Muller a final sweet smile, which she hoped convinced him that she was just an innocent visitor.

'The number – I'm sorry I didn't get back to you quicker, but the phones are still going crazy. It was Santa Fe, and the subscriber is Mr Nicholas Nathan.'

'Thank you for your help,' she said. And despite his previous strictures, she slipped a hundred-dollar bill into his hand. He watched her leave, then turned to Vern Muller who had joined him.

'Who is that lady?' Muller asked him curiously.

'Mrs Page?' Fischer replied. 'She's a private investigator working on the Harry Nathan murder inquiry. She said she was working with the police in LA and had full co-operation from you.'

'Oh, yeah?' the officer said. 'If she has, it's the first I've heard of it. She looks more like a newspaper reporter to me.'

'Well, she's gone now, whoever she is,' Fischer said. 'Let's get on with it.'

Sonja tucked the comforter round Arthur: he was fast asleep and snoring. Sometimes he looked like a scruffy kid, and she felt such a touching warmth towards him. He took such care of her, and she loved him for it, had not realized how much until today. She moved quietly around the room, then went to a closet to select the clothes she wanted to pack and get out her case. She heard a car drawing up in the driveway and went into the other bedroom to look out to the front of the house. Vern Muller had sweat stains under the armpits of his blue uniform shirt, and was hitching up his navy police-issue trousers over his paunch. He tossed his hat into the rear seat, then looked at the house. Sonja saw him stop to admire her beloved garden before he set off up the path. She went downstairs and had the door open before he could wake Arthur by knocking or ringing the bell. 'Hi, Mrs Nathan. Sorry to bother you again,' he said, walking up the steps.

'Not at all, Vern,' Sonja said. 'Come on in.'

'I won't, Mrs Nathan, if you don't mind,' the police officer went on. 'I just stopped by to ask you if you know a lady named Lorraine Page.'

'Well, yes, I do,' Sonja said carefully. 'She called out here yesterday. She's a PI working for my late husband's lawyer in connection with the estate.'

'That's the story she told Fischer in the hotel, but when I spoke to her she said she was just a friend,' Muller went on. 'She told him and me another couple of things that weren't true, and she seemed pretty interested in this stuff about Raymond Vallance too – asked me if you were shocked and so on.' Sonja kept her face impassive. 'Wouldn't surprise me if she was some journalist come out here to dig dirt, or if you saw your name plastered with his across the papers,' the police officer concluded.

If that was all Lorraine was interested in, that was fine,

Sonja thought privately. 'Thanks for warning me, Vern,' Sonja said. 'I'll be careful what I say to her if she calls again.'

'Something about that lady makes me think she's looking to cause trouble for you,' Muller said. 'Take care now.'

'You too, Vern,' Sonja said, and closed the door. She leaned back against it for a moment. Upstairs Arthur lay sleeping. For the first time she had begun to believe that things were changing, that the dead hand of the past was losing its grip on her and a new life waiting to begin. There was only one person who could possibly stand in her way now – and that person was Lorraine Page.

Lorraine stared out of the window. There had been an accident, and the traffic tailed back for miles on both sides. They had been stationary for fifteen minutes, and the driver had got out to try to see what was going on. 'Nothing anyone can do,' he said, climbing back up. 'They're waiting for the recovery truck with a crane to drag two cars off the road, and there's a third overturned. Sorry, ladies and gentlemen.'

A collective moan went up, and Lorraine swore – she had been cutting it fine anyway, and now she doubted that she would catch the plane. The frustrating thing was that all she could do was sit and wait. She had been unable to concentrate on the book she'd bought, about art fraud through the centuries, so she opened her notebook. There were a few leads she could take further, but she was really no closer to finding either the missing money or the paintings than when she had first arrived.

She turned to a clean page. What if Nathan had

poured the money from the sale of the paintings back into his films? If that was the case, then there must be some record, but the investigation was cold. What if Nathan's brother had worked the fakes scam? He was family, would have got a slice of the money, and might even know where Harry had stashed it. She had to see him.

The bus jolted, advanced a few hundred yards, Lorraine stared out of the window. One of the vehicles going in the opposite direction was a cream Rolls-Royce, which brought Raymond Vallance to her mind.

What had made him kill himself? She turned to a fresh page in her notebook. Harry Nathan – dead, shot. Cindy Nathan – dead, probably murdered by Vallance. Kendall Nathan – dead, accidental fire? Raymond Vallance – dead, suicide. Lorraine tapped her teeth with the pen. Was it all a bit coincidental? Could Sonja have threatened him with the videotapes? What if there was no coincidence, but intent? She grimaced.

The bus moved forward another hundred yards before it stopped again, but Lorraine wasn't counting the minutes until her flight to LA. She had made up her mind that Santa Fe was her next destination.

CHAPTER 17

BY THE time Lorraine arrived in New York it was
almost eleven thirty p.m. and her flight to Los
Angeles had long gone. She booked into the Park
Meridian hotel and started to make some calls. She had
to arrange travel to Santa Fe, first thing in the morning,
and she knew she had to call Jake. As she dialled his
number, part of her longed to hear his voice, but the
other part, knowing what she was about to say, hoped
that his answerphone would pick up.

Jake answered the phone almost immediately it rang.

'Lorraine!' he said, pure pleasure in his voice. 'Where
are you? Do you want me to come pick you up?'

'Actually,' she began weakly, 'I'm still in New York.'

'New York?' he repeated, unable to mask his disappointment. 'What are you doing there?'

'Well,' she said, 'I got stuck in traffic and I missed the
flight.'

'What a drag,' he said sympathetically. 'Can you get a
flight in the morning?'

'Oh, sure,' Lorraine said. 'It's just that I have to make
a detour, just for a day, to interview someone.'

'Where to?' he asked.

'Santa Fe. Nathan's brother is an artist out there – I

think he might have been the one forging the paintings. I'm pretty sure it was him and that'll wrap up the case – I mean, I can't just dump Feinstein, I said I'd try to trace his art . . .'

'Lorraine,' Jake said gently, 'you don't have to make excuses to me about doing your job.'

'I know, it's just that I don't want you to think I don't care about you. I'd give anything to be coming straight home.'

'I know you would,' he said. 'Don't worry about it. When will I see you?'

'Tomorrow – or at worst the day after.'

'That's okay,' he said, with a laugh. 'I waited for you for forty-five years so I figure I can manage another forty-eight hours.'

'This is going to be the last time I go away like this,' she said. 'I'm winding up the agency after this case – just as soon as I can get Feinstein off my back.'

'You don't have to do that, sweetheart,' Jake said, clearly taken aback. 'Why don't we talk about it when you get back?'

'I don't need to talk about it,' Lorraine said. 'It's my decision and I've thought about it. Bill Rooney was right – you get dirty in this business, dealing with sick people, damaged people, crooks all day. I've had enough.'

'Well,' Jake said, 'let's see if you feel the same way when you come home. It sounds as though the case still has its teeth in you for now.'

'Yeah, I know,' she said wryly. 'Don't worry, I can cut loose.'

'Sure you can,' he said, with a laugh. 'Hurry home.'

God, she thought, what had she done to deserve a guy like that? And why had she put off calling him for so long? She had assumed he would be irritated and resentful that she had been delayed, but it was clear that his only concern was to make life easier for her. There weren't many like him out there.

Next she called Rosie, who had now met Jake when he had brought Tiger around. 'You're a lucky lady – he loves you, and he was open about it, came right out with it. He said he was gonna marry you, and me and Bill never even mentioned it, I swear.'

Lorraine felt warm inside. 'He said that to you?'

'Yeah, and to Bill – like he wanted our approval. He and Bill got on like a house on fire, and you know what a prick Bill can be. Well, they acted like old buddies, and the best thing is, Jake started asking about Mike and your girls. He said he felt you should get to know them. I think he kinda wants a family . . . are you there? Hello?'

'Yes, Rosie, I'm here.'

'He also said he was missing you and you didn't call often enough.'

'Well,' Lorraine said, 'I just called him, so that's taken care of.'

'About time!' Rosie said. 'This one you don't let off the hook.'

Lorraine felt so good she laughed.

Then Rosie told Lorraine that all she wanted was for her to find the same happiness she had found, and she reckoned that, of all the people she knew, Lorraine deserved it the most. 'See, I love you, and so does Bill.'

Lorraine lay back on the bed. 'I love you, too, and I'll see you both very soon.'

'How soon is that?' Rosie asked. 'Something tells me it's slightly later than planned.'

'Well,' Lorraine said sheepishly – how well her friend

knew her! 'I got a bit of a lead on this case, so I'm going to Santa Fe – just one interview, then I'll be on my way home.'

'Lorraine!' Rosie said, exasperation in her voice. 'There's some things more important than this case and that interview, you know. You gotta take care of the rest of your life.'

'Jake'll take care of me for the rest of my life,' Lorraine said, knowing that that was what her friend wanted to hear. 'Just after this one interview, okay? I'm still working for Feinstein and I can't just drop the case.'

'Okay,' Rosie said resignedly. 'We'll take care of Tiger, and I'll stop by your place and water the plants. It's hot as hell here.'

'Can you check my fridge too? And there's a crate of dog food under the sink.'

'Okay, he sure does eat. So when will you be back?'

'Tomorrow evening, next day at worst.'

'I'll be waiting.'

'Great, see you then – and, Rosie, give that Bill Rooney a big hug from me.'

'I will. 'Bye now.' Rosie hung up.

Lorraine rolled off the bed, her spirits high. She took a shower, washed her hair and got into bed. It was just after two, and she fell into a deep, dreamless sleep.

It was only six when she woke up, but she couldn't go back to sleep. As there was still an hour before the breakfast she'd ordered would arrive, she got up and sat at the writing desk in her room. Just as she had on the bus from the Hamptons, she went over the case – her last case, she said to herself, and as it was the last, she would not rest until she'd cracked it.

Something still unexplained which irked Lorraine was the phone call, apparently from Cindy, that she had received the day Nathan died. Lorraine would have bet her bottom dollar that it was either Kendall or Sonja, and if so, one of them had known about the murder virtually at the time it was committed. Or had Cindy called one of them to ask for help, and then that person had called Lorraine? Kendall would not have given Cindy the time of day, but Sonja had seemed to feel some measure of concern for her – that had struck Lorraine as odd because she did not consider Sonja either caring or altruistic.

She was still sitting hunched over her notebook when her breakfast arrived. Half an hour later, Reception called to say her car was waiting to take her to the airport.

Sonja lay back in the luxurious, king-sized bed, her breakfast tray beside her. She had arranged a hair-dressing appointment, manicure and massage in the hotel, leaving plenty of time to prepare for the flight, and was looking forward to being back in Europe again. She always looked on the Old World, where she had grown up, as home. Harry was dead, Raymond was dead, and she had vowed that the years of pain and obsession would be buried with them. She would choose the right man now where she had chosen the wrong one before, would choose a real life now over a living death. There was just one final statement she had to make.

Arthur, smart in a navy suit with broad pinstripes, walked in from the dining area with an armful of newspapers. 'Vallance got good coverage – they're using photographs of him from back in the fifties. There's the

New York Times, LA Times, Variety . . .' He had not questioned Sonja any further about Vallance's death, fearful of disturbing the fragile equilibrium of her mood.

Sonja read the articles, then turned to the arts page in the *LA Times*. She glanced over at Arthur. 'You read this?' Arthur sat on the edge of the bed and Sonja went on, 'It's about the fiasco in Spain at the Prado – they fired some art historian who wrongly hailed some painting found in the archives as an undiscovered Goya. It was already registered as a Mariano Salvador Maella.'

Arthur picked up a piece of toast and bit into the crust. 'He was one of Goya's contemporaries, lesser known, but how the hell they could confuse his work with Goya's is beyond me.'

Sonja continued to read, then looked over at him again. 'They only had a preliminary sketch listed as Maella and registered in their records.'

'Typical,' he said, shrugging. 'But these national art galleries have so many political strings attached and are run by assholes.'

'It says that they should have bought Goya's *Marianito*.'

'Better still, they should have snapped up *Condesa de Chinchon* – it's recognized as his best work. That's in private hands, though.'

'Is it?' Sonja peered at the paper. 'They say they don't have the funds to do renovations so that they can show one of the finest art collections in the world. It's bursting at the seams with nine out of ten of its treasures buried in vaults for lack of space . . .' She smiled at him. 'Would you like to be let loose in there?' He wandered to the window without replying. 'Could you do a Goya?' she asked, turning to the fashion page.

'No. I can't do anyone that good – every brushstroke is a signature. The stuff Harry had wasn't in the same class.'

She lowered the paper. 'Are you all right? Not nervous about the deal, are you?' He kept his back to her, so she crossed to him. 'What's the matter?'

'Nothing.'

He tried to move away, but she caught his arm. 'Tell me what it is.'

'It's nothing, sweetheart. Now, if you're going to get your hair done, I should—'

'I don't need to. I can stay with you.'

'Don't be stupid. Not that you need any primping – I love you any way you look.'

She reached up and touched his cheek. 'Thank you, but it gives me confidence to look good. You know how I hate standing up on platforms, let alone giving speeches. Though this will be the last one.'

'Sonja, don't talk that way. You'll work again if you want to. Just give it time.'

'I've given all the time I intend to give to my work in this lifetime,' Sonja said, a trace of bitterness in her voice. 'That's over now. Harry killed something deep inside me, and it just won't come alive again.'

She was about to say more, but Arthur swore, almost frightening her. The tension he had been suppressing since he walked into the room now rushed to the surface in a torrent of words. 'He's dead, Sonja, for God's sake – *the man is dead*. You make everything I am, everything *we* are, second best, second rate. Whenever you bring up that son-of-a-bitch – and you do, at every opportunity—'

'I certainly don't,' Sonja said, needled. 'I don't know

381

what more I could have done to put him out of my life. It was just that PI asking questions about him stirred up the memories again.'

'Really? Well, I'm sick of hearing his name, and I've been patient, but I don't know how much longer I can go on living with just the leftovers. I don't want to hear about him any more. Whatever he did, whatever happened between you, is in the past, and if you want to keep it in the present, then *I'm* past, Sonja, because I can't take it. I never wanted to get involved in this paintings scam, I did it for you. I—'

'It's going to make you very rich,' Sonja snapped.

Arthur moved quickly across the room and grabbed her. 'You don't hear me, Sonja. Believe me, I know how much we'll be worth. We've had to wait for it long enough, but without you, and I mean all of you, it won't mean anything. All I want is some kind of assurance that he's not going to dominate your life from his fucking grave. I don't understand how you can keep on and on about him, keep loving such a cheap bastard.'

'You think I still love him?'

'It's obvious. You can't stop talking about the man! You go on and on about him to anyone who'll listen, even to a woman digging around for stuff that could put us in jail. If that's not love, then . . .' He raised his hands in a helpless gesture.

Sonja put her arms around him. 'I don't love him, you big fool.'

He had to prise her away from him, wanting to look into her green-grey eyes see if she was lying. They were steady, and she didn't flinch from his gaze.

'I hated him, and I have hated with such intensity I have hardly been alive. He betrayed and destroyed everything I valued, he made everything I was meaningless. He threw all I had done for him back in my face, mangled all the love and care I gave him. It was as if he held me in his bare hands and kept wringing me like a rag, until—'

Arthur interrupted, his voice soft, 'I've heard this before, Sonja. I'm not listening to you, but you should listen to me. I don't want his leftovers, I need more – and if you can't be free of him, then, for my own sanity, I have to be free of you.'

The phone rang and Arthur snatched it up, exchanged a couple of curt words with the caller, then said Sonja would be right down. 'The hair salon – you're late.'

He made as if to leave, but she held out her arms to him in entreaty. This time he did not, as he always did, cradle her to him and say it was all right.

'I'll be ready in a couple of hours,' she said, letting her arms fall back by her sides. 'I'll never mention his name again.'

He wanted to smack her, shake her, throw her across the bed. He said, 'Not enough – *that's not enough*. I don't give a shit if you talk about him, that's not what I've been trying to get across to you and you know it. Whether it's love or hate is immaterial. I'm just sick and tired of him being between us. When he was alive it was bad enough, but now he's dead . . . I sometimes wish to Christ I'd pulled the trigger.'

She gave a strange, sad smile. 'No, you didn't, but I did.'

He felt as if he'd been punched. He swallowed hard. 'Go and have your hair done.'

'I love you,' she said softly.

Arthur halted in his tracks. 'Say that again.'

She was smiling again now, but a different smile of fun and pleasure. 'I love you.' She laughed.

'No, what you said before that. After I said I wished I'd pulled the trigger. Repeat what you said.'

'I said I wished I did.'

'No, you didn't. You said, "I did."'

'Artistic licence – I needed an exit line.'

'No, your exit line was after you said you loved me. So – was it a joke?'

She closed her eyes. It was not that she was afraid to look at him, she was afraid she might lose him, that as soon as she had decided wholeheartedly to commit herself to him, he would be the one to back away. Suddenly she knew that that was more than she could bear.

'Of course it was a joke,' she said. 'I mean, if you wanted to pull the trigger, do you think I didn't?'

'Open your eyes,' he said, bending closer, and she did as he asked.

'Give me the exit line, only this time look at me.'

'I love you,' she said softly.

'You got me,' he said, his voice gruff. He had waited a long time to hear her say it, and mean it.

Lorraine ate her plastic lunch on the nine thirty flight out of Newark, eager to get the interview with Nick Nathan over and done with, and hoping the journey wouldn't be a waste of time. She landed in Albuquerque just after lunch and stepped out into the surprisingly pleasant dry air of a high altitude and to the limitless New Mexico sky: even in fall it was like walking on the bottom of an ocean of blue, which made even the mountains surrounding the desert city seem only knee-high. She carried her jacket over her arm, her briefcase in one hand and made her way through the terminal to the travel agent's. She picked up a rental car, a Buick, then, armed with road maps, pulled out of town into the landscape of grey rock, desert pine and juniper to look for signs for the I-25 to Santa Fe.

As she joined the Interstate, Lorraine noticed on the map that its first thirty miles followed the course of the Rio Grande, and she could not resist turning off the highway for a few minutes to look at the great canyon, plunging down hundreds of feet to a truly breathtaking depth. Its sheer scale produced an overwhelming sense of the measureless, almost the eternal, and Lorraine understood now why so many artists and writers had chosen to make New Mexico their home. Still, she allowed herself only a couple of minutes' delay – one middle-aged painter was all the scenery she had come to see.

Sonja came back from the beauty salon feeling glossy, gleaming and beautiful from top to toe, and she knew that part of the feeling of newness and freshness had nothing to do with the beauty treatments or the new hairdo: she felt that she and Arthur had turned the corner at last. It had been her fault, she knew, that it had taken so long, but she would make it up to him now.

When she got back Arthur was not in the suite, but there was plenty of time to dress, and she decided to wear a tailored navy suit with a crisp white shirt, dark navy stockings and matching navy court shoes. She had a Valentino navy and white check trench-style coat that she would slip around her shoulders. She had made up carefully and slightly more heavily than usual, glossing her lips in a deep pink shade she had bought downstairs to match her expertly lacquered nails, and she smiled in the mirror at her new manicure. It had been months, years, since she had taken such care of her hands, but she could have inch-long talons covered in scarlet glitter now if she wished. It had been months, too, since she had bothered to accentuate her eyes, her most striking feature, with shadow and mascara and the fine tracing of dark liner on the lids, which extended their length. When she had finished she studied her reflection carefully – a new woman, she thought, or, rather, a transformed one, risen from the ashes of the old.

She checked her soft leather document case for her passport and tickets, then snapped it shut and cast an eye over the rest of the luggage, which she had lined up by the main door of the suite. She checked that Arthur's cases were packed and ready, then searched the room to make sure nothing had been left behind. The limo would be arriving any minute, and she wondered where Arthur had got to. She hated last-minute scrambles to get to airports.

The phone rang – Reception, as she had expected, to say that their car was waiting. She told them to send up a porter for the luggage, and to take the other items the concierge was holding for her to the car. When the porter arrived with the trolley and loaded the luggage, there was still no sign of Arthur and Sonja sat at the writing desk drumming her fingers.

She didn't hear him come in, but she turned as she heard his voice. He counted the luggage, and then, as Sonja had done, reminded the porter not to forget the other things with the concierge. 'They know, I told them,' she said, then gasped. Arthur was wearing a white shirt with a Russian collar and a dark grey pinstriped suit. His hair had been trimmed and he was sporting a pair of round Armani sunglasses with steel frames. 'My, my, you've been shopping,' she said, smiling, and he posed with one hand on his hip.

'What do you think? It's too straight?'

'You look fabulous – turn around.' He did so, and Sonja clapped. 'You look so good – I really like it. My God, new shoes as well.'

Arthur looked down and removed his shades. 'Yeah, got everything from the same place, and I had a haircut and a shave at the barber's in the hotel, and . . .' He dug in his pocket and produced a small leather box, which he tossed to her. Then he looked closely at her, and took in her appearance with surprise: it had been months since he had seen her looking so elegant, so feminine, and he was almost unnerved by it. 'You look very grown-up,' he said, walking round her.

'I've had all these things for ages,' she said. 'Just never got around to wearing them.' She opened the box and gasped – it contained a solitaire diamond ring. She snapped it shut as the porter wheeled out their luggage. 'Are you crazy? I thought we'd agreed to be careful until . . . afterwards. How much did this cost?'

He pointed to the box. 'That was a legitimate hole in my legitimate earnings. Now open it again. You're supposed to look at me, all dewy-eyed, then I put it on your finger.'

'What?'

'Jesus Christ, it's an engagement ring – didn't you look at it properly?'

Sonja opened the box again and started to laugh gently. 'Engagement? Aren't we a bit old for that kind of—'

Arthur took the box from her and removed the ring. He hurled the box across the room. 'Now, gimme your hand and let me do this properly.'

The ring was a little too large for her finger, but it didn't matter – it made Sonja feel happy and warm. Arm in arm, they went to the elevators, where the porter was waiting.

Sonja twisted the ring round and round her finger, then she held up her hand to look at the stone. Arthur laughed as she examined it closely, and by the time the elevator stopped on the ground floor they were both laughing: the jewel was a fake, but an exceptionally good one. Sonja kept turning it on her finger as she watched the luggage being loaded into the trunk of the limo. Arthur's 'wardrobe' of paintings had been sent ahead on an earlier flight so that the canvases would be stretched, framed and ready for collection on their arrival in Germany, as had the new piece of work Sonja proposed to exhibit for the first time in Berlin. While she was receiving her award, Arthur would be delivering his own exhibition to the small independent gallery in Kreuzberg – a cover for negotiating the sale of a second collection, accumulated over years and valued at twenty million dollars, with the list of private buyers he and Sonja had carefully selected.

After leaving the Rio Grande flood plain, Lorraine drove through a switchback of gently rolling hills before she reached the lower slopes of La Bajaba, and began the ascent of the notoriously steep mountain. At last she reached the plateau and the centuries-old settlement of Santa Fe came into view, surrounded by the same backdrop of mountain landscape against the huge, azure sky. She drove into town, chose a small motel near the downtown area almost at random and booked a room in which to change and make phone calls.

She rang Nick Nathan's number. A woman answered and was at first wary, asking how Lorraine had got their number. She told her that Raymond Vallance had suggested she call: she was opening a gallery and needed to find work by unknown artists. Vallance had recommended Nick. The woman kept her waiting for some time before she returned to give the address and a time at which it would be convenient to call. Lorraine had two hours to kill, so she decided to check up on some of the local galleries and enquire whether any of Nathan's work was on sale.

Lorraine walked past a number of galleries in the Plaza and the surrounding streets, and even without specialist knowledge of art she could tell that some of the works displayed were as sophisticated as anything she had seen in LA. It was clear that the old town was an art snob's heaven. Everywhere, too, was the beautiful American-Indian jewellery, glowing rows of semi-precious stones surrounded by silver settings, whose traditional designs Lorraine recognized as the height of current fashion. She studied piece after piece in turquoise, lapis, amethyst, citrine, rose quartz, freshwater pearls and a dozen other stones, whose names she didn't know, before eventually buying a serpentine ring for Rosie, some lapis cuff-links for Rooney, and an elaborate necklace of five inlaid hearts suspended from a beaded choker, all in precious minerals and stones, for herself. She savoured, too, the opportunity to look for a gift for Jake. It had been so long since she had had someone special to shop for that the time flew past. Then she saw two heavy silver cuff bracelets, set with bars of turquoise and speckled leopard-skin jasper. She went into the shop and bought them both. When the assistant remarked on how beautiful they looked on her wrist, she spoke without thinking. 'They're for my daughters.'

As she waited for the bracelets to be wrapped, she repeated, 'They're for my daughters,' in her mind. She knew that what Jake had said, and Rosie had repeated to her, meant yet another step towards her future.

When she returned to the car, she checked the map, then began to concentrate on how she would question Nathan, and, most important of all, what she needed to get out of the interview.

The narrow alleyway ran between two four-storey houses with shop fronts, situated in the most rundown part of town. She headed down the alley past boxes of old garbage from both of the shops, and found a peeling door marked 48. As it was ajar, Lorraine pushed it open.

The hallway was narrow, cluttered with bits of broken furniture and a mattress was propped up against a door. A girl of about nine was sitting on the stairs, whose bare boards were dusty and well worn.

'Hi, I'm looking for someone called Nick. Do you know which floor?'

The child wiped her nose with the back of her grubby hand. 'Up, number eight,' she said, and held out her hand. Lorraine opened her purse and gave her a dollar, and the little girl ran out, squealing with pleasure.

Lorraine tidied her hair, then tapped on the door. She could hear a male voice talking and laughing, so rapped again louder, then hit the door with the flat of her hand.

A chain was removed, and the door opened an inch. 'Yes?'

'I'm Lorraine Page – I called earlier.'

'Oh, yes, one moment.' A dark-haired woman unhooked the chain and opened the door wide, stepping back almost to hide behind it. 'Come in.'

Lorraine followed her into the apartment. The cramped hallway was dark, with coloured shawls tacked to the wall. A fishing net was draped over a doorway, and a large papier-mâché sun hung above a stripped pine door, which stood open.

Lorraine was surprised – the room was large, and very bright. The sloping ceiling and walls were painted white, while the bare floorboards had been stripped and stained, then varnished to a gleaming finish. All four windows were bare of curtains, as the room was obviously used as a studio, and the light was important. Paintings were displayed on easels, and stacks of canvases lined the walls, propped against one another.

The woman, who had still not introduced herself, moved with a lovely fluid grace from window to window, drawing down blinds for much-needed shade: the room was unbearably hot. 'We don't have air-conditioning,' she said.

Lorraine recognized her vaguely from Harry Nathan's funeral. She was pale, almost unhealthy-looking, with large brown eyes, quite a prominent nose, and a rather tight mouth with buck teeth. She was not unattractive, but there was a plainness about her, and her straight dark hair, swept away from her face with two ugly hair-grips, needed washing. She wore leather sandals and a loose-fitting print dress, which left her arms bare, and she held her hands loosely in front of her.

'Do you want some coffee?' Her voice was thin, and she kept her head inclined slightly downwards, as though she didn't want to meet Lorraine's eyes.

'Yes, please, black, no sugar – but if you have some honey . . .'

'Sure.'

She started to walk out, but stopped and performed a sort of pirouette when Lorraine asked if she was Nick's wife. 'I suppose so – I'm Alison. Please look around. He won't be long – he's just on the phone.'

As the door closed Lorraine smiled. She began to look first at the half-finished work on the easel, a portrait of a dark-haired man with finely cut features, but full, sensual lips, apparently looking through water, with flowers resting against his cheek and the lips slightly parted, as if he were gasping for air. The painting was unnerving, because Lorraine was sure the subject was Harry Nathan. She didn't like it, not that the work wasn't good, for it was, but it had a childish, almost careless quality. She turned her attention to some of the bigger canvases on the walls, all of which had a similar wash of pale colour in the background, and featured the same man from different angles and in a variety of poses – hidden by ferns, screaming and, in one, with a sports shoe carefully painted on top of his head.

Other canvases were traversed by a series of palm-prints, or featured pieces of fabric and leaves, but all appeared half-finished, as if the artist had grown bored mid-way and moved on to something else. Lorraine looked closely at a painting on the wall furthest from the door, which showed a group of tall trees with some scrawled writing superimposed on them.

She turned as Alison reappeared with a large chipped mug, and held it out to her. 'Coffee.' Lorraine took it, and the woman remained standing nearby, her head still bowed.

'Are you a painter?' Lorraine asked, with false brightness: there was a servile quality about Alison that made her skin crawl, as if she were afraid of something.

'No.'

She was tough to make conversation with.

'Have you lived here long?'

'A while.'

Alison straightened up and flexed her shoulder. She began to massage the nape of her neck, then gave a faint smile and left the room.

Lorraine could hear what they were saying in the next room.

'I'm going out now – I've got a class.'

'Okay, see you.'

She moved closer to the open door: Alison was standing in the doorway opposite and the conversation continued in audible whispers.

'Is she looking at them?'

'Yes, she was when I took her coffee in.'

'I'll give her a few minutes, then. What's her name again?'

Alison replied, but Lorraine couldn't hear what she said, nor could she see the man she presumed was Nick. A phone rang, and Alison turned to cross to the front door, but waited a minute listening. Nick said hello to the caller, and Alison left.

Lorraine finished her coffee. She was becoming irritated – the call went on and on. She set the mug down on the floor and started to detach some of the canvases from the stack – all of the same man. She moved to the next group. These were much better, stronger. She found one she liked a lot and pulled it out. It was a crude, but powerful, life-sized portrait – not, for once, of the dark man but of an Indian brave in feathered headdress. She put it to one side, planning to ask the price – it would make a nice present for Jake. She was about to move to the next group of canvases when she heard a loud shriek, sustained for some time. She ran over to the open door.

'It says *what*? Go on! How old does it say he was?'

The cries continued. Lorraine stepped into the hallway and made her way to the doorway at the end of the passage. She stood just outside the kitchen.

Nick Nathan had his back to her and was leaning against the side of a table talking on a wall-mounted phone. His dark, slightly greying hair was pulled back, as it has been at the funeral, with a rubber band. He was barefoot and wore torn, dirty jeans and a paint-stained cotton shirt, whose sleeves were rolled up to reveal muscular arms, one wrist encircled by a heavy silver bracelet, and a similar ring on the third finger of his other hand.

'*Vallance shot himself*? You're kidding me.'

He listened, then shrieked again in the same high-pitched fashion. He was almost bent double, and Lorraine realized suddenly that he was laughing. And whoever was on the other end of the line was telling him about the suicide of Raymond Vallance.

The call continued for another ten minutes. Lorraine returned to the studio, wishing there was somewhere to sit down. She lit a cigarette, and had smoked half of it when the shrieking stopped.

Finally Lorraine heard the receiver banged down. She hoped that Nick Nathan would finally come in and greet her, but then heard the clatter of dishes, and his voice calling the cat. At last the man came in like a whirlwind. 'Hi – sorry to keep you waiting. I'm Nick.'

He danced across to her, and pumped her hand up and down. His eyes had a manic look, and he was sweating profusely, his thinning hair sticking to his scalp. He darted close to her, then moved just as rapidly away, looking pointedly at the cigarette and opening a window.

'I'm sorry.' She gestured to her cigarette, but Nick shrugged.

'You want to die, it's your choice.'

He smiled suddenly, showing even white teeth, but his eyes were hunted, and he couldn't keep still, wandering around the room dragging out one canvas after another. Now that she had seen him, Lorraine wondered if the man in the paintings was himself, but he didn't have the same high cheekbones – his face was flatter and plainer than his brother's.

'I'm interested in that one,' Lorraine said, tossing the cigarette out of the window.

Nick whipped round to look at the painting she had pulled out of the stack.

'How much?' she asked, uncomfortable. She couldn't seem to get centred around Nathan – he was so off-beam that he unnerved her.

'Five thousand dollars,' he snapped, as if challenging her, but she didn't flinch.

'I'll take it,' she said calmly, and he beamed, picking the piece up to admire it himself. Then he started to drag out canvases at an alarming rate, laying them around the room. He babbled to her, asking about her gallery, if she was looking for a one-man show, or intended displaying a number of artists' work together.

'How did you find me?' he said, so intent on finding work to show to her that he didn't appear interested in her reply.

'Raymond Vallance suggested I call you,' she said, and saw him stiffen.

'He's dead,' he said, staring at her.

'I know, he committed suicide.'

She was wondering how in the hell she could start to question him – the reason she had come – but knew that she had to tread carefully. From what she had seen of his work, Nathan did not have the technical virtuosity to imitate better artists, and he seemed so mentally unstable that he would be too dangerous to have in on any scam – but she had come all this way to interview him and she intended to do so.

Lorraine took out her cheque book and started writing. 'Do you show your work mainly in Santa Fe?' she said, pretending to make conversation but paving the way for the real question she wanted to ask.

'I guess,' Nathan said. 'I've shown in California too.'

'Did you work with your brother's gallery?' Lorraine said casually.

Nick eyed her suspiciously. 'How do you know my brother had a gallery?' he asked.

'Oh, just contacts,' Lorraine said airily. 'I know a lot of people in the art world – I've come across Kendall too. It must have been very useful, having a gallery in the family, so to speak.'

Nick said nothing for a while. Then, 'I had a few pieces in there.'

'Did you ever live in Los Angeles?'

'No. I just stayed at his place a few times.'

Lorraine finished writing the cheque with a flourish and Nathan slowly relaxed. 'I hated LA,' he said. 'Full of fucking phoneys. They wouldn't know art if it walked up and bit them in the face.'

'That's a pity. I'm sure Kendall could have promoted your work.'

He sneered, 'The only person Kendall ever promoted was herself, money-grubbing bitch. My brother wanted more of my work, but she wouldn't have it.'

'Her gallery was successful, though,' Lorraine said.

'Bullshit! Filled with crap, wallpaper paintings.'

'Yes, some of those paintings look as though just about anyone could do them,' Lorraine said innocently. 'I'm sure you could do stuff in exactly the same style if you wanted to.'

'You bet I could,' Nick said. 'If I wanted to.'

'It must be a great temptation,' Lorraine said, flattering him, 'I mean, for a real artist, if money's tight, to know you could make a lot more just by imitating someone who happens to be flavour of the month.'

'Well,' he said, 'sometimes I've worked in a particular way because that was what a buyer wanted – that's the difference between working to a commission and working for yourself.'

'You haven't ever copied, say, a specific painting?' Lorraine went on.

'What? You mean an exact copy of a named work?' Nick said. 'Absolutely not – that's forgery, in case you hadn't heard.'

'But it must be quite a temptation,' Lorraine persisted.

'Not to me,' Nick said. 'I couldn't do it if I tried – it's a specific skill, and besides, my own work's too strong.'

'You don't know anyone connected with your brother who maybe . . . wouldn't have quite the same scruples?' she asked. She tore out the cheque and laid it on the table.

'Who the fuck are you?'

'Someone who's got five thousand dollars on the table for you, but I need you to answer a few questions.' He shook his head, and kept on shaking it. 'I'm a private investigator.' She flipped him her card, but he didn't take it. 'I've been hired by your brother's lawyer, Mr Feinstein. Do you know him?' Nick glared at her, his arms wrapped around his body. 'I've been hired to trace assets missing from your brother's estate.' This elicited a flicker of interest. 'Paintings.'

'What?'

She'd hooked him. 'Either there's a mountain of valuable art concealed somewhere, or there's several million dollars hidden in an undected account.' She took the list of missing paintings from her briefcase, and passed it to him. 'These are the works I'm looking for.'

He took a long time reading the list, then let the paper drop onto the table. 'I wouldn't pay a hundred bucks for any one of those assholes' pictures.'

'Maybe you wouldn't, but other people did – or at least they thought they did. Various buyers at Gallery One viewed an original, got it authenticated, but then someone copied it, and it was the copy that was hung on their walls.'

'Well,' Nick said, 'it was nothing to do with me. Nice scam, though – I wish the bastard had cut me in on it.'

Lorraine studied him. Her gut feeling was that he was telling the truth. 'You don't know of anyone Harry could have been working with?' she asked.

'Well, Kendall's a pretty obvious candidate, isn't she?' he said. 'She would have dug up her grandmother's grave if she thought there was a nickel in it.'

'She was certainly involved in setting up the initial part of the operation with Harry, but he switched the paintings again to cut her out. I was just wondering if that was all his idea, or if someone else was pulling the strings.'

'They must have been,' Nick said. 'Harry was never like that.' Unexpectedly, he started to weep uncontrollably, rubbing at his eye sockets while Lorraine watched in fascinated horror at this sudden switch of mood. The crying jag ended as suddenly as it had begun. 'Sorry,' he said. 'My brother was better-looking than me, better at everything. He was a hard act to follow, and all my life, until he died, I was kind of following . . . I still can't believe he's dead.'

'Kendall's dead, too, now, did you know?' Lorraine said.

'Yeah,' he replied. He was obviously not interested in discussing Kendall's death so Lorraine changed tack.

'What does Alison do?'

He smiled, and stretched out his arms. 'She's a dancer, but dancing's a hard world, almost as hard as painting.' Then he asked, 'You know Sonja?'

'I've met her.'

'She sent you here, didn't she?' he demanded.

'No, I told you, it was Raymond Vallance.'

He shrieked with laughter again, mouth wide open. 'That old queen! He clung to his past glories like a falling climber.'

'At least he had some to cling to,' Lorraine said quietly, but her sarcasm was lost on Nathan, who gave another loud hoot of laughter.

'He was in love with my brother, everybody was in love with him. Everybody always thought he was something special, and you know something, I did too. It wasn't until he was dead that I realized he was a loser.'

Lorraine had heard enough and Nick Nathan irritated her. The trip to Santa Fe had been largely a waste of time, but at least she knew he hadn't been responsible for the forgeries. It was interesting, too, that the family's suspicions, like her own, seemed to centre on Sonja . . .

'I have to go,' she said. 'Can you pack up the picture for me?'

He parcelled it in newspaper and handed it to her, saying that if she wanted any more of his work, all she had to do was call.

'Just for my records,' she said, 'could you tell me when you last saw your brother?'

'Must be a couple of years ago, just before he and Kendall broke up. Come to think of it, they were talking about getting some painting copied. I thought they meant onto a slide – it was one of that asshole Schnabel's.' He moved out into the corridor, heading for the stairs, and Lorraine followed.

'Was it just Harry and Kendall, or was anyone else there?'

'There was another guy – Arthur something, I don't know his last name. It was after a show Kendall had, and he and I had a kind of fight – over the Schnabel. I said it wasn't worth the hook it was hanging from and he kind of went for me. Fucking asshole.' Nick stopped on the landing to continue his tirade against Julian Schnabel, talentless bum, in his opinion, promoted by a clique of art insiders interested in lining their own pockets by inflating the prices of certain court favourites' work. 'Everything's fixed, you realize that? Art has got nothing to do with the market.' He jabbed his finger into Lorraine's chest. 'I've trailed my work round every fucking New York gallery. I send in my slides and they lose them. Then they buy a fucking piece of canvas with a wooden plank sticking out of it. That's not art.'

Lorraine stepped back to avoid Nathan's finger, and decided to risk interrupting him. 'Do you recall anything more about this Arthur?'

'Big guy, dark,' Nick said, setting off down the stairs.

'Do you know if he was a painter?' Lorraine asked, hurrying after him.

'I don't know. Bastards like Schnabel probably pay people like him to talk up their work. He hung around after the show, like he was waiting for me to go, and I thought, Fine, screw you, I'm just the guy's fucking brother, so I walked out. Then I forgot my jacket so I go back, and the three of them were out back in a kind of workroom, and Kendall and Harry were standing behind him, and he was using this big lamp, looking over the canvas, right, and . . .'

'What exactly did he say?' Lorraine asked. 'It's very important.'

'Oh, I can't remember. Kendall said something about

401

having a buyer and he said something about getting a copy made quickly. Maybe he's your rip-off artist.'

'Did you ever see him again?' Lorraine asked.

'No, I never went back to LA,' Nick said, then gave a boyish smile, and clapped his hands together, like a salesman who had just clinched a big deal. 'I hope you enjoy my work, and you have a real nice day. Been great meeting you, Loretta.'

Lorraine didn't correct him. 'Nice meeting you too, Nick,' she said, turning to go. Had he really just remembered this vital detail from the past, or was it a ploy on the part of Nathan's family to incriminate Sonja and her lover?

CHAPTER 18

LORRAINE RETURNED to the motel, her head aching. She called Feinstein and told him that she was beginning to find leads, and asked if her expenses could run to another trip, this time to visit Nathan's mother.

'Christ, she's in Chicago,' he demurred.

'I know, but it might tie up some loose ends.'

'Go ahead, then,' he said, and gave her Abigail Nathan's address and phone number.

Lorraine called Rosie to say she would not be coming home that afternoon, but would try for the following morning. Rosie agreed to keep Tiger for another night, and Lorraine heard Rooney in the background asking to speak to her.

'Lorraine,' he said, 'I've stopped by the office a couple of times and there's someone calling you all the time.'

'Well,' Lorraine said, 'if they're looking for my professional services you can tell them I'm about to retire.'

'It's not that,' Rooney said. 'Whoever it is hangs up the whole time – no message. Rosie and I thought it might be Jake, but you've spoken to him, haven't you?'

'Yes, I have. He's too busy for that kind of thing, anyway,' Lorraine said.

'That's what I thought. There's so many calls it's like someone's doing it deliberately, to make you realize someone's trying to get to you – it's like they think you must know who it is. I was just wondering if you've trodden on someone's tail.'

'Well, that's a possibility,' Lorraine said thoughtfully. 'How long has this been going on?'

'A few days,' Bill said.

That meant it could hardly be anything to do with Nick Nathan, which left only Sonja and Arthur, Lorraine thought, but said nothing to Rooney.

'Is there anything I can do from this end?' he asked.

'There is, Bill. In my office there are two plastic bags. They've got a lot of catalogues from art galleries, with notes from Decker. Can you go through them and find out about a painting by Julian Schnabel? It would have been in the Nathan gallery about four years ago. It's not on my list, but see if there's any record of it, and I'll call you from Chicago.'

'Okay, will do . . . and you look after yourself.'

She caught Burton at the station, and once she heard his voice she wondered what the hell she was doing planning yet another detour.

'So,' he said, 'I get three guesses, right? You're coming home late, you're coming home late, or you're coming home late?'

'Well,' she said, 'I did say it might be tomorrow.'

'I know you did,' he said, easily. 'I bought you an extra-specially non-perishable present.'

'I bought you one too,' she said. 'A timeless work of art by Nick Nathan.'

'Mine's pretty timeless too,' he said, and something in this voice told her immediately what it was.

'Oh,' she said softly. 'Do I get three guesses?'

'No,' he said. 'I don't want to spoil the surprise. Just get your ass back here fast.'

'Will do,' Lorraine said. 'I swear I'll see you tomorrow even if I pass all of Feinstein's paintings at a garage sale on the way to the airport.'

'If *that* happens,' he said, with a deep laugh, 'you can miss the plane. Otherwise, see you then.'

She was about to hang up when she remembered what Rooney had said about the messages left at the office. 'Just one thing,' she said. 'You haven't been calling my answerphone at the office for any reason? Rooney says there've been some weird calls.'

He laughed again. 'I'm flattered I'm the first person you thought of but, much as I miss you, the answer is no.'

After they hung up, she had another fifteen minutes of considerably less cordial conversation with an irate agent at the airline before she succeeded in rearranging her flight, but she was en route to Chicago by late afternoon.

Sonja and Arthur waited for their luggage in the terminal at Tegel, the airport at Berlin, having already enlisted the services of a porter with a trolley. They had arranged for a car to pick them up outside. Sonja got in and leaned back, closing her eyes. 'God, I feel nervous, now that we're actually here. I kept thinking someone was going to challenge us when we went through customs.'

'Why would they? The paintings are at the gallery now.' He took her hand and squeezed it. 'We're here, and the paintings are here, it's nearly over. Just stay calm. We've already got over the most difficult part.'

'Yes, but you've still got to do the deal.'

'Don't worry,' Arthur said. 'The buyers are lined up and waiting and they'll eat right out of my hand.'

Lorraine booked into the Chicago Hyatt, where the room was pleasant and well-furnished, and called Abigail Nathan at once. Her voice sounded young, and when Lorraine explained that she was working for Mr Feinstein in connection with her son's estate, she immediately said she was free that evening or Lorraine could call the following morning. It was already after ten and Lorraine asked if she could come at nine the next day.

She planned an early night to be refreshed and ready for Mrs Nathan, so she showered, booked an alarm call for six and went straight to bed.

Rooney let himself into Lorraine's office and crossed to check the answerphone: the light was flashing, and the new message indicator was displaying the figure twenty-two. He replayed the messages to discover that only one was legitimate, from Feinstein. On the remainder the phone had been put down. The caller's attempts to alarm Lorraine had, however, intensified, and there were ominous silences, sometimes heavy breathing, and, on the last, what sounded like six blasts of gunfire. This was clearly intended as a threat, and Rooney was certain that the caller believed their identity was known to Lorraine.

He picked up the plastic bags he had come to collect, turned off the lights and left the building.

Back home, Rosie was cooking up a storm, trying out a new recipe for pork tenderloin with a complicated pink sauce, and was red-faced and flustered. 'I don't know what I've done with this sauce – I put enough cornstarch in it to hang wallpaper, but it's not thickening like it should,' she said, waving a wooden spoon.

'Whatever you serve up, honey, will be fine by me.'

He went to get a beer, and they jostled each other for space in the small, but well-equipped kitchen. 'Go on, go sit down. Table's already set,' Rosie said, pushing Rooney away gently.

He plodded out with his beer, then turned back to her. 'Usual creepy messages on her answerphone,' he said.

'Probably Jake.' She laughed.

'Yeah, probably,' he said. He was on the point of telling her about the gunshots, but decided to wait until after dinner, not wanting to spoil the meal she had taken such trouble with: Rosie worried enough about Lorraine as it was. Almost as soon as they had finished eating, however, Rosie's former AA sponsor called and asked if she would help him out at a meeting where he needed someone to sponsor a young girl.

'Do you mind, Bill?' she said. 'I know I said I'd stay home this evening, but if someone had been too busy to sponsor me, I never would have quit drinking.'

'And you would never have been working for Lorraine and I would never have met you.' Bill smiled. He knew that Rosie had a genuine desire to put something back into the organization that had changed her life. 'Go on out – I'll go through this stuff of Lorraine's.' She dropped a kiss on top of his head, got her coat and hurried off, with a promise not to be too late.

Left alone, Rooney spread out the catalogues and thumbed through them, looking for the painting

407

Lorraine had mentioned. He found no record of it. He flicked through Decker's notes of dates and times for each gallery he had visited, saddened by the task – the boy had been so organized, such a good find for the agency, and it was dreadful that he had died in such a terrible way, so young and, as his voluminous notes testified, so eager to prove himself. Rooney kept on flicking backwards and forwards, matching catalogues to Decker's notes on the galleries, then saw something that made his blood run cold.

In Decker's neat handwriting was a name and address – Eric Lee Judd, employee at Nathan's art gallery. Rooney sat back and drank some beer. He couldn't be mistaken. He knew it had been a long time, but it was a name he would never forget. When she had been drunk on duty, Lorraine Page had shot a teenager. The boy's name had been Tommy Lee Judd.

Rooney put in a call to Jim Sharkey's home, but he was out on a case so he left a message asking him to call. It was after nine and he wondered if it was too late – bad district to go calling on anyone late in the daytime, never mind at night, but he mulled it over, and drained his beer. To hell with it, he thought, why not? His adrenalin buzzled like old times – it was too much of a coincidence, and he wondered if he had just solved the mystery of Lorraine's unidentified caller.

Half an hour later, Rooney was heading towards the eastern suburbs of LA, having packed a shooter – he wasn't taking any chances. Like Decker before him, he had a hard time making out the numbers of the houses on the side-street near Adams and, like Decker too, he passed the Lee Judd bungalow and had to reverse back to it down the street. Lights blazed, so he knew someone was at home. He got out, took a good look around, locked the car and walked up the drive to the front door. He rapped hard and waited several minutes before knocking again. This time he saw the outline of a figure shuffling towards the door through the dirty glass.

'Who is it?'

'Bill Rooney. Mrs Lee Judd? Is that you? I'm Bill Rooney – used to be Captain Rooney, you remember me?'

The front-door chain was eased off, and she peered through, fear on her big moon face.

'It ain't bad news? Please, God, you ain't come with bad news?'

'No, Mrs Lee Judd, no bad news, not this time, but I need to talk to you.'

The door opened, and the woman looked up with frightened hazel eyes. Her dyed blonde hair showed two inches of dark root growth, and mulberry lipstick ran in rivulets round her flaccid lips. She was grotesquely over-weight and her body gave off the distinctive stale smell of sweat. 'You ain't lying to me, are you?'

'No, ma'am, I'm not lying, but I need to talk to you.'

Rooney stared at the photograph. The boy was wearing the jacket with the yellow stripe down the back, his face half turned towards the camera. Unlike the other children in the photograph, Tommy took after his mother and was pale-skinned, while all his brothers and sisters had the dark colouring of their father, Joshua Lee Judd.

'Tommy's been gone a long time now,' she said sadly.

'Yes, a long time, Mrs Lee Judd, but never forgotten.'

She shook her head. 'You don't forget a boy you've

given birth to, no matter what he done, or what they say he done. He was my youngest, you know?'

'I know. Can I sit down?' he asked.

'Sure, you want something to drink?'

'No, nothing.'

She eased her bulk into a worn armchair, and Rooney sat opposite her.

'So, how have you been keeping?'

'My legs give out on me – knees all swelled up – and they say my heart's beatin' too hard or something, but I'm near sixty.'

There was a terrible tiredness about her, which made her seem much older.

'How's your family?' Rooney asked kindly.

She sucked her teeth. 'Joshua upped and left with some little girlfriend of his daughter's – may the good Lord forgive him, for I sure don't. I had six mouths to feed, and all he could think of was having his way with an eighteen-year-old. Some husband, some father.'

'I'm sorry.'

She shrugged her shoulders. 'Saved me from gettin' beat on regular, and good riddance, but sometimes he could be a real sweet-hearted man – it was just the liquor turned him mean. I've heard he's straightened out, got himself a regular job – not that he sends me no money – and got himself another couple of kids too, so I don't press for payments. I know it's takin' from the mouths of his new family, and you always got to put them first.'

'You're a good mother.'

'Yes, sir, when the good Lord takes me, he'll know that. It's all I was put on this earth for, 'cos God knows I ain't been good for much of anything but rearing kids.

Losing my little Tommy hurt me bad. When they die young, they stay young.'

'How's all his brothers doing?'

She took a wheezy breath. 'I got one working for a real estate outfit, suit an' all, another in a bakery, another in prison, and I got one . . . He was going bad, but he straightened out real good. He had a job uptown.'

'Doing what?'

'Odd jobs. For an art gallery – hanging paintings, sweeping up, cleaning. It was permanent, but the pay wasn't good, so he's looking elsewhere right now.'

'Was it the Nathan gallery?'

'Yes, sir, but a lot of bad things happened. There was a fire and she – the lady that owned it – was killed in it, so he was out of a job. Since then he's been looking hard.'

'That'd be Eric?'

'Yes, Eric, my oldest. I know he was in trouble a few times, but I swear to you, he's a good boy now.'

'He live at home with you?'

'Sometimes. He got his old room, but he comes and goes. He sees I don't go short, though. Why you come here? On account of my Eric?' She leaned forward. 'What you want here in my house?'

'I'm not sure – just an answer to a few things. Did you ever meet with a guy, maybe asking questions about the gallery?'

'No, sir.'

'You sure about that? Only I have some notes he made and, according to them, he paid a visit to you. It'd be a while back now.'

'No, sir, I had no one visit me.'

411

'How about someone calling to see Eric?'

'No, sir, no one has been here, I'd swear to that on the Holy Bible.'

'Is Eric around now? Could I see him?'

'No, he's out right now.'

Rooney was sweating – the cluttered room was stifling hot, even though only the screen door was closed. There was no breeze from the yard, and no air-conditioning.

'Does Eric drive?'

'Sure he drives. He needed a clean licence for his work at the gallery, and Mrs Nathan, she provided a van for him to deliver an' collect. He was workin' there quite a while.'

'Did you ever go to the gallery?'

'Who me? No, sir, I don't get to go no place, not with my condition.'

'Did you ever meet Mrs Nathan?'

'No, Lord have mercy on her, I never did. I'm praying my boy gets work soon – see, with her gone, who's gonna give him a reference? An' he worked a long time for that gallery.'

Rooney turned to the bank of family photographs, dominated by the large one of the dead Tommy.

'Which is Eric?'

She smiled and pointed. 'The sharp-lookin' one. He always was a fancy dresser.'

Rooney stared at the picture of Eric, gold chains round his neck, leaning against a wall and smiling to reveal a gold-capped tooth. Rooney had seen a few other photographs of Eric – in police files. 'So he's been straight since he got out?'

The big woman pursed her lips, then took a folded cloth from her pocket and dabbed her face and neck. She was sweating profusely. 'That is all behind him, mister. He swore on his brother's grave he would get out of that bad crowd he was mixin' with. It wasn't easy, believe me. You get into one o' those gangs round here and they don't let you out.'

'No drugs any more?' Rooney asked quietly.

'No, sir. Like I said, he swore on his brother's grave, day he came out of the pen. He went straight to the graveside and he got down on his knees, in front of me and his brothers and sisters, and he said he would stay clean. That was more'n seven years ago.'

'You sure now, Mrs Lee Judd? I mean he's unemployed right now, and, like you said, he comes and goes, so how can you be sure?'

She banged the side of her chair. 'One brother, one son dead is enough. He wouldn't do that to me.'

'Does he blame himself for Tommy?'

She dabbed her neck, then looked at him directly. 'There was one person to blame. We knew it, and you cops knew it too, but she never come to justice. She never come to court, she got away with murder, an' *no, no*, my boy don't blame himself. It was that bitch cop.'

'You recall her name?' Rooney asked.

'No, sir, I do not.'

'Does Eric know who she was?'

'I can't answer for what Eric knows.'

'So he blames her too, does he?'

She clenched the arms of her chair. 'You tellin' me he ain't got the right to blame her? She fired into that boy, kept on shooting. He was nothin' to do with what was going on, he was just an innocent boy, and she shot him down like a dog.'

'But he was there, wasn't he? Looked like he was being used by Eric as a runner.'

'Eric says it was a lie to get that woman off.'

'But there were traces of cocaine found.'

'No, sir, don't you tell me lies. They'd have had that poor child shooting up to serve their purposes, but he was innocent, and Eric swore on the Bible he was not using him. An' if you come here today to try an' rake up dirt for some reason, then you get out of my house, you hearin' me?'

Rooney stood up. Mrs Lee Judd was panting with anger, and he patted her shoulder. 'Now, don't you go gettin' all upset.'

'Why you come here? What do you want?'

Rooney hesitated, then looked at the big framed photograph of Tommy Lee Judd. 'Just making enquiries, Mrs Lee Judd, an' if you tell me Eric's a reformed character, then . . .'

She dragged herself up to stand in front of him, shoving her face forward. 'Like I said to you, Eric stood over that grave, an' I won't hear no bad things about him – he's a good son.'

'Well, I sincerely hope so, and more than that I hope he's not runnin' with the gangs again, because if he is I'll be right on his neck an' fast. I think your boy is looking for trouble, big trouble, so you warn him to stay in line. Warn him to back off – and quit making nuisance phone calls.'

Rooney got up. He had wanted to unnerve the woman, even though he wasn't sure that it had been Eric Lee Judd calling Lorraine. It was just that old second sense, plus the fact that Eric might have seen her visit the gallery.

'I'll see myself out. Just tell that boy of yours I was round, okay?'

She wouldn't let him go by himself, but shuffled after him, down the dark, dingy hallway. She wasn't going to let him wander around her house like those snooping cops were inclined to do – she wanted this fat man out, and the door bolted behind him.

Rooney heard the bolts being slammed across the front door, then the chain, and he knew she was watching him through the broken stained-glass window. He went straight to his car, and drove out of her drive.

He parked about a hundred yards away down the street and made sure all his doors were locked. He wondered how long it would be before Mrs Lee Judd contacted her son and told him about the visit – his old cop's nose knew she'd be trying, because one look around that cramped, dilapidated house had revealed a new TV set and video, fridge-freezer and washing-machine. They stuck out like a sore thumb beside the rest of the furniture, and were obvious signs of ready cash, signs of a kid handing over fistfuls of dollars to his mama.

Rooney sighed, and lit a cigarette: Lorraine had got off lightly from the Lee Judd episode. She was never called to court, as by the time of Eric Lee Judd's trial she was long out of the force, hell-bent on drinking herself to death. There had been a major cover-up – he knew that better than anyone, as he'd been responsible for most of it – but the boy was not the innocent his mother had tried to make out. They had found traces of cocaine on his hands and inside his jacket pockets, that black jacket with the yellow stripe down the back that little Tommy had coveted because it had belonged to his brother Eric. They had also taken statements from two other kids they'd picked up, who had said that Tommy was running for his big brother, who was dealing to some of the clubs, mostly cocaine and ecstasy. Six months after the trial, Eric Lee Judd had been arrested in another bust, and this time he had served three years.

Rooney smoked the cigarette down to the butt, and lit up another. Maybe he was putting two and two together and making five, but the whole thing was just too much of a coincidence. Maybe Eric had sworn to go straight on his kid brother's grave, but he might also have sworn some kind of revenge.

As soon as Rooney had gone, Mrs Lee Judd heaved her bulk up the worn stairs, one step at a time. She had a bed made up for herself downstairs, and hardly ever went up to the bedrooms – when any of the family stayed her daughters cleaned up there, and Eric changed his own sheets. She was frightened, not wanting to believe what Rooney had hinted at, just like she didn't want to believe that Eric had been up to no good since he lost his job at the gallery. She'd confronted him with it when he brought home the new TV set for her birthday, and he'd flown into a rage, saying that he'd spent all his hard-earned savings to make her happy, but he could never make up to her for Tommy. She always put Tommy first, just like she'd done when they were kids, and now he was dead he still got more love and attention than she ever gave to her surviving son. She had wept, and then he had put his arms around her, crying too, saying that all he ever wanted was to make up to her for what happened to Tommy.

She was crying now, as she heaved herself up stair after stair, because deep down in her weary heart, she knew that Tommy would have done anything for Eric. Little Tommy always followed Eric around like he was some kind of hero, had started to strut about the streets in his bomber jacket, and she had been worried he was getting into trouble, with his big brother leading him by the hand.

The bedroom was untidy, dirty, with old beer cans and bottles lying everywhere, and ashtrays piled high with cigarette butts. The wardrobe door was open, revealing rows of suits and shoes, and she rifled through the dresser drawers. They were full of shirts and T-shirts, some stuffed back dirty, likewise a drawer full of underwear. On the top of the dresser was a picture of Tommy, held in his brother's arms when he was no more than four or five, and she picked it up, kissed it, said a silent prayer for forgiveness for searching her son's room like a thief. As she put the photograph back on the dresser, she saw a smaller top drawer, open just a fraction, and slid it open. Inside was a tangle of jewellery – watches, bracelets, rings and heavy gold pendants with thick twisted-gold chains. There were also rolls of dollars, secured with rubber bands. She eased the top drawer closed then searched the others, finding two guns, knives and more rolls of banknotes. Her bosom heaved as she drew a deep breath, standing in the untidy room with her swollen feet planted wide apart to maintain her balance. Then, helping herself along the wall, she moved out and down the stairs, one by one.

Her breath rattled in her chest as she returned to the living room, picked up the phone and dialled a telephone number written on a pad beside the phone – Kelly, Eric's current girlfriend, whose number he had left in case of emergencies. There had been a lot of numbers over the years, always thoughtfully tucked by the phone. 'Kelly, honey, this is Eric's mama – he with you?'

She could hear loud music thudding in the background, heard Kelly shouting for Eric, who came quickly to the phone, his voice full of concern. 'Mama? You sick?'

'Yes, boy, I am. You come right home now.' She put the phone down before he could say any more, then eased her bulk into the sagging armchair. She picked up her walking stick from the side of the chair, raised it high, and brought it down on the new TV set, smashing it repeatedly against the casing, then thrusting it with all her might into the screen. The glass cracked, and still she kept on thrashing, as if she was thrashing Eric, the way she had when they told her about Tommy. She had beaten the hell out of him then, and now she attacked the fruit of his crimes with the same violence.

The pain shot down her left arm like a red-hot iron passing through her veins, piercing her again and again. The stick dropped from her hand as her body jerked in spasms of excruciating agony, and the last thing her frightened eyes saw was the picture of her dead son, Tommy Lee Judd, shot six times by a woman detective she'd heard was a drunk.

Rooney lit a third cigarette, inhaling deeply. He'd been outside in the car a good fifteen minutes. He could be wrong, he knew, she'd said the other kids were all in good jobs, and maybe they'd bought all the fancy new domestic appliances. He leaned forward to turn on the ignition, deciding he'd call it quits for the night, and check it out in the morning.

Not five minutes after Rooney had driven off a new black-on-black Cherokee jeep with black-tinted windows screeched to a halt in Mrs Lee Judd's drive. Eric, high on crack cocaine, ran from it and tried his keys, knocking when he found the bolts still fastened inside. He raced round to the back door, and kicked the screen door aside to see his mama lying face down, close to the fireplace, with her right hand outstretched. Just a few inches from her fingers was the framed picture of Tommy, the glass smashed to smithereens. In the last moments of her life she had tried to hold him – a last-born child is often the favourite, and Tommy had been hers.

Eric stood rooted to the spot, his head feeling as though it was on fire. He knew she was dead, that her big heart had burst in her chest, as blood oozed from her nose and mouth, and he didn't need to feel for a pulse. Slowly he stepped over her, and bent to retrieve the broken picture. He removed the jagged pieces of glass, and set it back on the shelf, his hand shaking. He felt it was some kind of omen, a message from the grave, and one that he would obey. The bitch cop would pay for what she had done. He'd make her pay.

Rooney let himself in, and was attacked by Tiger, though the dog was clearly more motivated by affection than any desire to guard the household. Rosie had already gone to bed, and Rooney undressed, cleaned his teeth, and got into bed beside her. She turned over and propped her head on her elbow.

'You know, you were making the floor shake. You

men are all alike, creeping round the bed, then sitting on it to take off your shoes.'

'I was trying not to wake you,' he grumbled.

'Well, you didn't succeed – first bang on the front door did it. You were gone a long time.' She stared at him, but his eyes were closed. 'Want to talk about it?' she asked.

He lifted one big arm up to let her snuggle in beside him, then drew her closer. 'I may be wrong, and I hope to God I am, but I think Lorraine may have a problem. You know the kid she shot? In a drug raid?'

'Yeah, I know about him.'

Rooney sighed. 'Well, he's got a brother, and this brother worked for the Nathan gallery, sort of handy-man-cum-driver-cum-delivery. Kid's been out of work since the gallery went up in smoke – and I just feel uneasy about it. Could be him making the phone calls. I kind of gave his mother a bit of a warning to back off just in case I'm right, that he's gonna try and take some kind of revenge on Lorraine.'

'You really think so?'

'Yep. There were another twenty-odd calls on her answerphone and one had what sounded like gunfire, six shots. She pumped the same amount into Tommy Lee Judd.'

'What you going to do?'

He sighed again. 'I'll talk to Burton, maybe see if he can sort it out, or run a check on the guy.'

Rosie lay on her back, staring at the ceiling. 'How did you find all this out?'

Rooney yawned. 'From the catalogues and stuff in that fag Decker's bag. His notes gave the Lee Judd address so I called round, talked to his mother.'

Suddenly Rooney sat up, and tossed the bedclothes aside. 'That accident, the crash that guy was in – it was on the intersection just a mile up La Brea from the Lee Judds' place.' He stomped out of the room, and Rosie grabbed a robe and followed him. He was banging around the kitchen looking for tea bags. Rosie reached up and took them out of a tin.

'It's another fucking coincidence, isn't it? He puts in his notebook that he's going to see Eric Lee Judd, the guy's mother said nobody ever came, but she could be lying, so what if Decker had come up with something, and . . .'

'But there was no other vehicle involved, apart from the garbage truck he drove into. It was an accident – he jumped the lights,' Rosie said, getting the teapot and setting a tray with cups, milk and a tin of cookies. She carried the tray into the bedroom, and poured tea for them both, but Rooney seemed disinclined to discuss Lorraine any more. 'Nothing we can do tonight,' he said. 'Maybe just keep this to ourselves – no need to get her all worried. Let me see if I can sort it out.'

Rosie sipped her tea, agreeing with him. She knew he was worried, as she was herself, but as he had said, there was nothing they could do that evening. By the time she put the tray on one side, turned off the bedside lamp, and settled back on the pillow, she thought Bill was asleep. But his hand reached out for hers and held it tightly. 'Nothing's going to happen to Lorraine, trust me.'

Lorraine went to the hotel gym for a workout, then returned to her room to dress and pack before going downstairs for breakfast and to settle her bill. At eight twenty, she took her luggage and asked the doorman to call her a cab. By ten to nine, she was drawing up outside Abigail Nathan's house in Norwood Park, an area north-west of the city centre. She was surprised that the house didn't match her expectations. It was in a nice white-collar area but it was small, an unattractive, square building. The lawns in the street had no fences and the properties abutted directly onto one another, divided only by garage drives and dinky, crazy-paved paths to the front doors. Mrs Nathan's drive was covered in leaves and rubbish, which looked as if it had been there for some time.

Lorraine stepped onto the veranda, which also needed sweeping. The lamp on the porch was broken, but antique. Lorraine rang the doorbell and waited. She could hear soft music playing. She rang again and a woman's voice called out that she was coming.

Mrs Nathan was wearing a satin floral print robe, which reached to her bare, mottled calves, and a pair of very old and worn pointed Moroccan leather slippers. She looked older than she had seemed at the funeral, but perhaps the deterioration in her appearance was due to grief. She put out a tiny hand, with thin fingers and arthritic knuckles. 'Hello. You must be Mrs Page.'

'Yes, thank you for seeing me, Mrs Nathan.'

Mrs Nathan ushered her straight into the drawing room, as there was no hallway. 'Sit down.' She indicated a satin-covered Victorian sofa, with curving sides and ugly, heavy legs. 'I won't be a moment.' She disappeared into the kitchen.

Lorraine looked around the room: there was a huge chandelier of fine Italian glass, and the place was crammed with antiques, ornaments and trinkets. A collection of hundreds of tiny glass animals and Victorian children's toys stood in several glass-fronted cabinets. Dust was thick on all the ornaments and furniture, and newspapers, empty envelopes and circulars were littered around the room – a complete contrast to her elder son's obsessive neatness. Lorraine wondered if the house had always been so neglected, or if Mrs Nathan had simply let everything go after her son had died.

She returned with a carved wooden tray, two chipped china cups and mismatched saucers. As there was no space on any of the tables, she set the tray down on a footstool, and asked how Lorraine took her coffee. 'Black, please, no sugar,' Lorraine answered. 'Have you lived here long?'

'Forty years,' the old lady answered. 'I meant to move when my husband died, but I brought my boys up here and you can't put memories like that in a packing crate.'

She carried her own cup to the big armchair, kicking aside the newspapers that covered the floor around it, and settled herself, like a small, rotund Buddha, her feet resting on an embroidered footstool in front of her. 'Also, of course, I can't bear the thought of having to pack up all these treasures – I'm a collector, as you see. I don't collect anything that isn't of intrinsic value, of course, I've never seen the point.'

'You have some lovely things,' Lorraine said.

'It's a sort of pastime for me, since I've travelled so much, all round the world so many times,' Abigail Nathan continued, seeming to want to make sure that Lorraine realized that she had been a rich woman and accustomed to deference. 'My boys came with me when they were young, and that's where they got their education. Artistic talent can't flourish, I've always thought, without the soil of culture,' she concluded grandiosely. 'I knew from the time the boys were babies that they would create.'

Lorraine made an effort to keep her face impassive as Mrs Nathan talked as though her elder son's vulgar movies and her younger son's daubs ranked as great art. 'You mentioned that you were working for poor Harry's laywer – did you ever meet my son?' Abigail Nathan went on.

'No, but I met Nick – in fact, I bought one of his canvases,' Lorraine said, hoping that she would be pleased.

'You'll be able to sell it for ten times what you paid in a couple of years,' Mrs Nathan said with complete confidence. 'I have high hopes that Nicky's work will be recognized. Ever since he was a small boy, painting has been his life.'

'Do you mind if I ask you some questions?' Lorraine said.

'Please do. I'm obviously interested – my son must have left a considerable amount of money. I haven't been told how the estate is to be divided, and when I telephoned Mr Feinstein, he said that woman' – clearly, as Raymond Vallance had said, there had been no love lost between Abigail and Sonja – 'has the house at least. I feel certain that there must be some mistake. Harry would not have forgotten his brother, of course. They simply adored each other. The boys always got along so well.'

Lorraine eased the cup and cracked saucer onto a table crowded with knick-knacks. 'It is indeed a considerable sum of money, Mrs Nathan, and there seems to be no trace of it in any of your son's known accounts. That means that it's likely he had banking facilities elsewhere – perhaps here in Chicago, I thought, or perhaps in other names?'

'I don't know anything about that. My son never discussed either money or business with me,' Abigail Nathan said, as though mentioning subjects unfit for ladies' ears.

'Did he visit here frequently?' Lorraine asked.

'He came when he could,' the old lady said. 'He had a busy life in Los Angeles, though he wrote me regularly and, of course, I used to visit with him, when he was married to Kendall.'

Lorraine seized the opportunity to embark on another line of questioning. 'Mrs Nathan, the primary assets missing from your son's estate are some valuable modern paintings. It seems that there may have been certain . . . irregular dealings on the art market.' She knew better than to accuse Harry Nathan directly of fraud to his mother. 'Which Kendall may initially have instigated.'

'Well, I find that simply impossible to believe,' Mrs Nathan responded, with a haughty sniff. 'I count myself a pretty fair judge of character, and Kendall was the only decent woman my son was ever involved with.'

'Can you think of anyone else involved in the art market whom Harry might have been working with?'

'I certainly can,' Abigail Nathan said with emphasis, then hesitated as though trying to bring herself to utter an indecent word. 'That wretched woman who wrecked my son's life. Sonja, whatever she calls herself now. I can tell you that if there was any kind of irregularity going on, that woman was behind it. She is a person without moral sense or scruple of any kind.'

'I have recently interviewed Sonja Nathan,' Lorraine said, keeping her voice expressionless. 'She denies having any sort of contact with Harry since they got divorced. The separation was not amicable, I understand.'

'No wonder.' Mrs Nathan snorted. 'Sonja couldn't stand the fact that Harry finally realized that he should have married a nice, sweet, normal, natural girl.' God knows how he ended up with Kendall in that case, Lorraine thought privately, but the older woman was in full flow. 'Sonja was a completely unnatural woman from the day and hour Harry met her, and she simply got worse with age. I blessed the day Harry got that woman out of his life, and it broke my heart when he started seeing her again.'

'What makes you think he *was* seeing her again?'

'He used to telephone her from here,' Abigail Nathan said, and Lorraine felt her pulse quicken. At last: someone had stated that Harry and Sonja Nathan had indeed remained in contact, but whether it was an indulgent mother's attempt to cover up her son's wrongdoing and incriminate a woman she disliked remained to be seen. 'It was the only time Harry ever lied to me. That woman had a hold over him of a kind I've never seen.'

'What sort of untruth do you mean?' Lorraine asked.

'He said he was talking to some business associate, fixing up meetings, but I knew it was her.'

'How did you *know* it was her?' Lorraine asked.

'Because I called the phone company and got a record of the long-distance calls made on my line,' Mrs Nathan said, giving Lorraine an arch look.

'I don't suppose you still have these records anywhere in the house,' Lorraine asked, glancing around the room – it looked as though nothing had been thrown out in a decade, and it struck her suddenly that if Nathan had been in regular correspondence with his mother, those letters, too, were in all probability nearby.

'I might have,' Mrs Nathan said, looking carefully at Lorraine, as though her appearance might yield some clue as to whether or not she could be trusted.

'Mrs Nathan, if Sonja is responsible for a substantial fraud and perhaps a more serious crime,' Lorraine said, meeting Mrs Nathan's eyes with what she hoped was a frank, honest gaze, 'then I will naturally be handing over the matter to the police.'

'I told the police that I suspected that woman was mixed up in my son's death and they pretty much told me to go home to my patty-pans. Just an old lady with a bee in her bonnet. They didn't have to say it, but that's what they were thinking.'

No doubt they were, Lorraine thought, and the fact that Harry Nathan had called his ex-wife a few times must have seemed innocent enough. But in the context of so many other circumstances that seemed to point to Sonja, and in particular the flat denials Lorraine had received from both Sonja and Arthur that there had been any contact between her and Harry after they divorced, it was important evidence. Though Nathan could, of course, have been calling to speak to Arthur – the two men had known one another for years, and it was possible that Arthur was helping Nathan with his forgery scam without Sonja's knowledge. Lorraine realized she had never asked Arthur if *he* had had any contact with Harry Nathan. But that had seemed unlikely – Harry Nathan had to be the last person with whom Arthur would secretly have been best buddies.

'I'm afraid that the police often take such allegations

lightly when they're made by a member of the public,' she said, 'but they might be more inclined to take it seriously against a background of other evidence coming from a . . . more professional source.'

'You mean from you,' Abigail Nathan said bluntly.

'Yes, I do.'

There was silence for a few moments while the old lady weighed up the pros and cons of trusting Lorraine. 'Well,' she said at last, 'I could go and look upstairs, if you have time to wait.'

'I'm in no hurry,' Lorraine said. 'Or I could come and help you, if you'd like.'

'That won't be necessary,' said Abigail Nathan. 'You wait right here. You can look around my collection.'

She got up, and Lorraine heard her slow footsteps climbing the stairs. Look around the collection was exactly what she would do, and particularly the collection of papers in the ginger jar. She waited until she heard the woman's footsteps overhead, tipped it out and flicked through the contents – Abigail Nathan had kept all sorts of junk, matchbooks, photographs, dinner menus and letters, but the most recent was from a woman friend, dated 1994.

There were papers all over the house, and Lorraine decided to investigate further. She opened the door to the next room noiselessly and found herself in a den full of trinkets and toys, bursting out of cupboards and balanced on a number of little spindle-legged tables. Looking round the room, her eye was caught by a most unusual display of carved red wooden devils, no more than a few inches high, with hideous faces and cloven hoofs, holding a pack of miniature playing cards. Lorraine bent down to look closer, genuinely interested, and saw, tucked into the corner of the cabinet, an airmail envelope with a German stamp. She eased it out, recognizing Harry Nathan's large, untidy handwriting. The postmark was a few months old.

'Mrs Page?' Abigail Nathan called. 'Are you down there?'

Scarcely thinking what she was doing, Lorraine reached under her jacket and slipped the letter into the back of the waistband of her skirt, then walked smartly out to see the old lady making her way downstairs.

'Yes, I'm here, Mrs Nathan. I just went to the bathroom.'

'I see. I have what you wanted here – I never throw anything away.'

She held out two sheets of paper. Lorraine's hand almost trembled as she took them. 'Thank you, Mrs Nathan,' she said. 'May I take these back to LA?'

'You take them wherever you like,' Abigail Nathan replied, 'if it'll help to get justice for my son.'

Lorraine placed the sheets of paper in her briefcase, and said, 'I'd better be on my way now, I'm afraid. Can I call a cab?'

'Certainly,' Mrs Nathan said graciously, waving her hand towards the filthy kitchen as though ushering Lorraine into a palace. 'Phone's through there.'

Lorraine found a card for a cab company pinned next to the phone and made a quick call. 'It'll just be a few minutes,' she said, hanging up. 'One last thing, Mrs Nathan. I don't suppose you know anything about a man named Arthur? I don't know his last name, but Harry knew him as a young man and he's living with Sonja now in the Hamptons.'

'You mean Arthur Donnelly. He and Harry were in

college together. He was a painter, he said, but I knew he'd never get anywhere. Masterly technique, of course, but simply nothing of his own to say. I told him he ought to count his blessings and join the family firm.' She laughed at the recollection.

'What was that, Mrs Nathan?' Lorraine asked curiously.

'Oh, an outfit in the antique trade. All reproduction.'

Another piece of the puzzle slotted into place, Lorraine thought, recalling the sticker Cindy had found inside the fake antique jar. It looked like Arthur had indeed taken Mrs Nathan's advice.

The doorbell rang and Lorraine picked up her briefcase. She thanked Mrs Nathan profusely.

'So glad to have been of assistance – if I have – and if you hear anything you will contact me, won't you?'

Once the cab was clear of Abigail Nathan's house, Lorraine reached carefully under her jacket and extracted the envelope. She took out a single sheet of folded airmail notepaper, with no address, simply the salutation 'Dearest, sweetest Cherub-face'. The first few lines expressed hopes that she was sticking to a diet, using her exercise bike and not, underlined, eating too many cookies. He went on to say that he was abroad for just a few days, and from Germany he would be going on to Switzerland, but then underlined was, 'No one must know, that also means do not' underlined 'tell even Nicky.' He said he would explain on his return. He went on to say that within a few months he would be mega-rich, that he was on to something that would set him up for the rest of his life. The writing was slapdash, and looked as if it had been scrawled in a hurry: some was in cursive script, the rest in capital letters.

Lorraine replaced the note in the envelope and slipped it into her case. There had been no record of this trip to Germany and, most importantly, to Switzerland on Nathan's official passport. This must be a clear lead to the secret bank accounts. She suddenly sat up. Germany! Sonja Nathan had said what? There was an exhibition of her work being shown in Berlin. Sonja was there now, and Lorraine did not doubt that it was in connection with the art fraud that she and Arthur had evidently been running with Nathan.

The net was closing, and Lorraine felt an almost ungovernable impulse to follow Sonja to Europe and run her to earth. She would have to act immediately – but the thought of telling Jake that she had to make just this one trip, follow this one lead, pushing his patience and understanding yet again was too much for her. She knew that next time he saw her, he wanted to give her a ring and make their engagement public. Suddenly she wanted nothing more than to see him, Rosie, Rooney, Tiger. She had been away too long.

CHAPTER 19

S ONJA STOOD in one of the airy, vaulted halls of the Hamburger Bahnhof in Berlin, the former railway station that had been stunningly restored as an art gallery. All the pieces she had executed during the past seven years were placed around her. People stood sipping drinks in front of them, but even more were gathered before her latest work, a huge rectangular structure draped in a black cloth, which was to be unveiled later in the evening. She scanned the unmistakably prosperous but vapid-looking crowd as she waited for Arthur to come back with her drink, and reflected that art snobs were the same all over the world.

Arthur returned with a glass of champagne for her just as she observed the two organizers of the exhibition bearing down on her. 'Arthur, I think I'm about to be carried off.'

He knew that she wanted him to go and, glancing at his watch, saw that it was almost time for him to pick up the car that would take him to Kreuzberg.

'Well,' he said, 'I'm afraid I have to run. Good luck, Sonja.'

Outside, the car was waiting, and Arthur switched his mind to the negotiations, which had been complex, though on the surface not illegal – none of the paintings he was about to sell were known to be stolen, none had been reported as such. By the time that happened he and Sonja would be long gone, and if the Japanese buyer he had lined up took the bulk, he wouldn't care. In Japan if a buyer of a painting could prove ownership for two consecutive years, the work became irrecoverably his or hers, and could be shown with impunity. This evening's sale had taken years of planning, years of secret meetings and hours of his time forging the artists' work. It was his own work now that he was thinking about: if this deal came off he would have the rest of his life to paint in luxury. If it went wrong, then he might spend it in prison. Either way, he mused, he'd be able to paint.

Because California time was two hours behind Chicago, it was only mid-afternoon when Lorraine got back to LA. She went straight to her office, eager to check Decker's research, but it wasn't until she was there that she remembered Rooney had it. She dialled Feinstein's number. To her irritation, he was in court, so she left a message. Next she called Rosie and Rooney, and left a message asking Rooney to bring Decker's carrier bags to her apartment as soon as he could.

At that moment Rosie and Rooney were with Jake Burton in his office. He had listened intently to everything Rooney had to say about Eric Lee Judd.

He had warmed immediately to the couple, knowing how highly Lorraine regarded them. 'Did she mention anything to either of you about her brake cables being cut and that someone broke into her office?'

They shook their heads.

'Well, whoever it was did some damage – didn't steal anything but made their presence known by using acid to destroy some tapes.' He shrugged. 'Could be whoever it was had been hired by one of the suspects and discovered something else in the office.'

'Like what?' Rooney interjected, leaning forward.

'That it was someone from her past who knew her, had a grudge against her,' Burton said.

Rooney looked to Rosie. 'I said there was some kind of hidden agenda, didn't I?'

Rosie was chewing her lip. She felt very uneasy. 'Do you think Lorraine knows?' she asked Burton.

'No, I don't, but she must be told. Have you any idea when she'll be back from Chicago?'

Rosie tried to recall exactly what Lorraine had said when they had last spoken. 'I'm sure she said she'd be back in LA this evening.' She looked up as Burton eased from his chair. He cracked his knuckles. He was obviously worried.

'Is she in danger?' Rosie asked.

'Not for the moment but, all the same, I want you to go back to your apartment in case she makes contact. In the meantime, I'll check out this Eric Lee Judd, maybe get someone to monitor what he's up to.' Burton put an arm around Rooney. 'I appreciate all you're doing for Lorraine, but don't worry, I won't let any harm come to her.'

Rooney coughed and stuck out his hand, which Burton clasped. 'I wasn't sure about you, not at first, but . . . we also appreciate everything you've done for our girl. She's very special.'

'Yes, I know,' Burton said softly.

As he closed the door behind the Rooneys he stood in the centre of the room. He could feel an ominous tug in the pit of his belly because just the thought of any harm coming to Lorraine made him realize again how much he loved her and wanted to protect her.

It was almost six when Lorraine was dropped outside her apartment, paid off the cab, and checked all her luggage and parcels. She had quite a few, plus the painting from Nick Nathan, so her hands were full as she opened the street door and climbed the stairs. The apartment door was ajar, and she smiled, sure that Rosie was inside. She called her friend's name as she pushed open the door with her case. 'Rosie? Are you here? Rosie?'

She put down the briefcase containing the phone records Abigail Nathan had given her, her overnight bag and painting, and turned to close the door. She didn't see or even hear her assailant, as the blow to the right side of her head had such force it lifted her off the ground. She tried to roll away, curling her body against the blows that continued to thud into her. One slammed into the small of her back and it felt as if her kidneys were exploding. She straightened out with a scream of agony, but the blows kept on coming, no matter which way she tried to fend them off. She couldn't tell if she was being kicked or punched. The pain was so vivid it was as if she was on fire. She couldn't cry out, she had no strength, and the last blow to the side of her head rendered her unconscious. Lorraine had not even glimpsed her attacker, who now, out of some reflex instinct for robbery, rapidly searched through her overnight bag. He found nothing of value, and as the briefcase was locked, he took it, throwing it into the back of his car before he drove off.

She lay motionless, face down, her battered body twisted like a broken doll, blood forming a dark pool around her head.

Sonja waited for the applause to subside as she stood on the small podium at the front of the gallery. 'Ladies and gentlemen,' she said, 'first of all I would like to thank the board of this exciting new treasure house of contemporary art,' she turned to smile at the two women behind her, 'for the honour they have done me in asking me to open the series of shows dedicated to living women working in sculpture. This will, however, be an occasion of endings as well as beginnings,' she went on, 'because as well as inaugurating a chapter in the work of this great new gallery, this evening will mark the end of my career.' She delivered the words in clear, ringing tones, knowing that they would take everyone present by surprise. 'My work has been my tyrant, my torturer, and it has come close to being my murderer,' she went on. 'It did not exorcize and transform the dark parts of myself, it fed and magnified them, and it has left me to live with the result, which is what I, and the man who has been brave – or foolish – enough to make a commitment to me, now intend to do.'

Somehow it was the mention of Arthur, of her private life, that turned the murmuring and head-shaking to hissing and booing: Sonja looked at the audience with the gaze of a heretic, hearing the crackle of her reputation burning around her.

Rosie was first up the steps. She knew something was wrong: Tiger was barking and yelping frantically, running from the open front door to the apartment and back inside. Rosie called Lorraine's name, but when she made it to the top of the steps she started to scream.

Lorraine lay slumped by the side of the front door, her face unrecognizable. Her shirt and shoulders were soaked in blood, which had sprayed up the walls and splashed over the door, and formed a puddle beside her head. Rooney pushed her out of the way and knelt down beside Lorraine, feeling for the pulse on her neck, then her wrist, shouting instructions to his wife to call the emergency services. He could feel only a faint throbbing, so faint that at first he had thought Lorraine was dead. 'She's alive – get me blankets, hurry. Are they on their way?'

Rosie was weeping, nodding, running into the bedroom. Rooney had to knock Tiger out of the way as he tried to get to Lorraine, then growled at him. He had to shout to Rosie to get the dog out of the room.

Rosie rode with Lorraine in the ambulance to the nearest hospital, St John's in Santa Monica, and Rooney followed behind in his car. He felt icy cold, shaken to the core, and he doubted that Lorraine would survive.

Jake had to sit down, his whole body shaking. It was some time before he could speak. 'How bad is it?'

Rooney wanted to weep, but gritted his teeth. 'She's hurt real bad. She's in a coma and they've taken her into Intensive Care.' He swallowed as the tears welled up. 'It's bad, Jake, real bad. They don't think she's gonna make it.'

'I'll be with you in ten, fifteen minutes depending on the traffic.'

Jake let the phone drop back onto the cradle. His body felt stiff and his mind blank. He was unable to take in what Rooney had said. He made himself go over the call again, then picked up his coat like a robot, and walked out. She was not going to die, he told himself. She was going to be all right.

Rosie handed Rooney a cup of coffee from the machine and sat close, resting against him. 'She's going to be all right, isn't she?'

'Yes.' He sipped the lukewarm excuse for coffee. 'She's as strong as an ox. She's gonna be okay.' But his words sounded hollow. Rosie's tears trickled down her face. They had been waiting for news, any news, for fifteen minutes.

Jake walked in, his features drawn and frightened. 'How is she?'

Rooney stood up, offering his hand. 'We don't know – they told us to wait here.'

'You want to tell me what happened?'

'We don't know. We got to her apartment and found her. At first I didn't think she was alive – she'd taken one hell of a beating. He used a baseball bat, left it by the door.'

'Who did you call?'

'Local guys, Pacific Area Homicide. They were on the spot within minutes, so were the paramedics. They brought her into Accident and Emergency to get her blood matched for a transfusion, and did some X-rays.'

Jake sat down and clasped his hands. 'You get a name? Someone I can talk to?'

Rooney wiped his face with his hand. 'Yeah, officer said his name was Larry Morgan.'

'I'll go call him.'

Jake was gone for several minutes. When he came back there was an almost pleading expression on his face – begging for news, good news, but there had been none. He sat down beside Rooney. 'They've taken the baseball bat for finger-printing, and they also got some bloody shoe-prints, some kind of sneaker. It looks like he broke in and was lying in wait – they found some screwed-up cans of Coke by the bed, as if he'd been waiting for her in the bedroom.'

Rosie said, 'I was there yesterday. I watered the plants, and there were no Coke cans then. I'd have seen them, put them in the trash can.'

There was an awful silence, as all three sat staring straight ahead.

'I've put out a warrant for this Lee Judd guy's arrest,' Jake said softly.

'Good,' Rooney said.

'You think it was him?' Jake asked, frowning.

'We'll soon find out. They get prints off the Coke cans?'

'Too early yet – it'll take a couple of days.' Jake got up, then sat down again.

Rosie took out a tissue and blew her nose. She had been crying off and on ever since she found Lorraine. No sooner did she get a grip on herself than the tears poured down her cheeks again.

Rooney lit a cigarette, ignoring a prominent 'No Smoking' sign. He leaned forward with his elbows resting on his knees, inhaling deeply and hissing out the smoke. He could think of nothing more to say to Jake, could think only about the lady he had grown to love and admire so much, sure that this couldn't be the end: life couldn't be that cruel.

Jake sat straight-backed, gripping the arm of the grey airport-style armchair, still in shock, still unable to believe that he might lose the woman he felt it had taken him his whole life to find.

The three sat in silence, but all with the same hope, that Lorraine would live. They were each wrapped in their own thoughts and memories of her, knowing there was nothing they could do but wait. That was the worst part of it all – the awful waiting, and the helplessness.

'Perhaps I'm addressing myself particularly to other women artists,' Sonja said. She had to raise her voice to be heard over the critical rumblings from the crowd gathered around the podium. 'The relationship of art to life is a complex one, on which wiser commentators and greater artists than myself have expended a considerable amount of thought. Whatever else is true of art, it is true that its practice changes the nature of one's relations with other people – and I think it deprives those relations of precisely the qualities of equality and repicrocity which women, in particular, cherish as ideal. For those reasons I think some women artists are not kept out of art by hostile conspiracies, but choose to remove themselves from it – as I now choose myself.'

The room erupted into chaos: Sonja's face had returned to mask-like impassivity, and she stood motion-less on the podium, as people continued to shout, jeer, and hurl incoherent questions at her.

As she turned to descend the steps, the crowd parted with ill grace to allow her to pass. She made her way to where her latest work was waiting to be unveiled. Taking a deep breath, she turned back to face the crowd.

'Ladies and gentlemen,' Sonja said, 'I consider art to be a sort of second-hand synthesis and simulacrum of other more truly destructive arts, acts in real life, of which the artist is also the author.' She finished quickly before the reaction to her words set in. 'That is certainly the case with this piece, my last, entitled *Quietus Est*, which I present to you now.'

She pulled the cloth off the sculpture, to reveal a huge glass tank full of reddish water. People crowded closer to observe the figure of a man floating inside it, the head hideously damaged and the face as though exploded.

Two more hours had passed, and Rooney and Rosie were still waiting in the small seating area outside Intensive Care, from which no amount of new carpet or pot plants could remove the atmosphere of anxiety and tension. Jake had gone to Reception to make some calls, and looked expectantly at them when he returned, but Rooney shook his head. No one had walked out of the unit, and the double doors had remained firmly closed.

'They just arrested Eric Lee Judd – holding him overnight for questioning,' Jake said. 'What do you think is going on in there?' He glanced at the doors.

Rooney lifted his shoulders with a sigh. 'Means she's still alive. That's all I can think.'

They all turned as the doors banged open and a small army of green-clad doctors and nurses appeared, removing their masks as they walked past. They looked exhausted. One youngish man lagged behind the others as he took off his mask. 'How is she?' Rooney blurted out.

'Are you relations?'

'Yes,' Rooney lied.

As the doctor slid off his green cap he seemed less young. 'I'm Dr Hudson – I've been heading the team. You mind if I sit down? It's been a long night.'

He sat, holding the cap loosely in his hands while his mask dangled round his neck.

'I might as well give it to you straight. She's in a very deep coma. She has a base-of-skull fracture and her right ear-drum is perforated, which means that she's losing fluid from the brain through the ear.' He rubbed his scalp, then took a deep breath. 'She is on a ventilator. Her ribs have been fractured, and have punctured the lungs, so both air and blood are escaping into the chest cavity. We've had a tough fight in there, as tests have also shown her kidneys are malfunctioning. The right cheekbone and right side of the jaw have been shattered, and there is also serious damage to the right eye.'

Rooney's heart was pounding. 'Is she going to live?'

Dr Hudson twisted his cap. 'She is critically ill and, as I said, in a very deep coma. We have a long way to go. We'll just take each day as it comes, and see whether she regains consciousness when the sedation is reduced. The main work we've been able to do this evening was to insert drains in the chest wall to clear air and blood from her lungs. We have to stabilize her breathing before we can carry out any other procedures.'

'Can we see her?' Rosie asked.

'You can see her through the viewing window outside the IC unit, but I'm afraid you will not be allowed inside.' He stood up. 'I'll ask one of the nurses to come and take you through. It may be quite a while.'

'We'll wait,' Jake said.

Hudson kept on turning his cap in his hands. 'I'm sorry it's not better news. Mrs Page is a very sick lady.'

He hated these sessions, trying to give hope, when in reality there was very little. In Mrs Page's case, it was already more than a probability that she had severe brain damage.

It was midnight before Sonja got back to the hotel to find Arthur waiting for her, a glass of whisky in his hand. 'How did it go?' he asked.

'Well,' she said, 'you won't believe it but it was one of the most bizarre evenings of my life. I announced that I was retiring and I couldn't resist telling them that art had all but wrecked my life and that I was getting out because I was sick of it and that I wanted a life with you.'

'You said that?' Arthur was incredulous.

'More or less. They went wild. But then I showed them the new piece and they went wild again – they

443

loved it. I think I just had the most successful show of my life.'

'Sonja,' Arthur said evenly, 'I haven't asked you this before, but what is your new piece?'

Sonja looked away. 'I'm sorry, Arthur,' she said, 'I had to do it to get rid of him.'

'Sonja,' Arthur said again, 'just tell me. I'll see it in the papers tomorrow.'

She said nothing for a moment, then looked him steadily in the face. 'It's Harry,' she said. 'It's Harry in the swimming pool. The way they found him dead.'

He knew then that Sonja had killed her ex-husband. For a moment he thought of asking her the question directly, but he knew there was no need to do so: they both knew the truth. Perhaps he, too, had become as detached, as amoral, as she was, for he found he was indifferent to Nathan's physical life or death: the invisible hold he had had over Sonja for so long was all that concerned him.

'So,' he said, 'they loved it?'

'They were practically jamming commissions into my coat pockets.'

'So what's the next project?' Arthur said, with a sudden bitterness. 'Son of Harry?' Sonja flinched, and he knew his words had hurt her enormously, but he carried on. 'Or should I say ghost of Harry?' He was almost shouting at her now. 'How long is this going to go on? We talk about it again and again, but nothing ever changes. Your heart belongs to Harry, winter, spring and fall.'

It was the crudest and most painful speech anyone had ever made to Sonja, and it was only with an intense effort of self-control that she prevented herself from weeping. 'On the contrary,' she said, standing very still and upright, 'I will not be working again, no matter what commissions are offered to me. I meant what I said – it is finished.'

Arthur saw a tremor run through her and he knew that, no matter what Sonja said about wanting to give up her work, it was a sacrifice, and one that cost her dearly . . . Or maybe now that she had destroyed the man who had inspired and obsessed her, her art had simply left her as a bird takes flight from a tree. An abyss of doubt suddenly opened in front of him as he looked at the ring he had put on Sonja's finger and wondered what bargain he had made, what it was to which he had pledged himself. A murderess? A woman who was finally prepared to commit herself to him, to make sacrifices for his happiness? Or just an empty shell? One never could know the secrets of another soul, he thought, and suddenly he knew that he did not care what she was or what she had done: what he felt for her lay deeper than any question, any answer, any doubt.

'I'm sorry,' he said, moving close to her and putting his arms around her. 'Perhaps I'm the one can't stop talking about him now.'

'It's all right,' she said, her voice oddly thick. 'It really is finished now.'

There was silence for a moment, and then she broke away. 'How was your evening?' she said with a smile, her tone normal. 'Are we in the clear, or on the run?'

He smiled back at her. 'The former, it seems. It went even better than we hoped – the money will be transferred into the Swiss account by nine tomorrow.'

'How much?' she asked.

'Twenty million dollars.'

Sonja inhaled deeply, then let out her breath slowly. 'My God, I don't believe it.'

'You'd better, it's taken long enough but . . . we did it.'

He crossed to the mini-bar and she watched him take out a half-bottle of champagne. 'I think we should drink a toast.' He opened it and handed her a foaming glass. 'To Harry Nathan,' he said, and saw her eyes widen in shock.

'Arthur . . .'

'No,' he said. 'Lay the ghost. To the man who made possible both our successes this evening. Harry Nathan, RIP.'

'RIP,' Sonja echoed. 'I never want to say his name again.'

'Well, then, that's a second toast,' he said. 'To us.'

She raised her half-empty glass, and he saw that she closed her eyes as she drained it, as though holding her nose to jump into a new and strange sea.

'To us.'

Lorraine's head was swathed in bandages to just above her eyes, and her face was grossly bruised and discoloured. Drips for fluid, plasma and blood fed into her arm, while others had been inserted in her mouth. Her arm was encircled with a blood-pressure cuff, and she was connected to a cardiac monitor. The rhythmic hiss of the ventilator, pumping air into Lorraine's lungs, and the dreadful bubbling noise of her breathing were the only sounds. A probe-like clip to measure the levels of oxygen in her blood was attached to her finger, and she lay perfectly still, unaware, in some limbo between life and death.

'Oh, God,' whispered Rosie, her hands pressed against the glass partition.

'There's nothing we can do here,' Jake said quietly.

'Come on, Rosie, let's go home,' Rooney said, taking his wife's arm.

'No,' she whimpered.

'We'll come back tomorrow, and we've got to take care of Tiger.'

They left, unable to speak. Seeing Lorraine so isolated, so vulnerable, so distant from them, frightened them. Having seen with their own eyes the terrible punishment she had taken, it was hard to believe she could ever be the same Lorraine again.

'She's a fighter,' Rosie said hopefully, as she got in beside Rooney and slammed the car door shut.

'This is one fight she might not win, Rosie. We got to face up to that.'

Rosie wouldn't look at him. She clenched her fists. 'Well, maybe I know her better than you, Bill, and I'm telling you she's as strong as an ox. She'll beat this, I know it.'

'I hope so, darlin'. I sincerely hope so.'

Lorraine was closely monitored through the night: she remained in a deep coma, her pulse low. She showed no sign of movement in any of her limbs, and as yet they had been unable to establish the extent of the brain damage she had sustained. When the surgeons and staff reconvened the following morning, it was suggested that

Lorraine's close relatives be told to be ready to come. There had been no progress; if anything she had regressed, and there was little hope of recovery.

Rosie had stayed with Tiger at Lorraine's apartment. She packed nightdresses and toiletries ready to take to Lorraine as soon as she was allowed to have visitors, but she knew when Rooney called at eight thirty in the morning, it was bad news. At nine o'clock she and Rooney called Lorraine's ex-husband to inform him of the situation. Mike Page was shocked, asked which hospital Lorraine was in, and if he would be allowed to visit. Rooney suggested he call the hospital himself, saying only that he had been asked to inform Lorraine's immediate family and that she remained on the critical list.

Mike replaced the receiver, shaken. Although he had not seen or spoken to his ex-wife in over two years, he was still affected emotionally by the news of what had happened to her. He immediately saw in his mind the Lorraine with whom he had fallen in love, the Lorraine who had worked day and night to allow him to gain his law degree, the Lorraine who had given birth to his two beautiful daughters. All memory of the violent drunkard, the pain-racked woman he had been forced to divorce for his own survival, was gone.

Sissy, his wife, walked into his study with the morning's mail. 'You're going to be late, darling, and the girls are waiting for you to take them to school.' She stopped, and took a good look at him. 'What's happened?'

He took a deep breath. 'It's Lorraine, she's . . .'

'Is she dead?' Sissy asked.

'No – on the critical list. It didn't sound very hopeful. Not that they'd tell me much over the phone.'

'I'm sorry,' she said, putting her arms around him.

'I'll go and see her this afternoon.' He hesitated. 'Do you think I should take the girls with me?' Sissy shrugged her shoulders, and began to tidy his desk. He took her hand. 'Just stop that. I mean, she is their mother.'

'Well, she hasn't been one for a long time, Mike, and they're so settled. I just don't want them upset. The last time she visited – the only time – Sally was in a terrible state, and Julia . . . Look, it's not up to me, but I'd think twice about it. Maybe see her first and then decide.'

'Okay, I'll go straight to the hospital after lunch.'

'What happened?'

'I don't know. As I said, they weren't too forthcoming over the phone. They just said the outlook wasn't good.'

'Was she drinking again?'

'I don't know, Sissy. I'll find out, and I'll call you.'

As he left, Sissy could hear the girls, waiting outside by the car, calling him to hurry up. She crossed to the window and watched them drive away, then went back to his desk, covered with family photographs – their son, away at camp, and the two girls. No one could believe they weren't Sissy's daughters: they were as blonde as she was, both tall for their age, both pretty, but so like their mother, Lorraine . . . It made Sissy feel sad just thinking about what Lorraine had lost, their growing up, their first prizes at school, their first tennis matches, their first time swimming without water-wings, the trill of their voices calling, 'Mommy,' because they both now called Sissy by that name – had done so from almost the start of her relationship with Mike.

She picked up one photograph after another – herself with the girls, Mike with them, the family all linking arms on a forest trail when they had been on a camper trip. Lorraine had never been any part of the girls' lives, and now she had appeared again. Sissy was fearful of what it would do to them, and to Mike especially. She knew Sally and Julia would have to be told and, if Lorraine was as ill as Mike had implied, they should at least have the opportunity to get to know her before it was too late. Sissy had no idea that it was already too late: that Lorraine was dying.

'I found these,' Rosie said, producing two gift-wrapped packages, one marked 'Julia', the other marked 'Sally'.

'She must have bought them for her daughters. Maybe she was planning what Jake suggested, getting in contact with them again.' Rooney sniffed, and turned away. 'Maybe we should call him, give him an update.'

'Yes, we should,' Rosie said sadly, then forced a smile. 'She's going to pull through this, Bill, I know it. Do you feel it too?'

He didn't say anything – he couldn't, because deep down he didn't believe what Rosie had said.

'We'll take that goddamned dog with us then, shall we?' he said.

Rosie's face puckered, and she went into the bedroom. Tiger lay stretched full-length on his mistress's bed, with her nightgown, dragged from beneath her pillow, in his mouth. He didn't know what was going on, but when

Rosie tried to get him off the bed he flatly refused to move, and when she tried to take the nightgown out of his mouth he gave a low growl.

Rooney and Rosie left Lorraine's apartment, dragging Tiger by his lead. Neither had been able to prise open his jaws to remove the nightdress, and it trailed on the floor, clamped in his teeth. They packed the car with everything they thought Lorraine might need, and then drove off. Rosie turned to look back at the apartment.

'Don't look back, darlin', it's unlucky,' he said quietly, and suddenly Rosie had a terrible premonition that Lorraine would never come home. She started to cry, and he patted her knee, near to tears himself, but the sight of Tiger's grizzled head on the back seat, still with Lorraine's nightdress between his jaws, touched him more than anything else. It was as if some sixth sense had told the dog, too, that Lorraine wasn't coming back.

Feinstein was told what had happened later that morning – Burton had called him after he had checked Lorraine's answerphone and collected her mail. He'd even watered her plants before he'd locked up and returned to the station.

By now they had questioned Eric Lee Judd, who maintained that he had been with four friends the entire evening, and was adamant that he didn't even know Lorraine Page or where she lived. The four friends were contacted and each verified Eric Lee Judd's alibi. Without further evidence, he would be released.

No prints were found on the baseball bat, none on

the crushed Coke cans. Whoever had attacked her was a professional, Burton knew, and had been careful to avoid leaving any trace detectable by the forensic lab. The bloodstains on Lorraine's clothes were found to contain no other blood group but her own. However, the bloody footprints taken from the carpet, and from the vinyl flooring by the stairs at the entrance to the apartment, were size nine, and showed the clear outline of a sneaker sole. Eric Lee Judd allowed the police to take samples of all his footwear. Nothing matched.

By twelve fifteen that morning there was no evidence against him and Eric Lee Judd was released from the police station. He was cocky and self-assured, warning officers that if they continued to harass him he'd take legal action.

Detective Jim Sharkey had been the main interrogator, and he had stared with loathing at the boy, then shaken his finger. 'You tread very carefully, Mr Lee Judd, because I am going to be right here.' He tapped the young man's shoulder. 'You put a foot out of line and . . .'

Eric Lee Judd glared back. 'What'll you do, mister? Get some drunk cop to fire six rounds into my back? That what you'll do, huh? Then cover it up, so they get away with it? Fuck you.'

'One foot out of line and I'll fuck you, son – just remember that. Now get out of my sight.'

Eric Lee Judd whistled as he strolled down the corridor. He stopped in his tracks when Lieutenant Burton stepped out of his office and their eyes met.

Lee Judd had no notion of who the tall, fair-haired man was – all he knew was that his eyes were like lasers, and those eyes watched his every move as he passed and bored into his back as he continued along the corridor. He turned back, a little afraid now but unable to resist another look, then kicked open the double swing doors leading into the last corridor before he made it to the street. He began to run then, run like his kid brother had all those years before. But that was settled now: the bitch had paid the price, and he had got clean away with it.

'How is she?' Sharkey asked Burton, who was still standing as if frozen.

'No news yet. No news.' He lowered his head, then gave Sharkey a small, bleak smile. 'Thanks for asking.'

Burton turned on his heel and returned to his office, closing the door quietly, leaving Sharkey alone outside. Sharkey went to the incident room: work would continue as usual – nothing ever stopped at the police department, not even when the life of someone many of the officers knew hung in the balance.

Burton's door opened again, and he snapped out Sharkey's name. The officer whipped round. 'In my office, Detective Sharkey, in fifteen minutes. I want you to go over some files I've taken from Lorraine Page's office. It's the Nathan case.'

Burton's door slammed shut with an ominous bang, and Sharkey sighed and muttered as he continued up the corridor, wondering what that damned woman might have found that he hadn't, and sure that he was going to be bawled out. Old Rooney had always maintained she was one of the best. He didn't notice that he was already thinking of Lorraine in the past tense – as if she was already dead.

CHAPTER 20

MIKE PAGE met Jake Burton in the hospita
reception area: neither knew enough abou
the other to be embarrassed, nor were the
there to find out about their respective places in Lor
raine's life and affections. They shook hands and went to
the small hospital coffee shop, stood in line to order thei
coffee, and didn't speak until they sat down at a smal
corner table.

Mike pulled at his collar with nerves. 'I haven't beer
allowed to see her yet. The head honcho was in the unit
said maybe in half an hour.' He sipped his coffee and
coughed. 'They told me there had been no improvemen
– did they say that to you?'

Jake nodded. He had seen Mike arrive and had
introduced himself: Mike had been a little confused to
begin with, presuming he was there in his police capacity
but then Jake had quietly told him that he and Lorraine
had planned to be married.

'Do we know what happened to her?' Mike asked.

'All we know is, she was attacked on entering he
apartment. We had a suspect in custody, but we released
him – no evidence.'

'Does anyone know why it happened? I mean, I know

she must have met some unsavoury types, but was she investigating something or . . . Was she still not drinking?'

Jake stirred his coffee. 'She was on a case, but as yet I haven't found any connection to her death. We're still checking it out. She was not drinking.'

'So this suspect – was he found there?'

'No.'

Jake was still deeply shocked and unsure how much he should tell Mike. He was unsure about everything but his own despair.

'Who was the suspect?' Mike enquired.

'He had a possible connection to an incident that happened a long time ago.'

'Like what?'

Jake looked away. 'He was the elder brother of the boy Lorraine shot.'

'Oh, Jesus, God . . .' Mike bowed his head. There was a lengthy pause during which neither man could say anything, each immersed in his own thoughts, until Mike looked at his watch. 'Time to go to the unit.'

Jake pushed back his chair. Then, as he stood up, he asked if Mike minded him saying something personal. 'Sure, say anything you want,' Mike said apprehensively.

'Bring her daughters to see her. Just before this happened she and I talked. I know she wanted to be reunited with them and . . .'

'I don't know if it's such a good idea. They haven't had any communication with her for a long time, and it would be unsettling for them.'

'She's their mother,' Jake said quietly, and Mike flushed.

'I'll think about it – I'd like to see her first. Been nice

meeting you, and I'm very sorry. Maybe she'll pull through. She always was a fighter, and she's taken a lot of punishment in her life.'

Jake walked past him, teeth gritted. 'Nice meeting you.'

Mike was ill-prepared for Lorraine's appearance. He focused on her hands, resting on top of the linen. They were white, with an almost bluish tinge.

He sat in a chair beside her and just said he was there, then slowly inched his hand over the sheet to touch hers. There was no response, so he withdrew it, and stayed for another few minutes without saying anything, just remembering. 'I'll bring the girls to see you,' he whispered. Again, there was no reaction, and he left the unit quietly. He asked to speak to whoever could give him most information about Lorraine's condition. What he heard was not good: there had been no improvement since Lorraine had been brought in; she remained in a deep coma, unable to breathe unaided; her pulse rate remained low; they were concerned about her kidneys and had a dialysis machine standing by.

Jake Burton came twice and also sat with Lorraine, talking and talking to her, willing her to react, but there was no response. He returned to the station, where Jim Sharkey and two other detectives were scrutinizing her files and notes, first with regard to the murder inquiry, then poring over the art scam, of which they had not previously been notified. When Burton returned they discussed it with him and he suggested that perhaps they should interview Feinstein. If their first suspicions regarding Eric Lee Judd had proved unfounded, perhaps Lorraine's attacker could be connected to the art fraud.

Feinstein was irate. He did not wish to bring charges as he was dealing with a client's private affairs, and if he did not wish to press any formal charges then the police had no right to do so. He also knew, without a shadow of a doubt, that none of the other police who had been stung by Nathan would want their names associated with a police inquiry.

Sharkey tried to change Feinstein's mind: what if the murder of Harry Nathan was connected to the art fraud? Maybe *he* was content to let whoever was behind the scam walk away scot-free, but perhaps someone else had cared enough about it to shoot Nathan? Feinstein almost wet himself, but refused to pursue any further enquiries in relation to the fraud. Sharkey asked if the money could be traced. But Feinstein refused to be drawn. How could he know what a dead man did or did not do? Yet again he insisted that he did not wish to pursue the fraud.

Sharkey stared at him with distaste, then rose slowly to his feet, buttoning his jacket. 'Thanks for your time,' he said curtly.

'So that's it, is it?' Feinstein hovered at the side of his desk.

'Might be for you, Mr Feinstein, sir, but we will still be investigating the art scam's possible connection to the murder of Harry Nathan.'

'But I refuse to press charges,' Feinstein said, his voice rising an octave.

'That is your prerogative, sir, but whether you like it

or not it's a police matter and it will therefore be treated as an ongoing investigation.'

'But everybody connected is fucking dead!' Feinstein screeched.

Sharkey was at the door, his back to the room. 'Yeah, I'd say that was a pretty good reason not to try to sweep it all under the carpet. Maybe you won't have to give evidence. There again, you just might not be able to get out of it. Have a nice day.'

Feinstein slumped into his leather swivel chair, took a deep breath and turned slowly towards the large empty space on the wall that had once been occupied by one of Harry Nathan's fakes. The faint dust line indicated the painting's proportions and the spotlight fitted to show it off was still trained on the blank wall. He didn't scream the words as he usually did, but almost spat them with venomous hatred: 'God damn you, Harry Nathan, you bastard!'

Burton rocked in his chair, drumming his fingers, his mouth down-turned. Feinstein's refusal to co-operate infuriated him.

'Any news?' Sharkey asked. Burton shook his head. 'Holding her own, is she?' he persisted, then saw that Burton could hardly answer.

'Not quite . . . but we're hoping. Okay, thanks for the extra work, I appreciate it.'

Sharkey and the two other detectives walked out to the nearest bar.

'That Feinstein is a prick,' one detective said, as Sharkey carried the beer to their table.

'Yeah – what kind of guy can be stung outa that much dough an' not want to do something about it?'

'Not just him. How many others got stung? Mind-blowing. I mean, if some shit diddled me outa a hundred bucks, I'd have to go after him. Wouldn't you, Jim?'

'Yep, but that's the difference between you and me and the likes of Feinstein and his rich clients. They got more fucking money than they know what to fucking do with, and he'll more'n likely make it up off their bills. So if they don't miss it, fuck 'em. They'll hopefully be made to look like real assholes by the press. I'd like to see them get a hell of a lot more, but you know how long these fuckin' fraud cases take to unravel. Not like somebody got away with murder . . .' He didn't finish the sentence, but took a deep gulp of his beer.

'You know some son-of-a-bitch just might,' said one, a thin film of beer froth on his upper lip.

Sharkey turned his head. 'What?'

'Well, they got nobody for Lorraine Page's beatin' and word is she's not gonna make it.'

Sharkey drained his beer in one, and banged down the glass.

One of the men had known her from the old days, when she had partnered Lubrinski, and he grinned. 'But she ain't dead yet, an' that lady's one hell of a fighter. Did I ever tell you about that story, with this guy, he's dead now . . . Yeah, Jack Lubrinski. Well, they go to this bar right, downtown someplace . . .'

They continued telling anecdotes about Lorraine and Lubrinski, and, as often happens, the good memories obliterated the bad. It was like some kind of wake. No one spoke of the shooting of Tommy Lee Judd, and

Lorraine Page's decline into alcoholism and drug addiction. They were remembering her as a good cop, the one that took the hassle and never made a complaint.

Three days later, to the amazement of everyone, Lorraine was still hanging on to life. She remained in a coma, still on the critical list, and the specialists testing her brain were noncommittal.

Reports of Lorraine's condition were relayed to Rosie and Rooney, and they were heartened to hear that she was still battling for life, but they knew that even if she did pull out of the coma, there was a strong possibility of permanent brain damage, causing severe physical incapacity.

'Is she paralysed?' Rooney asked.

'We're unable to do tests to ascertain the degree of paralysis with coma patients,' Hudson told him. 'As the sedation wears off and time passes, all we can do is wait and see if motor function returns.'

Day four, and still she clung on, the medical team reporting a slow improvement in her breathing.

Mike Page visited every other day, while Burton, Rosie and Rooney came daily. On day six Mike brought his and Lorraine's daughters. Rosie had been told they would be there and she brought the gifts Lorraine had bought for the girls in Santa Fe. They clung to their father as they were led into the unit.

The girls sat in awed silence. The bandaged woman in front of them was a stranger, and they didn't know what to say to her. When Mike encouraged Sally to touch her mother's hand she wouldn't, whispering that she was too frightened.

The doctors and all the staff were kind and thoughtful, suggesting to the girls that although their mother could not respond, they should talk to her to let her hear their voices. The girls looked at each other. Hearing this woman called their mother felt wrong, and Julia began to cry, saying she wanted to go home.

Two weeks passed slowly and the number of tubes attached to Lorraine's body gradually diminished. More tests to determine brain damage had been done, but she remained in a coma. The healing process of the external damage had been rapid though: she no longer looked like a monster for the terrible bruising to her face was fading and the bandages were removed.

The girls came regularly now, and the more they got used to seeing her, the more freely they chatted about ordinary, girlish things. They never called her Mom, but Sally often touched her hand, and Julia stroked her mother's pale arm. Both girls wore the bracelets she had chosen for them.

Rosie and Rooney divided their visiting time between them, and talked and talked, never giving up hope of a response. Jake came before and after work, spending hours sitting beside her, planning their wedding. He brought the ring he had bought for her, and asked her if he could put it on her wedding finger.

Christmas was now a week away, and Lorraine was still in a coma, her eyes closed, as if she was sleeping. The ventilator tube had been moved from her mouth to pass through a tracheotomy incision in her neck, and there was hope, hope that none had believed possible. She remained in the intensive care unit, as she still needed to be monitored round the clock. She was dressed now in her own nightclothes, and Rosie combed her hair and cared for her. She read magazines and books to Lorraine, played music tapes, and when she was through, Rooney took over. He talked for hours, all about his old work, and found it quite therapeutic to chat to Lorraine, asking her if she recalled this or that case.

Jake would take over from him, and sat holding her hand, willing her to acknowledge him. He brought fresh bouquets every other day, unable to bear the sight of flowers wilting, always insisting that fresh ones replaced them. Like Rooney, he talked about his work, discussing things with her as if she was replying. When it got to week eight, everyone was tired – and angry that Lorraine was still a prisoner in some alien world. She looked almost like herself – and yet she wasn't there. Rosie had brought in a small artificial Christmas tree and had decorated it with baubles and ribbons. Small gifts for the nurses were arranged beneath it, all bearing tags: 'Happy Christmas, with love from Lorraine.'

The first time she heard his voice was at the moment he had put the ring on her finger. She had started talking to him, saying how happy she was, and asking him why he didn't reply to her questions. It was frightening that she could hear them talking to her but they couldn't hear her.

The visits were the worst, when they seemed to ignore what she was saying, talking at her, not to her, not hearing when she called their names. Then she listened intently, and realized that the high-pitched chattering voices she had been hearing day after day belonged to

462

her daughters, talking about what they wanted for Christmas. She wanted to cry with happiness that they were there with her – but *why* couldn't they hear what she was saying? She could hear Mike, and told him how pleased she was that he had brought the girls, asked him if he had met Jake. She asked so many questions, and sometimes she laughed at what they were saying, especially old Bill Rooney, forever droning on about some case he knew he should have beaten, then complaining that Tiger had chewed up his best sweater. Her visitors came and went, not hearing her answers, her voice, and when it was night she wept, because it felt as if she would never see them again, and she couldn't understand what had happened, or where she was. She started to be strict with herself, telling herself to pull herself together, that she had to straighten out. Crying every night was not doing any good: it was just using up all her energy, and she had to start thinking about other things. She forced her brain to be active, even though it hurt to think – yet she had to do something.

Lorraine felt as if she was gritting her teeth with determination, that if she could just get through the pain barrier her mind had erected, then she was sure she would be able to see again, see her loved ones. She told herself that she was having a nightmare, that she'd wake up soon, but that she had to make herself do it by retaining a mental connection with her active, waking self and her life, and convince herself that she would soon be coming back to them.

Worst of all were those silent night hours when all she heard was the clatter of things around her, the alien whispers, sounds that reminded her of a hospital, and her mind drifted back to the last time she had been in a hospital, when she'd had the plastic surgery on her cheek to get rid of the scar in an expensive private establishment. She made herself visualize the place, taking herself on a tour of her room, the corridors, the television lounge, the day room, the other patients.

Lorraine had had no visitors then – no one had even known she was undergoing surgery – so she spent many hours alone in the sunny, comfortable TV lounge, not that she had ever had much interest in television but this was the only room in which patients were allowed to smoke, and she had passed the time by watching the others, playing detective as to their real ages and backgrounds.

Most were women between forty and sixty, and some had already had so much surgery that at first sight they looked much younger, but there was always some incongruity between their faces, uniformly taut, tanned, slightly android-looking, and the way they dressed, moved or, most noticeably, spoke, that betrayed their real age. There were other dead giveaways too: the slight slackening of skin tone on the under surface of the arm that no amount of exercise could firm, plus, of course, the hands and feet. There were a couple of veritable Zsa Zsa Gabor lookalikes, dyed blonde hair piled up, stretched and lifted faces that could have passed for mid-forties, but with the liver-spotted hands, thickened knuckles and prominent tendons of old age. Only a lucky few seemed to escape *that* tell-tale sign of time's passing. There had been a woman in a wheelchair, wearing dark glasses and still bandaged so that virtually none of her face could be seen. Lorraine had assumed, from the few visible strands of white hair, that she must be in her sixties or seventies, but she had noticed that the woman's large, fine, restless hands were those of someone much younger, conveying an unusual impression of simultaneous flexibility and strength. She remembered noting how short the nails were cut, and had thought at the time that the woman must use her hands – perhaps as a musician or, at her age, a music teacher – which would explain how they had escaped shrivelling into an old lady's claws. Now she knew that the woman was no musician, no teacher, and no old lady: it had been Sonja Nathan, she would have taken an oath on it.

The woman had kept herself to herself, only coming into the TV lounge once and taking no part in any of the casual conversations that were going on around her. Lorraine had thought, though, that she had seemed to pay attention when she herself had revealed to a chatty lady who worked for a real estate company that she was a private detective – they had commented quietly that they seemed to be in a minority here of working women: most of their fellow patients were pampered wives. When Lorraine had said she might be looking to rent a new office shortly, the woman had insisted on knowing Lorraine's full name and the name of her company, Lorraine remembered, and she remembered, too, how she had thought of trying to draw the bandaged woman into their conversation, but some separateness and aloofness in her demeanour had deterred her from doing so. It was that indefinable *froideur*, as much as anything in Sonja Nathan's physical appearance, that now made Lorraine certain it had been her.

Sonja Nathan had left the clinic knowing exactly who Lorraine was and, weeks later, had been able to recall those details.

Sonja had said that she had not been in Los Angeles

at all for the previous year. That was a lie, and Lorraine was positive now that Sonja had also lied when she had said she had not made the call to Lorraine's office on the morning of the murder. Lorraine already had documentary evidence – presumably lying in her apartment, she thought, in her briefcase – that Sonja and Harry Nathan were in contact after their divorce. Now she had the last piece of the jigsaw: proof that Sonja Nathan had been in LA the day her ex-husband was killed. She was sure now that if she ever got out of this goddamn hospital and was able to get voice experts to analyse the recording Decker had made of the call which had to be somewhere on that tape, they could identify some feature of Sonja's mid-Atlantic, faintly European accent. That would be the final link and would put the woman behind bars.

It was painful to drag up each memory, worse than any headache she had ever known. The pain was excruciating, but Lorraine wouldn't, couldn't stop. Now everything had fallen into place, and Lorraine understood Sonja's odd concern about Cindy, her saying that she wished she had given her more time – 'or assistance'. Sonja's lack of interest in the fact that so much money was missing from the estate had also seemed strange – but not, Lorraine thought wryly, when one knew that the assets had been taken *before* the bizarre sequence of events that had left Sonja, ironically, Harry Nathan's legitimate heir.

Sonja Nathan knew the house, the gardens, and more than likely her ex-husband's routine – or she could readily have arranged to meet him in advance. Sonja was clearly capable of premeditation, as she must deliberately have hired a jeep identical to Kendall's to conceal her comings and goings at Nathan's house – perhaps she had even hoped to incriminate Kendall, Lorraine thought, and she had managed to take every nickel of the woman's money through the art fraud. Even if Kendall's death really had been accidental, Sonja bore some indirect responsibility, as it had been after realizing that she had lost her stake in the paintings that Kendall had been tempted to try to burn down the gallery for the insurance. That must have given Sonja considerable satisfaction, Lorraine thought, for, as Arthur had said, she was all too human – or inhuman – under the cool, superior façade, and had clearly hated Kendall as intensely as she had ever loved Nathan.

As for the paintings, Lorraine now knew that Harry Nathan had been to Germany, to make preparations for the sale of the real works of art, and she was sure, too, that once she got out of here and could get to Berlin, she could find out exactly how Sonja and Arthur, the expert copier, had stepped into Nathan's shoes and netted the proceeds of sale.

Lorraine's head throbbed, but she carried on, piecing the jigsaw together. All the dead faces floated in front of her – Harry Nathan, Cindy, Kendall, Vallance – faded, and then became clearer, but her concentration was wavering like a guttering torch. It was on Vallance's death that she tried to shed the last of its light. Lorraine knew now how Sonja had killed him – or made him kill himself – by threatening to release the porn videos, the murder weapon Jake Burton had innocently sent her. Sonja could not, of course, be made to bear legal responsibility for that murder, or for Cindy's death, for which she was also morally responsible: Vallance had strangled his former mistress, believing mistakenly that she, not Sonja, had killed the man he had idolized and lusted after all his life. Christ, Lorraine thought, that this should be the woman to whom she had poured out her own most private griefs to turn Sonja's mind from suicide – but once she got out of here . . . The faces blurred and parts of the conversations she was trying to recall began to crackle and echo in Lorraine's brain. The pain grew worse and worse: she was losing her grip, unable to think any more. She screamed in agony, as if a red-hot iron were forging up from her spine, blinding her, exhausting her, and she couldn't take it any more.

Rooney went pale. Even though he was outside Intensive Care, on his way to see Lorraine, he knew something had happened. Nurses and doctors, running as if for their own lives, entered the unit, and the curtains were drawn across the viewing window. Lorraine was shielded from his sight, and the last thing he saw as they clustered around her was the heart monitor, bleeping loudly.

A little later, Jake Burton walked up the corridor with fresh flowers, and Rooney turned to him. 'Something's happened, I don't know what, but they shut the curtains and there's got to be eight of them round her. I don't know for sure, but I think it's her heart.'

Sonja had had one white wedding, and she had decided that this time she would get married in deep red, a rich colour more suitable for both a Swiss wedding in winter, she thought, and for a mature bride. The close-fitting crimson suit, with rich brown fur collar and cuffs, accentuated her tall, slim figure, while she had bought a

468

frighteningly expensive hussar's cap in the same fur, which she was now wondering whether or not to wear.

She put it on, took it off, fluffed out her hair, then crossed to the far side of the room across the expanse of pale green carpet: she and Arthur had booked the Grace Kelly Suite in the best hotel in Geneva, with private sitting and dining rooms and a marvellous view of the lake. She walked towards her reflection in the long cheval mirror, studying it intently.

'Too much fur?' she asked, as Arthur appeared. 'I don't know whether or not to wear the hat.'

He was wearing a smart suit, with a rose in the buttonhole, and a matching waistcoat, and was knotting his tie. 'Put it on and let me see,' he said.

Sonja did as he asked and turned to face him: she looked beautiful, he thought, but she was different now, and it wasn't just the unfamiliar new costume. For all these years he had yearned to possess her without Harry Nathan, but now that Nathan's shadow had gone, she was not the same woman, less driven, less intense, as though someone had dropped the end of a rope she had pulled against for years, sometimes seeming younger, sometimes older. Was she free now, he wondered, or adrift?

She had always been able to read his moods, almost his thoughts, and it was as though she sensed his scrutiny. 'You're sure you want to do this?' she said quietly. 'You know you can still back out.'

'I don't want to back out,' he said. You could never tell with love, he thought, whether it would last or fade, stay constant or change. You just had to trust and step in. 'Wear the hat.'

Sonja looked at herself again in the mirror, then turned. 'Shall we go?' she said, her expression grave.

Arthur tossed something towards her. 'Here – this time it's not a fake.' She caught the ring box in both hands, knowing that the price of the jewel didn't matter now: all the money had been transferred to Switzerland, and they would decide later how to move it back to the United States if and when they needed it.

He watched her take the ring from the box, admire it, then hold it out. 'You put it on.'

He took it and held her hand, slipping it onto her wedding finger. Then he bent down to kiss her.

'Well, we did it,' he said softly, then smiled. 'And we got away with it. Was it worth the wait?'

'Yes, yes, it was.' She was not looking at him. 'Believe me, it was worth it.'

She turned away to catch another glimpse of herself as Arthur checked the time. They should go down to Reception, the limo would be waiting. Arthur crossed to the doors: as a small surprise, he had ordered some deep red roses as a bridal bouquet.

'Give me two minutes . . . I'll join you,' she called.

He held the door half open.

'Two minutes. See you down there.'

She waited for him to leave, adjusted her hat, needing a moment alone to look in her room of memories one last time before she turned the key. She remembered crossing the lawn, seeing Harry towelling himself dry after his swim. She had not decided then that that would be the day she killed him – a day she had been thinking about for a long time, and neither of them had known then that everything Harry Nathan did that day he was doing for the last time. It was when she had seen the gun on the table, one of Nathan's own guns, and had known that there would be no difficulty in disposing of a weapon, that she had felt she had received the signal to put the plan into action, had known that there would never be a better chance.

Harry had tossed aside his towel, not bothering to cover his nakedness in front of her, vain as ever of his body. Sonja had taken a handkerchief out of her pocket. He had paid no attention when she picked up the gun, turning it in her hand and covering it with the cloth. It felt cold and heavy – like her heart. She had raised it first to his chest, then a little higher, and he had smiled, told her to be careful as it was loaded. Then his face had slowly drained of colour as she aimed it at his neck, then tilted the barrel to his face.

'I've wanted to kill you for a long time, Harry, and until now I never thought I could. But you know something, Harry, I can.'

He had backed away, terror visible in his face, as his eyes widened in fear. Then she had pulled the trigger, and he stumbled two steps forward, then toppled into the pool. She had stood there, watching the petals of blood unfold from his head, as he floated face down, arms outstretched, the image that had never left her, and that she had felt driven to replicate, partly as a triumphal shout, a final exorcism – and partly as a confession that no one had heard.

She had then picked up her shoes, and walked back across the gardens, returning to the rented Mitsubishi jeep – Harry had agreed she should get one as close to Kendall's as possible just in case anyone saw her driving in and out of the house for their meetings and to remove the paintings. Suddenly she knew how fortunate that was. Sonja could not have cared less if the phoney, odious Kendall ended up paying the penalty for Harry Nathan's death.

No one else could possibly be incriminated, she had thought – but Cindy had been her one mistake. She had thought Nathan had told her on the phone, when they arranged the meeting, that he and Cindy had had a fight and she had left. It was only when she had heard the girl's scream after the killing that she had realized that she must have misunderstood. He must have said that Cindy had threatened to go, or was about to. Poor Cindy, she had thought. She had had no desire to see the pathetic, abused girl stand trial, and it must have been fate that had ensured she had not only met a local private investigator a few weeks previously but had remembered the woman's name. She had stopped the jeep at once, had got the number from Information, then called Lorraine Page's office from a public phone.

Her plane trip back to New York was, as always, booked in a different name, and she had carried the paintings like posters in rolls of cardboard. She was never stopped or questioned.

By the time she had returned to the Hamptons, the news had broken that Harry Nathan had been murdered and Cindy Nathan arrested. Next day, it had transpired that things were worse than Sonja had thought: the gun she had used had been Cindy's.

After that she had just sat back and watched the aftermath. Now there was no one left to hate, no one left to blame. She had told the world of her guilt, but no one had noticed, and it was over at last, she thought. *Quietus est.*

*

Rosie was out of breath as she joined Burton and Rooney – she'd rushed to the hospital as soon as she had heard.

'What happened? Is she all right?'

Rooney sat her down. 'There've been complications. Her breathing has deteriorated, and her temperature's started rising. She's holding her own, but now they're worrying that her heart's been under too much strain.'

Jake took Rosie's hand. 'Mike's on his way in, and the girls. It's just a matter of time now.'

'No, no, I don't believe it – she was getting better. They said her breathing wouldn't stabilize – well, it did. She'll get over this relapse – it's just a kind of a relapse, right? Look, I know her, I know her, and . . .' Rosie's face crumpled but she kept on talking about how she and Lorraine had first met – how ill Lorraine had been, how she was so thin and weak that no one would have ever believed she could recover, quit her alcohol addiction . . .

'It's part of the problem, Rosie, sweetheart. Her body took so much punishment for so long, it's just tired out.' Rosie started to sob and Rooney gripped her hand tightly. 'Now you listen to me, her daughters are coming in, and we don't want them upset and scared. Just pull yourself together – there's been enough tears, and you don't want Lorraine to see you crying.'

'She can't see me, she's in a coma,' Rosie said, wiping her nose.

'I know, but nobody knows if that means she can't hear. So dry your eyes, and go freshen up.'

Rosie went to the powder room, and Rooney felt exhausted. He had no tears left to cry, and he looked at the quiet, composed Jake. 'You okay?'

Jake was far from okay, but he nodded, and Rooney

sighed heavily. 'You know, maybe it's for the best. I mean, it's likely she's got brain damage, and I wouldn't want to see her all crumpled up, unable to do anything for herself. I know she wouldn't want that either.'

Both men stood up as Dr Hudson came out of the unit and gestured to them to sit down. He asked if Lorraine's daughters were coming in to see her, and Jake said they were on their way.

'You want it straight?' he said, pulling at the collar of his white coat. They both nodded. 'I've always been level with you, and I've got to admit I didn't think we'd be able to hold her for this long, but this recent development . . . Her organs are just giving way, and I am afraid there's nothing more we can do. It really is a matter of hours. She's in no pain, but her heart is now in trouble, and what with that and the cumulative malfunction of her kidneys and lungs . . .'

'How long?' Jake said quietly.

'I doubt if she'll last the night. I'm very, very sorry.'

Jake stood up and looked at Rooney. 'I'd like some time alone with her, before her daughters arrive.' He turned his gaze to the doctor. 'Can I go in?'

The doctor nodded: the staff were already making Lorraine look more presentable by removing some of the drips and machines from the room, which was already screened off from the rest of the unit to give more privacy. 'The nurse will come out in a minute, but I'll be here if you need me. Just tell the duty nurse, or Reception to buzz me.' The doctor hovered for a moment, then walked away from the tiny overheated anteroom with a grave nod.

Five minutes later, when Rosie had returned, a nurse

came out. She smiled cheerfully and held the door ajar. 'You can see her now. Thank you for all the gifts.'

'They were from Lorraine,' Rosie said firmly. The nurse moved away, and Rosie saw as she went in that the little Christmas tree had been taken down.

Sonja and Arthur exchanged their vows in a quiet ceremony, with only one other person as a witness, a clerk from the mayor's office, a small, balding man who had obviously performed this function on innumerable occasions. He gave them an encouraging smile, signed the register with a flourish, and wished them every happiness in their future life. They walked out arm in arm, Sonja's bouquet of roses matching Arthur's buttonhole.

'Holy shit, they gone an' put my nightdress on back to front,' Lorraine said, then angrily told Burton that one of the nurses should be fired as she had a rough bedside manner. He drew up a chair and sat close to the bed.

'I have to say you must have shares in a florist!' Lorraine joked. 'I mean, this is getting to be ridiculous. When I get out of here, I'm taking that bunch with me, the lilies – I always liked lilies, it's the smell. I've been meaning to ask you, though it's a bit embarrassing, do I smell? I know they clean me up, but that fucking nurse, the one with the frizzy hair, I don't think she's a pro. She almost had me out of the bed earlier you know, whipping out the fucking tubes as if she was playing an organ.' He touched her hand, and let one finger trace the dark bruises where the needles and drips had been attached. 'I know – they think they're digging for gold trying to find a vein.' She laughed, then frowned.

'I worry about wearing this ring – I don't know if you can trust these nurses. I remember when my dad was in hospital, you couldn't leave fifty bucks. Mind you, he wasn't in a private ward like this. Thank Christ I blew so much on a private medical plan.'

He gently traced her fingers, touching each nail. 'I love you, will never forget you, and with this ring I thee wed. You are the wife I always wanted and never believed I'd find, but we did find each other, didn't we? If just for a short while.'

'Yeah, we sure did, and you know I've never been the romantic kind, but . . . remember the beach? The first time you came walking with me and Tiger – I knew I was in love with you then. Actually I knew when you knocked on the door. Did I tell you that? You have a way of holding your head, on one side, and when you're going to say something romantic, you get these two red dots in your cheeks. You've got them now . . .'

'Remember the first time we walked on the beach?'

'Yes, I just said that. But it was even better later with all that takeaway food – my God, we ordered every single thing off the menu. You know I truthfully never thought I'd have someone love me.'

'I love you.'

'I love you, too, with all my heart, and . . . Hey, where you going? Don't go yet, I want to kiss you. Don't go, let me kiss you.'

Jake got to the door, stopped, turned back. He found it almost unbearable to see Lorraine propped up, but with her eyes closed, just as if she was sleeping. He returned to the bed and gently kissed her lips, then rested his head against hers and touched her cheeks. For the first time her flesh felt cold.

'I don't call that a kiss, and listen, we have to talk before you go. Listen to me, it's very important. I cracked the Nathan case. Sonja Nathan killed him, I'm sure of it. I know I've got nothing but circumstantial evidence, but you've got to get my briefcase and get some phone company records out of it, and contact the clinic where I had my scar fixed. I'm sure she was there. You've got to get the tape recording Decker made of that call that was made to my office too – the one Cindy never made. He couldn't find it, but it's just got to be there somewhere. It was Sonja. Why don't you listen to me? Where are you going?'

Jake leaned out into the corridor. 'Bill, you want to come in? I'll just take five minutes, go to the john.'

Rooney came in, sweating as usual, wanting to take off his jacket, but not sure that he should.

'Sit down, Billy, before he gets back. We got to talk – he doesn't seem to take me seriously, but I think I cracked the Nathan case. I'll need help, and there could be big bucks in it if we can recover the stolen art work. It's worth millions and I have a damned good idea where it is. Germany. I also know Sonja Nathan killed her husband.'

'Rosie's with me, she won't be a minute.'

'Okay. Let me get this sorted out before she comes in. First you have to check out Nathan's fake passports, there's a letter in my purse he sent to his mother from Germany. I think – in fact, I'm sure – Sonja Nathan was working with her ex-husband on this art fraud scam. It's big money, Bill, not a few hundred thousand dollars, but millions.'

He looked at her, lying so still, eyes closed as if she was sleeping.

'You look beautiful, darlin',' he said softly.

'Oh, quit with the flattery. Listen to what I'm saying. We trace those paintings, we'll all be in for a few bucks to retire on, Billy. I'm out after this case, and all I want to do is crack it – you know the way I am. Now, I need you first to contact Feinstein, then get my briefcase out of the apartment, Bill. Then you and Rosie do another trip to Europe. I want this case cleared before I quit, know what I mean? I get married to Jake and . . . You like him, don't you? He's an okay guy, isn't he? And I'm going to tell you something. I was so scared, Bill – you know, I didn't think I had any right to love or be loved. He loves me, Billy.'

'We're taking care of Tiger,' Rooney said, trying to think of something to say, then told her how the dog had already destroyed their new sofa.

Lorraine laughed, that big, bellowing laugh of hers. 'Hey, Bill, did you ever tell Rosie about that guy, remember him? With the lottery ticket? God, that was funny.'

Rosie came in, smiled at Bill, and drew up a chair.

'Hey, Rosie, did Billy ever tell you about Chester Brackenshaw? When we were working together. Well, this guy Chester was a real pain in the butt, always going on about what he would or wouldn't do when he won the lottery, and he was a real practical joker, wasn't he, Bill? Anyways . . .'

'She looks beautiful,' Rosie said.

478

'Thank you, but my nightdress is on back to front. Anyway, Chester goes every Friday to this club, an' me and the guys work this scam out – like I said, he was a real practical joker – and we get his lottery ticket numbers. It was you, wasn't it, Bill? You got 'em out of his wallet. Anyway, hasn't Bill told you this, Rosie?'

'She's got her nightdress on back to front,' Rosie said, fussing.

'I know, I know . . . but listen, he goes to the club, right? And we get the DJ in on the joke and tell him to announce the winning lottery numbers. So he stops playing records and he announces all Chester's numbers, and we all expected him to start buying drinks for the house. After we'd got him to spend his wages, we were going to let him in on the joke, but . . . he did nothing. Like, we saw him check his card, but he puts it back in his wallet, right, Bill?'

'Shall I comb her hair?' Rosie said to Bill.

'Leave it, just leave it, and listen . . . we all think he knows he's been had, and we're all waiting for him to get back at us some way, but he doesn't, but then as we're all leaving the place, he suddenly throws his car keys at his wife, Sandra – her name was Sandra, wasn't it, Bill? Yeah, "Sandra," he says, "take the car, it's yours, and you can have the house. I hate your guts and I've been screwing your sister for two years, but I've won the lottery, so fuck you!"' She roared with laughter, seeing all the guys lined up behind Chester trying to make him shut up.

Lorraine fell silent then as Sissy, Mike's wife, appeared in the doorway. 'Mike's coming, he's in court,' Sissy said, ushering in the girls. Just hearing her daughters made Lorraine feel so emotional she couldn't joke any more.

479

The two girls took Rooney and Rosie's chairs, side by side, and she was so proud of them.

'Come on in, Sissy, don't be embarrassed, I'm not. In fact, I'd like to say something to you. It's . . . well, it's thank you. You've taken such care of my girls, and I want you to know I don't resent you. I did, but I don't now. In fact, I'd like to kiss you.'

Sissy leaned over the bed and kissed Lorraine's cheek. 'I'll be outside if you need me,' she said to the girls, then left them alone with Lorraine.

Julia was the first to reach out to the still, cold hand. 'I'm wearing the bracelet you got for me.' She hesitated and then said softly, 'Thank you, Mom.'

'Oh, now, don't you cry – I don't want to see you crying,' Lorraine said, but then was so close to tears herself she couldn't continue.

Julia turned to Sally: 'Say thank you to Mommy, Sally, go on.'

Sally gently touched Lorraine's fingers. 'Thank you, Mommy.'

Lorraine burst into tears: she had never believed she would hear them call her that again. She told them how proud she was, that she knew Julia was a great tennis player and Sally was a gold medallist at her college for swimming. 'One day, maybe you'll understand – I wasn't really me for such a long time, but all the times I wasn't with you, all the times I should have been there, I never stopped loving you both with all my heart. I want you to have a good and happy future, and I know you've got a good father . . . because I loved him too. Hey, Mike, I was just talkin' about you.'

Mike came and stood between his daughters, then took Lorraine's hand and kissed it.

'Say goodbye to your mom.'

Both girls whispered goodbye, and Lorraine was upset that they were crying – she didn't want them to cry. She watched them leaving the room, and called after them, called each daughter by name, and they turned and looked at her.

'I love you, babies. I love you.'

She wanted Jake again, needed him, in fact wanted him to be there more than Mike or the girls. She felt so light, as if she were floating, and she wanted him to hold on to her. She had the eerie feeling she was going somewhere, and she called out his name.

He stood in the doorway, and she sighed with relief. For a few moments she had thought he had gone, but he came to her side. 'I'm here, darling, I'm here,' he said softly, and she began to relax, knowing he was holding her hand.

'I want you to know, I don't care how long it takes, but I'll get him. We even had him in custody, but we had nothing to hold him on – there were no prints on the baseball bat, nothing.'

She was confused for a while, not understanding what he was talking about, but then he said the name. Eric Lee Judd. Where had she heard that name before? Then she remembered the alley and the moment she had shouted at the boy to stop. She remembered it all now, all the years she had tried to bury the guilt with drink and wanted to pay for what she had done: now she knew that at long last she was paying the ultimate price.

She knew then that it was over, and the last thing she heard, and would ever hear as she floated free of pain was Jake's voice, filled with love, the love that had given her a happiness she felt she had no right to enjoy, and that now absolved her of guilt and gave her final release. She began to float, way above the bed, and the pain stopped. It was such a relief when the awful pain in her head stopped, and she felt at peace. Hearing him say that he loved her had freed her soul: it was the best way to go.

Lorraine had left life surrounded by people who loved her dearly, and reunited with her daughters. But she would never be able to tell anyone the solution to her last case.

None of her private analysis of the murder had been discussed with anyone, none of her notes made on her travels had been read by anyone. Lorraine's last case appeared to have died with her – the only time a case had not ended in success. Sonja Nathan had not only got away with murder, but with a massive fraud that netted her twenty million dollars.

Lorraine had been at rest for six months when a battered briefcase, its lock forced, was found by a garbage sifter. Lennie Hockum made his living scavenging in garbage dumps, salvaging anything he could recycle and sell on. It often surprised him just how much some of the junk he collected was worth. The briefcase was leather with a suede lining and he was sure he could fix the locks, or make them look good enough for a local garage sale.

Lennie did not inspect the contents of the briefcase thoroughly until he was back at his trailer. There was nothing of immediate value, not even a pen, but there were hotel receipts, sales stubs from various stores and a few business cards in the name of Lorraine Page Investigations. There was also a thick notebook with scrawled writing covering almost every page. Lennie skim-read it, flicking the pages over with his gnarled thumb. Some pages had lists of names with some underlined, but nothing made much sense to him. But he had the woman's card, he had her address. Maybe he could make a few more bucks if he returned the case to its rightful owner.

Lennie took the case to Lorraine's office, but he was disappointed when the valet told him the office was closed and had been taken over by another company. He held up the case, asking if the valet knew where he could find the woman.

It was almost a month before Jake Burton was contacted and the briefcase brought into his office. He sat staring at it, then slowly ran his hands along the top. It smelt of mildew and leather polish. Inside there were water stains and the suede had green mould at the edges. The thick notebook seemed fatter due to the damp and some of the pages were stuck together, but he recognized Lorraine's handwriting. Burton read every page, made copious notes as he went along. Then he had to wait a further week before the Nathans' housekeepers were traced. He used favours to gain access to their personal finances, but it was evident that they had improved considerably lately: they had purchased a small but quite expensive condo, just off the Ventura highway. They also owned a new Pathfinder and appeared not to be employed.

Using Lorraine's notes, and with Sharkey as backup, Burton questioned and requestioned Juana and Jose, putting pressure on them to give details of their income. They insisted that they had simply been paid their back salary from the Nathan estate, but when they were informed that it would take only a phone call to verify their statement they began to waver. When they were taken to the station for the interview and questioned separately the cracks began to show. Juana broke first, sobbing hysterically and insisting it was money they were owed, that they had had no choice and had been forced to agree or they would not have been given what was rightfully theirs.

'I am sure you *were* owed a lot of money, but as you were not paid out of the Nathan estate, who did pay you?' Burton asked. He repeated, 'Who paid for the apartment, the car? Please answer the question. Who is financing you?'

Jose was the one to admit that it was Sonja Nathan and, like his wife, he started to weep. They had promised Mrs Nathan they would use the money to return to Mexico, but had changed their minds. He kept insisting they had done nothing wrong except lie to Mrs Nathan about moving back to Mexico . . .

Distressed, Juana revealed that Sonja Nathan had always been kind to them, had promised always to take care of them. 'She was only keeping her promise. She was a good woman . . .'

Burton kept up the pressure. He was calm, encouraging, and yet relentless. 'So, on the morning of the murder, you have stated that you saw no one and that you did not hear anything, but were drawn towards the swimming pool when you heard Cindy Nathan screaming. Do you still maintain that to be the truth?'

Sharkey waited as the couple sat, heads bowed. The room so silent you could hear the desk clock ticking.

After an interminable silence Burton softly asked again: 'Did you see anyone else on that morning?'

No reply.

'Did anyone you know arrange to be at the house on that morning?'

No reply.

Sharkey shifted his weight, looking from Juana to Jose as they sat, their hands clasped tightly in front of them. He then looked at Burton, who was staring at a large silver-framed photograph on the desk. Sharkey couldn't see the front, but he knew it was a photograph of Lorraine.

Burton continued, in the same calm, almost disinterested voice, 'Did you see anyone in the grounds of the house on the morning Harry Nathan was murdered?'

'Yes.'

It was hardly audible. Sharkey had to lean forward to hear it.

Juana reached over to hold her husband's hand. 'Tell him. Tell him. I don't want to lie any more.'

Jose clung to his wife's hand and took a deep breath, but refused to look up and meet Burton's eyes.

'Sonja Nathan.'

Sharkey's jaw dropped. Burton sat down. 'Thank you, that will be all for now. I suggest you get legal representation before we question you again. You may take one of the tapes we have used to record this interview. Thank you for your co-operation.'

Sharkey ushered the couple out and into the corridor. As he looked back into the room, Burton was sifting through a notebook, head bowed.

'Pick up Sonja Nathan?' Sharkey asked.

'Yes.'

'She almost got away with it,' Sharkey said, closing the door.

Burton sighed, running his hand over Lorraine's closed notebook, then laying his palm flat against it. He looked sadly at the photograph on his desk. Her face smiled back. It was a photograph he had taken on the beach: she had been so happy, so full of life, her head tilted back, her arms lifted towards the camera, as if about to break into laughter. He knew she had been happy – it shone out of her like the sun that glinted on her silky blonde hair.

'Well,' he said softly, 'you got your man and you'll be pleased to know you got your killer too.'

POCKET
BOOKS

Lynda La Plante

Cold Shoulder

'Lorraine Page, officer, wife and mother, is as tough as they come' *Sunday Telegraph*

Lieutenant Lorraine Page had everything – a devoted husband, two beautiful daughters and an impressive career with the Homicide Squad. It's impossible to believe that she could be thrown out of the police force and end up on Skid Row.

Lorraine's ex-colleagues soon forget her, as the hunt for a nightmare serial killer spirals into an all-out search for a missing witness: a victim who escaped.

Lorraine Page is that witness. Against her will she is drawn into the investigation, and forced to face her past and her overwhelming guilt...

ISBN 978-1-84983-262-5
PRICE £7.99

POCKET
BOOKS

Lynda La Plante

Cold Blood

'Lynda La Plante practically invented the thriller. She is
without a doubt one of the best writers working today'
KARIN SLAUGHTER

Suspicion and fear surround the mysterious disappearance of a
movie star's daughter. The race to claim the reward for finding
Anna Louise Caley - dead or alive – spirals into a deadly
voodoo trail in the French quarter of New Orleans.

In her desperation to succeed in this, her first case as a private
detective, ex-Lieutenant Lorraine Page is caught in a web of
deceit and violence that threatens to drag her back into the
murky world she has fought so hard to escape.

Continuing the investigation means risking everything. But the
million-dollar bonus is one hell of an incentive not to back off
from a case that could kill her – or give her the future and the
professional respect she craves.

ISBN 978-1-84983-264-9
PRICE £7.99